STAR
WARS
FATE OF THE JEDI
CONVICTION

BOOKS BY AARON ALLSTON

Galatea in 2-D

Bard's Tale Series (with Holly Lisle)
Thunder of the Captains
Wrath of the Princes

Car Warriors series
Double Jeopardy

Doc Sidhe Series
Doc Sidhe
Sidhe-Devil

Star Wars: X-Wing series
Wraith Squadron
Iron Fist
Solo Command
Starfighters of Adumar
Mercy Kill

Star Wars: New Jedi Order series
Rebel Dream
Rebel Stand

Star Wars: Legacy of the Force series
Betrayal
Exile
Fury

Star Wars: Fate of the Jedi series
Outcast
Backlash
Conviction

Terminator 3 series
Terminator Dream
Terminator Hunt

AARON ALLSTON

BALLANTINE BOOKS • NEW YORK

2012 Del Rey Mass Market Edition

Published in the United States by Del Rey, an imprint of The Random House Publishing Group, a division of Random House, Inc., New York.

Del Rey is a registered trademark and the Del Rey colophon is a trademark of Random House, Inc.

Originally published in hardcover in the United States by Del Rey, an imprint of The Random House Publishing Group, a division of Random House, Inc., in 2011.

This book contains an excerpt from *Star Wars: Fate of the Jedi: Ascension*. This excerpt has been set for this edition only and may not reflect the final content of the forthcoming edition.

ISBN 978-0-345-50911-6
eBook ISBN 978-0-345-51958-0

Printed in the United States of America

www.starwars.com

www.delreybooks.com

9 8 7 6 5 4 3 2

Del Rey mass market edition: September 2012

Acknowledgments

Thanks go to my editor, Shelly Shapiro, and my fellow writers on this series, Troy Denning and Christie Golden, for inventiveness and patience; to Sue Rostoni, Leland Chee, and all the other fine folk at Lucas Licensing for their help; to my agent, Russ Galen, for his work on my behalf; and to all the fans, for their good wishes.

THE STAR WARS NOVELS TIMELINE

OLD REPUBLIC
5000–67 YEARS BEFORE *STAR WARS: A New Hope*

***Lost Tribe of the Sith*†**
Precipice
Skyborn
Paragon
Savior
Purgatory
Sentinel

3954 *YEARS BEFORE STAR WARS: A New Hope*

The Old Republic: Revan

3650 *YEARS BEFORE STAR WARS: A New Hope*

The Old Republic: Deceived

***Lost Tribe of the Sith*†**
Pantheon
Secrets

Red Harvest

The Old Republic: Fatal Alliance

The Old Republic: Annihilation**

2975 *YEARS BEFORE STAR WARS: A New Hope*

***Lost Tribe of the Sith*†**
Pandemonium

1032 *YEARS BEFORE STAR WARS: A New Hope*

Knight Errant

Darth Bane: Path of Destruction
Darth Bane: Rule of Two
Darth Bane: Dynasty of Evil

RISE OF THE EMPIRE
67–0 YEARS BEFORE *STAR WARS: A New Hope*

67 *YEARS BEFORE STAR WARS: A New Hope*

Darth Plagueis

33 *YEARS BEFORE STAR WARS: A New Hope*

Darth Maul: Saboteur*
Cloak of Deception
Darth Maul: Shadow Hunter

32 *YEARS BEFORE STAR WARS: A New Hope*

STAR WARS: EPISODE I
THE PHANTOM MENACE

Rogue Planet
Outbound Flight
The Approaching Storm

22 *YEARS BEFORE STAR WARS: A New Hope*

STAR WARS: EPISODE II
ATTACK OF THE CLONES

22–19 *YEARS BEFORE STAR WARS: A New Hope*

The Clone Wars
The Clone Wars: Wild Space
The Clone Wars: No Prisoners

Clone Wars Gambit
Stealth
Siege

Republic Commando
Hard Contact
Triple Zero
True Colors
Order 66

Shatterpoint
The Cestus Deception
The Hive*
MedStar I: Battle Surgeons
MedStar II: Jedi Healer
Jedi Trial
Yoda: Dark Rendezvous
Labyrinth of Evil

19 *YEARS BEFORE STAR WARS: A New Hope*

STAR WARS: EPISODE III
REVENGE OF THE SITH

Dark Lord: The Rise of Darth Vader

Imperial Commando
501st

Coruscant Nights
Jedi Twilight
Street of Shadows
Patterns of Force

The Han Solo Trilogy
The Paradise Snare
The Hutt Gambit
Rebel Dawn

The Adventures of Lando Calrissian
The Force Unleashed
The Han Solo Adventures
Death Troopers
The Force Unleashed II

*An eBook novella
**Forthcoming
† Lost Tribe of the Sith: The Collected Stories

REBELLION
0–5 YEARS AFTER
STAR WARS: A New Hope

Death Star
Shadow Games

0

STAR WARS: EPISODE IV
A NEW HOPE

Tales from the Mos Eisley Cantina
Tales from the Empire
Tales from the New Republic
Scoundrels**
Allegiance
Choices of One
Galaxies: The Ruins of Dantooine
Splinter of the Mind's Eye

3 *YEARS AFTER STAR WARS: A New Hope*

STAR WARS: EPISODE V
THE EMPIRE STRIKES BACK

Tales of the Bounty Hunters
Shadows of the Empire

4 *YEARS AFTER STAR WARS: A New Hope*

STAR WARS: EPISODE VI
THE RETURN OF THE JEDI

Tales from Jabba's Palace

The Bounty Hunter Wars
The Mandalorian Armor
Slave Ship
Hard Merchandise

The Truce at Bakura
Luke Skywalker and the Shadows of Mindor

NEW REPUBLIC
5–25 YEARS AFTER
STAR WARS: A New Hope

X-Wing
Rogue Squadron
Wedge's Gamble
The Krytos Trap
The Bacta War
Wraith Squadron
Iron Fist
Solo Command

The Courtship of Princess Leia
A Forest Apart*
Tatooine Ghost

The Thrawn Trilogy
Heir to the Empire
Dark Force Rising
The Last Command

X-Wing: Isard's Revenge

The Jedi Academy Trilogy
Jedi Search
Dark Apprentice
Champions of the Force

I, Jedi
Children of the Jedi
Darksaber
Planet of Twilight
X-Wing: Starfighters of Adumar
The Crystal Star

The Black Fleet Crisis Trilogy
Before the Storm
Shield of Lies
Tyrant's Test

The New Rebellion

The Corellian Trilogy
Ambush at Corellia
Assault at Selonia
Showdown at Centerpoint

The Hand of Thrawn Duology
Specter of the Past
Vision of the Future

Scourge

Fool's Bargain*
Survivor's Quest

*An eBook novella
**Forthcoming

THE STAR WARS NOVELS TIMELINE

NEW JEDI ORDER
25–40 YEARS AFTER *STAR WARS: A New Hope*

Boba Fett: A Practical Man*

The New Jedi Order
- Vector Prime
- Dark Tide I: Onslaught
- Dark Tide II: Ruin
- Agents of Chaos I: Hero's Trial
- Agents of Chaos II: Jedi Eclipse
- Balance Point
- Recovery*
- Edge of Victory I: Conquest
- Edge of Victory II: Rebirth
- Star by Star
- Dark Journey
- Enemy Lines I: Rebel Dream
- Enemy Lines II: Rebel Stand
- Traitor
- Destiny's Way
- Ylesia*
- Force Heretic I: Remnant
- Force Heretic II: Refugee
- Force Heretic III: Reunion
- The Final Prophecy
- The Unifying Force

35 *YEARS AFTER STAR WARS: A New Hope*

The Dark Nest Trilogy
- The Joiner King
- The Unseen Queen
- The Swarm War

LEGACY
40+ YEARS AFTER *STAR WARS: A New Hope*

Legacy of the Force
- Betrayal
- Bloodlines
- Tempest
- Exile
- Sacrifice
- Inferno
- Fury
- Revelation
- Invincible

Crosscurrent
Riptide

Millennium Falcon

43 *YEARS AFTER STAR WARS: A New Hope*

Fate of the Jedi
- Outcast
- Omen
- Abyss
- Backlash
- Allies
- Vortex
- Conviction
- Ascension
- Apocalypse

X-Wing: Mercy Kill

*An eBook novella
**Forthcoming

Dramatis Personae

Luke Skywalker; Jedi Grand Master (human male)
Ben Skywalker; Jedi Knight (human male)
Vestara Khai; Sith apprentice (human female)
Leia Organa Solo; Jedi Knight (human female)
Han Solo; pilot (human male)
Allana Solo; child (human female)
Tahiri Veila; defendant (human female)
Natasi Daala; Chief of State, Galactic Alliance (human female)
Jaina Solo; Jedi Knight (human female)
Wynn Dorvan; government aide (human male)
Valin Horn; Jedi Knight (human male)
Jysella Horn; Jedi Knight (human female)
Corran Horn; Jedi Master (human male)
Drikl Lecersen; Moff (human male)
Haydnat Treen; Senator (human female)
Seha Dorvald; Jedi Knight (human female)

A long time ago in a galaxy far, far away. . . .

CONVICTION

Chapter One

INFIRMARY LEVEL,
JEDI TEMPLE, CORUSCANT

THE MEDICAL READOUT BOARD ON THE CARBONITE pod flickered, then went dark, announcing that the young man just being thawed from suspended animation—Valin Horn, Jedi Knight—was dead.

Master Cilghal, preeminent physician of the Jedi Order, felt a jolt of alarm ripple through the Force. It was not her own alarm. The emotion was the natural reaction of all those gathered to see Valin and his sister, Jysella, rescued from an unfair, unwarranted sentence imposed not by a court of justice, but by Galactic Alliance Chief of State Daala herself. Had they come to see these Jedi Knights freed and instead become witness to a tragedy?

But what Cilghal *didn't* feel in the Force was the winking out of a life. Valin was still there, a diminished but intact presence in the Force.

She waved at the assembly, a calming motion. "Be still." She did not need to exert herself through the Force. Most of those present were Jedi Masters and Jedi Knights who respected her authority. Not one of them was easily panicked, not even the little girl beside Han and Leia.

Standing between Valin's and Jysella's hovergurneys

with her assistant Tekli, Cilghal concentrated on the young man lying to her right. His body gleamed with a trace of dark fluid: all that remained of the melted carbonite that had imprisoned him. He was as still as the dead. Cilghal pressed her huge, webbed hand against his throat to check his pulse. She found it, shallow but steady.

The readout board flickered again and the lights came up in all their colors, strong, the pulse monitor flickering with Valin's heartbeat, the encephaloscan beginning to jitter with its measurements of Valin's brain activity.

Tekli, a Chadra-Fan, her diminutive size and glossy fur coat giving her the aspect of a plush toy instead of an experienced Jedi Knight and physician, spun away from Valin's gurney and toward the one beside it. On it lay Jysella Horn, slight of build, also gleaming a bit with unevaporated carbonite residue. Tekli put one palm against Jysella's forehead and pressed the fingers of her other hand across Jysella's wrist.

Cilghal nodded. Computerized monitors might fail, but the Force sense of a trained Jedi would not, at least not under these conditions.

Tekli glanced back at Cilghal and gave a brisk nod. All was well.

The pulse under Cilghal's hand began to strengthen and quicken. Also good, also normal.

Cilghal moved around the head of the gurney and stood on the far side, a step back from Valin. When he awoke, his vision would be clouded, and perhaps his judgment as well. It would not do for him to wake with a large form standing over him, gripping his throat. Violence might result.

She caught the attention of Corran and Mirax, parents of the two patients. "That was merely an electronic glitch." Cilghal tried to make her tones reassuring, knowing her effort was not likely to succeed—Mon Calamari voices, suited to their larger-than-human frames, were resonant and even gravelly, an evolutionary adaptation that allowed them to be heard at greater distances in their native underwater environments. Unfortunately, they tended to sound harsh and even menacing to human ears. But she had to try. "They are fine."

Corran, wearing green Jedi robes that matched the color of his eyes, heaved a sigh of relief. His wife, Mirax, dressed in a stylish jumpsuit in blacks and blues, smiled uncertainly as she asked, "What caused it?"

Cilghal offered a humanlike shrug. "I'll put the monitors in for evaluation once your children are checked out as stable. I suspect these monitors haven't been tested or serviced since Valin and Jysella were frozen." There, that was a well-delivered lie, dismissing the monitor's odd behavior as irrelevant.

Valin stirred. Cilghal glanced down at him. The Jedi Knight's eyes fluttered open and tried to fix on her, but seemed to have difficulty focusing.

Cilghal looked down at him. "Valin? Can you hear me?"

"I . . . I . . ." Valin's voice was weak, watery.

"Don't speak. Just nod."

He did.

"You've been—"

She was interrupted by a stage-whispered notification from Tekli: "Jysella is awake."

Cilghal adjusted her angle so she could address both siblings. "You've been in carbonite suspension for some time. You feel cold, shaky, and disoriented. This is all normal. You are among friends. Do you understand me?"

Valin nodded again. Jysella's "yes" was faint, but

stronger and more controlled than Cilghal had expected.

"Your parents are here. I'll allow them to speak to you in a moment. The Solos are here, as well." *And little Amelia and her pet Anji, both of whom smell like they've been rolling in seafood shells left rotting for a week.* Cilghal had to blink over that fact. The child should have received a thorough disinfecting before being allowed in this chamber. Come to think of it, Barv also reeked. Where could a youngling and even a Jedi Knight go in the clean, austere Temple and end up smelling like that?

She set the question aside. "Bazel Warv is here, and Yaqeel Saav'etu, your friends. They can answer many questions about an ailment that afflicted the two of you just prior to your freezing."

Jysella looked around, barely raising her head, her attention sliding across the faces of friends and loved ones, and then she looked at Valin. He must have felt her attention; he looked back. A thought, the sort of instant communication that only siblings can understand, passed between them. Then the two of them relaxed.

Jysella looked again at her parents. "Mom?"

At Cilghal's nod, Mirax and Corran came forward, crowding into the gap between the hovergurneys. Tekli moved out of their way, circling the head of Valin's bed to rejoin Cilghal. She craned her neck to look up at the Mon Cal. "All signs good."

Cilghal nodded. She turned to the others in the room. "All but the immediate family, please withdraw to the waiting area."

And they did, exiting with words of encouragement and welcome.

In moments, only the Horns and the medics remained

with Valin and Jysella. Cilghal took a few steps to the nurses' station and its bank of monitoring screens, giving its more elaborate readouts a look . . . or pretending to. Tekli found a mist dispenser and sprayed its clean-smelling contents around the chamber, driving away reminders of Amelia's, Anji's, and Barv's recent presence. Then she rejoined her superior.

If Cilghal's predictions were correct, Valin and Jysella would be reaching full cognizance right about now, if they hadn't already. And if the madness that had caused them to be subjected to carbonite freezing was still in effect, their voices would be raised in moments with accusations: *What have you done with my* real *mother, my* real *father?*

That was the insanity that had visited them, the manifestation of the dark-side effect of their connection with the monster known as Abeloth. But recently, Abeloth's power over the "mad Jedi" had been broken. They had all returned to normal—all but these young Horns, their recovery delayed by their suspended state.

Valin's voice was raised in a complaint, but it was not an accusation of treachery and deceit. "I can't stop shaking."

"It's normal." His father sounded confident. "Han went through it years ago. He said it took him quite a while to warm up. This gurney is radiating a lot of heat, though. You'll be warm enough before you know it." He frowned. "He also said his eyesight was gone right after he woke. How is it that you're seeing so well?"

"We're not." That was Jysella, raising her arms above her to stretch, an experiment that caused her to wince with muscle pangs. "I'm seeing mostly with the Force."

Valin nodded. "Me, too."

Cilghal and Tekli exchanged a glance. That was a relief. The conversation was idle chat, and would soon turn to minute discussions of who had been up to what while Valin and Jysella slept. All was well.

Unless . . . Cilghal still had one more test to run.

She raised her voice to catch the attention of all the Horns. "Excuse me. I must interrupt. We have to let the monitors get several minutes of uninterrupted data, and all this talking is interfering. I must ask you two to withdraw for a while."

Mirax gave her an exasperated look. "After all the time we've waited—"

Tekli held up a hand to forestall her. "After all that time, you can afford to indulge in a few minutes of quiet relief with your husband." She made a shooing motion with her hands. "Out."

Grudgingly, the older Horns withdrew. They'd be joining the others in the waiting area.

From a cabinet, Cilghal took a pair of self-heating blankets. She approached the gurneys and spread one blanket over each patient. "Tekli and I need to make some log entries about your recovery. Josat will be here in a moment—ah." As if on cue, and it was indeed on cue, a teenage Jedi apprentice, cheerful and maddeningly energetic, entered the chamber. Red-haired, lean with a teen's overactive metabolism, he offered Cilghal and Tekli a minimally acceptable respectful nod and immediately moved over to the nurses' station monitor to familiarize himself with his two charges.

Cilghal finished adjusting Jysella's blanket. "If you need anything, Josat can provide it, and if he is not here, say 'Nurse' and the comm router will put you in contact with the floor nurse."

Jysella glanced over at her brother. "I have just been tucked in by a large fish."

He smiled, and when he spoke, there was amusement in his voice. "Maybe you're hallucinating."

* * *

The waiting room was a long chamber decorated with plants from a dozen worlds and a wall-side fountain shaped to simulate a waterfall on the planet Alderaan, destroyed so long ago. The air here was fresher than that in the infirmary chambers, smelling of oxygen from the plants, mist from the waterfall—

Fresher in most ways, fouler in others. Leia turned to Allana and crossed her arms. "Sweetie . . ."

"I know, I know." The child did not sound at all childlike, but she hugged her pet nexu to her with what looked like a need for reassurance. "We smell bad."

"What did you get into?"

Allana's shrug was uncommunicative. "I don't know."

Leia glanced at Barv, but the Ramoan Jedi Knight, big and green with ferocious tusks, avoided her eye.

Well, of course he didn't want to explain. He'd been entrusted with watching over Allana, and he'd failed to keep her out of mischief. This was the sort of humbling experience young Jedi needed to have from time to time.

Han leaned into the conversation, but his attention was on his wife, not his granddaughter. "Garbage Compactor 3263827."

Leia scowled at him. "Oh, shut up."

Han grinned, and there was a bit of mockery in the expression. He switched his attention to Allana. "Sweetie, I can remember when your grandma smelled just like that. And unlike you, she was rude and ungrateful, too."

"Han—"

"Go get cleaned up, and sanisteam Anji if you can, while your grandma and I discuss the impossibility of keeping children—or teenage princesses—clean."

"Yes, Grandpa." Allana scurried while the scurrying was good. She didn't have to look back to detect the glare Leia was visiting on Han.

* * *

Cilghal and Tekli walked toward an office at the far end of the hall from the Horns' chamber, just short of the waiting room.

Cilghal had Josat's script timed and running in her head. He would now be moving around the Horns' chamber, humming to himself, cautioning Valin and Jysella not to move or talk—the monitors needed stillness to do this evaluation—but *he* could talk, fortunately, for it was impossible for him to keep quiet, or so his family said . . .

Tekli interrupted the holodrama in Cilghal's head. "So what *did* cause the pod monitor to fail?"

"Maybe what I said. And maybe it was a spike of the ability Valin manifested when he went mad."

"The one that blanked out the encephaloscan?"

"Yes. He was probably using the technique when he was frozen. The monitor failure would have been the last bit of that usage."

"Hmm." Tekli didn't comment. She didn't need to: Cilghal knew what she was thinking. Retention of that scanner-blanking ability was not an indication that Valin retained the madness, as well, but neither physician liked mysteries.

When the two of them entered their office, the main monitor on the wall was already tuned to a hidden holocam view of the Horns' chamber. They could see Josat indeed bustling among the cabinets, assembling a tray full of beverages, receptacles for medicines, blood samples, swabs.

Tekli heaved a sigh. "So far, so good."

Cilghal offered a noncommittal rumble. "Time will tell."

Josat moved to Valin and then Jysella, offering drinks. His voice was crisp over the monitor speakers. "We gave you the farthest room from the turbolifts and offices and waiting room. Much quieter here. If there's an emergency, though, it's safer to head to the stairs instead of the turbolifts. Right next door, take a left when you leave this chamber, it's the door straight ahead, you can find it in pitch darkness. That can be important. I never used to pay attention to things like that, but since I started studying nursing, I have to know these things. Jedi Tekli will make me run laps if I ever don't know where the emergency exits are from any of my stations. Were your Masters always assigning you exercise when you messed up? Don't answer, the monitors need quiet."

Cilghal blinked, pleased. "He worked that in very well."

"About the punishment?"

"About the stairs."

"I know."

Cilghal sighed. "Mammalian humor. Deliberate misinterpretation."

"Tends to drive a Master crazy, doesn't it?"

Josat now stood beside Valin's gurney, his lightsaber swaying on his belt within Valin's easy reach. The apprentice eyed one of the wall monitors. "Slow progress on your evaluation. No matter. Nobody will come back to bother you until it's run its course. Half an hour at least, I'm guessing."

Cilghal nodded. "The last of the bait. He is not a bad actor." Under ideal circumstances, Valin or Jysella might feel a trace of deceit from him through the Force, but now, still suffering a little from the aftereffects of carbonite freezing, they were unlikely to.

They were, however, likely to add up four important details. First, they were in a room at the end of the corridor, away from most visitors and medical personnel. Second, they were next to stairs that would allow them to reach any level of the Temple while bypassing well-traveled turbolifts. Third, they had half an hour before their absence would be noticed. And fourth, they had ready access to a lightsaber.

If they were still mad, and merely concealing the fact, could they resist the bait?

But neither Horn made a grab for the lightsaber.

If they had done so—well, it wouldn't have been too damaging. The lightsaber would not have ignited. Switching it on, or having Cilghal or Tekli press a button on the comlinks they carried, would cause the false lightsaber to emit a powerful stunning gas. The Horns would have been felled without violence, never having even reached the corridor. Josat would have been felled as well, but it would have been easier on him than being thrashed by two experienced Jedi Knights.

But clearly, escape was not a priority for them. Which meant that they, too, were sane. Cured.

Valin had felt nothing but warmth and relief from his parents—

From the man and woman *masquerading* as his parents.

As he lay listening to Josat's endless, maddening blather, Valin forced himself to remain calm. Any distress might send a signal through the Force to his captors, a signal that their deception had been detected.

And perhaps, *perhaps*, the man and woman who wore the faces of Corran and Mirax Horn didn't even know that they were imposters.

What a horrible thought. Perhaps they were clones, implanted with memories that caused them to believe, in their heart of hearts, that they were the real Corran and Mirax. What would happen to them when the truth was revealed? Would they be killed by their secret masters? Were they even now implanted with strategically placed explosives that would end their lives when they were no longer useful?

Valin clamped down on that thought, suppressing it.

Again Josat came near, chattering about his studies, about politics, about the best mopping techniques for apprentices assigned to clean Temple corridors. Again his lightsaber swung invitingly just within Valin's reach.

But, no. He and Jysella needed to know much more than they did now if they were to stage a successful escape. They needed to be rested, informed, and somewhere other than deep in the enemy-occupied Jedi Temple before they struck out on their own.

So he looked at his sister and offered her a smile full of reassurance. That emotion, at least, was real. In all the universe, the one person he knew to be true was Jysella. He'd known it from the moment they had reached for each other in the Force. Dazed, barely conscious, dreading what they would find, they had still connected, and they knew they were not alone.

She smiled back at him, an expression he felt more than saw.

They had each other, and for now, that was enough.

Chapter Two

MELIFLAR STATION, MENDENBATT SYSTEM, NEAR ALMANIA

AT MAXIMUM GAIN, *JADE SHADOW*'S SENSORS SHOWED the distant space station as a small, irregular cluster of pods and modules, an ad hoc arrangement familiar anyplace in the galaxy where hardworking spacers made do with less than the newest, shiniest vehicles and habitat components.

Ben Skywalker, in the pilot's seat, straightened from scrutinizing the main data monitor. Still faintly visible on his neck and cheek was the wide crisscross pattern so recently cut into his skin by Lord Taalon's Force net. He looked over at his father, seated at the navigation console. "It's, uh, uninformative. Nothing in *Jade Shadow*'s database, either." He shrugged. "I'm guessing pirates or smugglers."

Luke nodded, his thoughts elsewhere. He could feel the space station ahead, both as a small pulse of ordinary Force energy indicating that there were living beings aboard it, and as a separate sensation, a faint but distinct flavor, unsettling and elusive, of dark-side Force energy.

Which meant, quite possibly, that their quarry was there, as well. The Dathomiri blood trail he'd established between himself and Abeloth had led him here—

but it was faint, complicated. The pulse of dark-side energy was reassuring.

"She's there." Vestara Khai currently occupied the copilot's seat. As always, Ben couldn't tell if she was smiling slightly, or if it was merely the effect of the small curved scar at the corner of her mouth. This time, he decided, it was probably just the scar. All her concentration was forward.

Luke looked at her. "You have some special reason to believe she is actually there?"

Vestara shook her head. "Just shapes and shadows in the Force. I can almost see her and Ship arriving there."

"Almost." With that single word, Luke offered a mild rebuke, cautioning the younger Force-user not to assume too much. Still, she was more closely attuned to the dark side than either Luke or Ben. Perhaps she could detect patterns in it that the light-siders could not.

He slid into the rear seat and felt a wash of relief. An injury to his knee, sustained on Almania, plagued him. Too intent on pursuing Abeloth to wait for bacta treatment, he was forced to move around on a leg that was damaged, bandaged, and benumbed by medicine.

He returned his attention to his son. "Set up a transponder signal, one of your mother's alternate identity packets, way down on the list. A smuggler. Then move in and request docking instructions."

"Yes, sir."

Once again, he was reassured that he had made the right decision to alter so little of the *Jade Shadow* after Mara's death. He felt close to her on this ship, despite the sadness the reminders sometimes evoked, and there was no doubt that some of her own tools and supplies could come in quite handy at times. She'd been nothing if not resourceful.

Ben activated the sublight thrusters and made a smooth, slow approach toward the station. With a touch of a button, he began transmitting, and filled Luke and Vestara in on the necessary information. "We're the *Black Diadem,* a courier yacht belonging to a Hapan nobleman under suspicion of piracy and smuggling." Which was not unusual, as many Hapan males found the freedom their culture withheld from them at home in the more illicit spacefaring trades.

Ben's comm board dinged and text scrolled across it. He gave it a look. "We're cleared to dock on spar three, module eleven. They're requesting our trade manifest."

Luke offered a little smile. "Transmit 'three occupants, combat and insurgency skills.' "

Ben looked disappointed. "That's not even a lie."

"Sometimes a Jedi must deal with the disappointment of having to tell the truth."

Ben brought the yacht to a smooth dock against the extender boarding tube protruding from an ancient KDY deep-space warehousing module. Luke stood by the air lock, checked and confirmed the boarding tube's pressure seal, gave a quick look to the atmospheric analysis board to make sure the breathing mix was right for humans and not toxic, and then activated the air lock's outer door. It hissed open, revealing a cylindrical corridor, once white, now dingy, with sputtering glow rods overhead and a tattered black grip surface below. The air lock hatch at the far end was closed but showing green for readiness.

No one waited there.

Luke patted the folds of his robe, making sure his lightsaber was still concealed, and glanced at his two companions. Like himself, they were shrouded in travelers' robes, their lightsabers out of sight.

They moved along the corridor, feeling their own body weight diminish as they passed out from the simulated gravity of *Jade Shadow,* through a border area, and into the grav effect of the station. The far air lock opened to admit them. Moments later it was cycling, the door behind them sealing, the indicator in the door ahead going from red to green. Except for the hiss of the atmosphere pumps, all was silent.

Ben glanced at his father, an I-don't-like-the-feel-of-this look. Luke gave him a little shake of the head, cautioning him to silence. There was no telling how many sensors might be active around them.

The air lock opened into a large chamber, poorly lit by more sputtering or flickering glow rods inset in the ceiling six meters up. The chamber was thick with shelving twice the height of a human, but few of the shelves were loaded with stores or wares. Luke saw shipping containers from dozens of worlds, many of them marked with the names of their contents—mainly preserved foods.

And still there were no people to greet the three travelers.

No people to be *seen*. Luke could feel a growing sense of anticipation, not his own emotion—something felt by others, not too far away. He could tell from their faces that Ben and Vestara, too, detected the rising tide of emotion.

He sighed. This was not going to go well. Perhaps an appeal to common sense—reinforced by his reputation—would save some trouble and a few lives.

He threw back the hood of his cloak and raised his voice. "My name is Luke Skywalker. I'm the former Grand Master of the Jedi Order. We're not here to close down your operation . . . but it would be best for everyone if you dealt with us peacefully."

Ben dropped his own voice to a whisper. "Nicely intimidating, Dad. Very aggressive."

"Shhh."

Vestara merely grinned.

Two shelves over, a blue-and-white container labeled NERF LOAF collapsed. It was not a collapse into ruin; the lid flew up, the front panelΔ33 fell forward on a hinge, the two side panels swung away. Revealed within was a squad-level blaster cannon and a crew of two humans, men wearing dark pseudo-military jackets and bandoliers of vibroblades and extra blasters.

Three lightsabers were in hand and igniting as the blaster crew opened fire.

Ben went left, Vestara right. Luke stayed where he was, both to act as a focus of the enemy attention and to favor his injured knee.

A stream of blasterfire poured toward him. Luke braced himself, partly with his good leg and partly with the Force, and got his blade between his body and the bolts, deflecting the first one up into the ceiling, angling his weapon so that the rest followed. Each bolt—and they came in an automatic-weapons barrage—hammered at his control of the lightsaber, threatening to knock it aside and plow through into his body, but he held fast.

Vestara vectored, effortlessly tucking and rolling across the nearly empty shelf unit between her and the blaster nest. Ben skidded, then was gone—Luke glimpsed his son going high, leaping straight up to the top shelf of the closest unit.

The blaster crew jerked the tripod-mounted weapon left and right, trying to put bolts into the bodies of both Luke and Vestara. They had no luck; the tactic gave Luke split seconds to recover, and Vestara was simply too fast and agile for them.

Luke realized he was deflecting stun bolts, not blasterfire. That was not too surprising. Missing living targets with blasterfire in an environment this old and rickety would surely punch holes in exterior surfaces, causing decompression. Stun bolts hitting the same surfaces would do no harm. These attackers, successful or not, were at least disciplined.

Vestara came to her feet in the gap between shelves. The blaster crew turned its entire attention on her, as she was now closest and therefore most dangerous. Their choice freed Luke to act. He gestured, a heaving motion, an instinctive directive for an outpouring of the Force, and a small crate one shelf up hurled itself off the near shelving unit straight into the blaster cannon. The weapon slammed into the two operators, who momentarily ceased fire.

Luke could hear Ben now, or at least infer his position from the volley of small-arms fire sounding from off to his left. He could see the flashes of more stun bolts, but none came near him.

Vestara leapt to land in front of the tripod blaster. She lashed out, her lightsaber moving almost too fast to see, and the blaster fell into two pieces, severed just in front of the trigger housing. She instantly positioned the tip of her red blade under the man's chin, allowing portions of his black beard to fall into it, sizzle, and vaporize. "I suggest you call off the attack."

"I'm not in charge." The man's wide eyes belied the ferocity suggested by his wild mop of black hair and drooping piratical mustache. His voice emerged as a desperate squeak.

"Try anyway."

"Mates, we're caught! Shut down, shut down!"

The black-bearded attacker had told the truth. He wasn't in charge, and none of the other attackers paid heed. Luke heard them keep up their volley of small-arms fire, heard the hum of Ben's lightsaber, heard the number of weapons shooting diminish at a terrific rate. There was one scream and the air was suddenly flavored with the odor of burned flesh.

And then, silence—but for the hiss of air pumps and

the hum of lightsabers. Moments later Ben led the other attackers back to his father, five men and two women, one man with an arm severed just above the wrist; pale and shocky, he kept a greasy black bandanna wrapped around his cauterized stump. None of the new prisoners looked too pleased with the situation.

Luke looked at the assailants. "Which one of you is in charge?"

They looked at one another. One, a Devaronian male with illuminated glitter decorating his horns, finally spoke. "Hallaf's in charge."

"Take me to Hallaf."

"Hallaf's in the brig."

Luke blinked. "Hallaf's in charge but is in the brig?"

Another attacker, a rotund dark-haired woman whose crossed bandoliers were now empty of weapons, spoke up. "Hallaf *was* in charge. He was going to do things the way *she* wanted them done. Bad business sense, no profits. So we threw him into the brig. I'm in charge now. I'm Cardya."

"And who is this *she* you refer to?" Luke was pretty sure he knew the answer.

Cardya merely shuddered.

It took some time to sort out the details. *She*—a slender woman, brown hair and silver eyes, robed, flying a small ball-shaped vehicle of a type these smugglers had never seen—had arrived and spoken with the band's leader, Hallaf. She'd left soon after, to the relief of all the others, who were intimidated by her forbidding manner. Hallaf, shaken, emerged to say that three Jedi would be arriving soon—

"*Three* Jedi?" Vestara sounded offended.

Ben grinned at her. "Smugglers know Jedi represent law and order, so that made us three targets they'd want to kill, not just two. Hey, welcome to the Order."

She did not look at all happy with the unofficial membership.

Three Jedi would be coming, and the crew of this station would kill them in a fast and efficient fashion: by planting explosives on the boarding tube with an automated detonator. When the three visitors were in the tube, the explosives would blow, vaping the Skywalkers and Vestara Khai. *Jade Shadow,* naturally, would drift away, damaged or destroyed, and perhaps be irretrievable.

Luke fixed Cardya with a querying look. "Which wasn't what happened."

She shrugged. "We got the sensor data on your yacht. Nice, expensive yacht. We decided we wanted it. Which meant capturing it intact."

Luke nodded. "For once, greed was our savior."

Cardya shrugged again, unrepentant. "So we threw Hallaf and his daughter in the brig and set up the ambush."

"Hm." During the account, Luke had been broadening his senses again, and now he could once more feel the pulse of dark-side energy that had drawn him to this station. If Abeloth had left, what was the source of the energy? He pointed in that direction. "Take us that way. And if anyone else from the station attacks us, we'll just let their blaster bolts hit you before we start blocking them."

"Understood." With a long-suffering sigh, Cardya led them from the warehouse module—and took extra moments to activate her comlink and tell others on the station to stand down.

Luke's sense of the dark-side energy led them through several other spokes and hubs, until finally they reached a larger module, which Luke recognized as a century-old Corellian module normally used for medcenter stations. It had to have been stolen from somewhere; it was neither old nor damaged enough to have been decommissioned.

"Our command center." Stone-faced, Cardya led them into its center and to the station's brig.

Only one of the eight cells was occupied. In it, sitting on the cell's sole chair, was a middle-aged man, short, skinny, and gray-bearded. Beside him, stretched out supine on the cot, was a young woman. Lean, angular, and dark-haired, she might have been as old as twenty. Her eyes were open, but rolled up in her head so only the whites showed, an unsettling look.

And from her radiated the dark-side energy Luke had felt all this time.

The Force-users and Cardya entered the cell. Luke glanced at the girl on the cot. She seemed stiff, unresponsive. "Who is this?"

"My daughter, Fala." Hallaf did not stand, and his body language said that he was as dejected as a man could be. "She's going to die." His eyes narrowed, suddenly full of fury, which he turned on Cardya. "Your fault. Her death is on your head."

Cardya shrugged. "By the way, I quit."

Hallaf scrambled to his feet, but Ben gave him a little shove and he fell into his chair again.

Luke approached Fala and put a hand on her forehead. This close, he could tell that the dark-side energies she radiated were characteristic of, flavored of, Abeloth. "Has she studied the Force for many years?"

"Never." Her father's voice was hoarse, despairing. "She's quick, she feels things the rest of us don't . . . but she's no Jedi."

"How did she come to be this way?"

"She was in my offices when that woman came. That woman wanted wine, so I stepped out to fetch some. When I came back, Fala was like this. That woman said that she would die . . . if you and your crew didn't."

Luke frowned, considering. With a look, he caught the attention of Ben and Vestara. "There are spots where continued dark-side use for ages, or the presence of creatures instilled with that energy, can cause the places themselves to radiate the power of the dark side. My old Master's home on Dagobah was near a site like that. I think we're looking at something similar . . . but accomplished in a matter of minutes instead of centuries."

Ben shook his head. "I'm not sure I understand."

"I think Abeloth tore off little pieces of her own energy, in a sense, leaving it behind like crumbs of ryshcate for children to follow to danger. And it has poisoned this girl."

Vestara looked unconvinced. "Dark-side power doesn't poison."

"That's debatable, but we're not even talking about the dark side as the Sith use it. We're talking about tiny portions of Abeloth's own being, energy interworked with her own nature. It turned Fala into a beacon and is keeping her unconscious."

"Can you do anything?" That was Hallaf, sounding as though he were being choked.

"Maybe. Give me your chair."

Hallaf rose, and Luke sat. He kept both hands on the girl's forehead. "The energy clings to the girl like a feeding mynock. It will be dangerous to try to ease it free."

Ben's eyes said it all. *Dangerous to you, too?*

Luke nodded.

Vestara frowned. "We're losing time. And you might hurt yourself doing this. Let's just go."

"I might. But Abeloth had to have been planning, adjusting her goals, when she did this to Fala. Perhaps some sense of what her plans were remains within, bound up in that same energy. This could actually *save* us time."

Vestara fell silent. Indifferent or not to Fala's fate, she clearly recognized the merit in Luke's tactic.

Luke turned to his son. "Ben, get to the command chamber. Lock everything down, put the *Shadow* and occupied areas under surveillance. I don't want to be surprised while we're doing this."

Ben nodded. He gave Hallaf a look that spoke volumes: *I feel about my father like you feel about your daughter. Mess with him and you won't like the results.* "I'll need your security codes. Right now."

"I'll give them to you."

Chapter Three

Ben and Hallaf left. Vestara kept her eyes on the silent, sullen Cardya.

Luke could feel the energy within Fala slowly building, slowly moving its way through her mind, touching and changing everything. She was clearly a Force-sensitive, but without the training to recognize and understand what was happening to her, she would be far more vulnerable to the corrupting influences of the dark side than even a novice Jedi. What Abeloth had done to her might not kill her, but it could transform her into something dangerous and unpredictable, something that influenced beings and situations toward dismay and death.

And there, beneath the feelings and unconscious thoughts of Fala, were others. Touches of memories of the Shelter Jedi Knights, the young Jedi Abeloth had made mad, all of them now recovered. But Abeloth wanted them back, was hoarding her energy to call to them again.

There, too, distant, was the sad, self-sacrificing personality of Callista, with whom he had once shared so much. Luke couldn't afford to dwell on that now. He went even deeper.

He saw and felt dark places, gems that thought, insects that stole thoughts—

Of course.

Luke was dimly aware of Hallaf's return to the brig cell. He paid no attention, trusting Vestara to continue to guard him. He turned his mind away from the shadows of Abeloth's memories for the moment and to Fala, to the alien energies that were wrapped up within her.

He extended himself, a subtle but pure wave of light-side energy, flowing through his body and into hers.

His energies, Abeloth's energies, light and dark, both of the Force, two sides of the same coin, bonded. And with the infinite care of someone carrying a planet's last trickle of water in his cupped hands, Luke drew both sets of foreign energy out of Fala's body. He held them suspended before him, noted Vestara's quick understanding of what was happening.

Slowly, with meticulous care, he separated the two forms of energy from himself. They had nothing to hold them, nothing living to sustain them, nothing but each other to cling to, and they began to dissipate. In moments they were gone.

He felt weary. Well, wearier. That last fight on Almania had stolen a lot of his strength. Keeping himself going despite his injury had taken more. And now this . . . What he had sacrificed he would eventually regain, after rest and food and meditation, but for now he felt tired to his bones. He wondered if the same was true of Abeloth.

Fala's eyes fluttered open. "Papa?" Then her gaze fell on Luke. She lay there, confused for a moment, and then, evidently recognizing him, gasped and drew away.

In a moment Hallaf was by her side, holding her. "It's all right. You're all right."

"It was . . . I couldn't think, couldn't move . . ."

Luke rose and stepped away from father and daughter. He rejoined Vestara and activated his comlink. "Set the lockdown to continue for ten minutes," he told Ben. "I don't want them training their blasters on us or interfering with our departure. Come on back."

"Copy, Dad."

Ben, his step bouncy despite his injured shoulder, rejoined them within moments. He glanced at his father, and his expression became one of concern. "You look pale."

"I'm fine." Luke turned to Fala. "Keep a close eye on yourself for the next few months. Look for sensations, emotions that seem out of place, dreams that aren't quite right. If you begin to experience them, set your scruples aside and go consult a Jedi. Your life and your future may depend on it."

Hallaf rose from his daughter's side, his expression confused. "You're not going to bring in the authorities?"

"Currently we don't represent them, and we have bigger issues to deal with. Such as the kind of being who could do that to your daughter just to distract her pursuers." Luke let a touch of durasteel creep into his voice. "A little smuggling does not offend me. But the kind of individual who uses others—and uses *up* others—invites me to retaliate. You understand?"

Hallaf nodded stiffly. "Thank you."

Luke spun away, his cloak fluttering, and, ignoring the pain in his knee, led the way back toward *Jade Shadow.*

"Where are we going, Dad?"

"Nam Chorios. We have to hurry. I could sense that she's calling to the Shelter Jedi Knights, to renew her bonds with them. She's too weak now to reestablish those severed bonds, but if she becomes stronger . . ."

ERRANT VENTURE, ALMANIA SYSTEM

Raynar Thul's StealthX, its S-foils locked together in standard flight configuration, rose into the belly bay of the red Star Destroyer orbiting the planet Almania. His fighter had a little scoring along the port side, the result of cruising just a trifle too near a missile detonation, and it would have to be patched if he hoped to retain full stealth capability in time for the next engagement—wherever that might be.

Rising into the bay, he could see the majority of the other Jedi StealthX fighters already at their landing spots. He nudged his craft in the direction of an empty spot, marked off by yellow reflective tape laid down on a temporary basis, and settled in beside the fighter of Master Kyp Durron. Moments later, canopy raised, he ignored the offer of a ladder from a support worker; he merely dropped over the side and landed between his fighter and Kyp's.

Kyp stood there with his astromech, scrutinizing his starboard S-foils. Of average height, handsome, with graying brown hair worn long and currently matted by sweat and hours under a helmet, Kyp did not look much like the Jedi Master he was; his dark StealthX pilot's jumpsuit was rumpled and he had a faint reddening of skin on his face, similar to a sunburn, suggesting that a laser volley had been stopped—*mostly* stopped—by his forward shields.

Still, he looked normal, and Raynar felt a small pang of envy. His own features had been restored to nearly normal by numerous surgeries, the extensive burns he had experienced years ago detectable only as a few patches of slightly glossy skin resembling textured plastic. His face would no longer cause children to scream, and he had much to be grateful for—especially the fact that the Jedi had once again accepted him as one of their own.

But occasionally he did feel a distant longing for an even greater degree of normalcy.

He pulled off his helmet, then removed his gloves and dropped them into it. "Master."

Kyp looked his way. "Jedi Thul. You did well out there today." It was the sort of encouragement a Master tended to offer an apprentice or a newly elevated Jedi Knight, not one of Raynar's experience, but Raynar knew what it meant. *You've come back a long way from your own dark times. You're doing fine. Keep it up.*

"Thank you. Master, is there any update?"

Kyp shrugged. "We're recovering EV pilots now. The Sith force has regrouped in a tight defensive formation, very disciplined. They apparently got one of their disabled frigates moving again just before we took out the seventh, so their net loss is six. We expect them to enter hyperspace at any moment."

"The Grand Master?"

Kyp became just a little more somber. There were, of course, two Grand Masters, in a sense—Luke Skywalker, in exile, and Kenth Hamner, who had succeeded him. And Hamner was dead. Details were still sketchy. Only the Jedi knew anything at all; some of them had dimly felt it happen.

Kyp knew which Grand Master Raynar meant. "*Jade Shadow* went into hyperspace hours ago. While we've been mopping things up here, there's been no further word from Master Skywalker. And there've been no instructions from the Temple." He slapped his gloves against his thigh, a show of irritation or impatience not characteristic of most Masters.

Another StealthX rose into the bay, a ferocious shower of sparks spewing from its starboard thrusters. Its pilot maneuvered it skillfully enough, landing it well away from other fighters to keep its fiery exhaust from damaging them.

Kyp watched it for a moment, then sighed. "We don't know what to do. Until we know where Abeloth went, where the Sith are going, how the situation on Coruscant is shaking out . . ."

"Understood."

"Have Calrissian arrange a conference room for us. Ask Masters Ramis and Katarn to meet me there in half an hour. We need to make some contingency plans."

"Will do, Master."

"I'm going to see if I can sanisteam the stink of this battle off my skin." Kyp managed a little smile. "Let me know when everything's set up." His step jaunty, or perhaps just plausibly jaunty, he headed off to the temporary pilots' quarters.

Chapter Four

ARMAND ISARD MAXIMUM SECURITY CORRECTIONAL FACILITY, CORUSCANT

THE GUARD-DROID, BULKY AND INTIMIDATING, ITS smooth, black surface offering no place for an attacker to grip, came to a halt at the end of the industrial-green corridor. The blast doors slid aside ahead of it, and it gestured for Tahiri Veila to continue alone.

Tahiri, clad in the strident yellow jumpsuit intended to alert the public that its wearer was a dangerous prisoner, walked through and down the ramp into the exercise yard.

Of course, it wasn't a yard at all. Yards had access to the sky. This large chamber, buried deep within the prison, afforded those in it no opportunity to scale a wall or receive aid from an ally on a speeder bike. Its walls and ceiling were disingenuously painted sky blue, and large monitors on the walls displayed soothing nature scenes. Air blowers set in the high ceilings provided intermittent breezes carrying simulated forest scents. A sophisticated sound system provided background noise, bird calls and other animal sounds, that one might find in nature. Altogether, they provided an atmosphere that was only slightly less claustrophobic than that of an ordinary large subterranean chamber—and was no doubt intended to lull prisoners into passivity.

At the bottom of the ramp, as the blast doors closed behind her, Tahiri took a look around. The chamber had perhaps a hundred inmates in it, all of them clad in yellow jumpsuits. Some ran along the oval track laid out just inside the wall. There was a ball game going on in a wire mesh-enclosed court. Most of the pieces of exercise equipment, especially weight machines, were occupied.

And except for Tahiri, every prisoner present was male.

Tahiri frowned. This prison had inmates of both sexes—all sexes, actually, when certain nonhuman species were factored in—but as a practical consideration the genders were kept separated except in circumstances where there were few prisoners and many guards, such as group emotion therapy sessions and some work environments. But in this chamber there was no guard in sight, either flesh or droid. Of course, the exercise yard would be under constant holocam surveillance, but clearly something was not right.

"Look at this." The words were spoken in the gravel-toned voice of a Mon Calamari male. The salmon-pink skin of his head and hands was thickly decorated with crude black tattoos, many of them gang markings or kill silhouettes Tahiri recognized. The Mon Cal stood in a group of other inmates, perhaps a dozen; they had been doing calisthenics when Tahiri arrived.

She felt her heart sink. She knew this Mon Cal. But she kept her dismay from showing. "Hello, Furan. It's been a while."

"Since just before the war. When you decided to frame my little social club. Fabricated evidence of grand vehicle theft against us."

"Fabricated?" Tahiri let some contempt creep into her voice. "You and your motor-pool buddy were stealing and chopping army hospital shuttles. My evidence didn't convict you. Your buddy's testimony did."

"Too bad he's dead now and can't recant it." The Mon Cal twisted around to face the other way and raised his voice. "Gaharrag, Leurm, look who we have here."

Across the chamber, two other inmates, one involved in the ball game and the other lounging near it as an observer, raised their heads. Tahiri felt her heart slip down a few centimeters more. The first was a Wookiee, his fur marked by patches shaved away in gang markings. The other was a Hutt, large for his kind. Both left their places to move toward Tahiri.

Tahiri took a deep breath. No, her presence here was no accident. Three of the most murderous criminals she'd put away during her career as a Jedi were here, with no guards present.

The rest of Furan's buddies were moving, not being too obvious about it, several of them repositioning themselves to get to her sides and back, the rest simply giving themselves a little more space.

She could see the situation play out in her mind's eye. The Wookiee and the Hutt would arrive and crowd in. Taunting would continue. She'd be shoved—shoved *at*, since she was not likely to allow herself to be touched. She'd have to leap clear to get fighting space, and given the arm reach of the Wookiee and the ability of the Hutt to lash with its tail, she might have odds as poor as fifty-fifty to get clear. If she did, everyone in this chamber would be on her. If she didn't, she'd die at that moment, her body snapped by the Wookiee's tremendous physical strength.

She didn't even know whether it was a touch in the Force or just her own tactical sense that showed her these things. Nor did it matter. She wasn't going to wait for the situation to unfold that way.

Furan turned toward her again. His eyes vibrated in what Tahiri took to be expectation. "You shouldn't—"

She turned to the right and brought her left leg up, planting her foot between his eyes at the perfect point in her delivery. She felt his skull flex under the impact. He staggered back into the arms of two of his yard buddies, the strike so sudden and effective that he didn't even have time to grunt.

While the other inmates around her recoiled in sudden surprise, Tahiri leapt toward Leurm.

Simple tactics. Gaharrag was the most dangerous of her opponents on a being-by-being basis, but not as dangerous as Gaharrag plus Leurm. So she had to eliminate Leurm first, and fast.

Her leap brought her directly in front of the Hutt. He wasn't prepared for her swift arrival and was still in full-speed forward slither. He slowed himself, his greasy mass going flat on the flextile floor for more traction, and she continued forward, bouncing up over him in a flying somersault. He reached up for her as she passed, but his arms were too short.

She landed on his back, struggling for balance as his uneven contours rippled beneath her feet.

His arms were the key. Spindly as they might look in comparison with the rest of his body, they were powerful by human standards . . . but not as well protected by sheaths of fat and muscle as the rest of his body. As Leurm twisted to spin around, she grabbed his lead arm at the wrist and kicked out as hard as she could against his elbow.

The blow snapped his arm to full extension and beyond, breaking it at the joint, a clean break. Leurm shrieked, a gargling, burbling noise only a Hutt or a superheated mud hole could have made.

Gaharrag would now be almost on her. She leapt off

Leurm's back, landing immediately beside the Hutt and facing the Wookiee.

Gaharrag was there, approaching at controlled speed, and lashed out at Tahiri with one big, furry paw.

She ducked, rolling out in front of Leurm. The Hutt took the Wookiee's blow. The huge, furry fist hammered the Hutt's head, knocking him over onto his broken arm, which collapsed under his mass with a grinding noise. The Hutt's screaming grew more shrill.

Tahiri came up on her feet within reach of an inmate, one who'd been at the rear of Furan's pack a moment earlier, a Bothan whose white fur was dyed bloodred in spatter patterns. She gave him no time to react either with fight or flight instincts. She hit him, open-palmed, in the jaw and felt it break under the impact. Unconscious where he stood, he stumbled a step and crashed to the floor.

It ran counter to her instincts to attack someone who had not overtly demonstrated hostile intent. But if Tahiri were to survive, she had to win this fight both by force and intimidation. If she managed to put the Wookiee down, there was the rest of the room to consider. If they were too intimidated to attack, she would survive . . . and fewer of them would be hurt.

Gaharrag turned, roaring, and came after her. That roar, sounding like an entire jungle's worth of rage, was supposed to freeze enemies with dread for a critical second. Tahiri grinned. She'd trained so often against Lowbacca, the Wookiee Jedi, that the roar seemed almost welcome.

Training against Lowbacca had other advantages. She knew where a Wookiee's vulnerable points were. There weren't many. But with older Wookiees—and Gaharrag was no youngster—the knees were the first to go.

As Gaharrag came within reach of her—his reach,

not hers—Tahiri ducked under his grasp and rolled to her left. She slapped out with her arms, anchoring herself in place on her side, and, as Gaharrag's weight came down on his right leg, she lashed out at it. The kick took him in the side of the knee.

With a gruesome crack, his leg folded sideways. Roaring in pain, Gaharrag toppled toward Tahiri. She rolled out of the way and came up to her feet as he crashed to the flextiles. Then he folded up around his injury, howling.

Tahiri took a couple more steps back, to be out of his reach in case he decided to renew hostilities, and turned to look around. Though some of the other inmates had been in midstride forward a moment before, they were all now frozen in place, looking at her.

She pointed at the nearest one, a Sullustan. "You want to play? Come here." He shook his head.

She gestured toward a far corner of the room. "Get out of my sight." She turned to the next nearest one, a heavily scarred human who massed roughly three times what she did, almost none of it fat. "You?"

He shook his head, his expression stony.

She gestured. He withdrew.

The others began sidling away without further invitation.

She looked back at her downed opponents. The Bothan was facedown, blood pooling on the floor under his mouth. Furan, the Mon Cal, was clearly unconscious, his eyes closed, his body unmoving; the two inmates who had broken his fall were in slow retreat. Leurm and Gaharrag lay where they'd fallen, both conscious and in pain, the one issuing burbling whimpers, the other offering up little growling moans and curses in the Wookiee tongue.

There was another noise, too, a faint mechanical

whine. Tahiri looked up toward the ceiling, seeking its source.

A metal cylinder half as long and wide as a human male had extruded itself from the ceiling. At its bottom end was a blaster barrel—aimed at her.

She jerked into motion but heard the weapon fire before she'd moved a handspan. Then everything was blackness.

Her wrists and ankles encased in bulbous durasteel shackles, with metal cables running from wrist to wrist and ankle to ankle, Tahiri was led by a guard-droid into the office. She had to shuffle; the cable between her ankles was too short to allow her to walk normally. Not that she would have been very energetic in any case. The stun bolt she'd sustained, scaled to bring down Wookiees and Hutts, was still affecting her, leaving her pained and listless even hours later.

The office was large but sparsely furnished. There was a desk with a black nerf-leather office chair on the far side and two visitors' chairs on the near. The entire left wall was a square viewport looking down on a real exercise yard, a walled enclosure open to Coruscant's sky, with towers at intervals on the walls and less ferocious prisoners down at ground level, three stories below.

And all over the walls were framed holos, some still and some moving in perpetual loops, showing the prison's warden in happy times. Accepting awards from prominent politicians. Shaking the hands of celebrities. Posing with his arm around the shoulders of prisoners who constituted particularly heartwarming success stories of rehabilitation. In the holos, the warden, a rotund pale-skinned human with wispy gray hair, seemed just the sort of grandfatherly man for whom rehabilitation was a paramount concern.

The man himself sat in the office chair. He was studying a datapad on the desk before him and he was not smiling. Without the smile, he seemed far less grandfatherly.

He did not glance up. "Sit."

Tahiri took one of the visitors' chairs. The droid remained back by the door.

One of the holos on the wall, a moving image, showed the warden shaking hands with Admiral Pellaeon. Its frame was prominent and central on the wall. Tahiri felt an electric thrill of anxiety. This was not going to be a fair hearing.

Finally the warden did look up at her. "Jedi Veila—"

"I'm not a Jedi anymore."

"Don't interrupt me again. Jedi Veila, obviously you are not at this time serving a sentence here. You have not yet been convicted or sentenced. You have been remanded to our custody because of the danger you pose due to your Jedi warrior training. And we've worked under the assumption that you are innocent until proven guilty . . . even though no evidence in your trial suggests that you did not kill a great and important man.

"But this morning . . ." He shook his head. "Very unfortunate that a clerical error placed you in the high-security exercise area at the same time as the male prisoners, but the situation did not call for you to attack and brutally injure them."

"'Clerical error.' Do you really imagine that a clerical error put me there? It was a setup, someone hoping I'd be killed."

"Nonsense. Though I will make a note here about your possible paranoid delusions, in case it's of interest to the prosecution." He paused to type a few words.

"And I was the one under attack."

He glanced up at her again. "I've just reviewed the recordings. I saw the inmates speaking to you and gathering around. There was no attack until you assaulted

Furan. Who has, I might add, sustained a serious concussion. I imagine he probably was taunting you . . . but in my prison you may not respond to taunts with lethal violence."

Tahiri kept silent. Even if this man was as impartial as he pretended to be, the excuse that her opponents were merely repositioning themselves so that her murder would be quick and inevitable was not something she could prove.

"For the protection of my other inmates, you will remain in shock cuffs. They will be removed only when you are returned to your cell or surrendered to the marshals for transportation to your trial."

"I assume I'll be confined to my cell when not coming or going from the courts?"

He shook his head. "Solitary confinement is a punishment, Jedi Veila. Since you are not a convict, I'm in no position to punish you for infractions. No, you'll eat at the common mess and have your daily exercise, education, work, and therapy privileges, of course."

"Ah." Now she understood. The situation that had been set up for her had more than one level. If she did not die at the hands of Gaharrag and his fellows, then she would be rendered almost helpless while being exposed to the ordinary dangers of a maximum-security prison stay. Whether it happened today or at some near-future date, she was marked for death.

"Any questions, Jedi Veila?"

"No, you've answered them all."

The warden looked past her to the droid at the door. "Take her away."

Chapter Five

BORLEIAS, PYRIA SYSTEM

IT WAS A DULL LITTLE WORLD WITH AN INTERESTING past. Thickly overgrown with tropical trees and underbrush, lightly settled, it was a convenient stepping-off point between the Core Worlds and more distant reaches. It had intermittently been a useful outpost for the military leaders of whoever had ruled Coruscant in the past.

Once, its main military complex had housed Imperial biological development facilities, the type governments generally didn't want the public to know too much about. Later, it had been the jumping-off point for the New Republic's successful efforts to capture Coruscant and drive off the government that had gained control of the Empire after Palpatine's death. Later still, when the Yuuzhan Vong invasion had reached Coruscant and the New Republic government itself had fled, Borleias had been the site of a holdout force, a target for the Yuuzhan Vong, its continued resistance giving the New Republic leaders time to escape and regroup. Most recently, it and Bilbringi had been traded to the Imperial Remnant by Jacen Solo in return for military aid. After Solo's death, the government of Admiral Daala, unwilling to have such a valuable waypoint belong to a foreign power, conducted an aggressive negotiation with the

Empire, resulting in Bilbringi remaining Imperial and Borleias staying with the Galactic Alliance.

But for all that, it was really just a place where old military careers went to die. Here were officers and personnel who needed a last chance to demonstrate basic competence but were not really expected to do so successfully, or who needed a place to serve out the remaining years of undistinguished careers. The outpost, one combined-forces military base, was noted for good communications and sensor gear, for self-destruction capabilities, but not for might.

There were, however, some opportunities for the smart fellow. Sergeant Dolo Karenzi, de facto night-shift quartermaster for the outpost, knew he was a smart fellow. Now he tried to keep the excitement off his face as he realized the opportunity he was being handed on a datapad. A spacer's son who had made the military his home because no one else would have him, he was always alert to opportunity—just not always good at covering up his tracks.

The woman facing him, young, redheaded, and graceful, gave him another maddening I'm-way-out-of-your-league smile and offered the datapad again. "I don't care. It's paid for, the manifest is correct, you can sign for it and we can off-load, or you can refuse it and we take it away and try to figure out who fouled up."

Dolo took the datapad and ran the situation through his mind one more time. The transport *Dust Dancer* was in orbit carrying a load of consumable luxury items with a listed destination of the Borleias outpost. The manifest included expensive wines, exotic foods, fresh sabacc decks, entertainment datapads, candies, pastries . . . all of it in high demand.

It was a mistake, of course. The quartermasters of this base had not been notified of any such delivery, and given its specialized nature, they ordinarily would have been. So something had happened in the ordering process, delivery locations had been scrambled or swapped, and a shipment designated for some deep-space hotel or rich individual's estate had been diverted here.

All he had to do was sign for it—as illegibly as possible—and take possession. He could warehouse it in some little-trafficked storage pod, wait to see if anyone came looking for it, and, if not, arrange for it to be sold for a small fortune.

He scribbled his name across the datapad's touch screen and handed it back to the young woman.

She dimpled another smile at him and handed him a datachip. "Your copy of the manifest. If you'll give us landing authorization, we'll bring the *Dancer* down and off-load."

He smiled back, no longer caring that she was out of his league. "Consider it done."

His good mood lasted barely half an hour.

The *Dust Dancer,* eighty meters of Kuat Drive Yards mechanical efficiency, had a ball for the command center at one end, a mass of engines at the other, and a connecting spar thickly clustered with cargo pods and shuttle attachment points dominating the middle. He had seen numberless ships like it before. It came in for a smooth landing at the dirt-topped field most distant from the base center of operations, and its small crew began off-loading Dolo's precious new acquisitions.

Then the base sirens sounded, filling the air with a noise like a city-sized dragon mourning the death of its offspring. The base lights came up. Its squadron of starfighters began lighting off, readying themselves for space.

Dolo, at his desk, monitoring the off-loading of the *Dust Dancer* cargo, cringed. His chances of getting his goods hidden away before they were detected were dropping fast.

He stepped outside the dome-shaped prefab where the quartermaster offices and facilities were located. The landing field was now bathed in lights and busy with personnel running to the bare dozen starfighters that defended this world.

He managed to grab a soldier passing by, a Rodian corporal and motor pool mechanic he regularly played sabacc with. "Vez, what's happening?"

The corporal cocked his head at Dolo. His voice emerged in the classic Rodian singsong, so imitated and mocked by comedians. "A Star Destroyer dropped out of hyperspace. It's entering orbit."

"So? Alliance or Empire?"

"Neither. Private. Wanted for action against the Alliance. The *Errant Venture.*"

"Oh . . . stang."

Rumors had spread days before, of course. The *Errant Venture* had been hosting a high-stakes sabacc tournament, the sort that every player worth his or her skifter salivated at. Combine a luxury cruise, the wealthiest card-playing opponents, media, free-flowing wine and other spirits, companionship . . . it was to have been a once-in-a-lifetime experience.

Well, it was, except perhaps not in the way the organizers intended. The Star Destroyer left Coruscant, aiding a wing of Jedi who, in defiance of government orders, had fled the world in their StealthX space superiority fighters. No one had known whether the card players were hostages or just innocent bystanders swept along in some mad Jedi plan.

And now they were all here. Dolo's heart sank. It was very hard to do a bit of honest stealing while under intense military and media scrutiny. Not impossible, but hard.

* * *

The base starfighters did not launch. The general in charge knew, as did every soldier and support staffer on Borleias, that an assault on a Star Destroyer, even one with a reduced number of weapons emplacements, was a suicidal act to be taken only if there were no other options. Word was that the general was in frantic hypercomm contact with Coruscant.

The *Errant Venture* did not wait. Immediately after it achieved orbit, it began sending shuttles down. It did not request landing instructions, merely offered a stern transmitted warning that firing on the shuttles would be a very bad idea. The shuttles began landing at Dolo's field, and he saw them discharge their contents.

Their contents? Sabacc players.

Some were happy, some confused, others morose or spiteful. Some had been awake for days. Some could not get it through their heads that they were not back on Coruscant, despite the fact that the landing field was surrounded by thick stands of trees rather than skyscrapers. There were card players, reporters, companions and camp followers, piles of luggage, bottles, streamers and bunting, glittering confetti, music blaring from datapads . . . The *Errant Venture* had delivered the sputtering remains of a galactic-level party to this remote outpost.

Dolo brought his office chair out of the dome and set it down in the fresh air to watch things unfold. He'd managed to get the *Dust Dancer* cargo under wraps. Now he was hard at work falsifying a second manifest, a list of ill-fitting uniforms and tasteless preserved rations already in storage, that he could claim was the *Dust Dancer*'s delivery if all went well. When not copying and pasting items from list to list, he watched the events taking place on the field.

He recognized several of the celebrities brought down

from the Star Destroyer—holodrama stars, famous dancers, millionaires, risk takers, politicians, high-ranking military officers. Dolo took a little time to make recordings of them. The recordings would at least be souvenirs, proof that he had been here on this historic night. Maybe, if he was lucky, some might serve as blackmail evidence.

It was once again turning into a good night.

One of the arrivals was Wynn Dorvan, chief of staff to Admiral Daala, the Galactic Alliance Chief of State. He was not drunk, not bewildered, but he still felt a bit shell-shocked.

When the Borleias base general arrived, the man deployed his command staff as shields, using them to keep outraged or incoherent celebrities from engaging him while he headed straight for Dorvan. He only had two aides left by the time he reached his objective. He held out a hand. "Wynn Dorvan? General Eldo Davip."

Wynn shook his hand and gave him a close look. Davip was large, nearly two meters in height, and filled out his uniform to an extent that suggested a more strict diet and exercise regimen would have been a good idea. Wynn knew the man's reputation: A lackluster career officer, Davip had been here on Borleias during the Yuuzhan Vong siege and had distinguished himself. Through the rest of the war and in the years since, he'd served well and intelligently. But doing his duty and following his orders, he'd ended up under co–Chief of State Jacen Solo's command during the Second Galactic Civil War. Never accused of impropriety or complicity in Solo's ruinous plans, he nonetheless was tainted by association, and had maneuvered for a transfer to this little-noticed outpost. It was a good way to retire inconspicuously while still drawing pay and doing a little good.

Dorvan nodded. "Glad to meet you."

"You seem to have a small animal in your pocket."

Wynn glanced down at his suit's breast pocket. Nestled there, his pet, all orange stripes and sleepy eyes, peered out at the general, then settled down for another nap. Wynn grinned. "Pocket's a lot of fun. I sometimes try to convince people that they have animals in their pockets, too."

"Ah." Davip didn't rise to the bait. "Will you come this way?"

"Thank you."

They walked clear of the party atmosphere and the worst of the noise, to the general's personal landspeeder. They boarded, but the general did not signal his pilot to move out. "It's calmer here."

"I could use some calm."

"I've been in direct contact with the Chief of State and have given her the preliminary report that you're fine. She wants you to get on the holocomm and report as soon as possible. But the security and survival of this outpost is *my* first concern, so I need you to tell me what I can expect from *that.*" He jabbed a finger upward, pointing at the *Errant Venture,* a tiny triangle orbiting far above, so high that it was in sunlight, a red arrowhead.

Wynn shrugged. "I don't think you can expect any action, actually. As far as I can tell, Booster Terrik and the Jedi have just one agenda here—staying clear of the Alliance military—and no plans to do Borleias or anyone else any harm. From what I could overhear as we were being lined up for the shuttles, they plan to leave the Pyria system as soon as the last shuttle returns. I think they want to stay clear of any capital ships coming out of Coruscant or other Alliance naval bases."

The general offered an irritated grunt. "I don't think there will be any capital ships."

"How's that again?"

"I've been informed of no relief coming our way."

Wynn blinked. That made no sense—

Oh, yes it did. Slave revolts were now popping off all along the galactic rim like celebratory fireworks, and the Jedi departure from Coruscant had to have suggested to Admiral Daala that she had enemies capable of doing tremendous harm to her military close to home. She doubtless did not want to pull any forces from the fleet guarding Coruscant. To do so would weaken the planetary defenses, weaken herself.

He sighed. "Any idea how we're getting home?"

"I've been given broad discretionary powers to deal with that. There's a transport here—it was grounded by the *Errant Venture*'s arrival while delivering consumables. I intend to press it into service to deliver all of you back to Coruscant. It'll be a little cramped, I suspect, but it's only a short run."

"I look forward to getting home."

"By the way, who won the tournament?"

Wynn felt a little flush of emotion, but wasn't sure whether it was more pride or embarrassment. "I did."

The general looked at him as if he'd just magically transformed himself into a Twi'lek dancer. "Are you joking?"

"No."

"Well . . . when I retire from the military, I'm coming straight to you for a job."

"Make sure I get a private cabin back to Coruscant, and I'll certainly consider it."

"Pilot, back to Ops."

The pilot put the landspeeder in motion.

On the bridge of the *Dust Dancer*, the young redheaded woman who had received Dolo's signature sat in the copilot's chair and watched the final shuttle arrive. It would be carrying Lando Calrissian and his retinue. They'd be traveling back to Coruscant to present a credible case of being innocent of any complicity with the plans of Booster Terrik or the Jedi.

The young woman knew this, of course. Her name was Seha, and she had recently been elevated to the rank of Jedi Knight. Even more recently, she had flown shuttle missions—recovery of EV pilots—above the world of Almania.

After the Almanian engagement, events had developed with startling speed. The Masters along with the StealthX mission had emerged from a private meeting, including a holocomm exchange with the Masters back at the Jedi Temple, with a new set of objectives. Until the Sith were found, they had plenty to do involving Coruscant.

Booster Terrik, once a smuggler and presumably long retired from that profession, but with connections to that trade that never seemed to become fewer in number, had arranged for the *Dust Dancer* to be loaned to them. A legitimate cargo transport owned by a legitimate company, it had an unsullied record. That would probably change soon.

Booster had also arranged for many of the untouched stores brought aboard his ship for the sabacc tournament to end up in *Dust Dancer*'s cargo modules. The two shuttles connected to the freighter's main spar, repainted and with new false IDs, had shielded smuggling compartments.

By choosing a planet not too far from Coruscant but with limited transportation facilities, by positioning *Dust Dancer* there first, and then by commandeering all the celebrity players' own shuttles and transports before dropping the celebrities themselves off on the planet's surface, the Jedi had all but guaranteed that the

Dust Dancer itself would be commandeered to transport the players back to Coruscant.

Which meant that, in a few hours, their shuttles would quite probably be able to transport armed Jedi right into the Senate Building.

Seha's comm board blipped. She looked down to see a text message pop up. She read it over, then turned to the woman in the pilot's seat—her Master, Octa Ramis. The woman was nearly unrecognizable, her skin temporarily dyed dark, her hair bleached nearly white. "We have a message from Borleias Operations. They're requesting that Wynn Dorvan receive a private cabin for the trip back to Coruscant."

Master Ramis snorted, amused. "Our first special request. I wonder how many of the celebrities will be requesting—*demanding*—private cabins. Of which we have one, mine."

"You going to give it to him?"

"Sure. I'll make certain we have a listening device in place before he boards." She rose to accomplish that errand. "There's no hurry, I suspect. We're going to be herding unhappy, uncooperative drunks for the next couple of hours."

Seha gave her a wise-beyond-her-years smile. "Ah, the glamorous life of a Jedi."

Chapter Six

NAM CHORIOS, MERIDIAN SECTOR

It was a whitish pebble drifting in space, surrounded by a few gleaming specks of sand, all under the mild violet glow of the system's sun.

Luke gestured toward Ben, a circular motion ending on an upward stroke, and Ben obligingly dialed the visual magnification upward. The pebble grew larger, and the specks of dust around it resolved themselves into space stations—mostly Golan III Space Defense NovaGun stations, the same platforms, thick with domed turbolaser batteries, that protected far more populous, industrialized, and wealthy worlds of the Galactic Alliance.

One station was not a weapons platform. The largest, it dwarfed the others in size. A thick-bodied ring in silvery gray, its surface was mottled with docking ports and magnetic atmosphere barriers.

Vestara, in the navigator's seat, gave the shimmering sensor image a close look. "They've devoted a lot of firepower to keeping that backworld safe from intruders."

Luke shook his head. "Those stations are to keep ships from escaping, not arriving."

That earned him an arched brow. "Escaping?" she repeated.

"You're right that it's a backworld. But one of the naturalized life-forms, an insect species called drochs, carries a disease called the Death Seed. Heard of it?"

She shook her head. "But no one names a disease *Death Seed* if all it does is give you an upset stomach."

"You're depressingly logical . . . Drochs are tiny. They start out that way, anyway. They breed at ferocious rates in dark, damp places. When they encounter living tissue, of most species, they burrow in. Their gift is that they sample the host's body chemistry and electromagnetic characteristics, even tissue density, and mimic them, becoming all but invisible to scanners. They grow in the host's body, living off the host's life energy, and when they are numerous enough, when collectively they begin drawing enough life energy from the host, the Death Seed plague manifests itself."

Ben scrunched up his face, an expression of mild disgust suggesting he'd heard all this before and didn't enjoy hearing it again. Luke gave him an understanding smile.

"The skin begins to die. The drochs inside the body continue breeding, releasing more drochs to infect others. The victim experiences bodywide aches and listlessness, impaired thinking, impaired breathing . . . and then dies. The drochs that do not flee the body are seldom detected, so there are no bacterial, viral, or fungal infections to detect, no poison traces . . . just death. And under certain circumstances—such as control from a very old, very powerful, very large droch—the illness can be accelerated, claiming its victim when only a few drochs are in the body, killing so swiftly that the necrosis of the skin isn't even under way."

Vestara looked at the image of the planet with more distaste—or perhaps respect; Luke couldn't tell. "I'm surprised you haven't destroyed the world altogether."

Ben leaned back as if to put a few extra decimeters

between himself and the planet's image. "There are other life-forms on the planet—human settlers, and an indigenous crystalline life-form, the tsils."

"How can they survive there with these . . . drochs?"

"The violet light from the sun, processed through the tsils and other crystals, kills the drochs, and they just get absorbed harmlessly into the body. But you have to stay within reach of the tsils and the sun. Otherwise—well, make sure your last will and testament is up-to-date. Dad, are we going in as Skywalkers or what?"

Luke shook his head. "We don't want to invite scrutiny at this point. Send our *Black Diadem* ID again. Captain, Vestara Khai. Crew, Owen Lars, Ben Lars. Cargo, none. Purpose of visit, searching for relatives and genealogical information among the Newcomers."

Ben nodded and turned to his task. A few minutes later, he received transmitted text. "We're cleared to dock at Koval Station. The port authority sent a list of decontamination options. We can take *Jade Shadow* down to the surface, but on liftoff we have to return to the station and put the yacht through quarantine and decontamination—minimum of a full day and lots of credits. If we shuttle down as three passengers, the cost for getting offplanet is lots less and with much faster decontamination."

"We'll go the cheap, fast route. The other option is mostly for vessels delivering cargo."

Ben nodded and began inputting a course to Koval Station.

With the young, appealing Vestara up for the task of taking point, interacting with port authorities, and paying for everything with a credcard not traceable to the Skywalker name, it was simple for Luke and Ben to stay wrapped in their traveler's cloaks and remain anonymous.

The port authority representative, a youthful red-headed human wearing a gold jumpsuit with piping in burgundy, offered advice—rote advice that he'd obviously memorized years earlier. "Nam Chorios is at its farthest point from its sun, and that, plus axial tilt, means it's winter. Harsh winter. If you're away from shelter at night, you freeze and die. If you don't have heavy clothes, you can pick them up in Hweg Shul, the shuttle's destination." He set three small spray canisters on the desktop between himself and Vestara. "Droch repellent. Courtesy of the port authority, which means it's paid for by your decontam prepay. You can buy more planetside." He set three small glow rods with oversized battery packs beside them. "Very bright—don't look right into them or you'll damage your retinas, but they send drochs scurrying away. Or paralyze 'em so you can step on 'em. These you return when you lift, or incur an additional charge to your decontam account. Good luck finding your cousins." He sounded as though he had not the least interest in learning how the quest for fictitious cousins came out, but his tone was polite enough.

A few minutes later, loaded with their new anti-droch gear and duffels from *Jade Shadow* packed with winter garments, the three boarded an aged but meticulously maintained *Lambda*-class shuttle. A few minutes later, the passenger compartment also occupied by a Duros female in medical whites and a middle-aged human male in the shiny business wear affected by Meridian sector middle managers, they launched from Koval Station and began atmospheric entry.

Staring out the port-side viewport beside his seat, Luke reflected on the changes brought by the thirty years since his first visit to this world.

As they descended into the atmosphere, the colors, the textures of the world below were just as he remembered. There were vast plains of slate-gray stone and dust. There were patches of terrain that glittered, reflecting and refracting the sunlight in all the colors of the rainbow and more besides—plains of crystalline gravel, ravines filled with towering columns of crystal, some of them the sapient tsils, or spook-crystals, native to this world. There were dark ridges of basaltic mountain, many of them decorated with crystalline patches. And here and there, more numerous than on his first visit, there were small patches of green—communities clinging precariously to the small areas of arable land above subterranean water seams.

Not that farming sustained the planet's economy these days. Most of the remaining farmers were Oldtimers, descendants of the first wave of colonists, tough, hardy men and women content with the hardscrabble existence of agricultural production on an unforgiving world.

But for the Newcomers, the second wave of settlers, the aftermath of the events that had brought Luke Skywalker here three standard decades before had changed everything. Release of the Death Seed, discovery of the intelligent tsils, had forced the hand of the New Republic, which previously had had no interest in the self-governing world. Suddenly there were space platforms taking away from the Oldtimers and their ground-based weapons stations the responsibility of making sure no drochs ever made it offworld . . . and that no tsils were removed from the planet against their will. Suddenly medical facilities, both government and private, were establishing a new economy based on medical research and the production of medicines unique to this world because of the violet sunlight, the manipulation of that light by the tsils, and the healing techniques of the Theran Listeners, the Oldtimers who communed with the tsils through the Force.

Everybody had gotten what they wanted. The Old-timers, though their secrets were revealed, had help in keeping the menace of the drochs in check. The New-comers had a booming economy. The tsils no longer had to fear being ripped from their world by technology-producing corporations that did not understand, and in many cases would not have cared, what they were.

Everyone got what they wanted . . . everyone but Callista Ming, who had come here to learn to reconnect with the Force, and had failed. Callista, now part of the being called Abeloth. Callista, whose memories of the resources this world had to offer had doubtless led to Abeloth's choice to come here.

Luke caught Vestara's eye. "By the way . . . no using the Force."

Her eyebrows shot up. "What?"

"You don't draw on the Force here, period. Passive uses, perhaps. Nothing as active as giving yourself a boost of running speed or a few extra meters of jump distance. If you do, disaster results. People die."

"I don't understand."

"It's a unique property of the Nam Chorios environment. The crystals that lace the planet's crust magnify Force usage . . . and redirect it in random and destructive ways. You augment one of your leaps here, and somewhere else, a storm rises that causes catastrophe in a farmstead or a town."

"I wish you'd mentioned that before."

He managed a smile. "Consider it a test of discipline."

Luke couldn't tell how much Hweg Shul, the planetary capital, had changed in all these years. As the shuttle descended into the lower atmosphere, winds battered it, sending it slewing, and the winter storm they entered, scores or hundreds of kilometers in length and breadth, stirred up the planetary surface into a dust storm that obscured the town.

The thrusters and repulsorlifts of the Lambda whined as its pilot battled the winds, fought to keep control. Luke saw Ben and Vestara grimace. He felt the same way they did. From what he could tell of the winds they were experiencing and the pilot's control, the shuttle passengers were in good hands . . . but no pilot ever, *ever* wanted to be a passenger, especially in difficult circumstances. Every pilot wanted to be in control.

The businessman in the shiny suit, sitting one row up from Luke and on the other side of the aisle, began to change color. From the pocket under his armrest, he extracted an opaque flimsiplast bag designed to capture the contents of his stomach should they decide to escape. He did not use it immediately, just held it before him and contemplated it sorrowfully. He occasionally looked at the other passengers and seemed to grow even more unhappy as he realized that they were not as miserable as he was.

Then the thrusters cut out. Through the Force, Luke felt alarm from the businessman, none from the cockpit or the woman from Duro.

The shuttle turned slowly. Luke's view of driving wind and abrasive crystalline dust in a single, nearly opaque sheet was blocked as the Lambda's wings lifted into landing position. Then the shuttle thumped to a comparatively gentle landing. It began to rock at intervals under the pressure exerted by particularly hard gusts of wind.

The pilot's voice, that of a female, probably human, rich with humor, came over the intercom. "Koval Transport would like to welcome you to Nam Chorios, vacation capital of the Meridian sector, and Hweg Shul Spaceport. Please prepare to debark via the main boarding ramp. The temperature outside is negative ten degrees, but windchill brings it down to a far more comfortable negative forty-two, so please watch that exposed flesh."

Moments later, hoods up and eyes protected by goggles, the three of them marched down the boarding ramp. The bitingly cold wind tried to topple them as soon as it began to flow past their ankles. Outside, it plastered their insufficiently insulated clothes and cloaks against their bodies. All three instinctively turned their backs to it. In the near distance, they could see lights limning what had to be the main terminal dome, but the skin of the dome itself was invisible, obscured by the driving dust.

Ben managed a wintry smile. He had to raise his voice to a shout to be heard over the wind. "This planet is a hellhole." His breath emerged as a foggy plume that was ripped away from him.

Luke shouldered his carry bag and turned toward the terminal. "You're spoiled. I grew up on a planet like this."

"Not including Death Seed, Dad."

"Well, true." Not including Death Seed, ancient and insane Dark Jedi, synthdroids . . . Memories of Nam Chorios flooded him, and he could not afford to push them away.

Chapter Seven

CORUSCANT

"SOMETIMES I THINK THIS PLANET IS NOTHING BUT A hellhole." Chief of State Natasi Daala's voice was unusually soft, subdued.

But that was appropriate in this place. It was late at night in the medcenter. The brilliant, horizontal streaming lights of Coruscant's endless airspeeder traffic, outside the high-altitude chamber's viewport, were not accompanied by traffic roar; the room's sound insulation kept that noise at bay. Yet the streaks' steadiness and beauty were actually soothing. Faint light from dimmed overhead glow rods suffused the chamber, turning stark medical whites into calming grays, turning machinery-packed walls and corners into shadows illuminated by unblinking starlike glows.

And turning the bed's badly wounded occupant into what plausibly looked like someone who was merely asleep.

Admiral Nek Bwua'tu, head of the Galactic Alliance Navy, lay as he had for so long, unmoving, faceup. A sheet covered and concealed his still-healing injuries. One arm lay exposed across his chest. Not long before, it had ended a bit below the elbow. Now it was complete again, the prosthetic hand and forearm indistinguishable from a naturally furry organic limb, except for the band of very short fur where the prosthetic had been joined to flesh—his fur had yet to grow in, completing the illusion that his arm was undamaged.

An aging Bothan, he was strong and resolute, one of Daala's few confidants.

And she could confide in him even now. But he could not hear, could not answer, while he remained in his coma.

She continued, though, as if he were an active part of the conversation. "What amazes me is the struggle for power. I don't mean the jockeying to discredit a rival for a Senate seat or the rank of general. They constitute real power, worth real effort and risk. I'm talking about the way people will resort to the same viciousness for nothing. The office martinet who's willing to make lifelong enemies just so he can win the right to apportion the monthly allotment of datachips. The personal assistant who doles out the right to appointments with her obscure, irrelevant, powerless boss just so she can curry favor with people equally meaningless." She shook her head, a slow motion at odds with her usually brisk personality. "You'd think that they'd proportion their efforts to the value of the reward, but no. Treachery can be just as great when it's for control of a caf cart as when it's for control of an empire."

Nek didn't answer. He lay, eyes closed, this being in the midst of the hours when his eyes were scheduled for rest rather than data stimulation. His thoughts remained locked away in the damaged compartments of his mind.

Knowing that she was not under observation, for there was no one else in the chamber and her own security team swept the location prior to every one of her frequent visits, she reached out and put a hand on his chest, on the fur above the blanket's hem. She felt the slow, shallow rise and fall of his breath. "I'm going to stay the course, Nek. I'm going to crush the ones who pursue power. Leaders of the slave rebellions, who simply want to rule where others ruled before. Politicians who look on good men and women as nothing but meat standing in their way . . . or as disposable assets. Jedi, with their lawless arrogance. I'll crush them, and you'll come back to me, and together we'll figure out how to crush them for good. How to make them pay for their self-interest. Self-indulgence."

There was a single rap at the chamber door, the signal from one of her security detail that someone was coming, someone they weren't supposed to intercept. Daala jerked her hand back.

She was standing, posture-perfect, demeanor icy, when the door lifted and Desha Lor entered.

A female Twi'lek, green-skinned with darker stripes on her head-tails, she wore a blue gown that set off her skin color attractively. One of her brain-tails, or lekku, was wrapped around her neck; the other hung free down her back.

She bowed to Daala. "My apologies, Admiral."

"What is it?" Daala didn't try to keep the curtness out of her tone.

"*Dust Dancer* has entered the system. Wynn will be here within half an hour by shuttle."

Daala moved to and then past the Twi'lek, allowing her speed and decisiveness to suggest that she had already put Nek Bwua'tu from her mind. The door reopened for her and she swept out. She did not need to look—she could hear Desha's rapid steps as the Twi'lek tried to catch up to her, to keep up with Daala's longer stride.

Once Desha had drawn up alongside, Daala spared her a glance.

"Bring his shuttle to the Senate Building. I'll debrief him personally."

"Yes, Admiral."

JEDI TEMPLE

A crisis, Leia noted, far from the first time, cut through barriers of rank and social status like nothing else could.

The conference chamber, deep within the Jedi Temple, was packed with Jedi who seldom interacted in these numbers on the basis of equals. But here, anyone might throw out an idea that could save lives. Thousands of lives. Millions of lives.

She sat in a high-backed gliding chair next to her daughter, Jaina, who brushed a lock of chestnut hair back behind her ear and spared her mother a smile. Leia patted her hand and turned to listen, to ease into the flow of conversation and information.

Master Corran Horn, standing in front of his own chair, his green Jedi robes somewhat rumpled from his having occupied them for too many hours, was talking. ". . . telemetry indicates that it entered planetary atmosphere five minutes ago and is on an approach path toward the government district, perhaps the Senate Building." He glanced at a junior Jedi Knight, a dark-skinned human male, who appeared to be monitoring matters on a datapad. The Jedi Knight returned his look and nodded confirmation of what Corran had just said.

Saba Sebatyne, the Barabel Jedi Master and temporary leader of the Jedi Order, sat to his immediate right. She glanced at the Jedi Knight and then back to Corran. "What are the chances Master Ramis and Jedi Dorvald will be detected?"

Corran shook his head. "Minimal. Seha is the sole pilot, and she is not well known. Facial recognition scanners are going to be thwarted by plastinserts in her cheeks, which change the outlines of her face, and by her optical goggles. Octa Ramis and Kyp Durron are inside the shielded smuggling compartment."

Master Cilghal, to his left, turned her large, bulbous eyes onto him. "Two Masters. If they *are* detected entering the Senate Building under these circumstances, it will force Chief of State Daala's hand. She will—correctly—assume that she's under assault. It will be all-out war."

Jaina spoke up. "You don't win by playing a defensive game."

"Jedi Solo is correct." Saba shifted in her seat, an unconscious indication of discomfort. Though it had been a few days since her tragic duel to the death with Master Kenth Hamner, the injuries to her side were not fully healed. Cilghal and Tekli exchanged a glance, outwardly emotionless, but it was clear to Leia that both wished Saba would do what she had to do to rest and recuperate.

But Saba could not afford the time that a protracted stay in a bacta tank would entail. Her position slightly more comfortable, she continued. "Now we must figure out how to capitalize on this opportunity. How to manage the timing. How to keep it as bloodless as possible."

His formal report done, Corran resumed his seat. "We already have provisions in place to ground the shuttle in the Senate Building. But if Kyp and Octa are going to be able to move around in the building, we need to get them resources. Identification, for those times a Jedi hand wave won't get them through a security station. Makeup. Yes, Leia?"

Leia lowered her half-raised hand. She thought for another split second about saying, *Forget it, bad idea.*

But it wasn't a bad idea, just a betrayal of trust. Daala perhaps did not deserve to be able to trust . . . but Leia's instincts ran contrary to what she was going to suggest. "After the, um, less-than-entirely-friendly exchange Master Sebatyne had with the Chief of State the other day, we could propose a series of meetings. Han and I and the Chief of State. This would require regular, even daily, visits to the Senate Building. Opportunities to smuggle in necessary materials, a process my husband knows something about."

Corran nodded, his expression speculative. "But she's going to want to talk to Kenth Hamner instead. They speak—spoke—the same language. And until the news of Hamner's death breaks, he'll still be assumed to be in charge."

Leia sighed. "Here's our story. Kenth Hamner has withdrawn to a concealed location because his military mind tells him that Daala's best tactic would be a surgical strike against the acting Grand Master of the Jedi Order, himself. He has taken this drastic action to forestall such a preemptive strike, and appointed Master Sebatyne as his spokesbeing in his absence. He'll come out of hiding when relations between the Alliance government and the Order have normalized."

It was a big lie, a painful lie. Kenth Hamner never would have avoided the risks brought on by his office.

But Daala seemed to be increasingly paranoid, and this tactic was one a paranoid would understand and appreciate.

Jaina looked thoughtful. "That . . . might work."

"We will do it." Saba's voice was decisive. "Now we must plan contingencies for the removal of Admiral Daala. In the absence of knowledge of her schedule, her current resources, and her exact state of mind."

Corran managed a wan smile. "If it were easy, it wouldn't call for a Jedi."

* * *

Several floors up, the name finally came to Valin Horn: Nam Chorios.

It had been growing within his mind for days, a conviction that he needed to go somewhere—somewhere distant, a place where he could be himself, could achieve his destiny. With each hour that passed, his sense of it became stronger, sharper, more defined.

And now, sitting in the main Temple chow hall, a forkful of nerf steak raised nearly to his lips, the exact place flashed into his mind.

He knew about Nam Chorios, of course. Everyone knew about the Death Seed plague that had decimated Meridian sector thirty standard years earlier. Everyone knew about the extraordinary efforts by the New Republic, later the Galactic Alliance, Department of Health to keep the cause of the plague buttoned down on that dimly lit little world.

And now he knew that this was where he needed to go.

He glanced at his sister, sitting opposite him.

She flashed him a smile and gave him a small nod. She knew.

They couldn't talk, of course. Spies were everywhere. These false Jedi clearly remained suspicious, despite pretending to accept the two of them as their own, as trusted members of their subverted Order. So Valin and Jysella had said not one single word that could have let their captors and observers know that the two of them understood what was really happening.

But what to do? The best way to escape Coruscant would be in StealthXs, but almost every Jedi StealthX was now in space, hunting the Sith.

Master Kam Solusar, lean and weathered, a Jedi since the earliest days of Luke Skywalker's school on Yavin 4, moved up to stand at the head of their table. "May I join you?"

Jysella offered the older man a smile Valin knew she did not feel, and Valin gestured for him to sit. "Of course."

Kam did, his body language suggesting ease and confidence. "I hear from Tekli that your last sets of test results are in. No lingering effects from your lengthy carbonite imprisonment."

Jysella gave Valin an encouraging look, and Valin answered Kam. "Good to know. Except, of course, it means that our vacation is over. Back to work, I assume?"

Kam nodded. "I'm afraid so. I've scheduled the two of you for a light courier run to Corellia. You'll take a long-range shuttle to transport some lightsaber crystals and some medicines, a small payload, to our enclave there."

Valin felt his stomach tighten. Trap, it was a trap.

It had to be. A mission like this didn't require two experienced Jedi Knights.

The most likely scenario flashed through his mind. The shuttle would have a tracking device on it. Valin and Jysella were expected to take it up out of Coruscant orbit, put in a course to some distant point that was probably not Corellia, and make an escape attempt. A signal to that tracking device, which would be tied into the shuttle's computer, would shut down all but the shuttle's life-maintenance systems. The false Jedi would come, and, knowing at last that Valin and Jysella had not been subverted, would capture them again. Or kill them.

This was all so obvious that only a crazy person would step blithely into the trap. Did these impostors think Valin and Jysella were crazy? Or of diminished mental capacity? It was insulting.

Or maybe he and his sister were expected to refuse

the bait because it was so obvious—but if so, what then? Valin's thoughts began to circle ever more tightly as he sought to anticipate his enemies' anticipation of his anticipation.

Kam gave Valin a close look. "Are you all right? I felt a flash of . . . something."

"Disgust." Valin positioned his fork underneath Kam's nose. "Here, smell this."

"That's all right."

"No, really. I think it's canned and about a million years old." He moved the fork under Jysella's nose. "Smell."

She grimaced at him. "Don't do this to me. He's always doing this to me."

Valin returned the fork to his plate. "A mission like that doesn't call for two Jedi Knights. One Jedi Knight and a Kowakian monkey-lizard, maybe."

"That's the point." Jysella kept her face straight. "I'm the Jedi Knight. You're the monkey-lizard."

Valin made a shooing gesture at her. "Send her to Corellia. Put me in charge of security at some bathing-suit charity function."

Jysella grinned at him. "Sure. A Gamorrean charity bathing-suit function."

Valin shuddered.

"Good point." Kam rose. "Jysella, two hours. Valin, I'll find something else for you to do." He wandered to the next table, doubtless to impose a series of tasks on the Jedi Knights and apprentices there.

Valin relaxed, just a little.

He and his sister had passed another test. Jysella would go on her undemanding Corellian run and come back. The two of them would be that much more trusted, that much closer to finding their escape vector off this planet . . . and on to Nam Chorios.

Chapter Eight

HWEG SHUL, NAM CHORIOS

BEN DECIDED THAT HE'D NEVER SEEN A TOWN QUITE like Hweg Shul.

Not that he'd seen much more than a few meters of it at a time. The driving wind and the dust storm that blanketed the town made any comprehensive overview impossible, and the intense cold, threatening to strip heat right out of his body despite his winter cloak and insulated clothes, made him happy to scurry with Luke and Vestara from sheltered spot to sheltered spot without much time for sightseeing.

But Ben did have time to see the disparity of architecture in the town.

The majority of dwellings and businesses were built on stilts or pilings—some wood, mostly permacrete, a few of durasteel coated in corrosion-resistant ceramics. These stilts tended to be a meter and a half to two meters high, the buildings themselves permacrete or duraplast domes of various colors, their foundations, resting atop the stilts, of sand-scoured permacrete. A meter up on the stilts, on most buildings, he could see bright glow rod modules, shining even at high noon—a measure against drochs, he assumed.

The dome shapes were highly wind-resistant, but their undersides, the flat permacrete foundations, were not. An occasional wind at the correct angle and speed would sweep under these elevated buildings, making lifting surfaces of the foundations. They did not actually lift off their stilts; they were too firmly attached for that. But the contact caused a succession of shuddering booms as the wind hit underside after underside in turn. It sounded like a city being strafed.

These, his father had told him, were the Newcomers' buildings.

Less numerous and far older were the dwellings and businesses of the Oldtimers. Often built with angled walls or even with trapezoidal shapes to keep the winds from hammering them constantly at right angles, they were made of stone covered with stucco, or, in the case of more shanty-like dwellings, cast-off duraplast covered in stucco. The stucco itself, like the materials the Newcomers' buildings were made of, was wind-scoured.

Viewports on both types of buildings were small patches of transparisteel, usually scratched by sand until they better served as diffusers rather than admitters of light. Ben quickly realized that the homes of the wealthier residents of town were characterized by transparisteel panels that were regularly replaced or polished, and thus more transparent than those in the less wealthy homes.

And everything, at least indoors, had a faint, not-too-offensive chemical smell. It was sweetish, a little cloying. Ben didn't recognize it or know what it was until he unpacked his duffel and, at his father's suggestion, sprayed down his clothes and the bag interior with the droch repellent he'd been provided at Koval Station. *That* was the smell—every plastoid surface, whether it be chamber walls, carpet, or furnishings, was coated or imbued with something to keep the drochs at bay.

His father led the three of them out of the Admirable Admiral, the hostel where they'd taken two adjoining rooms, and through the streets of this wind tunnel masquerading as a town.

Again, Ben raised his voice to a shout in order to be heard. "Looking for something, Dad? Why not use the town directory?"

"What we're looking for isn't in the directory. I know—I looked."

That got Vestara's attention. "What is it?"

"Theran Listeners."

Ben shook his head. "I thought they were the planet's healers. Why don't they advertise? It's not like they're the Black Sun."

"Computers and data grids are newfangled. Not to their liking." Luke spotted something that must have looked promising to him. He headed in that direction. Ben and Vestara followed.

It was, to all outward appearances, an Oldtimers' hovel, larger than most, but with light shining out through every hazy viewport. It was, unlike many such buildings, set back from the street, with a few aging landspeeders and speeder bikes parked outside, rocking in the wind.

The front door was a vault-like durasteel portal, a very old-fashioned design that swung out on metal hinges, and Ben belatedly recognized it as an ancient air lock door, doubtless transported from some crashed ship or ancient installation to this place. As the three neared it, a short man in hide garments and coat, fur lining showing at the wrists above his gloves, finished pulling the door open and stepped inside. He looked back, caught sight of Ben and his companions, did a double take, and then pulled the door shut just as the three reached it. The cycle light, scratched transparisteel inset at eye height, switched from green to red.

Ben stared at the formidable portal. "Friendly."

Luke gestured at Ben's clothing, which, though modest and stylistically ubiquitous in the spaceways, was clearly dissimilar to that worn by the man who had preceded them. "We're obviously not locals."

Vestara quirked a smile. "Are they going to gang up on us and beat us up because we're strangers? Or because we have a vocabulary of more than twelve words?"

"Now, now." The cycle light switched from red to green, and Luke pulled the door open.

Just inside was a small chamber—gray permacrete floor and ceiling, comparatively undamaged stucco walls. But the door opposite was the counterpart of the one by which they'd entered. Its cycle light showed red; as soon as Luke pulled his door shut against the howling wind, it went to green.

They stepped through into the main room of a pub. The floor and walls were covered in what looked like dark green vines tightly pressed into an irregular wall but, on closer inspection, proved to be absolutely flat, the appearance of roughness and depth an illusion. There were several long wooden tables and even more small round ones, but only about a dozen men and women sat among them. They were all hardy-looking customers, a bit below average Galactic Alliance human height standards, brown-haired and brown-eyed, clothed in garments of thin hide or hard-wearing cloth of brown or green.

And as Ben, Luke, and Vestara entered, their conversation stopped. They turned to look at the three intruders, their faces impassive.

They continued staring, silent, forbidding.

Automatically, reflexively, Ben opened himself to the Force. Alertness to ripples and eddies in the Force would give him an instant's advance warning if any of these insular locals chose to attack.

But it was not their emotions he felt, not the expected

combination of suspicion and perhaps growing resentment or anger.

He felt . . . surrounded, as if he'd suddenly realized that he was at the exact center of an amphitheater with thousands of spectators in the stands. And the observers' emotions were cool, analytical, not heated.

It was such a jolt, to feel himself under such immense scrutiny when he thought he was in a room with fewer than twenty people, that his eyes widened. He tried to keep his sudden surprise off his face.

The barkeeper, behind the bar, wiping its surface down with a yellow rag glistening with some sort of oil or polish, was a bald man of middle years, more heavily muscled and thicker in the middle than most of his customers. He made a face as though he'd come to an unhappy decision, and then spoke. "Help you?"

Luke didn't throw back his hood or take off his goggles. "Looking for healing."

"You're not local."

"Looking for healing."

Ben rubbed at his goggles. Despite the anti-fogging surface on them, the temperature and humidity difference between the outside and inside was causing them to fog up. Plus, the action might distract observers from his sudden surprise of a moment earlier. He glanced at Vestara and saw that she, too, was looking around as if seeking the source of all those extra, unseen eyes.

The exchange between Luke and the barkeeper had been odd. Curt, primitive. His father didn't even sound like himself. His voice had taken on the flat, slightly monotonous character of the barkeep's speech.

The barkeeper just kept polishing.

Luke just stood where he was.

Another Oldtimer, a young woman, her face long and weatherbeaten but her eyes lively, finally spoke. "Sel."

Another, a gray-bearded man, nodded as if that hadn't occurred to him. "Aye, Sel."

"Huh." The barkeeper considered it, then nodded. He looked back at Luke and jerked his thumb toward the wall to Ben's left. "Two streets down, three streets over to the right. Blue Newcomer dome. Ask for Sel. She'll set you right . . . or send you home."

The second man who'd spoken snickered. "I vote home."

"Thanks." Luke turned back toward the door.

As Ben and Vestara turned to follow, Ben felt a light impact against his back. He spun in time to see an insect the size of his thumbnail leap free from his cloak, hit the floor, and scurry away on six articulated legs to the shadowy baseboard.

None of the Oldtimers had apparently moved. The one who had flicked the droch onto Ben's back was clearly adroit at covering up his schoolroom-style pranks.

The barkeeper smiled. "Looks like you've got a pet, newmer."

Luke pulled the old air lock door open and led them out.

Back in the windy street, Ben gave his father a curious look. "I thought you said things had changed here in thirty years. From what I've read about this planet, what we just went through sounds like what would have happened back in the old days."

Luke shook his head. "Things *have* changed. They didn't go after us with scatterblasters and clubs."

Vestara snorted. "Not yet. But I'm keeping my eyes open."

"And the Force." Ben tried not to sound as thunderstruck and naïve as he felt. "Is that what it feels like all the time?"

Luke's smile became a little more sour. "That's what it's like when things are calm."

* * *

The barkeeper's directions led them to a small sea-blue dome, its viewports scoured to a frosty opacity. Its fold-down front steps were retracted.

Beside the spot on the foundation where those steps accordioned was a glowing green button with an intercom grille beside it. Both were inset a little, providing some protection from side winds. Luke pressed the button.

A moment later a woman's voice, buzzy and poppy, sounded from the antiquated device. "What is it?"

"We're looking for someone called Sel."

The voice at the other end did not reply, but the stairs, skeletal durasteel ones painted in alternating stripes of black and yellow for high visibility, unfolded. When they were done, the lowest one was still a quarter meter above the ground. Luke led the others up into the front-door alcove, and the door slid to one side, opening for them.

Beyond was a small antechamber, and as soon as the outer door slid shut, the inner one opened.

Next was a medium-sized all-purpose room. Ben saw tight-weave green carpet, a stuffed sofa and chair in tan, a long white duraplast-topped table that could have served for family dinners or medical examinations, walls lined with shelves stacked with piles of flimsi printouts, a door in the center of the back wall. By his calculation, this chamber would take up half the ground floor, with a much smaller second floor, under the apex of the dome, above the door they now faced.

That door opened and a woman emerged, wiping her hands on an off-white cloth. She was lean and fit but elderly, with white hair cut in a flat-topped hairstyle. Her eyes were a light blue, her skin fair. She wore a utilitarian burgundy jumpsuit. She must, Ben decided, have been beautiful in her youth; she was beautiful now.

She gave the three visitors a smile, showing white, even teeth. "I'm Sel."

Luke pulled his hood back and removed his goggles. "I'm—"

"Luke Skywalker." Sel dropped her drying cloth on one end of the white table and advanced, her hand outstretched. "An honor."

Luke shook her hand. He turned to indicate Ben and Vestara. "And this is . . ." But his voice trailed off and he turned back to Sel, his eyes narrowing—not in anger, Ben thought, but in consideration, perhaps suspicion.

"Sel." Luke's voice turned just a little incredulous. *"Teselda?"*

The old woman nodded, her smile half fading away. "That's my full given name, yes."

"You don't remember me?"

"I know who you are."

"No, from before. From thirty years ago. You knew me as Owen Lars."

"Ah." Sel gave him a blank look. "I'll take your word for it. There are things I don't recall."

Finally, Luke remembered to finish introductions. "This is my son, Ben Skywalker, and our companion, Vestara Khai. Ben, Vestara, this is Teselda . . . perhaps the galaxy's oldest surviving Jedi."

Chapter Nine

LUKE ACCEPTED SEL'S INVITATION TO SETTLE HIMSELF on the sofa, but declined her offer of caf or wine. With the most imperceptible of gestures, he indicated to Ben and Vestara, sitting respectively on the sofa beside him and in the stuffed chair, that they should decline, too, and they did.

Sel settled in a chair at the table and turned to the two teenagers. "Master Skywalker is stretching a point, I'm afraid. I'm no longer a Jedi. Have not been since before I can remember. If anything, I'm a Theran Listener now, and a healer. And sometimes, the one the Oldtimers send strangers to in order to see if I can sort them out."

Ben shook his head. "You weren't really represented in my father's accounts of what happened on Nam Chorios all those years ago."

Sel glanced at Luke. He thought the look carried just a touch of gratitude. "I doubt I made a good impression." She fell silent for a moment. "But yes, I was a Jedi once. I have the faintest memories of some happy times on Coruscant . . . As a young Jedi Knight I was sent here with a senior Jedi Knight named Beldorian."

"*Him* I've heard of. The Hutt Jedi."

"This world is toxic for Force-users if they stay long enough, unless they have a very rare level of emotional grounding. Which the Listeners do, through their contact with the tsils. But Beldorian was too much of a

Hutt, fighting the greedier, more self-indulgent side of his nature while a Jedi, succumbing to it here. I was too young, too ignorant, too inexperienced; I hadn't attained sufficient skill even to make a lightsaber. I fell to the dark side . . . and then to insanity." Sel's tone was oddly light, as if she were explaining the details of a shopping trip made earlier in the day.

Vestara's eyes flickered; it looked to Luke as though she was doing some calculation. "This would have been—what? Fifty, sixty years ago?"

Sel smiled again and offered a little shake of her head. "Much longer than that. Centuries ago."

Vestara frowned. "But you look true human. You'd be dead."

"I am true human. Of Alderaanian and Hapan descent. And not a prosthetic or replacement part in my body—except for my teeth, which were damaged beyond repair long ago by neglect." She shrugged. "But even as my mind decayed and flaked away, my body was preserved. By the consumption of drochs."

Ben's eyebrows rose and he glanced, suspicious, at his father. "That wasn't in your official report, either."

"Do you imagine that I wanted anyone to think they could achieve quasi-immortality by coming here and becoming involved with the drochs?" Luke gave his son a shake of the head. Indeed, he felt as though there was considerable danger in Vestara discovering these facts. If her true loyalties remained with the Sith, if she did not gain a healthy respect and fear of the drochs and what they represented while she was here . . . "Besides, it's not an issue of coming up with a dish, a recipe, that you can prepare for its health benefits."

"No." Sel's voice took on a distant quality. "You have to eat them live. Pop them wiggling into your mouth. Sometimes they try to chew their way into your cheek or your tongue when you do so. You bite down on them, crunch crunch crunch."

Ben tried to suppress a shudder. He wasn't entirely successful.

Sel shook off the mood and looked at Ben again. "As you consume them in this way, they give off little bursts of Force energy, life energy they have consumed. These bursts, in conjunction with secretions from their exoskeletons, cause the body to perform little acts of regeneration and repair beyond what bodies normally do. Nerve tissue regenerates. Cells are replenished . . . But there are problems. The larger drochs, the ones with more energy, have also drained memories and thoughts from their victims. Consumption of these drochs causes you to absorb these memories in turn, fragmenting your own mind over time. And the drochs have achieved their growth in the first place by draining other living things. To benefit from them, you find yourself at the top of a pyramid scheme, staying alive at the expense of others, animals and people—dozens, maybe hundreds, maybe more over time." She offered the slightest of shudders, matching Ben's.

Luke, still wary because of the way he had been deceived by this woman all those years before, hoped she was telling the truth—hoped the sympathy growing within him for her had a basis in truth. "But you've given up consuming drochs."

"Long ago." Sel gestured at herself. "Look at me. Aging at a normal rate now. My life has a finite span again . . . but at least it *is* a life. Not a terrible, endless story told to frighten children."

Ben knit his brows, still putting things together. "The HoloNet resources on Nam Chorios talk about the drochs as the source of the Death Seed plague, and talk about Nam Chorios's new medical economy, but don't link them. All this new development is from exploring medical by-products from study of the drochs, right?"

Sel brightened but shook her head. "No. The Theran Listeners also promote healing. They do it by convincing the patient's body to heal itself. This is the basis of the new economy. Take someone who is ill, run a complete series of tests on his body chemistry. Then put him through a regimen of Listener healing. Run a comparison suite of tests. The patient's body will have manifested chemicals that were not present before—for example, to diminish or eliminate a cancer. Newcomer doctors analyze those chemicals, trying to replicate them. Sometimes they can, resulting in new medicines. Not just for humans. Duros, Chadra-Fan, Gamorrean, Wookiee, Twi'lek . . . I've seen so many species helped."

Vestara looked doubtful. "And that's why you stay on this sad excuse for a world? So you can heal ungrateful, insular farmers and the occasional desperate visitor one by one?"

Sel gave her a wan smile. "More because there is no place for me anywhere else. I was raised in the Jedi Temple. I never knew my family. My contemporaries, all dead. Even my enemies, my rivals . . . dead and gone. I feared and struggled against death for longer than some planets have been settled. Now I know that death is part of life, a part I embrace. I do not rush toward it . . . but I might as well meet it here as anywhere." She gestured around at her modest home. "At a certain point in life you realize how little you need. Now I enjoy days without hatred and insanity, nights without bug bites and bad dreams."

Luke caught her eye. "How were you healed? The last time I saw you . . ."

"I suspect I was not a pretty holo."

"No."

"There is a Listener technique. I needed many applications of it over many years. I apparently knew, when they explained it to me, that it would probably restore my sanity but would rob me of memories . . . because I was so far gone, of *most* of my memories. The Listeners call it vein routing, meaning that you completely grind out every memory contributing to some traumatic response or insanity. I call it mnemotherapy, a gentler term, less frightening."

Luke nodded. "Which is why you don't remember meeting me."

"Yes."

"Teselda . . ." Luke battled a mix of emotions as he leaned forward. Dimly remembered revulsion at what Teselda had been, anger at how she had tried to use him and Callista, warred with his native sympathy . . . and his need for help in the here and now. "I suspect you're in greater danger than anyone on this planet."

Her smile widened. "That will be a refreshing change."

"I'm not kidding. Something is coming here, or has arrived already. A great menace that preys on the vulnerable through the Force. Before, you were too undertrained to have even the basic set of Jedi techniques. And then you couldn't keep from falling to the dark side, couldn't keep madness at bay. Couldn't control me for very long even when I was a much younger, much more emotional man. Unless you leave Nam Chorios now, I doubt you stand a chance. Especially if, as you say, you're a Listener now. I suspect their techniques of opening themselves to voices in the Force will make them especially vulnerable to Abeloth."

She blinked, considering. "And yet, knowing me, you stand a much better chance of recognizing this Abeloth's influence if you can witness changes to my manner. My personality."

"That's . . . very noble of you, but you *don't* want to be Abeloth's tool before you die."

"And yet here is where I will die. I made that choice a long, long time ago. So, how can I help?"

Luke sighed. "We suspect, from asking around at Koval Station, that Abeloth has not arrived yet—she'd be in a very small, very distinctive ship. But we can't be sure. Do the Oldtimers still operate the old weapons emplacements?"

"Yes, as sensor stations only."

"Can you get me any reports of small craft entering the atmosphere in the last few days, especially if they bypassed Koval Station?"

"Probably."

"And I was hoping to learn something of the Theran Force Listening technique . . ."

"Which I'd be honored to teach you."

"But now, I think I'd also like to see this mnemotherapy technique."

"Which I can't teach you . . . but I can introduce you to someone who can."

"Thank you." It felt strange to be grateful to someone who, for the last thirty years, Luke had remembered as an object of revulsion at worst, pity at best.

She put her hands over his. "Welcome back to Nam Chorios."

SENATE BUILDING, CORUSCANT

The shuttle *DeepRay*, a *Lambda*-class vehicle much newer than the one Luke had boarded at Koval Station, glided through the open blast-style hangar doors south and west of the Senate Building's main entrance hall. Alone in its tiny flight deck, Seha Dorvald put all her attention on making the last moments of this flight smooth and unremarkable.

Ahead and below, a jumpsuited Gamorrean, his

greenish, porcine features disinterested, gestured with a pair of guidance glow rods for her to bring the *Deep-Ray* farther into the hangar. Seha did as directed, gliding forward on repulsorlifts only until the shuttle was directly over a landing spot limned by glows embedded in the gray permacrete floor—the entire hangar was like that, the layout of its landing spots computer-controlled and infinitely reconfigurable.

She brought the shuttle down to a landing smooth enough that it was almost undetectable as a cessation of motion. She began powering down immediately and toggled her comm board. "This is Pilot Dorn. Welcome to Coruscant and the Senate Building. I hope you enjoyed your flight." With no additional speech making, she tripped the switch to lower the belly boarding ramp.

In her peripheral vision, from the port side, she saw an interior hangar door slide upward, allowing a small party, mostly humans, to enter. She recognized Chief of State Daala, gleaming in a spotless white admiral's uniform. With her were a number of security agents and aides, including a green Twi'lek woman.

Seha pretended to pay no attention. She brought up a diagnostics screen—a *simulated* diagnostics screen—and began tapping each item on it in turn as she would for a normal power-down checklist.

She heard her passengers catch up their carry bags and briefcases. Noisily, they began trooping down the boarding ramp.

And then there was Daala's voice, drifting up from the ramp: "Wynn. General Jaxton, Senator Bramsin. Delighted to have you back in one piece."

The gruff voice of General Jaxton followed, but grew fainter with each word. "Good to be back. So I can mount an operation against the *Errant Venture* and the Jedi. Imagine the arrogance . . ." Seha saw the Chief of

State's party, now considerably larger in size with the addition of her passengers, move back toward the door.

Moments later there was a creak as someone moved up the boarding ramp too silently for footsteps to be audible but not so carefully that the ramp itself settling did not make noise. Then a man spoke from just behind Seha: "What do you think you're doing?"

Seha glanced up at him. He was youthful, nice-looking, with brown hair in a military cut. He wore a Galactic Alliance Security lieutenant's uniform and a scowl that suggested he needed her to be impressed with his sternness and force of will.

She smiled up at him. "Powering down. I'm getting some anomalous readings from the thrust generators."

He shook his head. "You're authorized only to set down, let your passengers off, and lift. You're going to have to leave."

She gestured at the monitor screen with the checklist on it, at the three items blinking red. "I'd really rather—"

"I'm sorry, I have to insist."

Seha let her tone turn frosty. "Well, then you have two seconds to get your rear end off my shuttle." She turned her back on him and began a fast restart of powered-down systems.

The lieutenant was halfway down the ramp when the right stern thruster blew.

It didn't explode, not really. The plastoid-shelled capacitor and associated chemical package wired into the circuitry there, activated by the power-up switch, discharged, frying all the circuitry in that module, as well as catching on fire and emitting a tremendous amount of red-gray smoke.

Seha let out a well-practiced yell of outrage and frantically flipped all the emergency-off switches within reach.

On the permacrete just ahead of the shuttle, the lieutenant stood, staring up into her viewport, looking stricken. She glared at him, then rose. She ran back and down the boarding ramp to confront him.

A holodrama stereotype of righteous hostility, she thrust her datapad, showing a feed of the new, revised diagnostics screen, toward his face. "You see this? Couldn't wait five minutes for a simple diagnostics check and slow restart, could you? What do I tell my captain? What do I tell the Senator? The whole thruster array is blown because *somebody* couldn't wait. What is your name, Lieutenant Used to Have a Career? The Senator's going to want to know." She didn't bother to say which Senator. It was better for him to assume it was the one the shuttle had just delivered.

The lieutenant's words came out in a desperate, disorganized string: "Didn't. Predict. Regulations. Fire."

Smoke, pooling up against the permacrete ceiling, triggered the hangar's fire-control system. Articulated tubes descended from the ceiling, aimed, made a coughing noise, and emitted a tremendous quantity of gray-white fire-smothering foam.

Seha and the lieutenant were drenched in it. Seeing his uniform suddenly become matted with material the approximate consistency of dessert topping, seeing his once-natty hat adorned with a large triangular quantity of the stuff, Seha burst into laughter and couldn't stop.

The lieutenant managed a few more disjointed words and then heaved a sigh. The tubes ceased spewing. The lieutenant's pose of military competence irreparably shattered, he gave Seha an apologetic half grin. "All right. Start over. What do you need?"

Seha managed to bring her laughter under control. "Um, extend my access until I can get a mechanic in to look her over?"

"Consider it done. Twenty-four standard hours, maybe more pending your mechanic's report."

"And take a lady out to dinner? Once she's cleaned up, that is."

"Also done."

"What *is* your name, anyway?"

"Javon Thewles. Lieutenant, GA Security."

She held out a hand lightly insulated in foam. "Sela Dorn."

Chapter Ten

OBRIDAGAR'S SIMULATOR PALACE, CORUSCANT

THERE WEREN'T MANY PLACES, MOFF DRIKL LECERSEN reflected, where an aging man, far older than any active-duty starfighter pilot, could dress up in the uniform of a TIE fighter pilot with a unit designation forty years out of date and attract absolutely no attention.

Obridagar's Simulator Palace was one such place. Lecersen, clad head-to-foot in that black uniform, wearing the unit patch of one of the squadrons that so famously and unsuccessfully defended the original Death Star in the Yavin system before most of the Palace's patrons were born, walked the aisles of this curious establishment and nobody gave him a second look. The forbidding but anonymous helmet he wore concealed the gray hair, fierce bristly mustache, and military manner made famous by his many appearances on HoloNews broadcasts and addresses to those he governed within the Imperial Remnant.

The Palace's main room and many of the branching side rooms were, of course, dominated by gleaming banks of the highest-quality civilian-grade flight simulators. The carapaces enclosed cockpits featuring state-of-the-art vidscreens and sound systems; their bases and ceilings were implanted with acceleration/deceleration simulators similar in design to the inertial compensators found in starfighters. Slide into a cockpit, issue a verbal command indicating which vehicle was to be simulated and which mission was to be flown, and the simulator would do the rest, reconfiguring the cockpit components and throwing up the video images appropriate to those choices. Elsewhere in the establishment, a patron could find room-sized simulators, rented by teams, that replicated the interiors of capital ship bridges and famous fleet actions.

Obridagar's went a step beyond many similar businesses by encouraging costumes. So long as the uniform a customer wore was either from a decommissioned service or was more than twenty years out of date, it was permissible. So, in addition to tourists in glaringly mismatched colors or anonymous traveler's robes and university students in whatever style had been predetermined to represent rebellion and individuality on a universal basis this season, there were customers in the uniforms of pilots, ship officers, and infantry of the Empire, the Rebel Alliance, the Old Republic, the Alderaan Royal Guards . . . Lecersen continued to be amazed at the variety of styles and the attention to detail that went into some of them.

He turned left down a side corridor. Five paces behind, two similarly anonymous TIE fighter pilots, not obviously accompanying him, followed. A few steps more and Lecersen reached a door flanked by potted plants and a handful of costumed ersatz pilots standing in a group and talking in low tones—not obviously blocking access to the door, but doing so from any perspective of practicality. These men and women glanced at him, and one woman looked down at a datapad in her hand—this one designed to receive a transceiver signal from a device Lecersen carried. The signals they exchanged were apparently correct; the pilot, dressed in a sixty-year-old style from Naboo, nodded and stepped aside.

Lecersen brushed past her. The door opened and he went through, emerging into a small private cantina, heavy with plants in the sort of long, thin boxes that were normally placed just outside viewports. The lights overhead were bright, the wood lining the walls dark. Lecersen's escorts did not enter with him, and the door slid shut. Lecersen removed his helmet, glad to have moving air on his face again.

The others were already waiting for him.

Senator Haydnat Treen of Kuat, her years not diminishing her alert eyes or perfect posture, wore a uniform matching that of the datapad sentry outside. On the card table beside her rested the antiquated helmet of a Naboo pilot. Her gray hair, though immaculately styled, bore the unmistakable signs of having been mashed by the helmet and then teased back into a semblance of its correct shape.

General Merratt Jaxton, Chief of GA Starfighter Command, burly and surly, sat on a stool at the bar. His costume was a mismatch of components: A jumpsuit, once probably orange, that had been imperfectly dyed into something that was now the murky green of a lizard's innards and subsequently patched. His boots, knee-high, had glaringly obvious sheaths for hold-out blasters and vibroblades clipped inside the upper cuffs. His nerf-hide flak jacket was stenciled on the back with kill markings—ridiculous ones: silhouettes of a city construction droid, a sarlacc, two communications satellites, a refueling station, and an Ewok. His helmet and face mask were of identical leather and lay on the bar to his right.

Senator Fost Bramsin, tall, ancient, and cadaverous, occupied a stuffed chair of black leather beneath the drooping fronds of a tropical fern. He was dressed as if for a day's activities at the Senate, in a dark, expensive, and immaculate suit, but draped over the back of the chair was the red robe of an Imperial throne room guard, the matching helmet resting on the floor by his feet. Over his steaming cup of caf, he gave Lecersen a cordial little nod.

And then there was the newest member of their conspiracy. Lecersen saw what she was wearing and stopped where he was. "That, my dear, is a genuinely sick joke."

Admiral Sallinor Parova smiled, taking the remark as a compliment—though Lecersen had not meant it as such. A dark-skinned human woman of over-average height, her short hair tightly curled, she sat opposite Treen in a costume that was at once childlike in its crudity and very sophisticated in the offense it offered.

It started with a white admiral's uniform, decades out of date, but the uniform itself was of the sort one might buy for a child at a novelty costumer's—it was made in a single piece, like a loose-fitting jumpsuit, of slick woven flimsiplast, the uniform details printed on its surface in color rather than being actual components such as trousers, jacket, and buttons.

On the felt tabletop before her lay the costume's other components, a simple, inexpensive mask of a Bothan head and matching gloves.

She held up a hand. "Wait, you have to get the full effect." Her voice was surprisingly low and rich; it seemingly belonged to a much larger woman, one who might perform opera.

Senator Treen shook her head sorrowfully and, theatrical in her movements, buried her face in her hands. Obviously she had seen this before.

In moments Parova donned the mask and the gloves. Lecersen could see that the right glove was larger than the other.

Parova turned to face Lecersen, then flung up her

hands as if trying to take command of a meeting. Her right glove slipped off and went flying; Jaxton fielded it. Parova had already withdrawn her hand into her sleeve, so the effect was as if her hand had come flying off.

She shrugged. "Whoops!" Her voice was merry, and she broke into laughter as attractive as wineglasses shattering on a permacrete floor. She was still laughing as she pulled the mask and other glove off.

Lecersen shook his head and joined Jaxton at the bar. He set his helmet on the bar to one side. "Even sicker than I had guessed."

Jaxton looked over at him and gave a small, glum nod.

Lecersen did not know Parova well. She had been maneuvered by Jaxton, Treen, and Bramsin into a position within Admiral Bwua'tu's command hierarchy after the conspiracy had been formed. And though the eventual assassination attempt on Bwua'tu had failed—it had resulted in internal injuries, the loss of his right arm, and a coma—it had been just as successful as if it had been carried off as planned. Parova had been appointed by Chief of State Daala as acting Chief of Naval Operations, giving her all the power, influence, and resources she would have had if Bwua'tu had died.

Lecersen's due-diligence research on the woman strongly suggested that she was competent, resourceful, and dedicated to the conspirators' common principles of order, unity, and dispassionate rule of law . . . but this display gave him pause. Bwua'tu had been an impediment, an obstacle between them and their mutual goal, but he was an honorable warrior, deserving of respect, not mockery.

The bartender, a silvery protocol droid styled as a female, moved to stand before Lecersen. "May I bring you a drink?" The droid wore a restraining bolt, the large variety called an Inhibitor, which, when pulled, would take with it every recording made by the droid during the time it wore the bolt. This was an admirable security touch, a device that made any droid temporarily pressed into service a nonthreat to security.

"Sonic Screwdriver." Lecersen turned to face the others. "Well? Any progress while Jaxton and I were hostages of the Jedi?"

Treen smiled. "I think so, but it is Jaxton himself who offers confirmation."

Lecersen looked at the general. "Well?"

"I just spent about an hour being debriefed by Daala." Jaxton took a small sip from his drink, which smelled like something warm composed of caf, cream, and Corellian brandy. "She was under perfect, rigid control. Like the string of a musical instrument tightened until one note played on it will cause it to snap."

"Excellent. So now we may just need that one little pluck to set things into motion."

Bramsin shook his head. "If I may introduce a metaphor that could prove painful to the two of you, we want to program a skifter first."

A skifter was a rigged card used to cheat at sabacc. Lecersen did not allow himself to react to the reference, but Jaxton shot the aged Senator a dirty look. Lecersen and Jaxton had each lost the million-credit stake with which they had bought their way into the celebrity sabacc tournament that had just been held on the *Errant Venture*. Lecersen saw the loss as one of the inevitable possibilities of a gamble, but Jaxton had apparently had more emotion invested in the likelihood of his own victory.

Bramsin continued. "Our odds of making this coup fast and bloodless increase if we can cause some mistrust by Daala of her security details. If she has reason to mistrust Galactic Alliance Security . . ."

Lecersen thought it over. "Then she'll rely on her first love. The fleet. The navy. Even if it isn't the navy of her early days."

Parova smiled. "And I would be very happy and proud to provide the Chief of State with an elite security detail."

Lecersen's drink arrived, and he took a sip. The protocol droid had provided an absolutely average, by-the-recipe-book Sonic Screwdriver, the standard proportions of fruit juice and liquor, indistinguishable from the drink as served in a million cantinas and spaceports. He set it down again. "What if she goes to the Mandalorians instead?"

"We don't think she will." Treen's voice was certain; the only thing not certain was whether she was speaking of the conspirators in general or employing the royal *we*. "As she is subjected to more and more stress, we believe she will continue to trust them to destroy her enemies, but not to guard her while she sleeps."

"She really is becoming the old Daala." Jaxton actually sounded a bit regretful. That was not too surprising; three or four decades earlier, as a starfighter pilot, he might have faced Daala's forces. "Talking in tones as if her speeches were being recorded for replay by the Imperial-era Moffs. Brooking no argument. Snappish. Brittle. Still raw from Grand Moff Tarkin's death. She didn't know the Mandalorians well then, but she did know the fleet."

Parova nodded. "And my father, who served with her once upon a time."

"Ah." Lecersen gave her a little nod of respect. "You have impeccable credentials."

"And they're getting more impeccable all the time."

"So." Lecersen considered their options. "If and when we can maneuver security out of favor and your security detail into favor, and it becomes time to act, how do we push her over the edge?"

Parova's expression suddenly became sober. "I have that worked out. It will be sad . . . but let's just say that it will serve two or more purposes, and that I have no room in my navy for a vessel whose commander consistently fails to exceed minimal expectations."

Chapter Eleven

HWEG SHUL, NAM CHORIOS

As night fell across this portion of Nam Chorios, even the listless heat provided by the violet sun diminished—and so did the atmospheric agitation on the planet's surface. Winds died; the dust storm that had blanketed the capital town throughout the daylight hours faded, leaving Hweg Shul caked with a new layer of dust the approximate color of dirty snow. Overhead, a starfield like an empire's collection of royal jewels poured carelessly across a bed of black velvet gleamed down at the residents of this rocky, unrewarding world.

So beautiful. Luke, standing outside the Admirable Admiral with his son and Vestara, looked at the expanse of shining, twinkling lights. *Farther out from town, where the inhabitants' lights don't interfere, it will be more beautiful still.*

It was a strange dichotomy, that a world so poor, which had provided such a mean and meager living to its inhabitants for so many hundreds of years, should be lovely in so many ways. Its ravines and rises full of gloriously colorful crystals below, its clear and unpolluted nighttime skies above . . . it was little wonder that so many hardy citizens had remained behind when the world opened up for trade and emigration thirty years earlier, or that the population had even grown in numbers since then.

In the stillness of the painfully cold night, Luke glimpsed a flicker of light far up the street. It was hard to make out at this distance, even with the air as still and clear as it was, but it had a familiar, almost organic quality, like a legless sidewinder species made of golden illumination hurtling toward them at Podracer speed.

He caught the teenagers' attention. "Brace yourselves. Don't resist it. Let it flow through you."

Vestara caught sight of it, now plainly visible, just a few blocks from them. Her eyes widened.

Ben, his attention on his father, didn't. "Let *what* flow—"

Then it was on them, under them, *through* them, a blinding flash of light and a tingling throughout their bodies as if each had accidentally brushed a high-voltage line. Luke felt his muscles spasm, felt his mind go blank just for an instant. He saw his son and Vestara fall. He himself stayed upright, not out of force of will, but out of control of the Force—he let the Force energy pass through him, barely a trace interacting with his body.

Then the light was gone, crackling across the ground behind them, curling serpent-like beneath the elevated foundation of the hostel and other Newcomer buildings before vanishing among the homes and streets a block away.

Ben scrambled to his feet, a little shaky. "Uh . . . can I take it that this was ground lightning?"

Vestara rose more slowly and gracefully. "It's like a tedious old nursemaid who wants to tickle you . . . except she's switched to using an electrowhip."

"Ground lightning, yes." Luke stretched his legs to make sure they were still limber. The ground lightning jolt had aggravated his injured knee, which throbbed.

"It can be surprising and sometimes painful . . . but it also kills drochs."

"Ah." Ben's voice became cheerful. "Then it's my new best friend. I want to bathe in it."

Moments later, Sel appeared, turning the corner a block up the darkened, almost empty street. Over her jumpsuit were a fur-lined jacket and heavy boots in cu-pa hide dyed bright yellow, plus a heavy tan hooded cloak. Her features were largely hidden by a woolen veil and goggles, but she waved as she approached. "Were you outside for that?"

Luke nodded. "I see some things haven't changed."

Sel reached them, did not break stride, moved past, leading them onward. "Yes. Some things are eternal."

Luke, Ben, and Vestara caught up to her, Luke falling in place to her left. "So, we have permission to see this mnemotherapy being performed?"

"Yes. The Listener-Master Taru will conduct."

"Did the Oldtimer weapons emplacements have any sensor data that might be relevant?"

Sel nodded. "Two nights ago, someone made an adroit atmospheric insertion in a craft the size of a small shuttle. The pilot had a good fix on the Golan platforms around the planet, limiting their ability to fire on it—which they wouldn't anyway, since it was arriving, not departing—or to get useful sensor data. The ground weapons emplacement at Bleak Point got a fuzzy image of it. The operator says it was roughly spherical, but larger than a TIE fighter."

"Bleak Point." Despite himself, Luke was drawn into his memories for a moment. Bleak Point was where his first trip to Nam Chorios had ended—where he'd been taken after crash-landing and persuading the tsils to destroy the craft carrying the Death Seed offworld, where he'd been reunited with Leia.

Where he'd seen Callista for the last time, waving her

a farewell he did not know would be a final one. Where he'd taken a giant step toward abandonment of unhealthy attachment in his life.

For years afterward, he'd borne a diminishing sadness resulting from that good-bye, but had been certain it had been the right thing to do. Now, recently, doubts had arisen to plague him. If he had gone to her then, somehow persuaded her to leave Nam Chorios, persuaded her to follow some other road in her quest to regain her ability to connect with the Force, might she have avoided the Maw? Might she have escaped the fate that awaited her with Abeloth?

"We're here." Sel stopped and gestured for the others to enter a long, low, darkened Oldtimer building.

Luke snapped out of his reverie, glancing at Ben and Vestara to make sure they had not noticed his distraction. They appeared not to have. Luke followed Sel through the outer door.

In this place, there was an anteroom but no inner door. Instead, the doorway out of the antechamber was blanketed by heavy folds of woolen cloth, another insulating layer between the house interior and the subfreezing outer air.

Sel parted the blankets and led them into a chamber that might have been another pub's taproom; its tables were of similar make and antiquity. But some of them had thin, uneven bed-mats on them, and folded blankets. There were a few chairs, and also a couple of rolling racks holding bins of old-fashioned examination instruments—directional glow rods, tongs, galvanic response meters, encephaloscanners, sonic probes. There was only one person in the chamber, an elderly man seated on one of the chairs; he waved at Sel, then went back to reading a flimsi printout.

Sel took them through a curtained, round-topped entryway at the back of the chamber. It led to a flight of stairs that looked as though they'd been cut long before from the living rock beneath Hweg Shul. Sel headed down.

Luke hesitated for just a moment. He had bad memories of stone steps leading into darkness on Nam Chorios. Leia's memories, he knew, were even worse. But he could feel none of the consumption and waste of Force energy, as if the Force itself were rotting in a swamp, that had characterized the nests of drochs that had given him such trouble thirty years before. He headed down, Ben and Vestara following.

The chamber beneath was about the same size and shape as the one above, but had a higher ceiling and was dominated by a centerpiece—a crude hemisphere like half a gigantic geode, two and a half meters in diameter, positioned as if balanced on one edge. The crystals lining the hemisphere's interior were of all colors, predominantly blue, green, white, and violet.

Directly in front of the geode was a raised cot of metal, like a gurney without wheels or repulsorlift buoyancy tanks, and on it lay a young woman. She was perhaps twenty, small-boned, with facial features characteristic of the Oldtimers, and she wore the rough, simple garments of the Oldtimers. Her dark brown hair was worn in a long braid that mostly lay beneath her, and her eyes were closed.

Beside the cot stood another Oldtimer, a strongly built man of thirty or forty, his dark hair graying. He turned toward Sel as she led the others into the chamber. He wore a trim beard more appropriate to a dashing smuggler than a farmer, and his eyes were dark, expressive.

Sel gestured back at her companions. "Taru, I bring you Master Luke Skywalker, Ben Skywalker, Vestara Khai. This is Master Taru Durn, head of the healer hall of Hweg Shul."

Taru shook hands with all three, in the fashion of someone familiar with offworld customs, and turned to Luke. "I know you both from holocasts and from the memories of the tsils."

"I'm surprised to be remembered."

Taru shrugged. "They remember everything. You have special meaning to them, though. You promised to bring back the tsils that had been taken offworld and enslaved, and by and large you made good on your promise."

Luke nodded. He'd certainly tried. Tragically, some of the sentient crystals taken offworld and programmed as central processing units for droids, droid starfighters, and other devices could not be found, and others had been destroyed. But—with invaluable help from Leia, then the New Republic's Chief of State—he had returned most of them, and the search still went on for the missing ones.

Taru turned to the woman on the cot. "This is Thei. When she was five, she and her mother departed their farmstead for Ruby Gulch on a cu-pa. Two days later, she came wandering in out of the barrens alone. She had no memory of how this came to be. She was adopted by a rock ivory mining family and lived a normal life until recently. Six months ago, she married a Newcomer speeder mechanic here in town . . . and shortly after began experiencing emotional breaks, total collapses. Triggered, often as not, by the smell of topato soup."

Ben blinked. "If I didn't suspect there was a tragedy behind that, it might even be funny."

Taru nodded. "But mundane details can be strongly tied to memories. Smells are especially evocative."

Vestara glanced around. "If she's recently married, where's her husband?"

"They have differing opinions about the efficacy of

Oldtimer healing. Her husband is all for modern medical techniques and looks on what the Listeners do as superstition."

Ben's frown was thoughtful. "It's not a good idea for husbands and wives to conceal big things from each other. That can lead to tragedy, too."

Taru opened his mouth to respond, but Luke interrupted, deflecting the conversation in a new direction. "The geode. What's it doing here?"

"Normally, the vein-routing technique—which Sel insists on calling mnemotherapy—is conducted by one healer, one patient, and a trance-inducing medicine, nothing more. But that gives nothing for learners to witness. We use reflecting bowls like this to allow others to witness and understand what's going on. Since, with Thei's permission, we will have witnesses today, we will conduct this session with a reflecting bowl. Please, bring up stools."

They did. Vestara, first to sit, frowned. "If this is a Force technique, and use of the Force causes dangerous storms—"

Taru nodded, obviously having heard the question before. "The techniques taught to us by the tsils don't cause the Force storms. Oh, every use of the Force has a magnified effect here, but very minor uses, and uses involving tsil techniques, are channeled by the tsils and manifest themselves as ground lightning. Harmless."

When all were seated, Taru continued. "Thei is currently in a mesmeric state, one that enhances her mental connection to the Force. She will hear only me . . . I hope. Thei, can you hear me?"

The young woman spoke, her voice very quiet. "Yes."

"You know where you are. Safe, surrounded by friends and protectors."

"Yes."

"We are going to recall an earlier time, but you will

remember always that you are here, that there is no danger to you."

"I'll remember."

"It's just past the spring planting. You're five years old. You and your mother are going in to Ruby Gulch. Why?"

"Cloth . . . There are bolts of cloth to pick up. I'm going to have a dress . . ."

"You ride out on your cu-pa."

"Her name is Sparkle."

"Yes, Sparkle. Can you *see* Sparkle for me?"

The young woman did not answer, but glints of light appeared at points on the geode's interior, then flashed from crystal to crystal. In moments the glows resolved themselves into a wavering image of one of the two-legged beasts, this one long-furred, young, unusually long-legged. It turned its head to look at the viewers.

"Good. Now you're on Sparkle, heading to Ruby Gulch."

The image wavered, and abruptly the cu-pa was saddled, with an adult woman and a little girl, both brown-haired and similarly bundled against cold weather, in the saddle. The cu-pa vanished, replaced by a view of its neck and head from directly behind, a child's-eye view from the back of the riding creature. Now there was noise, too, vibrating from the geode as though it were a speaker of ancient design, the *thup-thup-thup* of the cu-pa's stride in the dust.

But the image would not stay consistent. First it showed a bleak gravel-encrusted wasteland ahead, then a woman's face from below, then views of Sparkle without riders, with or without saddle, from the side, all in a swirling kaleidoscope of brief glimpses.

The images began to cycle, repeating themselves with variations.

Taru glanced at Luke. "She doesn't want to go forward."

"Ah."

"It's here we define and insulate the first memory vein." Taru reached a hand, flat, palm down, over Thei's forehead and closed his own eyes.

Luke felt something, a tenuous vibration in the Force. The image in the geode contracted just slightly, was outlined in a faint golden glow.

Taru opened his eyes. "Now we have identified a specific set of memories—with some patients, they could be hallucinations instead—that abut the ones that truly cause trouble. We surround them with our own identities, our own projections in the Force, like sheathing them in a flimsiplast casing."

Luke glanced at the youngsters. Both were rapt, their attention on the geode images and Thei's face.

"Thei, you need to go on."

"No."

"Why not?"

"I don't know."

"You're safe. I'm here. There are Jedi here to protect you. Nothing will hurt you."

Thei whimpered. But she did go on. Suddenly the image's surroundings were foothills, crags of stone and spurs of crystal, as night fell.

Then they were in a cave, deep within it, the outside suggested only by a distant patch of stars at ground level—the cave mouth. Much closer, Thei's mother had set up a little grill—a stainless-durasteel grating, half a meter square, atop a rectangular pan just smaller than that. In the pan was a can of heating fuel, ignited, and atop was a good-sized saucepan with liquid in it, beginning to simmer.

Taru gestured at the geode, a complex series of hand

motions that reminded Luke of the sort of signed Basic used by elite military forces and deaf species.

A smell flowed through the room. Luke saw the others react to it, too. Topato soup, thick and heavy, flavored with spices. It startled Luke to be smelling a meal from fifteen years earlier. He could sometimes do that within his own memory, but to experience it from someone else's was a novelty.

The image changed again. It had to be showing a later hour, still within the cave. Thei's mother was asleep, bundled in her cloak and bedroll, a blaster rifle and glow rod near at hand. Sparkle could be seen just beyond her, lying on its side. The angle of the image was such that it had to be from the child Thei's perspective, nestled up against her mother. The smell of the soup was reduced in strength but still distinct.

There was a crack, a sound like stone shattering.

The eyes of Thei's mother opened. Sparkle sprang to its feet, making a startled noise, then seemingly collapsed again, though there was no sign, in the blurred and confused image, that the cu-pa's legs had folded.

Sparkle wailed, then sank instantly out of sight.

Thei's mother rolled away from Thei as if helpless to prevent the motion, toward where Sparkle had lain. She shoved Thei, and the girl's point of view tumbled, became incoherent.

It steadied again as the child Thei rose. The smell of soup was gone, replaced by another odor—

Luke felt his stomach lurch. It was the moist, enzymatic, decaying smell of a droch nest, a big one. He winced, knowing what had to come next.

The girl's point of view moved forward. Where the cu-pa and her mother had been, there was now a hole in the cave floor, sign of a collapse. A chittering, skittering noise emerged from the hole, punctuated by shrill screams from the cu-pa, wails of fear from the woman.

Chapter Twelve

In the image, which was increasingly clear, increasingly real, the shrieks of both human and cu-pa grew in volume.

The little Thei's small hand reached down to pick up the glow rod, to activate it, to shine its light down into the hole.

The portion of the cave floor where Thei's mother and Sparkle had lain, weak for who knew how many centuries, overburdened by the cu-pa's weight, had collapsed into a lower cave. Its floor was some ten meters down.

And it crawled with drochs, a carpet of the tiniest ones, moving lumps the size of fingernails.

Sparkle struggled frantically, its legs clearly broken, and atop its flank was a droch the size of a Wookiee's spread-fingered hand: a huge one. It turned to look at Thei, its multifaceted eyes evaluative, intelligent.

Thei's mother stood at the edge of the cave, scrabbling against the wall, trying to climb it. But the stone there was too smooth, and she could get no purchase. Drochs had swarmed up her legs and back. They had already drawn so much strength from her that it was clear her legs were failing, trembling, barely able to support her.

Her eyes connected with Thei's, and she managed two words: "Run, baby." Then she toppled over backward and the drochs swarmed over her.

A sharp, high-pitched peal rose from the image, a child's scream, and drochs by the hundreds or thousands began to climb the wall toward Thei.

Then the image jolted, blurred. Suddenly it was outside, under the stars, with dawn gleaming violet in the east. And the child's scream continued as the little Thei ran . . .

"Come back to us. Come back to the present, where you're safe. Don't think about the cave. Think about your husband. Think about your baby to come." Rubbing his chin, Taru sat back on his stool, leaning away from Thei and the geode.

The image in the geode faded, though the golden outline around its circumference lingered.

Ben whistled. He had paled.

Luke knew what he was thinking, what he was feeling. He'd lost his own mother only a few years before. It had been very hard to deal with. What it must be like to be five and go through that . . . Luke reached out, gave Ben a reassuring squeeze on the shoulder.

Then he turned to Taru. "What next?"

"First, I need to confirm something." From a side table, Taru retrieved a datapad, an older model with a scratched, scuffed case. He brought up a viewer and began scrolling through a set of holocam images. He angled the device so Luke could see its screen, but it showed only ordinary domestic scenes: Thei and the happy dark-skinned man who was clearly her new husband, the husband laboring away beneath an airspeeder, a living room, a kitchen—

"There." Taru froze the sequence on one of the kitchen images. It showed the husband standing beside a stove, saying something back over his shoulder to whomever it was taking the picture, presumably Thei. "See anything?"

Luke glanced at the image, shook his head, then

frowned and narrowed his eyes. He tapped the stovetop. "That saucepan. It's identical to the one in her memories."

Taru snapped the datapad shut. "Not of local manufacture. And a distinctive design, unusual scrollwork on the handle. So this girl leaves her home, moves into her new husband's dwelling, he has a saucepan identical to one she last saw in association with her mother's death . . ."

"And memories start surfacing." Luke considered. "What do you do now?"

"Just the revelation of the source of her terrors would probably suffice if she wanted to confront them. She could take that knowledge to a Newcomer mind doctor and spend the years, credits, and effort necessary to diminish those terrors. But we spoke of this earlier. She knows something awful had to have befallen her mother and doesn't want to live with that. So we will be doing the vein routing." Taru leaned toward Thei again. "Normally it takes months or years to learn the beginnings of this technique. But I suspect you constitute a very advanced student. Still, you'll need to join with me to the extent you can, a melding through the Force . . ."

"One of my specialties." Luke closed his eyes and extended his awareness through the living energy that surrounded them.

Once again, he was rocked by the sense that he stood in a crowd of giant, impassive observers. But he ignored them, shoved aside the self-consciousness that this world's Force presence invariably produced, and sought Taru.

He found the man's presence in the Force almost instantly—his, Ben's, Vestara's, and that of the girl Thei. Thei's presence was shining, as if illuminated by a bank of industrial-strength glow rods.

Within the Force, Luke reached out for Taru and

Thei, his energy connecting with, interacting with, theirs. He opened his eyes.

Taru shook his head, clearly impressed with Luke's speed and skill. His voice dropped to a whisper. "Now you see the portions of her memory that I have outlined and surrounded. Join me, find the same borders."

Luke tried. It was diabolically complicated. He could see Taru's energy, see its parameters, but not the memories themselves—as if, told to look at a river, he could only estimate its course by looking at dry riverbanks. Working with memories was not like working with Force energy . . .

Wait, it was. For all these memories had a distinctive characteristic, the primal terror experienced by a little girl. Emotion could flavor the Force, and he sought out that emotion, tasting its flavors, sensing where it turned more benign at the boundary of other experiences.

There was a recollection of the twelve-year-old Thei catching sight of herself in a mirror, gauging the changes time was making, reflecting that ever more she was coming to resemble her mother—and then, a blast of terror inexplicable to the adolescent Thei. But it was explicable to Luke, to Taru, for her eyes in the mirror had the same pleading quality as Thei's mother in that final moment and were suddenly bound up forevermore with fear. They surrounded that memory.

Another memory, this one by the then-teenage Thei, seeing a fallen cu-pa wailing in a corral, victim of a broken leg. Again, there was terror the girl did not understand. Again, Luke and Taru did, seeing in the scene a reflection of Sparkle's final moments. Again, they encapsulated the recollection.

Luke and Taru flowed along the contours of Thei's terror until they could find no more matching the flavor of fear they sought. There were other terrors in the girl's life, other tragedies, but none connected even peripherally with her mother's death.

"Very good, Master Skywalker. Now, ever so gently, we pull."

They did, together.

Luke had trained in many combat styles, against masters of many arts, and one thing he had learned early on was that the holodramas vastly exaggerated the ease with which a simple blade could be drawn from a body into which it had been thrust. Organic tissues tended to close over simple metal surfaces, preventing easy withdrawal. This was why primitive blades were often engineered with fullers, inaccurately referred to as blood grooves—they made that withdrawal a bit easier. This was why lightsabers and vibroblades were far superior to simple blades. Their very nature made them easy to withdraw instantaneously.

Pulling the toxic memories from Thei was like drawing out a simple blade. Despite her conscious wishes, her unconscious mind resisted their extraction. The very nature of memory resisted. The effort took a consistent application of Force by Luke and Taru, a slow, measured, implacable pull. Thought by thought, memory by memory, Luke and Taru persisted, and the set of horrifying images slowly released its hold on the young woman.

Luke could sense that it would be possible to apply more strength, less control, and wrench those memories free. He could not imagine the damage such an act would cause to Thei's psyche.

Within minutes, though he could not see them as images, Luke could sense the presence of the extracted memories as a hovering matrix of thoughts, bound to the Force but not to a body, floating before him and Taru, each of them touching it.

Taru turned to him. "Do you want them?"

Appalled, Luke stared at him. "*What?*"

"Thei loses them. She does not want them. But they are important, human experiences. We cannot dishonor memory by letting it fade to nothingness. Masters of this technique take those memories into themselves so that they will not evaporate."

Luke seldom found himself shocked, but the notion of internalizing the horror of a five-year-old girl watching her mother die floored him. At the same time, he understood what Taru was saying. "How many—how much of other people's grief do you carry in you, Taru?"

Taru gave him a bitter little smile. "How much do *you* carry, Master Skywalker?"

"No, I don't . . . I don't want these memories."

"Then you must release them."

Luke did, and felt a sudden easing of tension he hadn't realized he was experiencing.

Taru raised his hands. His eyes closed.

There was no visible change, but Luke could feel the alien Force element flow into Taru, become part of him. Taru shuddered once. Then his eyes opened. He looked tired. "Done."

"That was . . ." Something occurred to Luke. "I've done that before."

"I thought perhaps you had. You took to it very quickly."

"Not memories, not as such. But I've rooted out Force energies that didn't belong . . ." Luke felt tired himself.

"You know you are hurt." Taru glanced down at Luke's knee.

"My leg?" Luke flexed his injured knee experimentally. "It's healing quickly."

"If you want me to look at that—you know bacta isn't allowed on Nam Chorios, since it exacerbates the effects of the Death Seed plague . . ."

The scuffed datapad rose from the table where Taru

had replaced it. Suspended by no hand and no wire, it floated in midair, then opened of its own accord.

Luke glanced around at the others. "Who's doing that?" He couldn't detect any of them acting through the Force; the routine interference of omnipresent, dispassionate eyes prevented him from determining the effect's source. "Stop it at once."

Ben shrugged. "Not me."

The others began to shake their heads.

The datapad flew a meter to crack into the side of Taru's head. The blow toppled the Listener from his stool. He fell, landing on his buttocks and lower back, and an expression of pain shot across his face.

Luke was on his feet in an instant but did not stoop to help Taru. He knew what was coming, knew he could not take his attention off his surroundings. "Force storm! Prepare yourselves."

Ben, Vestara, and Sel rose, unconsciously took back-to-back positions. Taru rose, moved beside Thei, and angled his body over hers protectively. A thin line of blood crawled down his cheek from the cut inflicted by the datapad.

Vestara's lightsaber rose, tugging at the clip that held it to her belt. She grabbed it. Its activation button depressed of its own accord. She twisted the hilt, and the red blade sprang into life, pointing away from her. She held on to the hilt in a death grip, her expression surprised.

There was a crash from above, then a muffled explosion and a cry of pain. Sel ran for the archway to the stairs. Luke joined her, passed her by a few steps up, and left her behind, emerging into the main room above well before she did.

A few medical instruments, the most advanced ones, floated around the room, swirling in the air in the middle of the chamber like a miniature whirlwind outlined by the contents of a physician's office. The elderly man who had been reading was now hunkered down behind a stout wooden table. Atop another table were the ruins of a blaster pistol. Its battery pack appeared to have exploded, separating the weapon into several pieces, of which the handle and barrel recognizably remained on the tabletop. The old man's cheek was split as if by shrapnel.

There were howls and cries of alarm from outside. Luke charged in that direction, throwing the blanket curtain aside and hurling the door open.

Outside was a vision of chaos.

The instant Luke emerged, a late-model landspeeder rolled past, mere meters from him, end over end as if kicked by the galaxy's largest rancor. Three computer monitors, moving in formation like starfighters, flew by overhead, banked, then smashed straight into the wall of an Oldtimer house. Luke heard cries of alarm from within.

A block to the left, a whirlwind composed of glittering dust, chunks of speeder bike, glow rods stripped from building stilts, bales of wire, girders, and droid parts grew to an undulating shape ten meters tall and began moving away. A block straight ahead, a dome, a Newcomer building, jerked and rattled as if straining to break free of the ground.

Ben and Vestara appeared to either side of Luke. Ben's eyes were wide. "Stang."

Luke's reply was curt. "Dome." He sprinted ahead, angling left to follow a side street toward the twitching, heaving Newcomer dwelling.

As he skidded around the corner and the dome came fully within sight, it was clear the building and its inhabitants were in serious trouble. Two of the stilts had snapped, lengths of durasteel rebar showing in the broken permacrete posts. The dome on that side rose two meters into the air, then came crashing down on the broken piling stumps. The white dome cracked but did not collapse, leaving a jagged break across the front facing of viewports and the main entrance. There were cries of dismay and pain from within.

Luke charged forward and leapt up into the dome's recessed entryway. It was a difficult leap—he did not draw on the Force and had to perform most of the maneuver with his uninjured leg—but he landed where he intended. The light above the door sputtered.

The door itself did not open for him. Luke braced himself against the side of the entrance and kicked, but the dome rose and fell again as he did so. He was hurled up to crack headfirst into the entryway's ceiling. Despite the shooting pain to his skull, he managed to come down on both feet and not lose his balance.

To his right, Vestara leapt, a beautiful ballistic arc that brought her slamming against the dome exterior. In the doorway recess, Luke could not see where she hit, but the sound of impact was the dull clang of meat hitting thin metal instead of permacrete, so she must have been aiming for one of the viewports. There was a muffled clang that had to be the viewport giving way under her impact.

To Luke's left, Ben tried the same stunt. He hit harder, and had greater mass than Vestara to begin with. The sound of his viewport being punched free from its frame was distinct and gratifying.

Luke kicked again, this time completing the maneuver. The door, though a sliding barrier, catapulted free of its frame, giving Luke access to the interior, a living chamber the same size as Sel's.

Then the dome rose again on one side. Luke braced himself on either side of the entryway.

Instead of coming down, the dome twisted laterally. Luke heard another permacrete post crack. He looked over his shoulder to watch the world veer as the dome pivoted on its one remaining post. Centrifugal effect nearly threw Luke clear of the entryway—he certainly felt as though his stomach contents were about to be thrown free. He gripped harder, determined not to use the Force to anchor him in place, and heaved, propelling himself into the living chamber.

This room had started out more crowded with furniture than Sel's, and now those furnishings were scattered, strewn as if by the breath of some giant being. Electronics—datapads, entertainment monitors, art holoprojectors—rose to smash into the ceiling, crashed to the floor again, rose once more, hurling sparks in all directions as they performed their aerial dance of self-destruction. Luke saw a stuffed chair beginning to ignite.

Luke also saw a human arm flailing from beneath an upside-down sofa. He ran to it, uphill part of the way, downhill the second half of the distance as the dome's floor tilted crazily, and stooped to heave the furniture away from the victim it trapped.

Beneath was a white-haired man, lean almost to the point of emaciation, with a look of pain on his face. As soon as he was free of the sofa, he rolled onto his back and clutched at his left arm. From his expression, Luke suspected there was a break there, at the elbow or just above.

Luke knelt, bracing himself against a dome exterior wall to help maintain his balance. He had to shout to make himself heard over the din of breakage, of sizzling electronics, of screams from elsewhere nearby. "How many more here? In this house?"

"Two." The old man struggled to sit up. "My daughter, her son . . ."

Luke picked him up and turned to gauge the return path to the outer doorway. A bookcase of simulated wood scraped and slid past between him and his goal, then fetched up against an exterior wall and was momentarily still.

Luke ran. The floor seemed to heave and drop, causing him to stumble forward off balance, and he did not draw on the Force to stabilize his run. He twisted sideways so that he slammed shoulder-first into the entryway rather than hammer the old man's head into the surface there. Then, staggering sideways, he made his way onto the recess just outside the door and leapt free.

He leapt farther than he expected to, actually, for the dome began another pivot as he jumped. He flew ten meters, took the brunt of the landing on his uninjured leg. His momentum was not checked, so he went forward into a somersault, wrapping his body around the old man's, and came down on his feet again and ran another five paces, slowing.

Then he could stop and turn.

Vestara was already out of the dome. In her arms was a little boy of maybe three. Vestara, too, was turning to look back at the dome. Then she glanced down at the boy. She wrinkled her nose as though discovering she had just come in contact with a smelly substance. She unceremoniously set the little boy down on the dusty street.

Luke realized that the dome had twisted to face opposite its original direction; he and Vestara now stood on the street that had been behind it. It still twisted like a living thing, like an animal intent on ripping its neck free of a restraining collar.

There was a series of thumps from the second-story viewport and that piece of scarred transparisteel came free, rolling down the dome's curved surface to crash into the dust below. Then Ben emerged, a young woman in his arms. He hopped onto the curved exterior surface and, quick and nimble as a monkey-lizard, ran down that curve, leaping free when he was three meters above the ground. He hit the dusty Hweg Shul street on his feet, rolled forward across his shoulders, came up on his feet again.

The dome pivoted around and its free end rose directly over Ben's head. It came down—

Luke began to shout a warning. But Ben reversed direction, jumping and then rolling toward the one surviving permacrete stilt. The dome came down with a crash, obscuring him, a portion of it breaking free, and then rose again, and Luke could see his son and the woman Ben had rescued lying unharmed at the base of that surviving post.

The remains of the dome flapped up again and finally broke completely free. It rose into the air, spinning with a sort of strange majesty like a tiny space station come nearly to ground, then floated away, flying over the city.

Luke set the old man down and ran to Ben's side. "You all right?"

Ben stood. He had a cut on his cheek, and his cloak was gone. His breath, like his father's, emerged as a cone of frozen vapor. "Just fine. Dad, Zara. Zara, meet Luke Skywalker."

The woman, dark-haired and big-eyed, no more than glanced at Luke before running to Vestara and her son. The little boy wailed—not in pain; he was watching his home sail away, borne by phantom winds.

The dome disappeared over the horizon of Hweg Shul's low skyline. Then they heard it come to ground, a terrible crunching and crashing in the distance.

That seemed to be a signal for the powers that tormented the town. All around, the dancing, whirling, zooming devices and building components that had made the neighborhood a nightmare of danger and mayhem crashed down to city streets and building roofs.

They fell, and then silence fell—silence broken only

by the gasps of the injured, distant cries of pain, proximity alarms being triggered.

Vestara rejoined them.

Luke looked at the youngsters. Vestara, too, was little damaged; her robe was ripped at the shoulder, and its lower hem was splashed by liquid that smelled as if it came from an aquarium.

Luke nodded at the destruction around them. "Let's get to work."

An hour later, they had done all they could—helping Oldtimers and Newcomers alike dig victims out of collapsed houses, helping find children separated from parents, helping round up cu-pas freed when a corral fence collapsed.

The flying dome had, fortunately, come down in a field rather than atop another dwelling. It had claimed no victims.

Reports were sketchy. It appeared that there had been deaths, one of a man electrocuted in his sanisteam cabinet, one of a teenage boy crushed by a tumbling airspeeder. There might have been more; some dwellings had caught fire, and their charred ruins had not yet been fully explored. There were indications, too, that other Nam Chorios towns and settlements had been hit by the Force storm.

But for now the chaos had subsided, and Sel led the three of them back to their hostel.

Ben shook his head, wondering. Or perhaps Luke mistook his constant shivering for a shake of the head; Ben had not found his cloak. But Ben's voice certainly sounded impressed. "So that was a Force storm."

"That was worse than any I've ever seen." Luke tried to recall the descriptions Leia had provided him of the ones she'd weathered. "Worse than any I've heard about, actually."

Vestara frowned, the expression barely visible under her goggles. "Why was it mostly electronics affected?"

"No one is sure." Sel's voice was heavy with regret. "And we haven't had any Force storms in thirty years to evaluate. But there's a theory that, since Force activity is magnified and scattered by the presence of the tsils, and since the tsils themselves are a crystal life-form resembling programmable computer chips, the Force energy is reshaped and resonates with computer circuitry. Everything manufactured these days has circuitry in it—even durasteel girders, for self-diagnostic purposes. A dome like that would have hundreds in it . . ."

Vestara sounded impressed. "Did we cause that?"

"No." Sel's voice was decisive. "No. Listener techniques don't do that. I'd have seen it happen before. This was . . . something different."

"Abeloth." Luke repressed a sigh. "She's here. Somewhere. Experimenting. Using the Force with greater strength than I ever did, certainly. And not caring what happens when she does so."

Sel caught Luke's eye and deliberately lagged a little behind. Luke matched his pace to hers. The two teenagers drew ahead.

Luke heard Vestara's voice rise, her tone one of accusation. "That's just a ploy, Ben."

"No, it's not. I'm *freezing*. Look at me."

She sighed and opened her cloak, wrapping it around him as well. He tucked in close to her, and they shared its warmth.

Sel kept her voice low so Ben and Vestara would not hear. "I need to give you my key."

"The key to your dome?"

"No, to my mnemotherapy."

"I don't understand."

"Think of the mind as a computer system. The patient must trust the Listener, and they must work together to create a key, one that will give the Listener a back door by which he can invoke the mesmeric trance used in the technique. This was already accomplished on Thei before we arrived tonight. You understand?"

"I think so."

Sel passed him a folded sheet of flimsiplast. It was thin enough that Luke could see some of the notation through the material. It seemed to be a musical score. The lyrics belonged to an ancient lullaby of Alderaan; Luke had heard Leia sing it to Jacen and Jaina when they were little.

Sel returned her hand to the warmth of her jacket pocket. "That is mine. Taru and the other Listeners used it when curing me. You may have need of it, if you feel that I may have been . . . compromised . . . by this Abeloth. It might allow you to be sure."

"You're playing a dangerous game, Sel. You'd still be better off just leaving for a while."

"So would you."

"Point taken."

Chapter Thirteen

SENATE BUILDING, CORUSCANT

"YOU SEEM DETERMINED TO OFFER ME OFFENSE AT every stage of this discussion." Daala's voice was as frosty as Hoth in midwinter. Perhaps the spotless whiteness of her uniform and many of the furnishings in her Chief of State office contributed to that impression. "You refuse to allow me to speak to Kenth Hamner, and give me reasons for his absence that are patently insulting. You refuse to hand over information on the mad Jedi who assaulted Admiral Bwua'tu. You say you want to normalize relations between the Jedi Order and the government, but do nothing to support your claim."

Leia and Han exchanged a glance. It frustrated Daala that she could not read its meaning. Long-married couples possessed a language, one of glances and cryptic terms and throat clearings, that no outsider could interpret.

Han replied first. "We haven't seen any sign that the attackers *were* Jedi."

Wynn Dorvan, the fourth person participating in this private negotiation, gave Han a look that was all mockery. "No sign? Lightsabers? Forensic evidence that they knew how to use these weapons—not just to kill, but also to deflect blaster bolts? That's not something you learn from watching holodramas."

"Not everyone who knows how to use a lightsaber is a Jedi." Leia's voice was measured and polite but implacable. "There are ex-Jedi, of course."

Daala nodded. "Such as Tahiri Veila, the murderess."

"There are also, as you now know, more Sith in the galaxy."

"So good of you to have informed me of their existence before my intelligence forces discovered them. And I'm still waiting for a clarification on the difference between Jedi and Sith—a difference Jedi Veila and your son Darth Caedus could not seem to distinguish."

Leia was silent for a moment, and Daala wondered if she had finally pushed the doomsday button that would cause Leia to come over the desktop at her. But after the pause Leia continued speaking, with no change in her tone. "You yourself employed a lightsaber user, Zilaash Kuh, a bounty hunter, who was no Jedi. Where did you find her? Perhaps she can explain where Admiral Bwua'tu's attackers came from."

That rankled Daala . . . because Kuh had, shortly after her last mission with the bounty hunters employed by Daala, disappeared. Her ID documents proved to be masterful forgeries. Her true identity and current whereabouts were a mystery.

Daala did not allow this fact to intrude upon her point. "If you're hoping to recruit her, I regret that I do not feel obliged to help you. Back to the subject. The subject that has plagued me for many months. There can be no normalization of relations between the Jedi and the government until the Jedi Order acknowledges itself as, and behaves as, a government resource."

Han offered up a lopsided smile, a smuggler mocking authority. "Even if that's not what the public wants?"

Daala transfixed him with a hostile stare. "You think the public has any affection for the Jedi right now?"

Leia waved away the Chief of State's objection. "Now

may not be relevant. The Order waxes and wanes in public opinion . . . and is usually viewed in a heroic light, recent events notwithstanding."

"It doesn't matter." Daala offered a tiny, dismissive shrug. "The public doesn't want to be taxed, either. And without those taxes, the infrastructure of the Alliance evaporates, the armed forces cease to exist, some entire worlds become uninhabitable—Kessel, for example. The *public,* collectively, is not smart enough to make a decision like that."

Now it was Leia's turn to sound icy. "So the public has no right to demand that it be listened to, represented. Only ruled. Palpatine certainly thought that way."

"There's a difference between direction and distance, Princess. Palpatine went too far—vastly exceeded the distance he should have traveled. But his direction had merit."

Leia's expression froze as if carved in stone, and Daala knew they would find no common ground today.

Hundreds of meters away, in a secure hangar bay within the building, a Galactic Alliance Security two-person team carrying scanning apparatus descended the boarding ramp of the *Millennium Falcon.* The two women moved away from the saucer-shaped light freighter, casting not a backward look despite the vehicle's antiquity and fame.

In the cockpit, seated in the copilot's chair, C-3PO watched them through the starboard viewport. "Oh, dear. I wish they hadn't left so soon."

Behind him, standing in the cockpit doorway, R2-D2 tweetled musically.

C-3PO turned to glare at the dome-topped astromech. He knew he had no facial expressions with which to indicate his irritation, so he relied on posture and vocal tone. "Because, you assemblage of malfunctioning processors, now we have to do what Master Han and Mistress Leia asked of us. And I, for one, am not looking forward to it." He held up his arms so his photoreceptors could scan them. "Look at us, we're not even ourselves."

It was true. Where the protocol droid was normally shiny, if sometimes scuffed, gold and occasionally silver, he was now a matte metal-orange from head to foot, consequence of a session with a spray can. The orange color would peel away with a little work, and C-3PO wished that the work would begin immediately. The novelty of being in disguise did not endear the condition to him.

R2-D2 was similarly changed. All his blue coloring had temporarily been changed to black. He was disturbingly not himself.

Both droids also wore restraining bolts; C-3PO's was plugged into his chest. The bolts were false, inactive, but they looked identical to those with which droids temporarily visiting the Senate Building were routinely equipped.

R2-D2 tweetled with the old, let's-get-it-done manner that C-3PO found so irritating.

"Very well." Awkward, the protocol droid stood. From the pilot's seat beside him, he picked up a toolbox—innocuous looking, scarred from years of use, brushed durasteel with a black handle.

Together the two droids moved down the boarding ramp and headed for the interior exit, the one leading to the curved corridor accessing all the Level Two hangar bays. Two troopers in the uniforms of Galactic Alliance Security stood at that exit, talking, keeping an eye on the bay interior. One was a large Twi'lek male, blue-skinned, his brain-tails decorated with alternating yellow and red stripes like some sign from nature that he was a venomous reptile, while the other, a Bothan female, had fur that, had it been metallic, would have been an exact match for C-3PO's current color.

"Oh dear, oh dear, oh dear. I hate this part." Clutching the toolbox in both orange hands, C-3PO, affecting as nonchalant a walk as a protocol droid could manage, maneuvered to pass by the security operatives without engaging their interest.

"Halt," the Twi'lek barked.

C-3PO, programmed to obey the orders of living beings when they did not countermand more significant orders, jumped, then froze in place. "Sir?"

"You have no business here."

"Oh, please, sir, but I do. The mechanic who did the initial security evaluation of the Corellian freighter there is now in Bay 2315. He has left his auxiliary toolbox. I need to return it to him."

The Twi'lek exchanged a look with the Bothan and seized the toolbox. He opened it. The Bothan held up a hand scanner; the Twi'lek grabbed each of the box's contents in turn and held them under the scanner.

Hydrospanner. Data cards. Spray cans labeled as lubricant, preservative, and paint applicators. Meters. Datapads.

The scanner offered no blips of alarm, which seemed increasingly to annoy the Twi'lek. Finally he snapped the toolbox shut, shoved it back into C-3PO's hands, and glared at the droids. "All right."

"Thank you, sir—"

"It takes four standard minutes for a protocol droid to reach that hangar. I've timed it. If you're not back in ten minutes, if you leave the main corridor for any destination other than that hangar, I'll send lifter droids after you and have them crush you to a pile of flakes."

"Understood, sir. Very good, sir. Thank you, sir." His

speed boosted by fear, C-3PO hurried out through the exit.

The hall beyond was broad, its floor surfaced in permacrete rather than stone or some other pleasing material, and it was busy, trafficked by traveling parties headed to or returning from their shuttles, by miniature speeders hauling vehicle repair parts and battery packs, by beings from scores of worlds, many of them nonhuman. Despite his apprehension, C-3PO was cheered to hear so many different languages represented. They gave him a rare opportunity to exercise his multiple instantaneous translation faculties.

But then R2-D2, rolling along in tripod mode behind him, had to ruin it by communicating, a series of cheerful-sounding notes and blerts.

"Yes, Artoo, he *was* big, and I suspect he meant what he said."

Tweet, whistle, beep.

"Well, if we are delayed by circumstances beyond our control, we could very well end up in the crusher. Let's hurry a bit, shall we?"

Blert, tweedle, whistle.

"Yes, a Wookiee could decide to play with us, pinning us in place until the Twi'lek came for us. It's unlikely, it's a ghastly thought, but it's conceivable."

Tweet, toot-toot, blort.

"Artoo, I think you're having me on, and I don't appreciate it." But if he'd had the throat structure to do so, C-3PO would have gulped. All the many ways they could be delayed beyond their two-minute operating aperture . . . R2-D2's suggestions set C-3PO's mind racing, thinking of even more. A bolt failure causing his right leg to fall off . . . an impromptu parade cutting across their path . . . a malfunctioning set of blast doors . . . The possibilities were endless and horrible.

The two droids reached Bay 2315, which was similarly guarded by two security beings, a horned, red-skinned Devaronian male and a gray-skinned man from Duro. They, too, performed a scan on the toolbox contents, this time with slowness that agonized C-3PO, and then admitted the droids.

To C-3PO's relief, the shuttle from *Dust Dancer* was nearby, only one berth over from the doors. A male human mechanic was at work on the main thrusters at the stern, performing some sort of welding action that threw a glowing trail of sparks out to a distance of four meters. And—glory be—Seha was already at the foot of the boarding ramp, waiting. C-3PO came as close to running as he could in approaching her. "Mistress—"

"Sela, remember." Seha glanced over the protocol droid's shoulder, at the guards in the doorway.

"Yes, Mistress Sela."

"Stand still." Seha maneuvered herself so C-3PO was directly between her and the guards. She affected to open the toolbox and examine its contents. "Artoo?"

"Mistress, we're under considerable time pressure here—"

"Hush."

R2-D2 crowded in close. A small port on his dome slid open, and his spindly manipulator arm emerged. In its grasper claw was a silvery tube the approximate length of a lightsaber handle, but thicker along its length. Words were stenciled on it in black. He placed it in the toolbox and retracted his arm.

"Everything seems to be here." Seha's voice turned stern. "Don't let this happen again."

"Don't let *what* happen again? Oh. Yes. Forgetting. Although technically it was not *we* who forgot, but your mechanic." Which itself was a fabrication, since the mechanic had in fact not visited the *Millennium Falcon* at any point, but the lie was a plausible one.

Tweetle-tweetle-blort.

"Oh, goodness, time is running out." C-3PO spun in place. "Come, Artoo. If we're to avoid a fate even worse than being shredded . . ."

Seha watched the two droids flee. She glanced at her mechanic—the Jedi apprentice Bandy Geffer, who was black-haired, earnest, and good with mechanical tasks—and gave him a thumbs-up. Then she trotted up the boarding ramp.

In moments she had hit the button to raise the ramp to its up and locked position and had shut the light partition door between the cockpit and the passenger cabin. She moved to the back of the cabin, shutting the sliding covers over the side viewports as she went. Then she opened small hatches, ones that should have provided access to luggage storage, above the rear seats port and starboard. But these hatches showed emergency system backup controls—fire extinguishers, atmosphere, backup holocomm.

On the small keyboard of each panel, she typed in a short encrypted command. The panels slid forward, revealing that there were horizontal coffin-sized enclosures beyond, enclosures extending aft even farther than the passenger compartment did.

Enclosures containing Jedi.

Master Kyp Durron blinked at her, shading his eyes from the sudden light of the main cabin. "Delivery?"

"Finally."

Opposite, Master Octa Ramis pulled herself halfway out of her smuggling compartment, then levered her legs free and dropped nimbly to the floor. Dark-haired and appealing, she wore a white hooded rain cloak of thin material over the sort of dark, innocuous business dress that was ubiquitous in the Senate Building.

Kyp also pulled himself free, struggling a bit to fit his

broader shoulders through the aperture. He chose to fall face-first and roll to his feet. "Let's see it."

Seha handed him the toolbox. While Kyp laid out the contents on a shuttle seat, Seha brushed dust from the cabin floor off his back.

"Thanks. What do we have here . . . Identities. Cred-cards." Kyp held up the cylinder R2-D2 had given Seha and read its lettering. "TWO KILOS MALLEABLE EXPLOSIVE. DO NOT OPEN PRIOR TO USE."

Octa settled into the seat opposite. "The building's chemical sniffers will detect it once the container is open."

"Right. Um, makeup supplies, spray-on skin tone, and hair color."

Octa inserted one of the identicards into a datapad. She looked at the screen as data began to scroll by. "This one's yours, Kyp. You're Izzen Fray, a financial analyst with the tertiary support detail of Senator Treen of Kuat."

Seha offered a dismayed expression. *"Tertiary?"*

Kyp nodded. "Yes, she's known for maintaining lots of resources here. A good choice. She's also known for discouraging anyone prying into her affairs, meaning that many of her people don't know one another by sight."

Octa offered him a little grin. "Of course, as a Kuati male, you're a second-class citizen. Time to practice your bowing and scraping."

"Yes, madam. Hey, it's still a step up from a slave miner, which I've been for real." He inserted the other identicard in the other datapad. "You're Olya Merker. Same delegation. A comfort specialist."

Octa snorted, amused. "Ah, good, I'll need to sharpen my pillow-fluffing skills." Then something occurred to her. "Seha—how did the date go?"

Seha shrugged. "It was nice. Dinner, dancing. He was

just aggressive enough to show he was interested, but not so much so that I'd need to throw him out a viewport."

Octa gave her a cautionary look. "Remember, as nice as he may be, he's security. Naturally suspicious and probably inclined to poke around for information he shouldn't have. Plus, if he ever finds out you're a Jedi using him for access to the Senate Building . . ."

"Yes, yes." Seha rolled her eyes. "I can pretend to be living a normal life occasionally, can't I? For an hour?"

Octa and Kyp looked at each other.

He shook his head. "Nah."

She shook her head. "You're fooling yourself."

Seha sighed. "Anyway, one of these chips will have information on Senate Building offices not currently assigned to a delegation. If you can forge an assignment showing that another one has been approved for Senator Treen's use—"

"Then we'll have a semi-comfortable place to stay." Kyp grinned at Octa. "I get the couch."

"You get the floor. Or maybe the top of the desk."

Seha turned back toward the cockpit. "At least you'll already have your lightsabers past all the new security measures, and a constant flow of information and goods from the Solos. This should be an easy assignment. Right?"

"Nah."

"You're fooling yourself."

Half an hour later, Seha signaled Bandy via a single comlink beep.

Bandy, wiping his hands on an oily rag, walked stiff-legged up to stand before the cockpit viewscreens. Seha activated an exterior mike and speakers. "Yes?"

"All done."

"You're sure this time?"

He grinned. "You're going to get some smoke on activation. There's coolant pooled behind the exhaust vent, but it's ready to go. Guaranteed."

"Want a ride back to your shop?"

"Please. I'll get my tools."

Seha went aft and glanced at Kyp and Octa, who waited, with implacable Jedi Master calm, in their seats. "One minute." She activated the boarding ramp and trotted down.

At its bottom, she waved to get the attention of the door guards. "Can you switch off the fire system during our takeoff? We're going to have smoke here for just a minute, then we'll be gone. I'm sick of foam."

The Devaronian nodded. "Fine."

"It cakes in your hair. Takes several sanisteams to get out."

"I wouldn't know." He gestured at the top of his own head, gleaming, bald, and horned.

Bandy, tools in hand, trotted up into the passenger cabin. Seha followed and reentered the cockpit.

She powered the engines up, but did not raise the boarding ramp just yet.

As soon as the main thrusters showed all green for readiness, there was a mechanical coughing noise from the stern. Smoke billowed out the thruster.

Seha felt just a touch in the Force, a sign that the two Masters had run down into the smoke and then used their powers to boost their speed to get clear of the cloud before it dissipated.

She smiled, raised the boarding ramp, waved at the Devaronian, and lifted. She backed a few meters, turned the shuttle in a smooth pivot, and glided for the blast doors opening before her.

A moment later she was out in the sunlight again, breathing a sigh of relief.

Bandy moved up and settled into the copilot's seat. He pointed out the starboard viewport. "Hey, look."

In the distance, just leaving another Level Two hangar, was the *Millennium Falcon*. Seha gave the aging transport a little salute. "I suspect we had an easier time of it today than they did."

"Yeah, I guess stress comes with being old and famous."

Seha shook her head and began punching in a course for a climb to orbit.

For the Jedi, this was two missions accomplished—delivery of Jedi Masters, delivery of support resources to them—and nothing, absolutely nothing, had gone wrong.

So she hoped.

Chapter Fourteen

WILDERNESS, NAM CHORIOS

As Ben, boyish and unconcerned, piloted the landspeeder, Vestara used the best security available to encrypt the letter she was composing.

She had to. The letter was one she would never dare send, one she could never allow anyone to see. It would remain in the hidden reaches of her datapad's memory, something she would allow only herself to experience. She might have to purge it from her own memory if it threatened to expose what she was feeling.

Father—

No, that was how she normally would begin such a communication in truth, in the real world.

Dear Dad:

She rejected that as well. *Dad* was not right. The term was so very, very . . .

So very Ben.

The surroundings changed from bleak gray plains littered with crystalline gravel to hilly terrain, then dipped into a series of canyons. Rising from their depths were the chimney-like spars of crystal, blue and green and white, that constituted the largest and most impressive gatherings of tsils and inert stone found on this planet. Vestara barely registered their presence.

Papa.

That was it.

Dear Papa:

I hope you are feeling better, and that the hurts you have recently suffered have been well tended.

It was such a stupid way to begin, so strange to express such a thought. Of course his injuries would have been well tended. But to begin a communication with such a sentiment was itself a tremendous indicator of the difference between the Lost Tribe and the cultures of the Galactic Alliance. The words tasted strange in her mind, but she thought that she did not dislike the taste.

Nor did she necessarily dislike recasting her father, Gavar Khai, in a different light, softening his ruthless drive for perfection and accomplishment to something else. Something like Luke Skywalker.

The other night, seeing Ben blindsided by reminders of his mother, seeing how her loss still affected him, and seeing how his father instinctively reached out for him, to comfort him, I was of course reminded of you. And I wonder sometimes what I would be like if I had grown up with a sire—

She knew that was the wrong word. She backed up and corrected her words.

—grown up with a father who was cold and indifferent, or determined to drive me toward a hard destiny in a more cold and ruthless world. I'm not sure I would like myself, and I'm so—

The next word was almost impossible to add, so foreign was it to her nature. She forced herself to continue down that alien path.

—happy that you have always been kind and supportive.

Finally the lie was too big for her. She set the datapad down and turned away from it for a moment. She needed to regain her sense of self.

The very language she was employing was foreign, phrases and sentiments she'd heard when studying the holodramas of these people. They celebrated gooey, impractical emotions. They saw weakness as a virtue.

Except, perhaps, it was not precisely weakness. Ben was not weak. His sentimentality made him vulnerable, but she could no longer apply the word *weak* to him. What, then, was the right word?

Perhaps *supple*. She, Vestara, was like a hardwood tree, one that stood tall and proud no matter what was thrown at her.

Ben, instead, was a flexible tree, perhaps not capable of holding up so much weight, but also capable of leaning and bending to remain unharmed when the greatest winds came at him. Those winds might uproot Vestara, might topple her . . . kill her. And in the short time since she was separated from her fellow Sith—separated by more than distance, separated by her involvement with the death of their leader Taalon, which would earn her a death warrant from her own kind—she felt increasingly as if those winds were hammering at her.

She picked up her datapad again.

Luke told us a story the other night, a story of his first visit to this world. A woman brought him a tsil crystal, back before anyone knew they were living, intelligent things, and demonstrated how they could be reprogrammed through application of electrical current. She attached leads from a recharger to it, and the lines of its natural internal circuitry changed.

It also, it turns out, experienced the destruction of its mind, an event similar to a near-instantaneous, agonizing death. The experience was broadcast through the Force, hurting Luke badly, if temporarily. And shortly afterward, the crystal was dropped and shattered. Luke felt the tragedy of it all without understanding it. I have to wonder at the minds of the Newcomers here who still resist thinking of the tsils as sapient, who experience no sorrow at the thought of a needless, accidental death like that, an event that had to have been replicated by the dozens or the hundreds in those years . . .

Once again, the sticky sentimentality of her thoughts got the better of her. She saved her text and shoved the datapad back into her belt pouch.

One must do this sort of thing to understand the minds of potential enemies, she told herself. *One must understand their weaknesses if one is to exploit them.*

"Are you all right?"

Sel's question brought Vestara out of her reverie. She offered the old woman, who shared the speeder's backseat with her, a smile she hoped looked authentic. Then she remembered that it would go unseen under her goggles and cold-weather veil. "Just thinking."

Sel nodded, then turned forward again.

Taru's speeder bike was fifty meters ahead, making a left turn down a side canyon. Sel took a look around, orienting herself. "We're almost there."

"Good."

Moments later both vehicles came to a stop before a cave mouth. This was a large aperture in the canyon wall, tall enough for a Wookiee riding his brother's shoulders to stay upright as they walked in. Two more speeder bikes, another landspeeder, and three cu-pas were situated outside. Taru and Ben parked among them.

The five of them entered the cave. Its entrance, just inside, was flanked by two Oldtimers carrying modern, well-kept blaster rifles. These two men gave Taru a quick glance and then ignored him and the others.

The first cave was a bare and colorless thing, illuminated by a single high-powered glow rod. Toward the rear, its uneven floor sloped down at a steep angle. Steps had been cut into the floor there in some ancient time; they were now well worn with the passage of booted feet across the centuries. Taru led them down.

Deep within the canyon wall and well below the level of the canyon floor outside, the cave more or less leveled off. The half-natural stairwell opened out into a much grander cavern. Here, crystals were embedded in the walls; illuminated by more glow rods, they gleamed as if lit from within.

There were more men and women here, Oldtimers, most of them arrayed around an ancient black cooking pot from which smokeless heat emanated. Drawing close, Vestara could see that cans of heating fuel had been placed within it and ignited.

Taru brought Luke up before a man, as elderly in appearance as Sel. Tall for an Oldtimer, he was bald and white-bearded with intense eyes, black in these lighting conditions, that seemed fierce enough to stare clean through a person or a wall of stone. Vestara had seen eyes like his many times in her life, the eyes of Force-users with goals to pursue.

Taru made introductions. "Master Nenn, this is Master Luke Skywalker. Nenn is the senior Master of the Theran Listeners—as close as we have to a leader. Master Luke, of course, is head of the Jedi Order."

"Former head." Luke offered his hand.

Nenn stared at it before appearing to remember the Newcomers' way of doing things; he shook Luke's hand. "We of course know your name. I think I met you long ago, when you first began coordinating the effort to bring the lost tsils home."

"I believe so."

"Taru tells me you have disquieting news about Nam Chorios. I might have some disquieting news for you in return. Here . . ." He gestured to a rocky ledge, one nearly absent of crystals, and sat. "Please begin. Taru has told me what he understood, but I prefer to have such information firsthand."

Vestara settled in on the far end of the ridge to half listen. These were details she already knew.

If she switched herself over to the mind-set of the Vestara who had been composing the letter, Ben and Luke became different people. That was interesting. Yes, Ben was still infuriatingly boyish, in a way few Sith of Kesh ever were. Even Luke was sometimes boyish. But from that emotional perspective, this boyishness was not so ridiculous. Perhaps it was even attractive, in moderation.

Luke spoke of Abeloth, her ability to absorb others whole and take on their knowledge and identities, her desire to extend her very nature throughout the galaxy, her bleakness. Luke concluded with the warning he'd already offered to Sel. "Because the Listener techniques are so heavily involved in opening themselves to the Force, in listening to and interpreting the will of a difficult-to-understand species, I worry that they are vulnerable to Abeloth. If she—*when* she understands the tsils, she might be able to simulate their voices and thoughts very effectively, and persuade the Listeners to follow her. You and your followers may be more vulnerable to her influence than any other Force-using group I've encountered."

Nenn, eyes downcast for the last part of Luke's recitation, sighed. "You may be right. Perhaps we need to understand more of closing ourselves off from the Force. This is something we normally never need to learn."

"I can teach you. As can my son."

"And I." Sel offered a faint smile. "One of the few things I remember."

"So can I." Vestara surprised herself by saying those words. She was no stranger to working toward common goals, team goals—personal advancement sometimes called for that tactic. But she had as yet found no common ground with these Oldtimers and their insular, self-limiting ways.

"Now my news." Nenn raised his eyes to meet Luke's. "There was a Listener adept named Cura. Her body was found this morning."

Others of the Listeners murmured in surprise. Evidently that news had not previously spread to this entire gathering.

Nenn continued. "She bore terrible injuries on her body. They appeared to be the sort that would cause great pain rather than death under normal circumstances. We think she was tortured."

Ben frowned. "Why would Abeloth torture her when she could just incorporate her instead, and have all her knowledge?"

Nenn shrugged. "I don't know . . . perhaps Cura was too strong in the Force to be incorporated against her will. But she was not strong in body; her heart was weak. Perhaps Abeloth was wearing her down and her heart failed."

"Perhaps." Luke sounded thoughtful. "Could the killer have been someone else? A case of more ordinary murder?"

"Possibly. The other news is even less informative and even more potentially distressing. In Hweg Shul there is a doctor, a Latecomer scientist named Cagaran Wei."

Vestara had now heard the term *Latecomer* a couple of times, mostly at the Admirable Admiral. Oldtimers were descendants of the original settlers, Newcomers descendants of settlers who had arrived within the last century or so . . . Latecomers were those who had arrived in the wake of the New Republic's assumption of control of this world.

Luke frowned. "I know that name. He's been here for a while. I talked to him many years ago."

"Yes. He makes medicines for the offworld companies. He is also interested in the effects being a Force-user has on the body, and in all chemical and energy interactions of species from differing worlds. Drochs fascinate him."

"What about him?"

"He is gone. Disappeared. As of three days ago, when the Bleak Point station saw the arrival of what might have been your enemy. But he was not in Hweg Shul at the time, so it may be that he has a homestead out in the wilderness, a private one. A secret one."

Luke winced. "I hope you're wrong. It's not usually a good sign when a brilliant researcher chooses to maintain a secret facility."

"Yes, Master Skywalker. Especially on the world where the Death Seed plague survives."

"*Especially* here."

Nenn gestured at the Listeners in the cave. "I will begin a notification of all of our order to be aware, alert for possible signs of this Abeloth. I will supply you with Listener teachers who will learn your techniques of closing one's self off from the Force. My people will look for Dr. Wei."

Luke nodded. "As far as Wei is concerned, do you have anything to go on?"

"Yes . . . Perhaps his home in Hweg Shul will offer some clue as to the location of his other home. And his landspeeder is serviced in Hweg Shul. Its memory may have been backed up at the repair facility."

Luke opened his mouth as if to reply, shut it again.

Vestara thought she knew what he had intended to say. *Couldn't we have had this meeting in Hweg Shul? It's two hours' speeder time back to town. Four hours of search and investigation time lost.* But the Jedi Master withheld this implied criticism. He merely nodded. "Thank you for your help."

Chapter Fifteen

QUARTERS OF THE GALACTIC EMPIRE
HEAD OF STATE, CORUSCANT

SURROUNDED BY THE DARK, EXPENSIVE, INNOCUOUSLY tasteful furnishings and fixtures that suited Jagged Fel with such predictable and ridiculous accuracy, Jaina Solo sat on a black leather sofa, tucked against the shoulder of her future husband, and tried to think of something to say. "Did you get in touch with Tahiri's attorney?"

His eyes still closed, Jag offered a lazy nod. "I told him about Daala's discovery of the Sith you tried, in case it has some bearing on the way the prosecution portrays Tahiri's association with the Sith outlook on things."

"What did he think?"

"I can't say."

"Ah."

"What's going on with the Jedi Order?"

"I can't say." She was up to her ears in the Jedi plan to depose Chief of State Daala, and that was the last thing she could tell Jag. He might not be obliged to warn Daala . . . but he would surely take steps to protect his own people, and those steps might alert GA Security, which in turn might alert Daala.

"Ah."

She rubbed her cheek against his shoulder. "How

goes the investigation into the assassination attempt against you?"

"Can't say. How about the search for Abeloth?"

"Can't say." Finally it got to be too much for her and she began laughing.

He joined her, wiping at his eyes with his free hand. "Was it this hard for your parents? Just trying to *talk* to each other?"

"I don't think so. They weren't duty-bound to keep as many secrets. And in the early years, they were on the run together. Plus, Dad more or less gave up his profession as a smuggler. Which eliminated one source of stress in their situation. How about yours?"

He shook his head. "Well, for a while, they were basically on the run together. And Mother gave up her career as an actress . . ."

"Which eliminated one source of stress in their situation?"

"Yes."

"Well, that gives us a course of action."

He opened his eyes to look at her. "Go on the run together?"

"I'm all for it. You hide from your advisers and the Moffs. I hide from the Masters."

"And one of us gives up his or her profession?"

"I'm all for that, too." She poked him in the chest. "You."

He caught her hand and glanced down at the engagement ring on her finger. "Maybe we'll flip a coin to decide it."

"Sabacc tournament?"

"It's been done." He kissed her, but when he drew back there was a little sorrow in his expression. "For now, we can't *not* keep secrets from each other. All we can do . . ."

"Is not be angry for it. Ever again."

He nodded. "Preemptive forgiveness. For that and everything else."

"Oh?" She raised an eyebrow. "What else do I have to forgive you for?"

"Can't say."

She grinned despite herself. "I ought to smack you for that."

"No, you have to forgive me. Part of the new engagement contract."

"You win this one, Imperial swine."

Seventeen kilometers away, in the sort of tiny, tidy apartment suited to a budget-conscious security lieutenant, Javon Thewles stretched out on his own sofa, one far less expensive than the Imperial Head of State's, and luxuriated in his day off. Better still, the news holocasts showed citizens rallying, gathered in plazas, on elevated pedways, on rooftops, all within sight of the Senate Building, protesting Chief Daala and her vengeful responses to freedom and antislavery movements—and Javon did not have to work those potential security nightmares today. He didn't even have to listen to the holocasts narrating their movements, showing their placards, offering sound bites from their spokespeople.

Other things were going well, too. The young woman he'd met the other day was a looker and showing definite signs of interest. Javon was receiving glowing fitness reports from his superiors and anticipated doing well when he tested for captain.

He didn't feel quite so confident a moment later when his front door shot up and four military police in naval blues ran in, leveling blaster rifles at him.

He raised his hands, inadvertently spilling his drink all over the carpet. "The hell?"

The fifth person through his door—his ruined door,

for he could now see a curl of smoke rising from its security keypad—was a tall being in a naval captain's blues, his skin faintly green, his long black hair gathered in a topknot—Falleen, Javon thought. The Falleen moved to stand over him. "Lieutenant Javon Thewles?"

"You know I am. Can I sit up?"

"You're under arrest."

"Can I sit up anyway?"

The Falleen paused as if nonplussed by Javon's casual reply. "Don't you want to know why?"

"You're just the kind of clown who feels rewarded seeing people's expressions when you choose to tell them why. We have them like you in GA Security, too. Can I sit up?"

"The charge is conspiracy to commit murder."

"The sentence for which is not being able to sit up?"

The Falleen appeared to swell, and his color went from a faint green to a ruddy red. He held a datapad beside Javon's face. "Do you know this woman?"

Javon looked at the screen. It was a shot taken from a ceiling-mounted holocam, of himself talking with Sela Dorn almost the minute he'd met her, just before the fire-retardant foam had descended on both of them.

He glanced back up at the Falleen. "Do you know who my lawyer is?"

"No."

"Neither do I. But I bet he's going to tell me not to talk to you until I've talked to him first. What do you bet?"

"Yes, sit up."

"Can I get dressed?"

Two hours later, arriving at the Senate Building for their daily confrontation with Chief of State Daala, Han and Leia cleared the security check, recently made more strenuous, and then were escorted, not to Daala's antiseptic office, but to a larger conference room. It was already full when they arrived. Daala had the head chair, flanked by Wynn Dorvan and his Twi'lek assistant. Also present were officers of Galactic Alliance Security, Starfighter Command, and the navy. Leia recognized General Jaxton and Admiral Parova. Jaxton sweated excessively for the current air temperature, and his skin color seemed off, just a touch gray. The security officers looked unhappy, too, a despairing sort of unhappiness in contrast with Jaxton's brooding anger.

As the doors hissed closed behind the Solos, Daala pointed at two empty chairs directly opposite her. "Sit."

They did.

Han smiled. Leia knew it was a mask for irritation, knew he didn't care to be ordered around like a nek. He leaned back in his chair and laced his fingers behind his head. "Lot of protesters out there today."

"Not relevant." Clearly, it meant something to Daala; her face was as stiff as that of a duraplast doll.

"The holocasts estimate they're in the millions. That's a lot of protest."

"I'm not going to waste your time as you've been wasting mine." Daala was even more abrupt than during their previous visit. "Where is Jedi Knight Seha Dorvald?"

Leia and Han exchanged a baffled look. Bafflement was good. They genuinely didn't know where Seha was, and their ignorance on that point, and on how Daala might have rooted out Seha's involvement so soon, helped cover any telltale sign constituting admission that they knew what Daala was talking about.

Leia shook her head. "I have no idea."

Han mimicked her motion. "And what Leia doesn't know, I doubly don't know. That's the secret to a happy marriage, actually."

That got the faintest of grins from Wynn Dorvan. No one else appeared to notice his amusement.

"Have you contacted the Jedi Temple to inquire about her?" Leia tapped the pocket that normally held her comlink. "My communications have been taken away by building security, but I can put the call in for you."

"Don't play stupid." Daala sounded as though she could crack nuts with her voice alone. "We know she masqueraded as a shuttle pilot from the transport *Dust Dancer.* She poisoned General Jaxton and Moff Lecersen."

"What?" Leia couldn't keep the surprise out of her voice. Han slowly sat up straight and brought his hands forward, gripping the tabletop.

"She contrived to remain in the Senate Building for an entire day. We're now scouring the locations in the building she might have reached and are searching for more poison or other signs of sabotage. She is clearly another mad Jedi. You had best not be protecting her."

"I don't believe it." Leia didn't have to force a note of incredulity into her voice; her surprise was real. "General, are you all right?"

Jaxton made a sour face. "It was a slow-acting cardioparalytic. Fortunately, I had myself examined the minute I started feeling unwell. And even more fortunately, the medical droid ran some tests I won't ever again refer to as excessive or unnecessary, and detected the toxin."

Leia turned to Daala. "You can't think that the Order had anything to do with this."

"I don't think *you* would, and perhaps that means the Order as a whole would not." Daala steepled her fingers and stared over them at the Solos. "So I'll give you the benefit of the doubt. The benefit of the doubt says that Seha Dorvald went mad, decided to perpetrate murder, and fled . . . and the benefit of the doubt says that the Jedi Order will now find her and turn her over to me before I decide to withdraw the benefit of the doubt. We know what my displeasure can mean."

Han said it before Leia had a chance to kick him under the table. "Another failed assault on the Temple by the Mandalorians?"

Before Daala could rise to the bait, Leia interrupted. "What about Moff Lecersen? And the other passengers—Wynn, were you poisoned? The aides?"

Wynn gave her a little smile. "Thanks for asking. I'm fine, and the others are, too. Lecersen's poisoning was detected, and an antidote administered, as soon as we notified him of General Jaxton's troubles."

The doors slid open behind the Solos. A naval lieutenant—a Bothan female—hurried in, moved behind Admiral Parova, whispered in her ear, and, at the admiral's nod, repeated the process with Daala. Daala spoke to her, a few whispered words, and the Bothan departed as rapidly as she'd come.

Daala turned back to the assembly. "Fleet Intelligence has found at least one more component of Seha's sabotage. A small tank with a timer, spliced into the main Senate chamber's water supply, containing the same poison. Fortunately, it had not yet triggered."

"How . . ." Han wasn't acting; he was so surprised that his words started out stumbling all over one another. "How could she—Seha, I mean—have gotten access to those pipes? And how did this whole situation come to light?"

Daala jabbed a finger at the security officers. "Incompetence on the part of our much-vaunted security forces. One of them was *dating* your mad Jedi. We're still trying to determine how much information she seduced out of him. Fortunately, Fleet Intelligence was doing due diligence on the *Dust Dancer*'s part in transporting so many important people back to the Coruscant system, noticed some irregularities in their authorizations, and went from there."

Leia kept her face impassive as her mind roared through the possibilities. Seha had taken her shuttle back to orbit yesterday, rejoined *Dust Dancer,* and accompanied the transport on its exit from the system—an exit to a location very different from the course it had filed with Coruscant authorities. She should have transferred to another vehicle and returned to Coruscant yesterday, but Leia had not followed her movements, was not sure if that had happened as it was supposed to. In any case, GA forces looking for *Dust Dancer* at its destination of record would not find it. Unless Han and Leia were immediately arrested, they'd be able to get back to the Temple and get a transmission to the transport, letting its crew know it was being sought.

Now to test the waters and find out if the Solos were to be arrested. "As soon as we return to the Temple, I'll get word to Master Hamner and convey to him your wishes regarding Jedi Dorvald."

"See that you do." Daala gave Leia the unblinking stare of an enemy. "Immediately."

Han and Leia did not speak during their quick march back to the *Millennium Falcon.* In fact, they did not speak until they had landed the transport in the hangar bay at the Jedi Temple and had themselves gone through the similarly strenuous security check there. Only then, sure that they were not carrying new transmitters, did they convene with the Masters to report, and told their story.

Han, no stranger to being accused of crimes against

the government, sometimes rightly, was not furious, just curious. "We know Seha didn't poison anyone. So who *did* poison Jaxton and Lecersen? And why them but not Wynn Dorvan or the others?"

Corran Horn shook his head. "Find the motive, means, and opportunity, and you find the criminal. Head of State Fel, for instance, might have a motive to do in Lecersen, as there's some talk that Lecersen could have been behind the assassination attempt made against him." He cocked a brow at Han and Leia. "Which makes you two suspects as well, since you were endangered by that attack. You, like Fel, have access to associates with considerable skill and perhaps poisons. Means. And you, like Fel, have been visitors to the Senate Building recently. Opportunity."

Leia offered Corran an Oh-no-you-don't smirk. "But, Officer, we have no motive to harm Jaxton."

"Correct. Lecersen *and* Jaxton. Find the connection, find the motive. And then why the entire Senate chamber? One general, one Moff, and a lot of Senators?" Corran shrugged.

Master Cilghal heaved a rumbling sigh. "I wish they had mentioned the name of the poison. I could then tell you about its availability, characteristics . . . Will they give up that information?"

Leia shook her head. "Probably not. Daala only gave up as much information as she did in order to shake us, gauge our reactions, and embarrass her security detail for their failure. If we start making inquiries of her office, she'll seal up tight."

Corran looked thoughtful. "Back-door the query. Ask Wynn Dorvan. Or perhaps persuade Head of State Fel to ask Moff Lecersen."

"Is Jedi Dorvald back?" Saba Sebatyne asked.

"Back, and safe, and here at the Temple. Since she's

already wanted as one of the pilots who left with the StealthX wing, we made sure that her return to the Temple was by inconspicuous routes. And we'll get word to the *Dust Dancer* just as sneakily."

Han leaned back and stretched his long legs out under the table. "There's one good thing about her being suspected of attempted murder."

Cilghal gave him a disapproving eye. "Murder charges are not good subjects for jokes."

"I'm not joking. They think Seha's motive was an attempted poisoning. Or hundreds. This means they're not looking for Kyp or Octa."

Cilghal considered, then nodded. "You're right. That is a good thing. And not a joke."

"See, if I were telling a joke, it would start out, 'Two Mon Calamari and a Quarren swim into a cantina . . .'"

Saba offered a hiss of displeasure, interrupting. "This one dislikes the fact that there are unknown forces moving around us. This plan is dangerous enough. We must be even more cautious. Make sure the message getz to everyone who needs to know."

The others nodded.

"Let us return to our duties. Jedi Solo, this one has a special task for you . . . for your special diplomatic skillz."

"What's that?"

"This one wantz you to persuade Seha to turn herself in for arrest, trial, and possible execution."

In the Senate Building, the meeting was now finishing, with only Daala, Wynn, and Admiral Parova still present.

The admiral made her final statement as she rose. "I'll have the first team in place in five minutes, Chief Daala."

Daala nodded. "Be prepared for some resentment from security."

"Those who have failed always resent those who haven't. I'm used to it. And allow me to say, I'm proud, *we're* proud, to offer you our service, you personally."

"Thank you, Admiral. And well done."

Chapter Sixteen

HWEG SHUL, NAM CHORIOS

THE ITHORIAN WAS PHYSICALLY IMPOSING, AS THE hammer-headed species tended to be in comparison with humans, and not at all happy. "I have considerable difficulty thinking such disturbing things about Dr. Wei."

Luke, pausing midway through examination of a sheaf of flimsi printouts in Dr. Wei's small home office, nodded in understanding. "I can appreciate that, Mayor Snaplaunce. Can you tell me what you know of him?"

The mayor, standing in the office's doorway, offered a credible imitation of a human shrug. "He has been here nearly thirty years and has tried not just to get along in the community but to become a part of it. He was married for twenty of those years to a woman of the Newcomers, a jeweler, who died in a landspeeder accident. They have a son who is now studying medicine on Corellia."

From elsewhere in the doctor's spacious dome floated Ben's voice: "Doesn't he wear anything but *black*?"

Vestara, from another room, answered. "You're one to talk."

"Some people can pull it off, Vestara. Others can't."

Snaplaunce listened to the exchange, his head cocked.

"Your boy is very energetic. He seems quite responsible."

"He is. Mature beyond his age. In most ways. Not all."

"He and the girl, are they a couple?"

Luke cleared his throat. In some cultures, a question like that would never be asked by a stranger, but on a world like this, in a town where everyone knew everyone else, there was little regard for privacy. "No." *And let them continue not to be.*

"They argue like one."

"So you are a couple with every one of your political opponents?"

"Oh, well struck, Master Skywalker."

"And Wei? Other relationships, co-workers, colleagues?" Luke went back to paging through the sheaf of printouts. Most seemed to be meticulous, mind-numbingly boring accounts of the effects of experimental medicines on test creatures and computer simulations, with emphasis on the slightest variations in their responses.

"He technically is retired, now living on medicine patent royalties and interest on his banked capital. So he conducts his scientific explorations chiefly alone. When he wants an assistant, he hires someone from the staff of the hospital or the Enzymar Research and Development facility, usually a new graduate in need of a little more income. I'll put out word to find out if he has had any such in the last year."

"Thank you."

Ben stepped into view behind the mayor. Snaplaunce moved aside. Ben moved in, a sheet of flimsi in his hands, his expression grave.

"Let's see it," Luke said.

"I found it under his mattress." Ben handed him the sheet.

It was a page, slightly crinkled, dominated by drawings in black ink. Luke could see that the drawings had not been rendered by an ordinary stylus; the ink had flowed, smoothly and sometimes broadly, as if from an artist's instrument.

Part of the diagram was an outline of a human male viewed from the side—a silhouette with a hollow interior. The outline indicated no clothing, but there was something projecting from the back of the figure's neck. Lines radiating from the projection angled out to a box showing a blowup of that section of the diagram. The blowup was clearly a droch half the size of a human fist.

There were notations all over the page; the lettering was from a printer. Luke read some of them. "'Third thoracic placement—humans—for optimal effect. Signal strength and clarity drop-off not measurable at planetary distances, speed of light transmission the only limiter. Conditioning from childhood beneficial but not crucial. Average life span post-placement: seven point five standard years. Mutation remains a concern.'" The first few words created a flutter in his stomach, and it only worsened as he continued to read.

"May I see?" the mayor asked.

Luke handed the page to the mayor, who studied it intently, passing it first below one eye and then the other. "The ink is comparatively fresh. You can still smell it. But what does this mean?"

"It means, at the very least, that he's considering use of drochs on human hosts for some purpose." Luke sighed, suddenly weary of all the ways people, human or not, could imagine using, diminishing, and murdering one another for their own gain. "These drochs would have to be altered somehow to keep them from killing their hosts rapidly. Possibly the means of alteration is why he's concerned with mutation. I'm guessing that they'd serve as some sort of energy-transference mechanism, or perhaps a monitoring or even control mechanism."

Ben grimaced. "If he already knows how long a host normally lives after one of these things is attached . . ."

Luke nodded. "Then he's probably already experimented with the process."

The mayor handed the flimsi back. "There's something wrong with this."

Ben gave him a look of polite inquiry. "Based on your familiarity with Wei?"

"Based on my decades as a police officer."

Ben's expression changed to one of respect. "That's what you did before?"

"Yes." The mayor was looking at Luke. "I was so employed when I met your father—your father Owen Lars, that is."

Luke grinned. "I hope you've forgiven the subterfuge."

"Yes, of course. As for the diagram, why would he draw the man and the droch by hand, then let it dry and run it through a printer to add the text? Or go through those steps in reverse order? Why not do it all on the computer and print it out as a single step?"

Luke's comlink beeped. He brought it out of its pocket and activated it. "Skywalker."

"Luke, it's Sel. I've spoken to Dr. Wei's mechanic and he's allowed me to look at backups of his speeder's memory."

"Ah, good."

"There's not much to report. The mechanic's system is a bit of a mess, hard to navigate. One file I found, though, indicates that Wei regularly traveled a distance of exactly four hundred eighty-three kilometers each way from Hweg Shul. In what direction, it doesn't say."

Luke looked at the mayor. "Is it possible to plot distances from Hweg Shul to all known homesteads and facilities to see if one matches that distance?"

Snaplaunce offered a little bow. "Possible, and a matter of only a few minutes. I'll comm my office at once."

"Thank you."

There was one such site on record, a failed rock ivory processing camp in the mountains out beyond Bleak Point, uninhabited for years. But it exactly matched the distance shown on Dr. Wei's landspeeder memory backup file.

Luke assembled the others outside Wei's home. "Even with a good landspeeder, it'll take us hours to get there and back. I wonder if Koval Transport will let us charter a shuttle. Or, even faster, we could go up, bring the *Shadow* down, and use her. Though that means the slower decontamination when we leave Nam Chorios."

Mayor Snaplaunce shook his head. "No need. Take my shuttle. It will have you there in half an hour."

Luke smiled. "Perfect."

A few minutes later, Luke was no longer smiling. He was looking at a relic of his youth, a weapon of the enemy.

It looked like a TIE bomber—angled solar wing arrays like the more famous TIE fighter, with a double cockpit, two pods side by side. As if to mock its own sinister shape, this one was painted in bright yellow, with words on the outer wings in red: VOTE SNAPLAUNCE.

Luke looked at the mayor. "You have a TIE shuttle." Even to his own ears, his voice sounded as though he were informing the man of something Snaplaunce might not have realized before now.

Snaplaunce nodded. "Indeed."

"I'm not sure I can recall ever seeing one in private hands."

"A mechanic, late of the Imperial fleet, settled here about fifteen years ago and sold off several of the vehicles he had lovingly restored over the years. Seeing this one, how could I resist?"

"How indeed?" *Having painted it these colors, how could you resist activating the self-destruct sequence?* But Luke did not give voice to his thought.

He slid through the top hatch into the starboard-side pilot's pod as Ben and Vestara struggled into the port-side passenger compartment. While Snaplaunce checked him out on the vehicle's eccentricities, such as its lack of a laser weapon and the fact that its port-side ion engine had 10 percent greater thrust than the starboard, Luke heard his son and Vestara arguing over who should sit in front. Moments later they were ready to go; Luke and Ben dogged down their respective hatches, Luke brought the repulsorlifts and twin ion engines up, and they were airborne.

Airborne on a very precise course already transmitted to the port authority. "The commanders of the weapons platforms take a very dim view of spaceworthy craft rising from the surface and then deviating from filed courses," Snaplaunce had told him. "Best not to practice your astrobatics or to buzz Koval Station."

But restricted course or not, ugly paint job or not, Imperial symbol of terror or not, it was good to be behind starfighter-style controls again. And though the shuttle felt as maneuverable as a quartet of Hutts fastened together with space tape, it had fair atmospheric velocity. Luke brought it up to an altitude of ten thousand meters and luxuriated in the speed.

West of Hweg Shul, the morning sun had already caused ground-level dust storms to kick up. At this altitude, they looked like thick, motionless puffs of white or silver-gray plant fibers waiting to be harvested and spun into textiles.

Luke's feeling of good cheer lasted for twenty minutes. Then the aged shuttle's sensors picked up a signal, a small craft rising from a mountain range and coming up behind them. The pursuer kept a much lower altitude than the shuttle, two thousand meters, which meant that it was sometimes within the dust storms and sometimes above them. At this distance, it was too small to see anyway; on the sensors it was nothing but a blip.

Luke keyed his intercom. "Possible trouble, you two. Make sure you're strapped in tight."

"Understood, Dad."

The pursuer was faster than the TIE shuttle. It rapidly closed the distance between the two vehicles. Soon enough, even on the shuttle's ancient sensors, it resolved itself from a blip to a shape—a recognizable one.

It was spherical, with axial projections top and bottom and winglike projections laterally. At a tremendous distance, perhaps, it might be mistaken on sensors for another TIE-based vehicle, but Luke knew better. This was a Sith meditation sphere. This was Ship, the Sith-built, vaguely sentient vehicle now controlled by Abeloth.

"Potential trouble has turned into real trouble, kids. Ship is here."

"Great, Dad. Should I throw open the top hatch and hurl rocks at it?"

"Just bring up your own sensor board and lend me a second set of eyes."

"I'm in back—"

Vestara's voice cut in. "I've got it, Master Skywalker."

Ship closed to within a couple of kilometers behind, eight kilometers below. Its course was straight and true, just pacing them.

"Attack—"

Luke felt it as an electric thrill of danger as Vestara

spoke the second syllable, but he was already reacting to the alarm in her voice. He jerked the controls to port.

There was no flash of light, just the sudden appearance of a white smoke trail in the air from the point Ship had been a moment before to where the shuttle would have been had it kept its course. A moment later there was a distant *boom* from behind and below, a sonic boom.

Ship's accelerator weapon. An ancient device, it used high-order magnetism to accelerate masses of ferrous metal—usually durasteel spheres—to incredible speeds toward a target.

In space, debris and asteroid detection sensors would pick up those missiles. In atmosphere, those sensors automatically reconfigured themselves for the size of obstacles normally found in the air.

In other words, Luke was blind through the sensors, seeing Ship itself but not its supersonic missiles.

He could hear Ben and Vestara arguing on the intercom: "I know, Ben, I know, I can barely see the balls emerge."

"Recalibrate the sensors for vacuum!"

"We'll pick up every crosswind, every cloud and stream of dust. That dust storm will look like a giant mass—"

"Just do it!"

Luke kept his eye on the sensor screen, focusing on the aperture in the center of the spine emerging from the meditation sphere's top.

There was just a blur of movement—

He veered again, diving and banking to starboard. It was hard going, using pilot skill, muscle, and willpower to maneuver the sluggish shuttle.

The smoke trail, caused by the metal ball smashing through the atmosphere, friction alone igniting oxygen as it went, appeared to Luke's left. Moments later there was another distant *boom.*

"Civilian craft XV 119 'Vote Snaplaunce,' this is Koval Station Control. Cease your maneuvering and return to your original course."

Luke grimaced. He didn't know these controls that well, wasn't wearing a TIE pilot's helmet with a voice-activated mike, and couldn't take his eyes off the sensors long enough to find the manual trigger for the comm system.

Then he heard his son's voice. "Koval Station, this is 'Vote Snaplaunce.' We—"

There was a crackling noise, as if lightning had been set free to wander somewhere inside the shuttle. Sparks erupted from Luke's control board. His sensor-screen image contracted to a tiny white dot and stayed that way. His cockpit lights dimmed to nothingness. The engines skipped, coughed, caught again. Blinking yellow and red alerts began to flash on the main monitor screen, diagnostic warnings, and then that screen, too, failed.

And there was no more noise from the comm system.

"Ben? Vestara?"

"Here." Ben sounded aggrieved. "They're not responding."

"Getting it . . . Getting it . . ." Vestara said. "There. Sensors recalibrated."

"I can't see them. You're my eyes, Vestara."

"Understood. When I say 'go,' it'll—Go!"

Luke jerked the controls again, rolling to starboard, the roll narrowing his profile against the vehicle situated below him.

And, he discovered, from the enemy above. There was immediately another "Go!" and he halted the roll.

The universe above his top hatch flamed into incandescence as a capital-ship-level turbolaser battery discharge flashed just by the shuttle. It was not vertical; it came out of orbit at something like a forty-five-degree angle.

"Surface hit, surface hit." That was Vestara. "It took out an entire mountainside ledge. Go!"

Luke renewed the starboard roll, turning the shuttle upside down. He saw the smoke trail from Ship stretch, seemingly instantly, from Ship far above—below—to disappear behind his canopy. He finished the roll, returning to a right-side-up orientation.

This was not good. Attacks from below and above: below from a vehicle that was faster and more maneuverable than his; above from an enemy too distant to attack and which he could no longer communicate with . . .

Something clicked in his mind. He put the shuttle into a power dive.

"Dad, what . . ."

"Right now it's two weapons against none, Ben. Let's make it one against one. Dantooinian firing squad."

Everyone made jokes about the Dantooinians, of course, even when the remote planet was unoccupied. Residents of any rural, agricultural planet tended to be the butts of jokes about their intelligence, jokes made by more sophisticated neighbors. A "Dantooinian firing squad" was a ring of shooters intending to execute the prisoner at the center of their circle.

Diving let Luke pick up speed. Ship was slow to respond. Luke angled his descent to gain ground on his pursuer.

"Got it, Master Skywalker. You're five seconds from optimal placement. Four . . . three . . . Go!"

Luke jerked to port, minimally—he couldn't afford a more dramatic maneuver, which would cost him speed he badly needed now.

A shower of sparks erupted from the starboard solar

panel array. The shuttle shuddered. There was a *boom* from below and behind.

It was the most glancing of hits. One of Ship's shots must have just kissed the starboard wing, barely more than it would take to cause electrons to jump between the two masses.

But it was enough. The middle solar panel on that side began to peel away from the array. Suddenly the shuttle was trailing pieces of solar panel. The shuttle tried to heel over to the right—increased friction on that side. Luke fought the yoke, biting back a curse.

". . . One—Go!"

Luke reversed his intent, threw the shuttle into a rightward curve.

The world exploded again in illumination.

A blow, like from a thirty-kilo anvil swung by a rancor, slammed into Luke's head. He slumped, seeing his surroundings try to fade to gray. His hands, nerveless, slid off the control yoke. The shuttle began to tumble out of control.

Chapter Seventeen

LUKE FORCED HIMSELF TO THINK, SHOVED THOUGHTS through his sluggish brain.

Someone had just died. The death agonies had lashed out at him through the Force.

Ship, it had to be Ship. That was his intent, to put his shuttle and Ship along the same line of fire and hope that Ship, knowing the shuttle had no weapons, would be unprepared for a laser battery attack.

But Luke, too, would be dead in moments if he didn't regain control of the shuttle. He sat up again, forced his shaking hands to grip the yoke once more.

Outside the front viewport, the world spun. Dust storm below, sky above, dust storm, sky . . .

"Dad. *Dad.*"

"Got it, Ben." Even to himself, Luke sounded weary, hurt. He tried to regain control, watched the altimeter numbers plummet.

Four thousand meters. Sky—dust storm—sky. Thirty-five hundred. Dust storm—sky—dust storm. The starboard wing had now lost all three solar panels and was providing lift only with their support strut.

Lift. The fog began to clear from his mind. How good was Snaplaunce's repulsorlift landing system? Luke activated it, pulsing it at the same moment of each spinning rotation of the shuttle.

Three thousand meters. Twenty-five hundred. The

dust storm below was frighteningly close, and it could conceal jagged mountain peaks just below its surface. "Vestara, I need normal atmospheric sensors again." Sky . . . Dust storm . . . The rotation was slowing.

They plunged into the dust storm. Luke tried to ease the shuttle into a gentle starboard bank and descent.

Air bit wing the way it was supposed to. The shuttle made one more roll and came upright, the altimeter reading fifteen hundred meters.

Luke blew out a breath. "Sensors?"

"Nearest mountain altitude twelve hundred meters. Maintain current altitude and we're safe. Higher might be better."

"Above the dust storm, the Golan weapons platform will definitely see us," Luke said. "Now, they either can't, or are at least dealing with interference. I assume they vaped Ship."

"No, Master Skywalker."

"Come again?"

"It missed. It hit something down in a valley. That was the . . . death convulsion we all felt. I almost blacked out. Ship felt it, too. It wobbled, then turned away and ran."

"It hit a tsil." Luke felt deflated. "It killed a tsil."

A cough from the engines got his attention, but the main monitor was still inactive. "Look, I'm setting this baby down. Storm winds are kicking us around, and we need to know how badly we're hurt. Any idea where we are?"

"Dad, we're sixty-two kilometers southeast of our destination. Come to one-three-seven."

"In that direction, we're safe down to five hundred meters, and it gets better the farther we go—that's the descending slope of a mountain range."

Luke turned to the course Ben had recommended and began a gradual descent. There was a shuddering he didn't like from the starboard wing. The engines were losing power, and the less thrust they could provide, the less lift the damaged starboard wing would offer.

The repulsorlifts seemed fully functional, though. Under direction from his son and Vestara, he brought the shuttle down until he could occasionally see crystal-decorated hilly ridges just a few score meters beneath the keel. By eye and sensor reports, he slowed the shuttle and brought it down to fewer than five meters. A minute later, the shuttle was running like a landspeeder—repulsors keeping it off the ground while increasingly balky ion engines provided rear thrust.

"Snaplaunce is going to be mad, Dad."

"We'll get it restored for him. Assuming he didn't arrange this."

"Huh?"

Vestara sounded snappish. "Ben, be sensible. The mayor volunteered his shuttle and knew our destination. The systems that failed—did they do that because they were being overstressed? Or were they sabotaged?"

"I don't know."

"I don't, either, but your father is right. If Snaplaunce tried to kill us, we don't pay for his repairs."

Luke snorted, amused.

The engines continued to weaken, the right one giving out completely, as they completed their journey to the old rock ivory processing site.

It was, according to the data Snaplaunce's people had transmitted to the shuttle, situated in the foothills of the mountain range the shuttle had last cleared. Despite the uneven terrain, despite the way the dust storm winds grabbed the intact solar wing array and tried to drag the shuttle around by it, Luke was able to navigate through broad ravines and up gentle hill slopes, coaxing the shuttle as though it were an ancient landspeeder being towed behind a bantha, until the facility was, according to the sensors, three hundred meters away. That was when the second engine failed utterly.

The only sounds left in the cockpit were the hum of the still-functioning repulsorlifts and the howl of the winds outside, punctuated by scrapes and dings as small stones hit the shuttle's fuselage and scratched at the yellow paint. The wind pushed at the shuttle, compelling it to start sliding down the slope it had just grudgingly climbed; lacking thrust, and not daring to use the Force, Luke could do nothing to keep it moving in the direction he wanted to go.

Luke killed the repulsors, allowing the shuttle to settle down on the stony surface of the slope. The shuttle began to rock, pushed by the winds.

"Fun flight, Dad."

"Quiet, you."

Minutes later, wrapped against the cold and flying grit, they began their walk to the facility.

At a distance of twenty meters, the clouds of gray and crystal dust being driven past were thin enough that the three of them could see their destination. Situated in a cleft between two sloping ravine walls, it was a circular building of rough stones joined by permacrete mortar; it looked like the guard tower of an ancient city wall rather than a mineral processing plant.

And it was, as far as they could see, as dry and dead as most of this world. Its viewports, horizontal slits, were dark. There were no vehicles outside. But its main door, a slab of metal rare on a building this old on this world, was open, drawn halfway into the left wall section.

Vestara put her hand on her lightsaber hilt as if to reassure herself that it was still there. Her voice was muffled by her cold-weather veil. "Not a good sign."

Luke shrugged. "Look at it pragmatically. At least we don't have to climb a wall to get in."

The main door led to a broad channel between permacrete walls. This had been a lane for bringing in ore, Luke decided; its foundation, natural stone ground flat in some long-ago time, showed ruts where wagons had passed by the hundreds, perhaps across centuries. The channel was open to the air above, but at its end it entered an enclosed area that was dark, kept in shadow by the roof.

Once they were past the durasteel door they could see, just protruding from the shadows, a pair of leather, fur-lined boots. They were not decayed, crumbled wrecks, and they had not sagged flat.

Ben sighed. "Also not good."

They moved to the boots. Close up, they could see that this was a body, an unmoving figure lying mostly in shadow, facedown.

Luke opened himself up to the Force, seeking the distinctive, loathsome flavor of massed drochs, but he detected none. All he could feel were the looming presences of the tsils, watchful and intimidating.

He reached down to roll the body over. Vestara ignited a glow rod.

Once on his back, the victim proved to be stone dead, his body frozen. There was brown all over his chest, blood—practically freeze-dried by the surrounding air. His eyes were closed. His face was ruddy, not that of an Oldtimer, and his hair was graying black, tied back in a ponytail.

Luke knew his face. He'd seen it earlier today, many times, in holos.

Ben apparently had, too. "It's Dr. Wei."

They could not perform a full search of the old processing plant in just a few minutes, but a preliminary exploration did reveal that the place was plausibly unoccupied. There was no electronic equipment remaining, no food. There were a couple of muscle-powered machines still functioning, a wheel-shaped crank usable to open and close the outer door, and a hand pump that brought water up to a stone trough in the roofed area connected to the loading channel.

Their personal comlinks elicited no response from Hweg Shul, Koval Station, or any homestead.

Luke shook his head. "We may be too far from any receiver, or perhaps we're surrounded by mountain peaks. Or perhaps it's just the atmospheric conditions. We'll try again when the winds die down at night."

Seated on the water trough, Vestara looked at the body of Dr. Wei. They hadn't found any cloth or flexiplast to wrap him up and give him a little dignified concealment from prying eyes. "So I take it he *wasn't* working for Abeloth."

Ben made a disgusted face, though Luke could tell his emotion was directed at the situation, not at Vestara. "No. Or if he was, he didn't prove valuable enough to her. But I think he wasn't. He never was."

Luke gave his son a curious look. "How do you figure?"

Ben sat down on the trough beside Vestara. "Mayor Snaplaunce didn't think Wei was the kind of guy who'd mutate drochs to unleash them on the galaxy. Let's assume he was right. So how did all the evidence show that he was doing that? Well, first, there wasn't that much evidence. Just enough to get us up and running. It might have been planted. Let's say someone grabs Wei, kills him, flies his body out here in his landspeeder to have an authentic-looking record of the trip on his landspeeder memory. The killer dumps the body and goes back, then backs up the memory. Fiddles with the files, maybe, which is why Sel said they were a mess. And he—the killer, I mean—leaves that diagram for us to find."

Luke thought about it. "That's why the diagram was hand-drawn. Whoever drew it didn't know how to use the graphics capabilities of Wei's computer. Perhaps any computer. Which suggests it was an Oldtimer. And another one, one without any artistic ability, printed out the text accompanying the diagram in the first place." He sighed, vexed at himself. "That had to be what Snaplaunce saw but wasn't sure about. I saw it, too, and didn't recognize it. There were no other hand-drawn diagrams in all those printouts. Just the one that implicated Wei."

Vestara nodded glumly. "So they knew we, or at least you, would be coming out here to find Wei, which set you up for an attack by Ship. But they had to know that you'd be taking Snaplaunce's shuttle. Its electronics began to fail the exact instant we were talking to Koval Station . . ."

"So either Snaplaunce was in on the conspiracy, or he has a habit of lending out his shuttle to important visitors, and the habit was well known." Luke felt as unhappy as Ben and Vestara looked.

"Dad, how long do you think it will take us to repair the shuttle? And how much food and water are aboard?"

"Two days' rations for one average vigorous human. As for repairs . . . I don't know. When the sun goes down, we'll go out there and do an evaluation. We can jury-rig some heaters and run them off the shuttle's power. Let's hope the saboteurs left the tools in storage alone." Luke didn't bother adding what the two teenagers doubtless were already aware of: The saboteurs had known what they were doing. Yes, the three of them had survived Ship's attack, but they were still stranded out here for who knew how long. This was time the saboteurs could spend productively. Maybe harvesting drochs, maybe helping Abeloth subvert the Theran Listeners. Maybe both.

Something else occurred to him. "Though we do have one communications possibility they might not know about."

Ben perked up. "Which is?"

"Communing with the tsils."

Chapter Eighteen

ABOARD *FIREBORN*, HUTT SPACE

FROM THE OUTSIDE, GRUNEL OVIN REFLECTED, CC-7700 frigates were impressive things. Roughly triangular, evoking the decades-old dread of Star Destroyers but more rakishly arrowhead-shaped, they were fierce of appearance. It was a bit of an illusion; lightly armed and armored, equipped with a gravity-well generator, the frigate's main role was one of support, such as by positioning itself along a specific hyperspace route at a specific time and dragging a specific target out of hyperspace for capture.

But lack of firepower did not spoil its good looks. The running lights of this particular frigate, an aging ship of the Galactic Alliance Navy, gleamed against the darkness of deep space and outshone visible stars. And its turbolasers flashed brilliantly as it fired warning shots—such as it had when compelling Grunel's transport to heave to and prepare to be boarded.

From the inside, especially within the brig, the ship wasn't so impressive. Floors and other surfaces were not maintained at the level of sanitary cleanliness preferred by the GA's more hard-nosed naval officers. Crew uniforms were not pressed to stiff, crisp lines. Grunel had seen salutes thrown that would cause him to visit dire punishments on his own subordinates had they been offered to him.

When one was a leader of a desperate drive to free a slave culture, one had to be disciplined, hard, and merciless. Grunel was all three. And he was encouraged that the GA forces he faced were not as resolute as his own people. He was going to prison . . . but the movement would live on, perhaps led by his own brother. It would continue to swell, would achieve victory without him.

A larger-than-average Klatooinian, with the olive-green skin, heavy musculature, and severe, even brutish facial features common to his kind, Grunel knew he'd be a striking image on HoloNews during his trial. Perhaps this would not be the best way for him to serve . . . but it would still be service.

The door into his small, gray, solitary-confinement cell slid up. He looked over from his bunk. A Falleen male, lean and vigorous, in a naval captain's uniform stepped in. Behind him, a trio of guards waited. They disappeared from his view as the door slid into place again.

Grunel returned his attention to the ceiling. "You are my advocate?"

"No. I'm Captain Hunor. I'm here to discuss options with you." The Falleen sat in the cell's single chair, a spindly looking thing of durasteel tubing.

"I'll take the option where I go free and destroy your precious navy."

"Not available, sadly."

Grunel managed a weary smile. He knew it looked bestial to the humans and near-humans; the Klatooinian facial muzzle, not dissimilar to that of battle dogs but shorter, was intimidating to the more numerous small-chinned races. "I'm certain you are sad."

"I am. I'm caught between my duty to the navy and

my duty to sapient species everywhere. And increasingly, I choose to do my duty to the latter."

Curious, Grunel looked at him again. "And how do you intend to do your duty this time?"

"By killing you. With your cooperation. And making your death mean something."

ABANDONED ROCK IVORY PROCESSING PLANT, NAM CHORIOS

When night fell and the winds died down, Luke, Ben, and Vestara moved out to the TIE shuttle and got to work.

Luke let the youngsters attempt the resurrection of the shuttle. They had plenty of technical skill, and could call on him if they needed more.

For his own part, he went looking, climbing across the hilly ridges in search of crystals. He didn't need ordinary ones—he wanted those that resonated with the Force. He needed the tsils.

He found more than one such being occupying one of the elaborate chimneylike crystal formations, the kind that had collectively been termed *tsils* before that word had been revised to refer only to the sentient silicon life-forms of the planet. This chimney structure resonated with the Force, suggesting that there were two or three spook-crystals within; another one lay on the dusty ground less than a meter away from its base. The formation wasn't far from the shuttle. As he settled to the ground in a cross-legged position, his cloak under and around him, Luke could still hear Ben and Vestara talking.

Arguing, as usual.

"You have to admire his efficiency."

"No, you don't, Ben . . . *Whose* efficiency?"

"The saboteur. Looks like what he did was patch a high-powered capacitor straight into the electronics, triggered by receipt of any protracted signal on the official port authority comm channel. When it went off, every circuit chip and half the wiring in the shuttle fried. Probably no more than a five-minute job to set up the sabotage . . . days or weeks to repair it fully."

"And you admire this?"

"Just the efficiency. Next time I have to sabotage something, I'll have to remember this."

"Well, remember how cold you are before you express—hey."

"Hey, what?"

"The laser cannon was uninstalled . . ."

"We *knew* that. That's why Dad wasn't shooting back."

"But the support systems for it weren't. They were detached from the shuttle's other circuits but not removed. So we have a few control chips, plenty of serviceable wire, power output meters, emergency start-up capacitors . . ."

"Stang!"

Though heartened by the teenagers' discovery, Luke let his mind drift away from their conversation. He drew into himself, into his own ability to visualize, to communicate nonverbally.

The tsils were not remotely human. From his earlier contacts with them, they did not seem to be able to think purely abstractly. Even if they'd had ears, the spoken word "airspeeder" would not cause them to think of an airspeeder, nor would the word if written in text form, nor would even a simplified drawing of an airspeeder. But they *were* capable of some symbolic thought. One realistic image could be substituted for another, conveying an idea of association or comparison. That was how, three decades before, they had first communicated with Luke to inform him that crystals of their own kind were being brain-damaged, reprogrammed, and taken away to tragic lives of servitude as slaves.

And the tsils did care about living beings. Perhaps they did not truly worry about short-lived beings such as humans on an individual basis, but they cared about the survival of living, sapient species. They had struggled for better than seven centuries to keep the menace of the Death Seed plague, represented by the drochs, imprisoned on Nam Chorios, and this was in part over a concern for the fate of entire species other than their own.

Luke started with an image of a droch. He let it grow to a great size, the size of a human, the size of long-dead Dzym who had nearly escaped Nam Chorios three decades earlier. Luke modified the image in his mind, giving it many more legs and the greater angularity of the energy spiders of Kessel, but allowing it to retain the flavor, the Force-corrupting "taste," of the drochs en masse, memory of which could still make him shudder.

Then, preserving its menace and awfulness, he slowly, meticulously re-formed it into Abeloth's shape—humanoid but with a mouth broader than that of any human, with wavering tentacles instead of fingers, her body wreathed in mist. Then she changed again, becoming a human woman, silver-eyed and beautiful.

Luke was not done. He began creating other images to stand beside Abeloth. First was Callista, his love of so many years before. She stood, smiling and sad, beside Abeloth, so real in Luke's mind that he felt a squeeze across his heart.

Abeloth opened her mouth . . . and Callista was drawn, shrieking, increasingly tiny, into that maw.

And Abeloth became Callista.

Next was Dyon Stadd, the onetime Jedi applicant

who had helped Luke and Ben on Dathomir. He was dark-haired, natty, and vigorous, dressed in shorts and vest for tropical temperatures. Callista opened her mouth, and Dyon diminished in size. Thrashing and shrinking, he was drawn into her mouth.

A moment later Callista became Dyon.

Again and again Luke repeated this pattern, creating further images from whole cloth or basing them on characters from decades-old holodramas, showing the process of Abeloth absorbing lives.

He had just conjured up a beautiful blond human woman played by actress Wynssa Starflare, had her devoured by the particularly menacing but imaginary Devaronian man he had created just before, and had Abeloth assume Starflare's guise, when the next victim appeared without his participation. It was an elderly man, gray-bearded and fierce-eyed, wearing a patched blue jumpsuit appropriate to life on Nam Chorios.

Luke knew his face. The man was Nenn, leader of the Theran Listeners.

Luke felt a touch of grief as Wynssa Starflare opened her mouth and Nenn was drawn, flailing and screaming, into it. Then the actress became the Theran Listener.

And the cycle ended. Nenn simply stood there in Luke's imagination, smiling, his mouth open just a little, with the suggestion of movement within it—movement of dozens of beings now trapped forever within Abeloth.

The tsils knew. They knew even more than Luke did of Abeloth's activities here on this planet. Now, perhaps, they could suggest some course of action, some way to keep Abeloth from seizing control of the Listeners . . .

Luke's vision cleared and he found himself conscious once more.

Directly opposite him, wrapped up as he was, sat Vestara. She regarded him, her expression grave. "You've learned something."

"Nothing good. Abeloth has absorbed Master Nenn."

"Which would be *very* bad."

"Through Nenn's guise, she can probably seize control of the Listeners. Who can spread word that we three are enemies of the Oldtimers. The Oldtimers still outnumber the Newcomers and the Latecomers by orders of magnitude. And I'm not sure the tsils can persuade the Listeners to reject Nenn's words. Their voices are very soft and difficult to interpret; Nenn's will be forceful and clear. I hope *you* have better news."

"Some. Come on, I'll show you."

Luke bent over the crude diagram Ben had sketched out on a piece of salvaged flimsi. It rested on the starboard wing strut, motionless in the windless air.

Ben pointed out each feature in turn. "What we do is disassemble the solar wing arrays, the port side in three coherent sections, the starboard side for parts. We assemble them into a sail, the post mounted between the two main pods, cables attached to the trailing edges of the solar panels."

Luke nodded. "So what we have is a wind rudder."

"Co-rect. We'll pull the cables from our respective pod interiors—we'll rig pulleys, if we can figure out how, for efficiency. The repulsors work just fine. The port ion engine won't come up again, but the wiring on the starboard fared a little better. We can get maybe twenty percent output through it—but no variability. It's either all the way on or completely off."

Luke sighed. "We built junk racers more sophisticated than this out of spare parts when I was ten."

"Back in the old days. Back during the Empire. Back when starships were made of wood. Back when there were no holodramas, just puppet shows. Back when a hypercomm system was a long string stretched between two planets with a durasteel caf cup at either end . . ."

Luke snorted. "You're not helping. All right." He looked up in the direction of the rock ivory plant, hidden beyond an intervening hill ridge. "First things first. I'm going to go back to scuff out our footprints, if there are any, and pump out some water for our trip. We're not going to sleep in the plant. It's the one place they know to look for us, and as soon as Abeloth and Ship recover from being so close to the tsil when it perished, they'll be out looking for us . . . starting here."

Ben shrugged. "Then they'll find us. If they can see the plant, they can see the shuttle. Blasted yellow paint job. We can't fly her out of here even at ground level."

"We have no thrust, but that doesn't mean we can't move her. We're going to fire up the repulsors and push this baby as far away as we can reasonably move her." Luke pointed down the ravine they'd ascended to reach the vicinity of the plant. "I'll take one wing, you take the other, Vestara will shout directions, and we'll let gravity do as much of the work as possible. We should be able to get a kilometer or two farther away, and maybe find something to shelter us from overhead scans. Then, *there,* we effect repairs."

"Oh." Ben slapped the side of his own head, a gesture of self-rebuke. "Duh. All right, you still get to do some of the thinking for us."

Minutes later, returning with canteens filled with water, Luke paused on the ridge overlooking the shuttle on one side and the small tsil chimney on the other.

Something was different. He studied the vicinity of the tsils for a moment and knew what it was.

The spook-crystal that had lain a meter from the crystal chimney's base was gone.

He looked around. There were no footprints or other

tracks, excepting his own and the two teenagers', to be seen. But an Oldtimer scout familiar with this area could have crept up this close to Ben and Vestara without being detected, especially when they could not productively open themselves to the Force without risking a Force storm. Still, why would an intruder take a spook-crystal?

Troubled, he joined Ben and Vestara. "Ready to move out?"

"Sure, Dad."

"Vestara, fire up the repulsors."

Chapter Nineteen

JEDI TEMPLE, CORUSCANT

IN THE MASTERS' CHAMBER, SABA, CORRAN, CILghal, Han and Leia, Jaina, and Seha watched the image on the holoprojector. In it, Kyp Durron and Octa Ramis, dressed anonymously as Senatorial aides, stood to either side of their own projector.

Octa brought the projector online. An image swam into view, a high holocam perspective on the main Senate chamber. The chamber, shaped roughly like the interior of a giant egg, its walls lined with detachable speakers' platforms on repulsorlifts, was about half full and bustling with activity. The image, because it was a hologram projected within another hologram, was unusually fuzzy.

Octa waved a hand over it. "This is the Senate chamber this morning in an off-hour, as broadcast by HoloNet News. When conferences are in session, it's packed. This is an unusual amount of political activity, of attendance. There's a lot of discussion, formal and informal, on the situation with freedom fighters and slave rebellions, a lot of committee discussion of how these events affect committee duties, and a considerable amount of lobbying by corporations with interests both inside and outside the Alliance, attempting to maintain the status quo—to keep the Galactic Alliance from interfering on behalf of enslaved cultures outside the Alliance. The upshot is that any day we choose in the next few weeks, at least during prime arguing and posturing hours, we're likely to have a majority of Senators present."

Kyp tapped his control board. The image flickered and then gave way to a succession of recordings showing GA Navy personnel moving along the high-ceilinged hallways of the Senate Building. "We also have a lot of opportunities involving changes to security measures. Fleet Intelligence is now in charge of the Chief of State's personal security, and Daala has ordered GA Security to cooperate with Fleet Intelligence on all issues of Senate security, as well. What this means is that a lot of naval personnel who are not well known to existing security forces now have free run of the building. They have access to the security centers. Resentment is running high among the security forces, and we've had a lot of luck—a *lot*—just from Jedi mind-influencing techniques." He waved a hand, a casual gesture all those watching knew to be a minor distraction, the sort Jedi often used to presage a mind trick. "'You remember me from years ago when I was with security. You remember that I hate those navy pukes almost as much as you do.' This invariably gets me a few drinks in an office, accompanied by an hour's worth of venting about Fleet Intelligence interference . . . which comes with a lot of useful information about new procedures, new regulations, and so on.

"Also . . ." He tapped a control and the image switched to a still of a group of navy officers standing beside a wall panel, open to reveal a bank of electronics. "The navy is apparently being allowed to install monitoring hardware on many existing security stations and installations all over the building. We've been able to get to some of these units before they were activated, piggybacking our own hardware onto them. We now have holocam 'eyes' where we used to have none, and a couple of very valuable data conduits that are new to us. We can now forge self-erasing orders for personnel rotation that will allow us to bring two or three Jedi into the building with minimal security checks every shift. Not dressed as Jedi, of course. Dressed as naval personnel and sent straight to our auxiliary Kuat delegation office." He switched off the image of the naval officers.

Octa gave the viewers a satisfied smile. "If we can get some new data on the main building security center, then Master Horn's Plan Delta is, we think, viable. I expect that our opportunities to implement it will become poorer and more infrequent within the next week, though, in addition to the increasing likelihood that Kyp or I might be detected.

"So there's our report for today. May the Force be with you—and especially with *us*."

The hologram faded.

Han looked among the others. "Which one is Plan Delta? I only remember discussions of 'a plan.' What letter are we up to now?"

Corran gave him a quizzical look. "Can you read, Han?"

"Oh, very funny."

Corran smiled. "Plan Delta uses as many non-Jedi resources as we're able to pirate. Basically, we get as many Jedi into the building as possible. At a critical time, when the Senate is in session and as many politicians as possible are present, we introduce into the building's security computer a series of false events that trigger flags within the main threat-evaluation program . . . convincing the program that a massive planetary invasion has reached the plaza of the Senate Building."

Han blinked. "What sort of invasion?"

"Yuuzhan Vong."

"*Yuuzhan Vong?*" There was incredulity in Han's

voice. "Are you out of your mind? Nobody is going to take a Yuuzhan Vong threat seriously. They've been powerless for years."

"True, but you're missing the point." Corran rose, moved over to the chamber's holodisplay, and punched a series of commands into the console there. The display lit up, projecting a three-dimensional image of the Senate Building in the air. Moments later a large force of Yuuzhan Vong infantry, terrifying in their savage decorations and vonduun crab armor, began charging across the plaza toward sealed-up building doors. A pair of their starfighters, the bulky and nearly indestructible coralskippers, did a fly-by beside the building's upper tiers. "This is an animation developed as part of a defense plan put together in the months before the Yuuzhan Vong actually *did* take Coruscant all those years ago. It's still in the building programming—programmers never throw anything away until it begins to break down. So, we introduce enough false sensory data to convince the system that the Yuuzhan Vong are attacking. Several security measures that benefit *us* will activate before any living being can figure out what's going on and override them."

Corran tapped at Senate Building exits, hangar doors, and well-disguised exterior weapons emplacement ports in turn. "The building seals up. Many of the interior corridors seal, as well. The security centers issue an 'arm-up' code to all security personnel on-site. We will be at their armories, keeping their personnel out and letting ours in, meaning that we'll have armor, riot-control charges, gas charges, whatever we need. We'll also have a unit of Jedi within striking distance of the Chief of State's office. If we can secure Daala and the main security hub, we can keep the building shut down and address the Senate with an explanation that they're safe and that Daala has been taken as a measure to prevent further retaliations by her against slave populations and freedom movements."

Han whistled. "Control the leader, control the information flow, and portray yourselves as the do-gooders—"

"Which we are."

"Which we are. But what then?"

Finally Corran returned to his chair. He sighed. "Then we wait. We give the press everything they need to sell our side of the story to the public. We try to persuade the Senators that kicking Daala out will save thousands or millions of voters, which it will, and that they can present themselves as heroes to their constituencies. If we can get sufficient help from Daala's enemies in the Senate, and that number is already large and growing, we can justify our actions and end this ongoing conflict between the government and the Order before it blows up in everyone's face."

Saba turned to Seha. "Much dependz on you at this point. An easing of hostility from Daala. A distraction for the presz. And an opportunity to acquire the information we need about their security center. But the risk to you is serious."

Seha, grave-faced, nodded. "When I was a child, just getting something to eat was dangerous. I guess now it's time to pay for all those easy, safe meals I've had in the Jedi dining hall."

Wearing a jade-green jumpsuit instead of Jedi robes, accompanied by a squarish gold-tinted droid, Seha made her way across the plaza toward the main entrance of the Senate Building. Her path was impeded by members of the press who, tipped off by anonymous Jedi sources, surrounded her and hurled questions at her. The questions came with the rapidity and friendly intent of blaster bolts.

"Seha, why did you try to poison the Senators?"

Seha flashed the journalist a big, innocent smile. "Of course I didn't do that, silly. I'm innocent of all charges."

"Seha Dorvald! What's it like being a mad Jedi?"

"Don't be ridiculous. Mad Jedi think they're lost in a world of imposters. I know everyone around me is real, except maybe you." It hurt Seha's face to be cute all the time. Others had told her she was good at it, but it just wasn't natural for her.

"Seha! Why a droid attorney? Why not an organic?"

She rolled her eyes. "Really, a C-class VoxPop advocate droid is too much legal firepower for *this* case. I'm pretty sure a mouse droid with a two-bit logic chip could get me cut loose. I brought some credcoins to buy a ride back to the Temple when I'm freed later today."

It was all nonsense, of course. With Daala personally interested in the case, with the entire weight of the GA Department of Justice being brought to bear, Seha couldn't have wrangled her freedom with a squad of YVH combat droids masquerading as attorneys or a million credits to spread around as bribes.

But her droid did have some unusual features. In addition to the cultured speaking voice flavored with the traditional Coruscanti accent that once dominated the officer ranks of the Imperial armed forces, it was loaded with extrasensory apparatus, especially holocams—recording from artfully concealed, tiny apertures—that would document every centimeter of their movements even if the droid were shut down or shackled with a restraining bolt. If, as the Jedi Masters predicted, Seha was going to be hauled straight into the main security center of the Senate Building, the droid would emerge with invaluable information about that center's layout, personnel, and defenses.

With every question and answer, Seha and her droid got closer to the building's entrance. Now a dozen security troopers emerged from the entrance, marching toward her, and she suspected she wouldn't have to contend with the crowds for much longer.

"Why'd you choose here to turn yourself in?"

She blinked, all teenage-style innocence and good cheer, at the speaker and his holocam. "I was going to end up here anyway. I understand Natasi wants to chat with me. Maybe we'll talk about boys, or I can give her some good political advice." The use of Chief of State Daala's given name was improvised, but Seha suspected Han Solo would approve for its audacity and aggravation factor.

She hoped she didn't end up being tortured for it.

A second later she was surrounded by trooper uniforms. She and her attorney droid were hustled through the mob of journalists, many of whom gave way only grudgingly and with invectives shouted at the troopers, and then she was inside the main entrance.

She sighed, relieved. Maybe she *would* be tortured, but at least the reporters were gone.

A few hundred meters away, in the airy, light-drenched office of the Senator from Coruscant, Fost Bramsin nodded in approval, his attention fixed on the HoloNews broadcast. Seha's image, her questions and answers, were now being cycled through the analysis of the news commentators. "She plays well to the holocams."

In the visitor's chair on the opposite side of the desk, Senator Treen paused with her cup halfway to her lips. She sniffed, a disapproving noise. "I'm not at all happy with her surrender. If she'd stayed gone, no one would have had a chance to discover that she had nothing to do with the poisoning."

Bramsin gave her a reassuring, if weary, smile. "No one will. Jaxton and Lecersen aren't exactly going to admit that they allowed themselves to be poisoned.

Seha Dorvald's in the hands of Parova, which means *our* hands. No one will figure out what she was doing here . . . until *we* have figured it out."

"I just don't care for the notion that some mysterious agency, perhaps the Jedi Order, is active in ways that might interfere with us."

"She'll have confessed, to us alone, within a couple of days. Two minutes after that she'll be made to vanish from the scene, either until she's no longer a factor or forever. We have nothing to fear."

"Humph. Are you being gallant or stupid?"

"Gallant. I'm as worried as you are."

Finally she smiled. "At last, honesty in politics."

"A slip of concentration. It won't happen again."

CONFERENCE ROOM NEAR THE NINTH HALL OF JUSTICE, CORUSCANT

The elderly Bothan smiled. Tahiri knew it was supposed to be a reassuring smile: she had enough experience with Bothan body language to discern these things. But his words were not reassuring. "I'm sorry to say that they're not budging about a change of . . . accommodations . . . for you."

Tahiri shook her head. "I don't want to sound like a whiner. I don't object to danger—danger with a purpose. But I'm being kept shackled and surrounded by people who'd like to see me turned into fertilizer. And it's not for anything but the satisfaction of a warden who thinks he's the ruler of a petty kingdom."

Eramuth Bwua'tu sighed. "I know, my dear, I know. The problem is, the only evidence that can support your claims of excessive danger is being filtered by that selfsame warden. Naturally, he minimizes the danger. And the prosecuting attorney, who does play by the rules, has to base his arguments and objections on the evidence he has in hand—that same filtered evidence."

"So what do we do?"

"Short of one of your attackers voluntarily coming forth to testify that he had advance knowledge that you would be delivered to the wrong place at the wrong time so that you might be killed—"

"So not going to happen."

"—then we continue walking through the mud of the application process to get you transferred to another prison. We also exert under-the-table pressure on all parties concerned, especially the warden."

Tahiri frowned. "What sort of under-the-table pressure?"

"Suggestions reach the concerned parties' ears through diverse means they cannot follow back to their sources. For instance, I've made it clear to the warden that he is under intense scrutiny now. Every decision involving you is being analyzed. Every credit he drops on a luxury. Every charge on his expense account. Every purchase or service made on behalf of any member of his family. Known associates. It has been hinted to him that someone, he doesn't know who, recently sentenced to his prison is actually a Galactic Alliance Security agent investigating corruption in the Department of Corrections. Would that it were true . . . but any efforts on his part to root out the investigator will prove futile, so perhaps he will believe the investigator to be of extraordinary ability. If the warden has any sense, he will at least not resort to a tactic as simple as delivering you into the wrong exercise yard. I hope this will keep you safe. I expect it will, at least for a while."

"Good. That's something, anyway."

"And if I may be frank, the . . . effectiveness . . . of your spirited defense against your attackers has indeed convinced many people that you are not to be trifled with. But be wary of such things as sudden malfunctions on the part of your guard droid. It would not be a bad idea to occasionally switch places with other inmates when in line at the mess. All ordinary precautions. And I'll continue to work via the other means."

"Thank you, Eramuth." His words hadn't offered a lot of comfort, but they'd given her more than she'd had upon entering the conference room.

A tiny chime sounded from within one of Bwua'tu's many pockets. He drew forth a chrono and glanced at it. "Time to march into the Hall of Justice. Ready?"

"Ready." She rose.

He stood and smiled again. This time it was not reassuring. It was feral. "Let's destroy some prosecution witnesses, shall we?"

Chapter Twenty

WILDERNESS NORTHWEST OF HWEG SHUL, NAM CHORIOS

LATE THAT FIRST NIGHT, ONLY AFTER THEY'D CONcealed the shuttle beneath a rocky overhang and further disguised it with large quantities of crystal-and-gray sand poured liberally onto the vehicle from above, they saw Ship.

The Sith meditation sphere cruised high overhead on a straight line toward the rock ivory processing plant. Through his macrobinoculars, Luke studied the ancient craft's alien lines, the menacing pulsating redness of it, as it flew.

It circled over the distant plant for several orbits. Then its circle broadened; it spiraled out, an evergrowing pattern, as it searched for evidence of the Skywalkers and Vestara.

Luke smiled. He was sure they had left no sign they'd ever visited the plant. Dr. Wei's body was untouched. Any footsteps they might have left had been obscured by Luke, and any eddies of wind would have caused them to vanish completely.

Luke ducked under the overhang well before the sphere's orbit brought it on its closest approach to the shuttle. A few minutes later, he ventured out again. There was no sign of the craft. "All clear, you two."

Ben's head and shoulders popped up from the passenger-side hatch. He squinted toward the east, where a trace of violet light limned the peaks of the mountains, signaling the arrival of dawn. "Time to get some rest, too."

"You're right." Luke hopped up onto the port-side wing and climbed atop that pod. Moments later he squeezed into the passenger seat behind his son and closed the hatch. He didn't dog it down; in this sheltered ravine, the wind wouldn't be able to blow it open. In fact, he propped it open just a crack with some loose rocks, making sure that air could circulate.

They hadn't completed the repairs or the rigging of the sail. A few more hours would do the trick, but they wouldn't be able to do their work during the windstorm-battered daylight hours, so this was a time for rest.

Rest on restricted rations, already nearly half gone, on a hostile world. Things could be better. But Luke was a veteran of countless events that could have been described as *Things could be better.*

He listened as Ben made one last intercom check to make sure that Vestara, alone in the pilot's cockpit, was comfortable. Then, untroubled, Luke fell asleep.

Sleep was fitful during those hours. Luke would manage to sleep for an hour, for half an hour, and then a sudden rocking of the shuttle in the wind would rouse him, or a restless movement on Ben's part would do so. At times during the day, each of them had to exit the craft to relieve him- or herself and then would return, cold and dusty, to the comparative warmth of the shuttle interior.

Late in the day, each had managed all the sleep he or she would be able to get. They ate, a fraction of the calories they should be receiving, cold-stored rations several years old, and then contented themselves with time-killing tasks on their datapads.

Dear Papa:

The sleeping arrangements here are funny. Back at the hostel in Hweg Shul, Master Luke and Ben crowded into one room, while I had all the space I needed in the other. Here in the field, they crowd into the passenger pod and its two uncomfortable seats while I have the cockpit.

Master Luke is protecting Ben, of course, because I'm—

Because she was a Sith, of course, and not entirely to be trusted. But it was more than that. He was protecting Ben from possible mistakes of judgment, from any act that might bind Ben to her before her own loyalties and needs were clearly determined.

And that stung. It didn't bother her that she wasn't fully trusted. It was that Luke would protect Ben, while her own father, Gavar Khai, would offer her no such consideration, had not for years. He would simply assume that if Ben undertook any action Vestara did not care for, she would kill him herself. That was the Sith way. Like a reptile, walking away from the nest long before the eggs hatched, not overly concerned with the fate of its progeny.

She backed up a little in her letter.

Master Luke is protecting Ben, of course, just as you would protect me.

The letter stalled there. The lie, for the moment, was insurmountable. In her mind, the real Gavar Khai laughed at her for her softhearted delusions.

Suddenly she wanted to go home.

She wanted there to be a home to go to.

There wasn't one.

After dark, they resumed work on the shuttle. They activated the repulsors; vibration through the craft caused much of the piled-on sand to fall away, and Ben climbed atop the craft to sweep off as much of the rest as possible. They shoved the shuttle farther into the open and began the work of mounting the sail-rudder.

This entailed using the arc welder included among the craft's emergency tools, running off the shuttle's power, to burn two holes in the span connecting the port and starboard personnel pods, then fitting the rudder's main post down through the holes. After that, they attached wires and cables to the trailing edges of the solar panels and rigged the hatch-closing wheels as pulleys.

From a few meters away, they admired their handiwork.

Ben used his datapad to take some holocam stills. "Looks like bantha poodoo."

Luke nodded. "You're being generous."

Vestara took holocam shots of her own. "So what's our plan?"

Luke hopped up on the port strut and then moved to sit on the pod. "We have to assume that Abeloth-Nenn has seized control of some portion of the Theran Listeners. Which means that, for all practical purposes, all the Oldtimers could be against us. Which means we avoid human contact on the way back to Hweg Shul. We have the planetary map on our datapads, so we need to plot a course to Hweg Shul—flatlands only, since we can't steer this contraption well enough to navigate hills or mountains."

Ben frowned, clearly doing some mental calculations. "I'm pretty sure we can't get there by night's end."

"So we get there tomorrow night. Unless we stumble across some speeder bikes or landspeeders en route. We can't change what we can't change, Ben."

"I don't know about that. Obviously, we can build a landspeeder out of bantha poodoo."

Luke grinned. "Get in."

Steering was about as hard as they had anticipated.

Once the port ion engine fired, they could get up to speeds of nearly fifty kilometers per hour. That would have put them back in Hweg Shul after a hard ten-hour run, but only if they could have flown a straight line. The total trip, including zigzags to avoid mountains and hill ranges, was more like eight hundred kilometers.

They would run straight for an hour or two, then have to vector to navigate around a series of hills. That entailed Luke in the port pod and Ben, not strapped in, behind Vestara in the starboard pod, shouting at each other across the intercom—"Port! Port!" "I'm going!" "Keep going! Port! Stop stop stop!"—while manically spinning the improvised pulley wheels. Once the shuttle had finished its laborious, lumbering turn, they'd have to return the rudder to point straight back—"Starboard, starboard! Stop stop stop!" Within a couple of hours, both were hoarse.

But the kilometers flew past, and Luke's attempts to navigate by the stars, comparing the starfield above with data on his datapad, indicated that they were on a preposterous, overcorrection-driven, but roughly accurate route back to Hweg Shul.

At the end of that night, they cut the ion engine a hundred meters or so from a hilly ridge. Luke and Ben pushed the shuttle, still on repulsors, up against the ridge. Vestara killed the repulsors, and all three piled sand atop the vehicle.

Though the shuttle's comm system had been blown by the sabotage, they still had their personal comlinks, and these devices, in the last hour before dawn and the first hour after, picked up faint, distant comm signals.

". . . storm activity resulted in three deaths and hundreds of thousands of credits' damage to Hweg Shul. Authorities have offered no explanation for the freak events, which are similar to storms attested to thirty years ago and in the distant past . . ."

". . . launce still recovering from the savage beating he sus . . ."

". . . thority investigators are now on the ground, but restrictions on traffic to and from orbit are still in place, pending further . . ."

With the first winds of the day's dust storm, those tenuous transmissions faded away, replaced by static.

"Not good, Dad."

"Not good, Ben."

"Plus, I'm hungry and I smell bad."

Luke opened his mouth to answer, but Ben interrupted, an impersonation of his father's tone. "'Oh, but this is nothing like Dagobah, where mold rotted everything, duraplast included, and did it stink. Even my lightsaber blade stank. Food stank. Yoda stank. Distilled water stank, I'm not sure how.'"

Luke ruffled his son's hair. "If you're going to be my biographer, you're going to have to learn not to editorialize."

SECURITY CENTER, SENATE BUILDING, CORUSCANT

Shackled hand and foot, clad in prisoner's grays, her red hair a disarrayed mess, Seha moved as fast as her leg restraints would let her between two GA Security guards who insisted on walking just a bit faster than she could manage. Once inside the interrogation chamber, they pushed her down, not gently, into one of the two chairs at the table, then left.

Seha blew out a sigh and turned after them. "I miss you already." Then she turned to look up at the individual who stood, his back to her, on the other side of the table. He wore a crisply pressed Galactic Security officer's uniform.

She realized who he was a split second before he turned around. Her heart sank. "Oh, stang."

It was Lieutenant Javon Thewles. His face impassive, he seated himself opposite her. "Seha . . . Dorvald."

"My real name, you know that now. You shouldn't be here."

"I can't do my career any more harm. My career ended the instant you obliged me to take you out."

She offered him an expression of apology and sympathy. There was no deceit in it. "I didn't mean for that to happen. I'm so sorry."

"Why'd you do it?"

"Well, I was playing a role, and it seemed consistent with the behavior of the person I was supposed to be, and the old saying about men in uniform being especially handsome is true—"

He closed his eyes in a pained expression. "No. Why did you poison the Moff and the general? And try to poison all those others?" He opened his eyes again. His look suggested he really was trying to understand.

"Don't be silly. Of course I didn't do that."

"You were the only one with access to the poisoned men and to the Senate Building."

Seha's jaw dropped for a moment. "Are you crazy? Of course I wasn't. On the same shuttle were Wynn Dorvan and all their aides."

"None of whom had a motive to do it."

"Neither did I."

"Yet they were poisoned."

"When?"

Now it was his turn to look confused. "What?"

"*When* were they poisoned? Not on *my* shuttle. Maybe aboard *Errant Venture,* by political enemies. Except that wouldn't account for the same poison showing up in this building. So it had to be after they got here. Look, I have nothing to give you that you haven't already gotten from my earlier non-confessions."

"I haven't seen those recordings."

"Sure you have. Your superiors would have shown you at least a condensed version before sending you in here so you could guilt a confession from me."

He shook his head. "I'm not here on anyone's behalf but my own. I cashed in some favors to get a few minutes with you. I've already tendered my resignation from the GAS. As soon as it's processed, I'll be thrown out of the building, never to return."

"Oh." She slumped back in her chair. "I'm sorry."

"So what *were* you doing, masquerading as a shuttle pilot?"

"Can't say. I'm sure it will all come out at my trial."

He drummed his fingers on the tabletop and stared off into space as if Seha were all but forgotten. "So if you didn't poison those two, who did? And why? Step one is always to evaluate the consequences of the crime and see if one of them, plausibly, was the motive."

A trickle of alarm went through Seha. "Hey, wait a minute."

"What were the consequences? First, I was discredited, but I have no enemies. Only rivals I might be up against for rank advancement, and poisoning two Very Important People calls for resources way beyond those of another struggling lieutenant. Second, all of security was discredited." His eyes suddenly connected with hers again. "Was that it?"

"No."

"You become aware of some sort of conspiracy against Galactic Alliance Security. You bring Lecersen, Jaxton, and Dorvan here in such a way that this conspiracy can spot and exploit a security weakness. You do this to draw out the enemy."

A feeling of helplessness washed over Seha. This eager young officer clearly intended to jump aboard a white airspeeder and rush off to save the galaxy, and his suppositions were mostly wrong. She mouthed the words, *You're going to get yourself killed.*

"No need to whisper." He gestured around the chamber. "I made sure that the advocate–client confidentiality screens were functioning correctly, and I swept for listening devices."

"You're going to get yourself killed. You need to go home and start looking for a job."

"I have a job. An unfinished job."

"Look, um, I tried to kill Lecersen and Jaxton and all those Senators because I know the real ones have been kidnapped and these evil duplicates substituted for them, and I'm just trying to get rid of the duplicates."

"Too late, Seha." He moved to the door and keyed a code into its numeric pad, then stared into its retinal scanner. "I'm not angry anymore. It's obvious you were just doing your duty." The door slid up.

"Idiot."

"I know you don't mean that. Good luck." Then he was gone.

Despairing, she put her forehead down on the tabletop.

That was how they found her, a couple of minutes

later, the two security troopers. They hauled her to her feet. One, a dark-skinned human, gave her a close look. "Do you need medical attention?"

"I just need to learn how to keep my mouth shut. Forever."

Chapter Twenty-one

HIGH CORUSCANT ORBIT

PERHAPS IT WOULD HAVE BEEN BETTER IF THE GALACTIC Alliance government could have kept the tragedy a secret.

But it wasn't possible. Thousands witnessed it with their own eyes, as the GA naval frigate *Fireborn* passed between an orbital Golan gun platform and a hotel space station shaped like a child's top.

The event was promising to become a media circus. The government had already announced that *Fireborn* had been diverted from its normal picket routes so it could personally deliver its most famous prisoner, Klatooinian terrorist/freedom fighter Grunel Ovin, to justice. The stargazing decks and lounges of the hotel were packed with the curious—some of them, to the delight of news directors, wearing or waving banners with slogans such as FREE GRUNEL or GA OUT OF HUTT AFFAIRS—as the frigate cruised past.

Then *Fireborn* exploded.

It was so sudden that for several long moments the witnesses had no idea what had happened. The arrowhead-shaped frigate, headed for a low Coruscant parking orbit, was abruptly replaced with something resembling a tiny white dwarf star. The fireball swelled out as the crowds staggered back from it, many hundreds of people shielding their eyes. Then, as vision cleared, they stared at the spot where *Fireborn* had been—the spot where nothing now remained.

Moments later the first pieces of heat-warped debris slammed into the transparisteel viewing walls of the hotel. The huge viewports shuddered, some of them dimpling or actually buckling from the impacts. Atmosphere spilled out into space, not enough immediately to endanger the hotel guests, but decompression alarms shrilled their message of impending disaster, adding to the chaos and confusion of the moment.

Terrified guests shrieked and stampeded away from the suddenly fragile-seeming barriers, squeezing in crushing numbers through bulkhead portals that promised to lead to greater safety.

The viewports held, their structural strength witnessed by the bravest or craziest of holocam operators present. Those operators also captured images of the wounded: hotel guests trampled by their fellows in the mad rush to safety.

Within minutes those images were being broadcast across all holochannels, breathlessly narrated by anchors and field journalists, only to be shoved aside by the final message of Grunel Ovin. It was broadcast from an emergency beacon apparently launched from *Fireborn* moments before the explosion. The message was received, recorded, rebroadcast, and annotated by news services all across Coruscant.

In the message, Grunel Ovin sat, proud and defiant, his green skin clashing with the gray prisoner jumpsuit his naval captors had given him, and gave the viewing audience a victorious smile.

"By the time you listen to this recording, the frigate *Fireborn* will be destroyed and all aboard her, myself included, dead. I have done what I had to do in order to free my people. I have done this thing to make others understand they cannot own us.

"I allowed myself to be captured and taken aboard *Fireborn* so that I could accomplish the seemingly impossible, and you will never know how I have accomplished it. Understand, though, that every vessel of your navy is in danger. So long as you stand by while we are enslaved and oppressed, you can count on losing your defenders and loved ones by the hundreds and thousands.

"Let this serve as a challenge to all who think they can own sapient beings. You, too, will die at the hands of someone like me, and history will spit on your graves.

"My death also serves as a punishment for Chief Daala, who has always styled herself as an honorable warrior . . . yet has always behaved as a lackey, first of the Emperor and Grand Moff Tarkin, now of corporations that harvest profits from slaves outside the Alliance and then spend fortunes to buy Alliance laws that allow them to continue their crimes. Lick up their spittle, Chief Daala. I laugh at you from beyond your reach."

A HoloNews bureau chief, a gray-furred Bothan male in his division's main newsroom thousands of kilometers below the explosion site, viewed the first broadcast of the recording on the ridiculously oversized wall monitor overlooking his staff. He shook his head. "Daala's not going to take well to that."

His assistant, a male Chadra-Fan half his height but just as furry, seemed mesmerized by the image of Grunel Ovin as the message began to repeat itself behind a superimposed commentator. "No, she's not. Good news day, though."

"Oh, definitely."

Six hours later, Wynn Dorvan's heart sank as Chief Daala swiveled her conference room chair toward him, her face as stony as he had ever seen it, and announced her decision. "Mandos to Klatooine. Go."

He opened his mouth to offer yet another reasoned argument against her chosen course of action, then closed it. Reason wasn't working. Revenge, absolute suppression of defiance, was the order of the day. He rose and trotted to his office.

He knew this was not going to be good. The full strength of Daala's mercenary force would unleash its considerable expertise and advanced technology on the desert-dwelling Klatooinian group variously known as Ovin's Sand Panthers and the Sapience Defense Front. Daala's logic was that the sudden cessation of this group—substitution of a series of red-drenched craters for the wasteland encampments where warriors, civilians, and children had lived—would cause all such groups everywhere to reconsider whether destroying a capital ship of the Galactic Alliance was a good idea.

Wynn held the pragmatic opinion that the merciless extermination of a society was no better an idea than the treacherous bombing of a ship, but empirical data supporting such a theory was hard to come by and even harder to make meaningful to someone as angry as Natasi Daala.

This was not going to be his battle to win, so he did as he was told, and contemplated his retirement.

In her office kilometers away, after receiving Wynn Dorvan's encoded communication, Admiral Parova buzzed for Captain Hunor to join her. The Falleen male swept into her office at such speed that his ponytail took an extra half a second to sway into place against his back after he skidded to a stop. "Admiral."

She smiled up at him. He was such a good, obedient right hand. Once the Galactic Alliance and the Galactic Empire were reunited under traditional Imperial guidelines and nonhumans such as Hunor found their careers entombed beneath a transparisteel ceiling, he'd probably feel betrayed. But for now, he earnestly believed that the acts of sabotage, suborning, and murder he was accomplishing on the side were all solely for the removal of a Chief of State who seemed increasingly erratic.

She handed him a set of data cards. "Mandos to destroy Ovin's encampments. Leak these details to the usual resources. Then get over to the riot-control center and assume personal control in the Senate Building perimeter. I don't want protesters to be initially hindered, but I want Galactic Alliance Security efforts to keep them in line to be, um . . ."

"Intrusive? Ineffective? Tragic?"

"All three."

He took the chips, saluted, and was gone.

She shrugged, not displeased. After all the dust settled, Hunor might end up being a pretty good gardener.

She hit a desktop button to seal and sensor-insulate her office, then, from a drawer, withdrew a large, elaborate comlink. It broadcast on a specific comm channel to a receiver in this room. The receiver was hardwired to a repeater situated kilometers away.

She recorded a brief message. "This is Nona. On your way back home, would you pick up a container of blue milk? Thanks ever so." In seconds the circuitry in the comlink would modulate Parova's voice to more sultry tones, then transmit the recording to the personal comlinks of all the other members of her conspiratorial circle.

The words were innocuous enough, a plausible mistransmission. But everyone who was supposed to receive them would understand.

Daala had taken another self-destructive, citizen-enflaming step, one that the historical archives would, in their jaded wisdom, agree spelled the Chief of State's doom.

A pity about *Fireborn*. But no one would ever know that Captain Hunor, before leaving the frigate, had programmed an emergency marker buoy to broadcast Ovin's last message and had activated a self-destruct countdown authorized by the Chief of Naval Operations. It was the perfect "bombing"—no bomb necessary.

Parova deactivated the room's sensor insulation, summoned her aides, and rose. She'd spend the next several hours at the Senate Building. She wanted, needed, to be there for the kill.

In the Senate Building, in the increasingly crowded suite of offices appropriated by the Jedi for their own operation, Master Octa Ramis, studying the stream of data scrolling across her desktop monitor, suddenly sat upright. "*Kyp.*" Her voice was very intense.

Other Jedi and allies in the main office took notice. In a mixed group like this, one Master did not usually refer to another by his or her familiar name—such an informality normally arose only in more relaxed circumstances.

Zekk, dressed as a hangar mechanic, his hair spray-frosted blond and his face enhanced with a false beard, exchanged a look with his fiancée, Taryn Zel, who was dressed and made up as the sort of anonymous, generic office beauty whom many politicians wished to have nearby when holocams were present for recording opportunities. Standing beside the door, Jedi apprentice Bandy Geffer, picture-perfect as a scrubbed, eager naval ensign, looked worried. Masters Kam and Tionne Solusar, gray-haired and distinguished in the guise of expensively garbed ambassadors, focused on Octa from their seats on the sofa.

Kyp, dressed like Octa in Kuati political support team

member garments, moved over to stand behind her. He frowned over the stream of words and numbers flowing across the screen. "Node one-one-three. Which one is that?"

Octa consulted her personal datapad. "That's the monitoring unit the Fleet Intelligence team spliced into the comm trunk feed coming down from the executive-branch offices. We piggybacked a tap onto it. What's the office of origin?"

"X-wing Commenor Aldera two-four-seven-eight."

Octa's eyes widened. "Score. That's listed as Wynn Dorvan's inner office."

Kyp frowned as he puzzled out the unformatted blocks of text. "Am I seeing this right?"

"I think you are."

"Daala's issued an extermination order against a series of Klatooinian habitations. Mandos ordered to move in and leave them as smoking craters." He blew out a long breath. "If we don't move today, soon, this is going to happen. We have to execute Plan Delta now so we can call this Mando operation off."

Octa nodded. "I'll comm the Temple. Kam, Tionne, do you concur?"

The older Masters nodded. That made four Master votes to move. All the Masters remaining at the Temple would have to vote against to have a simple-majority override . . . and Octa couldn't imagine them doing that under these circumstances. This was a done deal.

She rose, preparatory to moving into the back chamber and the holorecorder there. "Maybe we can get one last team of Jedi in before things come completely unhinged. Everyone, prep for your assignments."

The monitors throughout the Chief of State's offices showed the main feed from HoloNews. In succession, they displayed images of crowds, growing in size and increasing in energy, massing in the vicinity of the Senate Building; of journalists offering interpretations of events; of stock recordings of Mandalorian transports; of Mando infantry operations in the past and their considerable destructive potential.

Wynn was watching the end of one of these rapid news cycles when his office door slid aside and Chief Daala, flanked by two Fleet Intelligence security agents, swept in. Wynn stood. The security specialists glanced around then stepped back out, and the door closed.

Daala gestured at Wynn's monitor, her hand shaking with her anger. "How did it leak? How did it leak *so fast*?"

Wynn shrugged, hoping it looked more hapless than uncaring. "The orders to commence an operation like this have to pass through several hands. Dozens. In theory, there could be a leak at any point. It could be something as malevolent as a traitor, or it could be a data tap placed by an unusually skilled newsbeing."

"It's the first one. I've been *betrayed*, Wynn. And this is a time of galactic crisis. Treason at this level is punishable by execution."

"I know that, Admiral."

"*Find out who leaked the information.* I expect arrests within the day. I'm also putting Fleet Intelligence on the search."

"We'll be stumbling all over one another, interfering with one another's investigations."

She fixed him with a cold stare. "I need the redundancy . . . in case *you're* the source of the leak." She turned and left, moving so fast that the door nearly scraped her face as it slid open.

Wynn gulped. He sat and returned to his monitor, issuing orders for trusted subordinates to begin the most intensive, no-stone-unturned investigation this environment had seen since . . . well, since the hunt for

Seha Dorvald's poison device, just a couple of days previously.

In between bouts of sending out orders, he continued to work on his letter of resignation.

Grudgingly, the Senate Building's security center issued authorization for the *Millennium Falcon* to land in a hangar bay. Han brought the transport in with his customary skill, the smoothness of the landing revealing no trace of the tension that gripped him, of the imaginary piranha-beetles flying formations in his stomach.

Once the transport was down, he commenced an abbreviated shutdown procedure, glanced at Leia, and looked back at the other two in the cockpit. "You two know what to do."

"Pardon me, sir, I'm not certain I do." C-3PO raised his arms in a vague and hopeless gesture. "I'm not even sure of the purpose of this errand. I assume you're offering Chief Daala comfort and wisdom in the face of the growing numbers of protesters outside . . ."

Han rolled his eyes. "Something like that. I expect she'll feel very different by the time we leave the building. Goldilocks, *your* specific task is to stay on the ship, to alert me or Leia if anyone comes aboard, and to follow Artoo's instructions if he offers any."

"Oh, sir, it's folly, very dangerous folly, to put Artoo in charge of anything. He's too impetuous, too much the daredevil . . ."

Han left, Leia beside him, the two of them breezing past R2-D2 at the cockpit entrance.

At the bottom of the boarding ramp waited Desha Lor, Wynn's Twi'lek assistant. Today her black suit seemed to match the mood of the surroundings, the growing hostility and seriousness outside. She shook her head slowly, causing her lekku to sway. "I don't think the Chief of State will be able to fit you in today."

Leia's voice was cordial but firm. "We'll stay in her waiting room. Please tell Wynn that we insist on seeing her today. We went to a considerable effort to find Seha and convince her to turn herself in. Daala owes us for this, and we demand to see her."

Desha gave her a little understanding smile. "I think I'll paraphrase that when informing Wynn."

"No, I insist you quote me exactly, and that Wynn does likewise when speaking to the admiral."

Han kept his emotions from his face. They weren't feelings of worry; they were the residue of what he'd felt during the hours, *hours,* Leia had fretted over the choice of her exact words. Those words had to announce the intent of the Solos; to annoy Daala enough that she would keep them cooling for a long time in her waiting area; but not to offend her to the extent that she'd have them ejected from the building.

Desha shrugged. "As you wish. This way, please. As usual, you'll have to endure the full security regimen . . ."

Chapter Twenty-two

THOUGH OUTWARDLY COLLECTED, INWARDLY DAALA felt like an insect being fried in the peripheral effect of an ion cannon.

The pressure *had* to relent soon. If only her enemies would stop besieging her administration, from outside and inside, for a few days, everything could be set right. If no one attacked her armed forces, her public infrastructure, she would not have to retaliate. If corporate lobbyists would just announce their wishes and quit pretending there were altruistic reasons behind them, she might perhaps gain a little respect for them, drive out the loathing that filled her every time she met with them. If all these things happened, tempers could cool. Politicians could go back to what they did best, transforming temperate oxygen into overheated carbon dioxide and eating appetizers. Journalists could return to talking about futile romances between holodrama stars.

The Jedi could—no, they wouldn't just shrivel up and die, would they?

A face appeared on her desk monitor, her scheduling secretary, a chalk-white Chev female with hair dyed a startling orange. "Admiral Parova requests a few moments, Chief Daala. She's not on today's schedule."

Daala blew out a silent sigh of thanks. Parova had the potential of developing into a friend, perhaps even a confidante. In rare noncrisis moments, they had recently even engaged in brief moments of girl talk—about which new capital ship designs looked promising, which teaching regimens appeared most efficient in military xeno-education. "Send her in."

The door slid open. The admiral stepped in, but not far enough for the door to slide closed. Her expression was serious. "Chief, given the rise in unrest outside and other indicators, I've brought in a new detail for your personal security. With your permission, I'd like to relieve the current detail."

Daala didn't hesitate. "Other indicators" had to mean that suspicion had fallen on one of her bodyguards currently on duty. Perhaps a Jedi had gotten to him or her with one of those accursed mind tricks. She nodded. "Do so at once."

Parova glanced at the two Fleet Intelligence security specialists situated inconspicuously at the back of the room. She gave the slightest jerk of her head. Both agents, without comment, filed from the office. Two more, a Falleen and a light-skinned human, both males, moved in and took their places.

Finally Parova stepped the rest of the way into the office, and the door slid shut behind her. She relaxed visibly. "That's better."

Daala gestured for her to sit. "There's some suspicion of the other two? Operatives you yourself assigned me just the other day?"

Parova sat and shook her head. "No, those two are among the best of the best. Incorruptible. Devoted to the Galactic Alliance over all other considerations. But that's actually part of the problem."

"What do you mean?"

"Well, I'll demonstrate." Her tone grew louder, more determined. "Chief of State Natasi Daala, in the name of—"

The office lights dimmed. A deep vibration, like a subsonic tone emanating from the lowest parts of the building, rattled the caf cup and writing implements atop Daala's desk. She felt the vibration in her fingers, in the long bones of her arms and legs.

A second later the vibration resolved itself into a low alarm tone, modulating between two ominous bass notes.

Daala's finger stabbed at the button connecting her monitor to that of her primary secretary. "*What is happening?*"

There was no reply. The monitor image clicked over to the secretary's desk, but he was not there. No one was.

A few seconds earlier, in the outer office, the chrono in Han's vest pocket beeped.

Daala's secretary, a gold-furred Bothan male, looked up at the noise. "What's the alarm for?"

Han grinned. "Nothing good. You know how we have to come in here unarmed?"

"Sure."

Beside Han, Leia rose to her feet, throwing her arms wide as if trying to get the attention of a crowd at a concert. "You are all my prisoners. Hand over your weapons."

Other important visitors waiting to see Daala—Senators, representatives of major corporations, ambassadors—gaped at her. At either end of the room, two naval officers reflexively reached for their holstered sidearms.

The instant their thumbs popped the restraining flaps free from the butts of the holstered blasters, Leia drew her arms in. The blasters flew from the holsters, one to her hands, one to Han's.

Without rising, Han switched his blaster over from blast to stun. Casually, he shot the naval officer to his left, traversed his weapon, and shot the one to his right. The secretary dived for the floor, thumping to the carpet behind his desk.

Leia spun, covering the door from the exterior hall into the waiting room.

Han smiled and waved his blaster in the direction of the other waiting dignitaries. "Nobody move. This is a holdup."

"Han."

"Oh, right, my mistake. Nobody move, this is a coup." He aimed at the prostrate Bothan. "Especially you, Fuzzy. You twitch a finger or make a noise I interpret as a warning for your boss and I'll fill you so full of stun bolts, you'll be able to light a glow rod for the rest of your life."

The office lights dimmed, and a low vibration rattled everyone's bones.

A few seconds earlier, Senator Bramsin joined Senator Treen in the latter's floating station in the Senate chamber. It was not floating now; it was firmly attached to its brackets against the curved wall midway between floor and ceiling. Together the old friends and conspirators watched the gigantic monitor at the chamber's summit; the screen showed the image of Deggan Rockbender, sandy-haired Senator of Tatooine. The young man's words floated down from the overhead speakers a fraction of a second after they emerged from the speakers at each station: ". . . expediency flies in the face of the principles that led to the foundation of the New Republic and the continuation of its ideals in the Alliance. An embargo against trade goods produced in territories where slavery is still permitted is an absolute ethical necessity, a declaration that we continue to be dedicated to the cause of . . ."

Treen sighed. "He does go on a bit."

Bramsin nodded. He checked his chrono. "But think about it. In moments, Parova will break in and announce that the armed forces have arrested Daala. In the midst of Rockbender's stirring speech about taking action against the forces of tyranny, Parova announces the deed's done."

Treen did think about it, and batted her eyes like a schoolgirl. "Rockbender's stock will go up immeasurably, and not just with his constituents."

"Correct."

"Perhaps I should be in a position to talk to him immediately after Parova's announcement."

"Also correct."

"Have you set up your priority override so you can take charge as soon as Parova is done?"

"Of course. The program's in place, and with the touch of a button . . ."

The chamber's lights dimmed. Treen felt her teeth rattle as a somber subsonic tone rippled through the assembly. On the big screen above, Senator Rockbender paused, looking around, confused. A data card on the desktop before Treen rattled under the vibration's influence and began to slide toward the desk's edge.

Bramsin gave her a puzzled look. "That's not part of the plan."

"No, indeed."

"I'd best get back to my station." He turned and left, moving faster than Treen had seen him walk since Palpatine had held the Imperial throne.

A few seconds earlier, R2-D2 tweetled, leaned back into tripod configuration, and rolled aft from the cockpit of the *Millennium Falcon*.

C-3PO hurried after him. "What message? I didn't receive any message."

The astromech ignored him. Reaching a specific point

along the transport's circular gangway, R2-D2 opened a port, extended his manipulator arm, and swung it out to bang against the floor three times.

"*Now* what are you up to—"

That section of metal flooring, and one next to it, rose.

"Oh, my."

Master Saba Sebatyne stood up from the smuggling compartment revealed by the raising of the floor panel. Nearby, Corran Horn and Jaina Solo stood up from an adjacent compartment.

"Master Sebatyne, Master Horn, Mistress Jaina. If I'd known you were here, I could have brought you some caf."

The three Jedi, climbing out of their compartments, barely glanced at the protocol droid. They replaced the hatch covers and raced to the top of the boarding ramp, then down into the hangar.

C-3PO could hear their progress. It was marked by the *snap-hiss* of lightsabers igniting, shouts, the crackle of blaster rifles firing, the sizzle of blaster bolts reflected into and extinguishing themselves against durasteel walls.

R2-D2 rolled after the Jedi, tweetling.

"What do you mean, accompany them? This is Jedi business, very dangerous. We have other orders."

The astromech gave an assertive tweetle as he descended the boarding ramp.

"Well, yes, one of our orders was for me to follow your instructions, but that was the preposterous one. Unfollowable, when you think about it." Yet curiosity and concern for the fate of his counterpart compelled C-3PO to waddle along in the astromech's wake. "Oh, dear."

The lights in the hangar dimmed.

* * *

The moment the lights dimmed across the Senate Building, a naval ensign loitering outside the entrance to the main security center perked up. He tugged his cap low over his eyes and clutched his briefcase close to him.

As the subsonic tone began to rattle the bones of everyone in sight, yellow lights flashed atop the entryway. Galactic Alliance Security and Navy personnel outside the entrance crowded in through it. The diagonal leading edges of the blast doors there flashed green, signaling the start of a lockdown countdown.

The naval ensign crowded in at the back of a group of security officers. He made it through the entrance as the blast doors' edges went from green to yellow, as the vibration became a modulated two-tone alarm.

The center was in chaos, a chaos that was only a few seconds old. Officers and troopers rushed to their duty stations. The level of noise, shouts for information, orders, the alarm tone, battered at the ensign's ears.

The ensign took a good look around. Everything looked different from the holorecordings supplied by Seha's attorney droid—the crowding and rushing of personnel made everything more difficult to comprehend.

But Bandy Geffer had studied the recordings for long hours. He knew the floor plan, could recognize the faces of many individuals, even knew the names and positions of some. He moved forward at a brisk pace, remembering to salute higher-ranking officers, catching no one's eye. As he turned rightward down a side corridor, in his peripheral vision he saw the blast door edges flash red; then they slid closed with a bone-rattling *thump*.

A few steps more brought Bandy to his destination, the marquee cells—a high-profile cell block where prisoners could be temporarily lodged and displayed before being turned over to other authorities. Each of these small cells featured a large transparisteel viewport instead of bars, giving an unimpeded view of the cell's contents—all but the refresher corners, which were screened off.

Seha Dorvald sat on the lower bunk of the third cell he came across. She watched the commotion outside her viewport with mild interest. As Bandy came into view, she waved.

Bandy set down the briefcase beside her gray durasteel door. He opened the case and pulled his lightsaber from it.

"Ensign, what's your post?"

Bandy grinned over his shoulder at the security officer, a human woman, facing him. "Lieutenant Zeiers! You look just like your holos. Uh, my post is the Jedi Temple."

"What did you say?"

He ignited his lightsaber. Its blue blade rose into shining coherence in front of his face. He looked at the door again and thrust the blade directly between the jamb and the numeric keypad beside it, cutting downward.

"Cell block alpha, we have an intruder!"

Bandy heard the words, heard the sound of a blaster pistol clearing leather. He spun, slashed upward, caught the pistol just forward of the trigger. The barrel flew free of the rest of the weapon.

Lieutenant Zeiers, unharmed but wide-eyed, stared at him. He returned his attention to the door. He heard her run off. Moments later his blade sheared through the bolt locking the door in place. After that, it took merely a wave of his hand and an exertion through the Force to slide the door open.

Seha stepped out, still hobbled by shackles. "Did you bring my lightsaber?"

"In the bag. Hands, please." As soon as Seha extended her hands, Bandy sheared through the shackles restraining them.

"How about some real food? What they give you here—"

"Sorry, no. If you're ever to have another good meal, we have to win this one." Bandy stooped and cut through the ankle bindings, scarring the floor beneath them.

Seha dug around in the briefcase, then straightened up with her lightsaber in one hand, a few centimeters of metal cable still dangling from each wrist shackle.

Together they charged deeper into the security center. Word of their presence had spread. Security officers from two armed forces scattered, took up emplaced positions, and opened fire with blaster pistols. Seha took point—a full Jedi Knight, she was much better at batting back blaster bolts. Bandy caught those coming at them from troopers they'd already passed, those whose weapons they did not shear through in passing.

The Jedi reached their destination, the center's armory. It stood resolutely shut and locked, the officers on duty not having had time to begin standard operating procedures on the arming of ready personnel.

Seha stood guard, catching and flinging back an ever-increasing barrage of blaster bolts. Bandy winced as he heard the occasional cry of pain. Seha wasn't deliberately aiming the bolts back at firers, but there were so many bolts in this target-rich environment . . .

Bandy plunged his lightsaber into the door, dragged it around to create an aperture a meter and a half in diameter. When the two burned edges of his cut met, he kicked the center of the circle and it fell into the armory. He jumped through, careful to avoid contact with the jagged, heated edges of metal, and once inside he slapped the button to open the door.

It still worked. The door slid open. Seha backed in. Bandy hit the button and it slid shut again. Now blaster bolts came in only through the hole Bandy had made.

He turned to look over the chamber's treasures. Stands of body armor, racks of blaster rifles, cases of grenades . . . "Gas masks . . . there they are." He grabbed two sets of protective breathing gear and several riot-control grenades. He placed one mask on his own face and one on Seha's, then began activating grenades and flipping them through the hole in the door.

So far, so good.

Chapter Twenty-three

THE NOISE MADE BY THE CROWD PRESSING AGAINST lines of security troopers at the outer perimeter of the Senate Plaza changed. In a second it turned from angry, full of false bravado, to curious and confused.

Javon Thewles, new civilian, a few ranks behind the front, craned his neck in an effort to see over the heads before him.

The building's doors—personnel entryways and hangar doors—were sliding shut, their movement simultaneous, clearly controlled by a central computer.

A tickle of alarm in his stomach killed his appetite. This could not be good. He pressed forward, shoving other onlookers out of the way. A security trooper, seeing his advance, gave him a close threat-evaluation look, but Javon drew to a halt at the barricade.

Now sections of permacrete at the base of the building drew aside and trapezoidal shapes of the same material rose into view. At the top of each was a cupola from which protruded a quad-linked laser array, quite sufficient to down starfighters, more than sufficient to annihilate scores of people with a single shot.

But Javon knew that the pillbox's automatic fire systems, or occupants if staffed by the living, were authorized to fire only if fired upon or if potential enemies came within fifty meters. And surely no one was crazy enough to approach weapons pods bristling with lasers—

At a point where security troopers were overburdened with the effort of holding back the crowds, a swell of pressure from onlookers moved barricades back and a civilian charged through. This was a human male, his hair black and military-short. On his shoulder was a holocam, a professional rig—he was either a newsperson or an amateur who liked expensive toys.

The troopers holding the line had their hands full. None could go after the errant holocam operator, who continued slowly moving forward, recording.

"Get back!" That was a trooper, a corporal, a Quarren female, her facial tentacles twitching with agitation. She stood only five meters from Javon, on the other side of the barricades. "Back!"

"Shoot him." Javon heard the words emerge from his own mouth, was surprised, and then realized they were absolutely the correct ones to shout.

The Quarren whipped around to look at him. "What?"

"He's going to trigger those lasers in a few more steps, and dozens will die—maybe hundreds. Switch over to stun and *shoot him,* Corporal." Javon put the full force of his command training into his voice, hoping the Quarren would respond to that and not to his civilian clothes.

The Quarren looked at him as if convinced that her tympanic membranes were playing her false. Then her fingers moved over the left side of her blaster rifle. She raised the weapon to her shoulder and fired.

The man with the holocam took the bolt in his side. He went down hard, his holocam shattering on the plaza's permacrete surface, his body spasming. His eyes closed.

The crowd howled with outrage. Holocams immediately swung around to focus on the Quarren. But the surge in the line the unconscious man had emerged from retreated. The troopers there shoved against the line of barricades and straightened it.

The Quarren turned to glare at Javon. "It pains me that you were right."

"Me, too, Corporal."

Fifty meters farther along the line of barricades, a yellow-skinned humanoid female with an omnidirectional mike in her hand stared gaping at what had just transpired. "That was—that was Tuvar, wasn't it? From Independent Voice News?" She looked back at her holocam operator for confirmation.

That individual, a Gamorrean male in permacrete-gray garments, held a holocam rig smaller and much less elaborate than that of the fallen man. It had a cradle for his shoulder, a diopter for his eye, and a trigger for on and off; everything else was automatic, making it an ideal rig for someone with a Gamorrean's intellectual shortcomings. In answer to the yellow-skinned female's question, he gave a porcine grunt of confirmation, but his attention did not waver; his holocam remained focused on his unconscious colleague, who was even now being approached by a security medic.

The female, lovely in a deliberately unthreatening fashion, made up to appear as though she wore no makeup, dressed in all-white to set herself off from most backgrounds when being recorded, turned to stare at the Senate Building. "I'd give a month's pay to know what's going on in there right now."

"The Jedi have stormed the building." The voice came from immediately to her left, pitched just loud enough to be heard over the crowd noise—from a distance of not more than five centimeters. The woman could feel the speaker's breath against her ear. Something about the words sent a chill through her, but it wasn't the speaker's tone, which was low, neutral.

As if expecting to see a flesh-devouring monster, she turned. But the speaker was a human male wrapped up in traditional robes that could have been Jedi dress. The hood of his cloak was up, shadowing his face.

He drew back a few more centimeters to give her space. He was young, early thirties perhaps, decent-looking. "They haven't admitted it, of course, the Jedi Masters, to the rank and file, but we know."

She narrowed her eyes, looking him over. "What exactly *do* you know—hey, I recognize you, don't I?"

"Yes."

"You're Valin Horn. Jedi Knight. Still being sought by the authorities after being broken out of prison. Along with your sister."

Valin jerked his head casually to his right. The woman glanced that way. Standing beside Valin was Jysella Horn, her cloak hood also up, her expression dispassionate as she watched the Senate Building.

"I'm Kandra Nilitz, Landing Zone NewsNet."

Valin bowed. "How do you do?"

"You can confirm that the Jedi have invaded the Senate? Hold on, let us get the holocam set up—"

Valin shook his head. "Not here. But if you can meet our terms, we'll give you an exclusive. Facts nobody else knows."

Kandra gave him a suspicious look. "What sort of terms?"

"Not wealth. Can you get hold of a hyperdrive-equipped transport or shuttle? And can you scan us for implanted transmitters? If you can, and if you can get the two of us up to where *Fireborn* blew up, we'll give you a story no one else is getting."

Kandra's mind raced. "I . . . can. We have to get back to the studio."

"We must go now, before the fa— before the Jedi finish their task inside."

Kandra signaled her holocam operator, and the two of them led the Horns through the crowd. Kandra's heart raced. This, perhaps, could propel her from location reporting of events picked up on comm scanners to anchor work with a *real* newsnet.

It was just that there was something odd in the manner of the Horn Jedi, something eerie.

Jaina's lightsaber finished traversing a circle in the dark durasteel blast door. She withdrew the blade and held the weapon away from the cut. She gestured with her free hand. The durasteel plug flew away from her, shooting into the section of corridor the doors had been blocking.

Behind her, Saba and Corran stood side by side, lightsabers lit, casually deflecting blaster bolts fired by the security troopers thirty meters back along the corridor.

Jaina peered through the hole she'd made. "All clear this way."

Saba glanced for a fraction of a second over her shoulder at Jaina, then returned her attention to the incoming bolts. "Get to the turboliftz. Give us accesz. We will hold here until that is done."

Jaina dived through the hole, rolled to her feet, and ran an additional twenty meters to the nearest set of turbolift doors. There were no people in this curved section of corridor; if there had been any, the sight of her lightsaber blade cutting its way through the doors had convinced them to flee.

She experimentally tapped the turbolift's access button, but the status display overhead gave no indication that it had accepted the command. Of course it hadn't. Security would have closed down all turbolifts except to those with priority access. But it sometimes paid to try the simple approaches. And Bandy and Seha might be able to turn turbolift control over to the Jedi, but that wasn't their top priority; it might happen too late to be useful here.

She popped the protective hatch free from the lift's control panel and patched in a datapad. It was an ordinary 'pad, but the program running on this one sent queries to the Jedi command center at the false Kuati offices, requesting data from the hardware modules Octa, Kyp, and others had piggybacked into the building's security systems. If this worked, it would be faster and less destructive than cutting another hole—

The turbolift door slid open. A split second later a lift car roared past, hurtling by on an upward course, the wind displaced by its passage nearly blowing Jaina over. Its inner doors were closed, so there was no split-second view of surprised lift occupants to see.

She yanked the datapad free. "Ready to go!"

Moments later Corran hurtled through the hole Jaina had cut in the blast doors, his lightsaber blade gleaming with purple light. He sprinted in her direction. An instant after that Saba leapt through and immediately rolled to the side, avoiding a barrage of blaster bolts pursuing her like angry flying insects. The bolts hit the corridor's permacrete floor, some of them burning themselves out of existence, a few ricocheting up to hit the corridor wall far past Jaina.

The two Masters joined her, and together they peered down into the turbolift shaft.

It was actually three shafts, no separations among them. Theirs, the central one, showed no car below; the car that had passed Jaina was stopped some twenty stories up. To the left, no car was visible in either direction. To the right, a car was descending from far above.

Jaina glanced back at the blast doors. At best, they had another ten seconds before the first, bravest, of the pursuing troopers would poke a head through and start shooting. From that point, the Jedi would once again be deflecting blaster bolts and would have to continue to do so until a suitable lift car came.

Somewhere else in the building, closer to the delegation offices than to the hangars, Tionne, Kam, Zekk, and Taryn would be doing exactly the same thing. That team had a different destination.

The car in the right-hand shaft roared down past them. Jaina saw it stop with startling suddenness four stories down.

The three Jedi jumped.

It was a fifteen-meter fall, but a touch of the Force allowed each of the experienced Jedi to land painlessly and gracefully atop the car.

The car got under way again, hurtling upward, its acceleration so great that Jaina and Corran were forced to their knees. Saba stayed upright, her legs and tail forming a triangle of support.

In moments the car stopped again with a turbolift's typical suddenness. These cars, equipped with interior inertial compensators, could do so without turning their occupants into broken-limbed jelly. On top, though, the three Jedi were propelled upward as if fired from a spring-loaded cannon at a carnival.

They flew up an additional two stories, then pushed a little with the Force and drifted a meter laterally to land on the centimeters-wide ledge at the base of another set of doors.

Corran glanced at the numbers stenciled on the inside of the door. "This is a chamber level. We're good . . . if that car doesn't come up and smash us flat. Give me some room." He ignited his lightsaber.

Jaina and Saba drew to either side, holding on to narrow grooves and durasteel plate joins on the wall, as Corran cut a way out through the doors.

The turbolift car below descended. A lift in the far-left shaft roared by from above.

Another one, far above in this shaft, became visible in a rapid descent. Saba hissed something unpleasant-sounding, activated her lightsaber, and joined Corran in cutting the hole. In moments, their blades met, buzzing and sparking.

Jaina dived at the circular plate they'd marked. Despite her comparatively light weight, she knocked the plate free and fell atop it on the corridor floor beyond. As she rolled to her feet, her shoulder grazed the superheated edge of the metal. Even with the protective virtues of her lightly armored robe, she felt the sudden sting of injury.

She came up on her feet. Ahead, just a few meters away, stood a row of security troopers aiming blaster rifles—

With no time to ignite her lightsaber, she dodged left, drawing their fire away from the hole. Bolts tracked her, smacking and sizzling into the wall and the other turbolift door now behind her.

Beyond the troopers, Jaina could see a low archway leading to a large, well-lit chamber beyond. The Senate chamber—

In her peripheral vision, she saw Saba leap through the turbolift hole, then Corran. A turbolift car descended so close to his emergence that his cloak was snapped from his body, jerking his head back before the clasp broke, slamming him back into the turbolift door.

Saba caught the next volley of blaster bolts as Jaina activated her lightsaber. Jaina spared a glance for Corran, but he waved her off, shaking his head. He rubbed his neck. Below his beard, an ugly welt was already beginning to rise.

Together the three Jedi charged the troopers.

* * *

"Wynn, what the hell—"

In Daala's monitor, her Chief of Staff looked haggard, as if he'd been working without rest or food for days, even though she'd seen him recently. He gave her a look of disbelief. "All indications, Admiral, are that we're under assault by the Yuuzhan Vong."

"Not possible."

"I know."

With an infuriated noise, half scream and half gargle, Daala switched the monitor back to the desk of her secretary.

The Bothan was still gone. But in his place sat Han Solo.

"Solo! What's going on out there?"

Han shrugged. "Your secretary served some snacks. Bug eggs on crackers, I think. Leia and I didn't have any but everyone else did. Then they all started running off for the refresher. Except the Hapan ambassador. She didn't make it in time and kind of disgraced herself. Your secretary ate the most of all and he passed right out." He looked down, apparently to where the secretary lay off-cam. "His fur is turning gray and curling at the ends. You might want to come out and give it a look."

Without answering, Daala switched to a data feed. She rose. "It's a Jedi assault. We're leaving." When she turned to face her back wall, she was pleased to note that the two navy officers already had their blasters in hand, ready to defend this chamber.

Parova stood, too. "You have a way out?"

"Of course." From a pocket, Daala fished out her comlink and spoke into the device. "Emergency override zeta thirteen."

A section of wall the height and width of a Gamorrean wrestler, unmarked by crease or line, suddenly withdrew a full meter.

Daala moved toward it. Then her body jolted as energy flooded through her.

She'd felt it before, years ago, in training and in combat—a stun bolt. Her vision contracted in an instant to gray nothingness.

Her last thought, before she hit the floor, before consciousness escaped her entirely, was: *How did they get in without me hearing them?*

Leia's voice was filled with scorn. "'You might want to come out and give it a look'?" She fired another full-strength blaster bolt into Daala's door, deepening the crater where she thought the locking mechanism must be. She desperately missed her lightsaber, but she could not have managed to bring it through the security check.

Han shrugged. "If it had worked, history would have said it was genius."

"Well . . . you're probably right." She fired again. The hole deepened another centimeter. The foam lining the interior of the door was already on fire. The smoke issuing from it stank with a sharpness that made Leia think of poisonous fumes.

"Besides, we learned something. She didn't ask about you *shooting her door.* Means it's so well sound-insulated that she didn't know you were doing it." Han kept his own blaster pointed in the general direction of the prisoners and the door out into the exterior hall. He thought he could hear blasterfire from beyond it, distant blasterfire. That probably meant the Jedi were coming. It also probably meant there were Senate Building defenders between the Jedi and this office, which could be problematic.

The Hapan ambassador, a woman of middle years with looks normally only found in very costly holodramas, glared at him. "I did *not* disgrace myself."

"Of course you didn't, sweetheart. But you still can, you know." Han reached down and hauled the Bothan secretary to a sitting position. "All right, last chance. Open that door or I shave you, dip you in gold paint, and sell you to Jawas for spare parts."

The Bothan winced. "I'm not a droid."

"I'll sell you to especially *stupid* Jawas."

The Bothan shook his head. "Forgive me, General. But I won't help you, and you won't sell me. You're a hero of the Alliance."

Han made a disgusted noise and let the secretary drop. "Leia, I swear, I hate having a good reputation. I *hate* it."

Not answering, Leia fired again.

The blasterfire outside was growing louder, closer. Han glared at the prisoners. "Drag that sofa over against the wall and get behind it." He glowered down at the Bothan. "You, too."

"Thank you, sir. I knew you were one of the good—"

"Shut up."

The prisoners had dragged the sofa and a couple of tables into place and were huddling behind them when the exterior door slid open. A pair of armored security troopers backed into the office, firing at targets outside.

Han aimed, careful and deliberate, at the neck of the nearer trooper. There was no armor there. He squeezed off a shot. That trooper uttered a grunt of pain and fell forward, out of sight.

The other one turned, swinging his weapon into line. Han fired again, catching him just below the bottom rim of his armor. That trooper collapsed, falling sideways into the office. The door closed.

The Bothan peered out from the sofa. "Shall I bring you their firearms?"

"Shall I shoot you in the face?"

"No, sir. Thank you, sir." The Bothan ducked behind the sofa again.

Han cautiously moved forward until he was within reach of the fallen trooper. He holstered his blaster pistol as fast as he normally drew it—

Tried to, actually. This wasn't his pistol and there was no holster there. Unthinking, he dropped the pistol to the carpet.

He growled a Wookiee curse, hoping Leia hadn't seen his mistake, and snatched up the trooper's rifle and switched it over to stun. "Leia . . ."

"Quiet, Han. This isn't working."

The exterior door slid open again. Han saw a wall of armored backs edging his way. He opened fire, spraying stun bolts among them. Troopers fell as if hit by a single giant hammer. The door slid closed again.

"Got that, Fuzzy? I just shot a bunch of troopers in the back. Would a hero of the Alliance do *that*?"

The Bothan didn't peer out, and his voice was muffled by the intervening sofa. "I bet you used stun bolts."

Han growled.

"Han, switch with me."

He did, clicking the rifle back to blasterfire. He spun and took a sideways step to be outside the direct line of fire from the exterior door, then opened fire on the interior. His blaster bolts chipped away at the crater Leia had made, filling the air with more smoke and burning insulation debris.

He heard the exterior door slide open again, heard Leia fire four times in quick succession. The door slid shut.

As the smoke drifted away from the interior door, moved by the room's air-conditioning, Han could see light through the hole he'd shot in his target. "We're through."

"Opening it." Leia moved up beside him and waved with her free hand. Han switched back to stun bolts.

This was the most dangerous moment, with both of them concentrating their attention on the interior door. Han's sense of timing said the troopers outside would spend a few seconds communicating their next plan of attack, then charge. But that gave him and Leia seconds to act—forever, to a cagy old smuggler and a Jedi.

With Leia's exertion through the Force, Daala's inner door slid up.

Two blurs in blue leapt out, firing blaster pistols. Han cut loose, traversing his aim across the two of them. A bolt passed between him and Leia, and it was not a stun bolt. Another hit the carpet just in front of his foot. Han felt the heat of it through his boot and jerked his foot back.

Both males, one Falleen and one human, wearing naval uniforms, hit the carpet, unconscious. Han maintained his fire through the door, spraying the office interior, though no targets were immediately in sight.

A moment later he heard a shout, a woman's voice strong enough to be heard above the blasterfire, from within: "Hold your fire! We surrender!"

Leia spun, covering the outer door again, but she kept her free hand up, clearly holding the interior door open.

Han left off firing but did not lower his weapon. "Show yourself."

Admiral Parova appeared in the doorway, her hands in the air. "Admiral Daala is down. You hit her with that last volley."

Han heard the exterior door slide open . . . and Leia did not fire.

He hazarded a look over his shoulder. Now entering the room were Masters Kam and Tionne.

Han returned his attention to Parova. "Take me to your leader. We come in peace."

"Han."

"Sorry, Leia. Sometimes I can't help myself."

Behind him, he heard the Hapan ambassador speak up. "Master Solusar, I did *not* disgrace myself."

Chapter Twenty-four

TREEN WATCHED THE THREE JEDI ASCENDING THE SENate chamber, leaping from platform to platform in a pattern that looked as random and graceful as a waterfall in reverse. The Senator had heard a few blaster shots before they'd entered the chamber, and she wondered if any members of the security detail guarding that entrance had been maimed or killed.

But it was only an idle curiosity. She had things to do.

With a little jerk of her head, she indicated that her aides should step off the platform and into its small access passageway. When they did, she stepped into place at the controls. Switching over to manual, she activated the platform's repulsorlifts and set it into motion, detaching it from its docking brackets and sending it floating out into the open air above the chamber proper. Above and below her, other Senators were doing the opposite—those who had been floating here or there on missions of discussion or collaboration were now scurrying back to the safety of their docks.

She maneuvered the platform so that it was above the ascending Jedi. Jaina Solo was in the lead, but in a moment she was overtaken by the reptilian Jedi Master, Saba Sebatyne.

None of the Jedi had their lightsabers switched on. To Treen, that was a good sign. And no other Senators were in the process of moving to intercept them, another good sign.

As Master Sebatyne came near, reaching an altitude of only one platform level down from Treen's position, Treen extended a hand and beckoned with a crooked finger. Master Sebatyne glanced her way and, after another bound up one level, leapt laterally, landing beside Treen, her weight causing the platform to dip a few centimeters.

The Barabel Jedi wore a look Treen interpreted as curiosity. "This one has only a moment."

"You may wish to take a moment more," Treen replied. "I'll conduct you up. I assume you're headed to the main speaker's area?"

"Yes."

Treen set her platform into a climb, sending it toward Senator Rockbender's location. "What has happened?"

"We have deposed Chief of State Daala."

"Ah. About time." Though Treen felt as though she had just been stepped on and smashed flat by a rancor, she was proud of herself for keeping her voice impeccably untroubled. "Are you also suspending the Senate?"

"No. There is no danger to the Senatorz or their role. We simply are assuming the functionz of the executive branch for now."

Treen kept her face impassive as her mind raced. She was momentarily unbalanced when Jaina Solo landed beside her and the ascending platform dipped again.

"You already have Chief Daala in custody?" Treen asked.

Master Sebatyne nodded. "We do."

Jaina glanced over the side, watching the ascent of Corran Horn. "She's in the hands of my parents. And the Masters Solusar, and others."

"You're facing a bloodbath, you know. A small force

like the Jedi Order, as capable as its individual members are, cannot hope to hold the government against the combined might of the armed forces and the will of the people."

"This one and all of the Jedi Council hope that we act *with* the will of the people," Master Sebatyne said.

The crude outlines of a plan clicked into place in Treen's mind.

She'd have to act on her own initiative. There was no time to run her idea past the committee. This would cause trouble, especially with the military contingent.

Too bad for them.

"Your action meets with my approval, Master Sebatyne. And the approval of others. If you could make me certain guarantees, I might be able to offer you the support not only of some key Senators . . . but also of the majority of the chiefs of the armed forces, all of whom have recently been chafing under Daala's irrational rule."

"Please, slow your ascent, Senator Treen," the Barabel said.

Treen did. A moment later the increasingly crowded platform swayed again as Corran Horn leapt on to join the others.

Treen spent the next several minutes on her comlink, the special one with scrambler functions, only occasionally tuning in to the speech Master Sebatyne was presenting mere meters from her.

The words were much the ones she expected to hear. ". . . acting in the interest of the Galactic Alliance . . . to prevent a catastrophe that might tear the Alliance . . . taken into custody . . ." Flanked by Master Horn and Jaina Solo, with Senator Rockbender conspicuous behind them, Saba's magnified image, stern but not ferocious, spoke down toward the assembled Senators.

One level below and well to one side, her platform now empty of all but her, Treen managed her own communications far more quietly. "We have no choice. We can either leap aboard this speeder or watch it disappear into the distance, carrying all our opportunities with it. We'll collect the pieces and suffer only a delay . . . if we cooperate with the Jedi right now. They need us. Yes, a unified front. I've been able to reach all relevant parties, even the one in custody."

She barely listened to Bramsin's replies. Nothing the man said meant anything at the moment. She made a few noncommittal noises of assent, then cut off the communication.

Resuming her place at the platform controls, she maneuvered so that her platform was next to Rockbender's. She locked its controls in place, then stared at Master Sebatyne.

Eventually the Jedi came to the end of her speech. She glanced over at Treen. Treen looked just as pointedly up at the main holocam unit hovering above the platform level.

Saba gestured for the holocam to switch its attention to Treen.

Though she was not staring at the gigantic monitors above, Treen knew when the image switched from Saba to her; the light intensity changed, reflecting the fact that the image, previously dominated by Saba's dark, scaly skin, now showed Treen's sky-blue robes.

She lifted her chin and stared into the holocam. "Though the action by the Jedi Order has no precedent, nor was the cooperation or blessing of the Senate or any of its members sought before this action, I now announce that the portions of our government still devoted to concerns of justice and rightness have chosen to lend our conditional support to this action. I have personally spoken with General Thaal of the army; Admiral Parova, acting head of the navy; and General Jaxton of Starfighter Command. They are in agreement that this unfortunate turn of events was the only one left to reasoning beings—the only option left by former Chief Daala. The armed forces will therefore not oppose the Jedi Order so long as the Order proceeds in a just fashion and works toward returning the executive branch to duly selected hands. A convocation of Senators, including myself, Fost Bramsin of Coruscant, and many others whose names I will list as soon as they cease to pour into my comm board, also support this action."

She saw, in her lower peripheral vision, activity on the platform's comm monitor. She'd taken thirty seconds to put up a Senatorial poll, whose title, enigmatic until her last few words, simply read, WHO IS IN ACCORD WITH SENATOR BRAMSIN AND MYSELF ON THIS ISSUE? Now names suddenly began appearing in the left-hand column, the YES column. In an instant the list of names stretched to the bottom of the monitor, and then the document's title scrolled off the top as more names were added.

"We encourage all citizens of the Alliance to remain calm. There is no cause for worry, and the functions of government will continue—far more smoothly and rationally than they have in recent months under former Chief Daala." She turned back to Saba and nodded, quietly ceding control of the transmission back to the Jedi.

Back in the Chief of State's waiting area, Han blinked as Saba's face once again filled the monitor. He turned back to his wife. She was flanked by Kam and Tionne. Zekk and Taryn held the inner office and the still-unconscious Daala. Late arrivals Kyp and Octa had already escorted the others from the waiting room out into the approach corridor and now held that door against possible strikes by security operatives. "We won."

Leia nodded. She looked a little shell-shocked herself. "That was already likely. Possibly inevitable. But we won *instantly.* No waiting for the armed forces and Senate to come around."

"So we can leave?"

"Soon, Han. Soon." She frowned, clearly troubled.

"What is it, sweetie?"

Leia shook her head as if dismissing what was bothering her. "It just felt a little like fleeing the first Death Star. Where we'd gotten some help that made everything easier . . . help that meant more trouble in the future."

"That was nearly forty-five years ago. No similarity." Han leaned back and put his hands behind his head. "What do you suppose will happen if we order something to eat?"

"Your Bothan's out in the hall. Ask *him.*"

News of the coup hit the holochannels the instant the Senate Building unsealed. It flashed to near and far parts of the Alliance, into Imperial Remnant space, into regions uncontrolled by those two political bodies, at hyperspace speeds.

News feeds exploded with noise and commentary. The recorded message queues of the comlinks of Han, Leia, Saba, Jag Fel, Treen, Bramsin, Rockbender, Jaxton, Thaal, Parova, Dorvan, and innumerable others filled up with desperate invitations to appear on holocam and explain what had just happened.

It was hours before the dust could even begin to settle, before all individuals in all corners of the Senate Building could be convinced that the situation was, for the moment, resolved, that blaster pistols and lightsabers were not about to flash into action once again.

Ambulances removed the few individuals injured in the Jedi storming of crucial points in the building, plus the many who had fallen victim to riot gas attacks in the main security center and the dozens who had collapsed from stress. Some awoke still thinking that the Yuuzhan Vong had attacked.

As peace—a tense, charged peace—settled on the seat of government, Wynn Dorvan, effectively under house arrest in his office for the last several hours, was ushered into the Chief of State's office by C-3PO. He looked at the damaged door into the inner office, propped open by a bookcase, and ducked to enter the office itself.

Inside, where Daala usually sat, stood Jedi Master Saba Sebatyne, her back to the door. She turned, careful not to let her tail sweep across the desktop or bookcases to the side as she did so. She gave Wynn a little nod. "This one appreciates your coming."

"As though I had a choice." He regretted saying that the instant the words left him. It might not be a good idea to irk the new, if temporary, masters of the Galactic Alliance. But he was tired, and his discretionary instincts had ebbed.

"You did have a choice. Would you care to sit?"

"Not if you're to remain standing."

"A practical necessity. This one failed to bring a chair suited to her structure."

Wynn remained standing regardless. From a pocket, he withdrew a small, sealed envelope and placed it on the desktop before Saba.

She glanced at it but did not pick it up. "A protest?"

"My resignation."

"Ah. Understandable. Honorable. But this one will ask you to retrieve it. And destroy it."

Wynn shook his head. "Chief Daala's political allies will not cooperate with me if I collaborate with you.

Her enemies will not cooperate with me in any case—they're too anxious to fill my job from within their own ranks. I'm useless here. And—let me be frank. Whatever you think of her, Natasi Daala is an honorable person. I'm not going to cooperate with a government that intends to hyperdrive her into a conviction and a prison term. I'm already hearing people talk about leveling charges of *treason* against her. I'm going to use my skills and my resources in her defense. That's it."

Saba regarded him steadily, long enough for her to take a few slow breaths. "This one commendz you and appreciates your candor. Now will you listen to what this one has to say?"

"Of course."

"The Jedi Order does not intend to remain in control of the executive branch, of course. Conquest was not our aim. Until a new Chief of State can be duly selected, we will be appointing a Triumvirate to act collectively as the Chief of State. It will consist of this one, Senator Treen, and General Jaxton."

"Representing the interests of the Jedi, the Senate, and the armed forces, respectively. About as appropriate an organization as one could hope for—but I'm surprised, even shocked, that former Chief of State Solo is not on it."

"Instead of this one?"

"Yes. Because of her experience with the office."

"Ah. But to have Jedi Solo here would suggest to the people that the Jedi intend to install her permanently, no?"

"Hm. Well, yes."

"Besides, we have other taskz for Jedi Solo's unique combination of political and Jedi skillz. Specifically, Klatooine. Newz of the intended assault there has stirred up a piranha-beetle's nest of protest and anger. She will quell it."

"And you want me for what, exactly?"

"A continuity of knowledge. We want someone who knowz the politicz, yet who would willingly abandon the opportunity to influence this office in order to defend a woman who is now the focus of the greatest political trial in many yearz. He who wishes to abandon power may be the one best suited to direct it."

"And Daala? What will you give me related to her situation if I agree?"

Saba sissed, a steam-valve noise bespeaking amusement. She recovered quickly. "Daala's defense team will doubtlesz want a change of venue so her trial does not take place on Coruscant or in some region hostile to her. The Triumvirate will ensure that the trial does receive a change of venue, and that the choice is made before we abandon the office."

"You have enough pull with the Department of Justice to do that?"

"It seemz so. They have already agreed to drop charges against Seha Dorvald, Booster Terrik, and Valin and Jysella Horn, and to set aside the plea bargain of Master Skywalker so that he might return to Coruscant. We are working on persuading them to drop the case against Tahiri Veila."

"Don't do that. Let that one go to trial."

Saba cocked her head, clearly curious. "Why?"

"First—unlike the case with Terrik, the active-duty Jedi, whose actions were clearly preludes to Jedi Order missions the populace basically approves of or should not have been prosecuted in any case, and Master Skywalker, whose trial and plea bargain were clearly the result of Chief Daala's specific interest—the Veila case is more murky. She did kill Pellaeon, and not for a clearly altruistic reason. Second, if you clear both Master Skywalker *and* Jedi Veila, critics of the Jedi will have an unimpeachable argument that you're using your new power for gain or personal reasons, but if you clear Master Skywalker and allow the case against Tahiri Veila to proceed, you divide your critics and weaken their opposition. Let's be honest, you can't stand too much opposition right now."

Saba was silent for a long moment. Then she picked up Wynn's letter of resignation and handed it to him. "Destroy this, please. Then assemble a list of ten worldz you believe can give Chief Daala a fair trial. Have it on this one's desk by tomorrow morning."

He looked over the envelope, its contents so carefully composed over so many hours, and accepted it from her. "Yes, Master Sebatyne."

"This one appreciates your help, Dorvan."

"You're welcome."

Chapter Twenty-five

HWEG SHUL, NAM CHORIOS

IN THE MOST STILL PREDAWN HOUR, THEY LANDED the shuttle, shut it down, and, bundled as well as they could be against the chill, hiked the few remaining kilometers in to Hweg Shul.

From a hilltop a kilometer off, Luke studied the town through his macrobinoculars. He could make out the government center, mostly domes and other raised buildings, and the area near the spaceport where the Admirable Admiral was located. But many things had changed in the couple of days they had been away. Nighttime overhead lighting was out in several sections of town; only when Luke switched the macrobinoculars over to starlight-vision mode could he make out details.

In the Oldtimer sections of town, there were men or women on the occasional street corner, dressed for the chill, standing stationary or pacing to keep warm. All were armed with blaster rifles.

There were also sentries on street corners in the Newcomers' and Latecomers' portions of town—uniformed police.

Everywhere there was to be seen the aftermath of Force storm damage. There were smashed landspeeders and speeder bikes here and there, one landspeeder atop another in a ruined heap just in front of a garage, another speeder nose-first halfway into a raised dome. One building in ten showed damage characteristic of battering by flying junk; one in twenty had collapsed entirely.

He handed the macrobinoculars to Ben. "They've been through a lot."

"They have." That was Vestara. She had her comlink in hand and an earpiece in place in her left ear, occasionally visible when she turned her head and her cloak hood gaped. Clearly, she was listening to broadcasts. "And we're being sought by the authorities."

"That's crazy." Ben studied the damaged town. "They're blaming us for the storms?"

"No, for the murder of Dr. Wei. We let a lot of people know that we were searching for him. Then we disappeared and someone else found his body out in the wilderness. The whole matter of trumped-up evidence suggesting he was engineering a new species of drochs seems to have been forgotten. Then there's the assault on Mayor Snaplaunce. He was stabbed at the site where he handed over the shuttle to us—most people seem to think we did it to steal his shuttle."

Luke glanced at her. "Did he survive?"

"Yes, and he's out of the hospital now. But he doesn't remember the circumstances of his stabbing, or whether it happened before or after we left."

Luke grimaced. "Force techniques may have been used to mess with his memory."

"Probably." Vestara hesitated before suggesting something Luke knew she never would have proposed a few weeks earlier. "Perhaps you should bring in some more of . . . your people."

Luke and Ben exchanged a look. Luke was still behaving according to the dictates of his plea bargain, not issuing orders to the Jedi. Ben, under no such restrictions, had listened to his father and, before planetfall on

Nam Chorios, sent off a holocomm transmission with some suggestions. But none of that would lead to Jedi coming to this world to aid in a ground search. The Jedi were needed elsewhere.

Luke merely shook his head. "We're on our own."

Ben raised the macrobinoculars to his eyes again. "Besides, it's a planet with an itty-bitty population. Two Jedi and a Sith should be able to handle anything they throw at us."

Vestara snorted. "Not necessarily including Abeloth."

Luke pulled his cloak more tightly around him. "Come on. Let's go in."

It was slow, careful work entering Hweg Shul. The task was made easier by the fact that it wasn't a walled community and by the fact that the damage to the lighting grid made it harder for the locals to detect them.

Staging their movements, remaining alert in all directions, and never yielding to impatience, the three made their way through the city outskirts and to the Newcomers' district, avoiding guards and eluding the views of elevated security holocams.

That brought them, half an hour before dawn, to the front of Teselda's dome.

Ben and Vestara kept an eye out while Luke leapt up to the entryway and ran a bypass on the entry keypad. A moment later the door slid open and the three of them entered.

The dome interior was mostly dark, illuminated only by colorful lights gleaming from various electronics, with only the hum and hiss of a heater to be heard—and then, from above, Sel's voice. "Is someone there?"

Luke gestured for the others to remain quiet.

A spiral metal stairway descended from the ceiling near the living room's back wall, unfolding like a musical squeeze box, and Sel descended. She was dressed in a downy nightshirt and leggings all in dark blue, and in her hand was an unlit lightsaber. When she caught sight of Luke and the others, she visibly relaxed and lowered the weapon. "Master Skywalker. I was worried about you."

Luke loosened his cloak, allowing some of the room's warm air to flow over him. "We're fine. We weren't *quite* shot down."

Sel reached the first-floor level. "They're looking for you. The authorities." The staircase rose behind her until it was flush with the ceiling again.

"*Just* the authorities?"

She cocked her head, puzzled. "I'm sorry?"

"Never mind. As you might expect, we didn't do it—whatever it might happen to be that they suspect us of."

"I knew that. Would you—would any of you like some breakfast?"

Luke cleared his throat. "Forgive me, but . . ." And he began to sing. The song had a gentle melody spanning a narrow range of notes, well suited to the average parent. "Green grasses beckon, soft and warm / My arms will keep you safe from harm / As thrantas dance across the sky / As stars smile down and south winds sigh / The scent of flowers fills the air / And sleep comes for Teselda fair . . ."

As he sang, he could feel the perplexed gazes of Ben and Vestara on him. But the song's effect on Sel was more dramatic. With the first few notes, she stumbled, her eyes fluttering, and dropped the lightsaber. It bounced on the carpet. Sel staggered over a meter and slumped onto her sofa.

By the time Luke finished the first stanza, Sel's eyes were closed. She breathed deeply in untroubled sleep.

Luke drew a hand over his brow, a mock expression of relief. "We're lucky that worked. I'm not known for my singing."

Ben moved over to look down on Sel. "What was that all about?"

"It's her trigger for the mnemotherapy technique. She gave it to me." Luke stepped beside his son and helped position Sel more comfortably on the sofa. "I need to know if she's been meddled with."

Vestara handed him Sel's lightsaber. "It looks old."

"Four centuries at least." Luke set the weapon aside and knelt. "Sel, can you hear me?"

Her eyes did not open, but she spoke, her voice low and languid. "I hear you."

"Do you know who I am?"

"You are Master Luke Skywalker. Leader of the Jedi. Enemy of the Listeners. Enemy of the Lady."

Luke smoothed down the hair on the back of his neck. It was abruptly threatening to stand up. "Where is the Lady now?"

"I don't know."

"How about Master Nenn? Do you know where he is?"

She turned her head, suddenly fretful. "I don't want to go there."

"You don't have to go there. You can stay here where it's safe. But I have to go there. Where is Nenn?"

"Below."

"Below, where?"

"In the pumping station. With the Listeners. With the drochs. In the dark."

This time Luke felt gooseflesh rise on his skin. He had bad memories of being in the dark with drochs.

"Here in Hweg Shul?"

"No, somewhere else."

"Where?"

"I don't know. The only pumping station I've ever seen is here. It isn't that one."

Luke sat back and sighed. "Of *course* Abeloth would

be in a place like that . . . Sel, you welcomed us when you realized who it was. You pretended there was no problem. What were you going to do with us?"

"Delay you. Keep you here. Alert the Listeners."

"So you have not alerted them?"

"No."

"Sel, you will sleep now. You're very, very tired. You will hear no voice but mine until you awaken. No voice, no alarm, no beep from your comm board, nothing. When you awaken, you will feel very good, refreshed, and you will marvel that you slept so long. But you will not recall that we were here with you."

"I understand."

Ben settled on a chair. "In the future, I suggest that we only ever fight guys who set up their lairs in posh hotel suites. With sunlight and buffets and sanisteams and dancers."

"Son, if you could figure out how to make that a reality, I'd make *you* the head of the Jedi Order."

Ben shuddered. "Pretend I never said that."

Vestara looked over the quiescent Sel. "Three of us to search a planet, and now it's more or less ruled, or at least influenced, by Abeloth, and we can't rely on our Force powers . . . Are you sure it isn't time to bring in your Jedi?"

Luke gave her a thoughtful look. Her words suggested that she really was dedicated to the elimination of Abeloth as a threat above all other concerns. That was a good sign. But still he shook his head. "The Jedi are needed elsewhere now."

"'One Jedi, one planet' is not a realistic motto to try to live by."

Ben grinned. "But we have *two* Jedi and one Sith. We have them outnumbered."

Vestara looked skyward as if seeking inspiration, and

Luke wondered whether the frustration-infused word flying around in her mind was *Jedi*, *men*, or both.

ABOARD THE SHUTTLE *VERNUS*, DEEP SPACE

Kandra sighed, frustrated. "You're not being very forthcoming."

Opposite her, in a rear-facing chair in the shuttle's passenger compartment, Valin Horn shrugged. "Some things are better experienced than spoken of. Jysella and I are taking you and your cam operator somewhere you can experience something remarkable."

"Where?"

"Nam Chorios."

The name sent a little thrill of childhood fear through Kandra. What had come out of Nam Chorios thirty years earlier had been the stuff of bedtime horror stories for those of her generation. "Does it involve the Death Seed plague?"

"Perhaps. It certainly involves a menace endangering our galaxy. Our very existence."

"But you won't tell me what it is, or how it relates to the *Fireborn* explosion, or to the Jedi takeover of the Senate Building . . ." She now knew, from scattered hypercomm reports picked up during their flight from the Coruscant system, that the Jedi had ousted and imprisoned Chief of State Daala. But Valin's hints, vague, tantalizing, and maddening, suggested that there was something far, far bigger going on. Some other reason the Jedi needed to be in charge.

"Correct. I won't. Some things are better experienced—"

"Than spoken of. Right. But—"

Valin rose. "It's about time for me to take over piloting duties from my sister." He moved forward, entered the shuttle's small flight deck, and shut the door behind him.

Valin settled into the copilot's seat with a sigh of relief. "She won't stop asking questions."

Jysella gave him a cool, emotionless look. "She *is* one of them. You could just space her."

"No, she may be useful to us when we get to Nam Chorios. As a distraction."

"I guess you're right."

"Just stay patient. We'll get through this. Even if we're the only real Jedi left in the galaxy, if we stay smart and let the Force guide us, we'll prevail."

Jysella gave him a troubled glance, clearly not convinced. "If you say so."

Chapter Twenty-six

NINTH HALL OF JUSTICE, CORUSCANT

LOOKING AT SUL DEKKON, THE CHAGRIAN PROSECUTING attorney, Tahiri allowed herself to feel another twinge of hope.

The attorney was not his usual crisp, upright self. Dressed in black robes that were positively funereal, he sat back in his chair at the prosecution table, watching with a marked lack of interest as Judge Zudan, up at the bench, sorted out her file printouts for the proceedings of the day to come. Though Dekkon's face betrayed no emotion, his body language was that of someone grappling with some unexpressed sorrow. There was a sort of waxy lifelessness to his blue skin and horns Tahiri had never seen before.

Anxious to have her suspicions confirmed, Tahiri turned to her own attorney, the Bothan Eramuth Bwua'tu. She lowered her voice to a whisper. "He looks rattled. Have we won?"

But Bwua'tu was none too cheerful. His eyes moved as though he were reading a text page no one else could see. He raised his eyes to meet Tahiri's. "We may be in trouble. He's just been dealt a new card, and I think he's playing it."

Her sorting done, the Falleen judge raised her head to

survey the courtroom. "Prosecutor, are you ready to proceed?"

"I am." Dekkon rose and moved around to stand in front of his table. He took extra moments to straighten his robes, then looked at Zudan again. "Your Honor, the prosecution rests."

There was a murmur from the audience seats. It wasn't much of a murmur. Tahiri's trial had not been truly newsworthy for days, and after yesterday's coup by the Jedi against Daala, the gallery had scarcely a dozen onlookers in it.

Judge Zudan blinked. "Are you serious?"

"Yes, Your Honor."

The judge turned toward the defense table. "Master Bwua'tu, are you ready to begin presentation of your defense?"

"If I could have just a few minutes to confer with my client, Your Honor."

"I think that would perhaps be appropriate. We will stand at recess for five minutes. Nobody go anywhere." Zudan rapped her gavel and returned her attention to her piles of printouts.

Now worried, Tahiri leaned over so she and Bwua'tu could speak and not be overheard. "I don't understand. You've been beating his case black and blue. You proved his star witness was a liar. You've been pulling his other witnesses' testimony apart like you were peeling fruit. And clearly he's giving up. Why are we in trouble?"

Bwua'tu gave her a look of sympathy. "Understand: Populations, represented in this case by the jury over there, do not generally approve of their heroes being killed. Our defense is predicated, among other things, on the notions that there are circumstances under which anybody would feel obligated to do such a thing, and that any effort to lie or manipulate evidence to convict a defendant must be symptomatic of a desperate need to ensure an unfair conviction—owing to the defendant's innocence. Yes?"

She nodded.

"Dekkon was indeed losing. And then the fates handed him enough ammunition to get back in the fight. The fact that the Jedi just seized control of the Galactic Alliance."

"But—wait. First, I'm not a Jedi anymore. And second, the Jedi didn't do that. They just ousted Daala, and now they're taking part in a transitional government . . ."

Bwua'tu shook his head, his expression sad. "Remember that the jury has been sequestered."

"So they shouldn't even have heard about the coup."

"But something like that can't be kept from even a sequestered jury. Crowds by the millions on the pedways, airspeeders flying by their windows trailing banners, hotel staff members speaking in hushed whispers—'What's happening? What's happening?' Inevitably the jurors will have heard something. The problem with their being sequestered then becomes the fact that they get only a part of the story. That part is that the Jedi have taken over."

"Which still has nothing to do with me."

"Ex-military still have friends in the military. Former workers from an office still have friends in that office. Ex-Jedi still have Jedi friends. And Dekkon shows up in court the morning after the coup, dejected, and rests his case, signaling defeat."

Understanding finally dawned. "Leading the jury to assume the trial doesn't matter. That even if the jury convicts, the Jedi are going to get me freed."

"Correct."

"But that's not fair. That's deceptive—"

"Is it? I have well-placed sources who say that, late yesterday, the Jedi Order made some initial queries to the Department of Justice about dropping your case and negating Master Skywalker's plea bargain. Dekkon may be responding with genuine dismay to anticipated interference with the process of justice. Or he may be play-acting to accentuate his case. I suspect both are true. Regardless, yesterday his chances of success were perhaps one in ten, and after the Jedi coup, this tactic has made them fifty–fifty. No better than a random throw of the dice . . . but far better than he had before."

Tahiri let out a long, slow breath. "What do we do?"

"We can choose one of three paths. Number one, we hope that the Jedi do indeed decide to oblige the government to drop your case. Number two, we proceed with our original defense course, extending this case for a few more weeks, and hope that during this time the Jedi do not lose the sympathy of the people. To achieve this, of course, they collectively would have to be superior politicians with a deeply ingrained understanding of motivating, encouraging, and uplifting large populations, as well as handling transition-era crises with superior diplomacy, which would be enhanced by the enthusiastic cooperation of the rest of the government. Or, number three, we can rely on the same fifty–fifty die roll that Dekkon has just made."

Tahiri thought that over. Her heart sank farther. "The die roll is our best option, isn't it?"

"Yes, my dear, I think it is."

"Go ahead and roll, Eramuth."

Bwua'tu turned to look at the judge. When she noticed, he gave her a little nod, indicating readiness.

She rapped her gavel. "Court is once again in session. Master Bwua'tu, are you prepared to commence the defense case?"

"Your Honor, the defense rests."

This time the judge did not even blink. She stared at the Bothan as if her eyes were being held open by adhesive. The low murmur began again in the echoingly empty gallery.

Finally she turned to Dekkon. "Master Dekkon, are you ready to begin closing arguments?"

"The prosecution has no closing arguments to offer, Your Honor."

That caused a noise to emerge from Bwua'tu, faint, a sigh of pain.

"Master Bwua'tu?"

"The defense has no closing arguments, Your Honor."

"How interesting. We will recess for another few moments while I send for the usual documents, and then I will issue final instructions to the jury." She rapped her gavel again.

JEDI TEMPLE

In the upper reaches of the Temple, below the Masters' chamber on a broad patio capable of holding a few hundred people, lay the bier of acting Grand Master Kenth Hamner, Hamner's body atop it. His robes were spotless and military-crisp, not the ones in which he had died, and his eyes were closed, but none of the Jedi and visitors filing past to pay their final respects offered the comforting, idiotic opinion that he looked as though he were only sleeping.

A very few of the mourners, having passed by him and offered a few words or a salute of respect, broke away from the line of people exiting the patio. These few stood in knots to watch the procession and speak in hushed tones. One was made up mostly of Jedi Masters, senior Jedi Knights, and their close associates—Saba, Corran, Han, Leia, Jaina, Amelia, Tionne, Kam, Cilghal, Jagged Fel, Octa, and Kyp.

Jaina caught Corran's eye. She kept her voice appropriately low. "Any word on Valin and Jysella?"

Grim, Corran shook his head. "It's pretty clear that they found someone who could do a sophisticated sweep on them for transmitters, found and discarded theirs . . . and then just disappeared. The only reasonable conclusion is that they're still suffering the madness effects that plagued all the Shelter Jedi."

There was regret in Cilghal's rumbling tones. "We must conclude that the fact that they were in carbonite suspension when the other Shelter Jedi Knights were cured prevented them from being cured, as well."

Corran offered an I-don't-care-why shrug. "And there's no telling where they might be hiding."

"Are you joining the search?"

If possible, he looked even more glum. "In any military, paramilitary, or security organization, including Corellian Security and the Jedi Order, there's a rule that is sometimes implicit, usually explicit. You're never assigned to a case involving your own loved ones, never allowed even to participate. Normally, I'm all in favor of that rule. At times like this, I just have to trust in others." He did not look as though he were a very trusting soul at that moment.

Jaina reached out a hand and gave him a reassuring squeeze on the shoulder. He nodded and turned away, standing a couple of paces apart from the others, watching the procession.

Wynn Dorvan had now reached the bier. Solemn, he said a few words to Hamner's body and moved on. Behind him, Senator Treen and General Jaxton paused to pay their respects.

Jag's mouth quirked just for a moment into a slight smile. "The Alliance's Triumvirate and the Empire's Head of State all gathered in one place, open to the sky, just one missile drop away from galaxywide chaos . . . my security people were *not* happy."

Saba offered a nod. "Some—the friendz of Master Hamner from the armed forces—have been saying that such a strike would be appropriate. Where this one is concerned, that is."

Jag gave her a look of sympathy, though the Barabel was not necessarily going to be able to interpret the human facial expression. "What about the Department of Justice? What's their reaction?"

Saba glanced toward the crowd on the opposite side of the bier. "That man, the tall human with white hair." Jag followed her gaze and saw an aristocratic-looking man, pale of skin, dressed all in gray, his left hand clearly robotic in origin. "Commander Makken. He has been appointed as special investigator on this matter. The Department of Justice does not yet know whether to charge an interim Chief of State, or even if a duel between Jedi should be considered a criminal offense, so they investigate."

Leia shook her head. "Even if they do decide to file charges, they won't do so until the Triumvirate has broken up and there's a properly selected Chief of State in place."

Saba regarded her. "Explain, please."

"I know it's only been a day, but the signs are already in place. The Senate has tabled most of its committee discussions and debates. No new bills were introduced today. They're going slack, Master."

"Why?"

"The less they do, the more you, Treen, and Jaxton *have* to do, if only through examples of leadership. This puts even more pressure on you to leave that post as soon as you can. Also, any political problems that arise while you're in charge can convincingly be blamed on the Triumvirate, meaning that problems the individual

Senators have been grappling with can be allowed to worsen—and all blame will be laid at your feet. In appointing a special investigator in the matter of Master Hamner's death, they demonstrate to their constituents that they're taking action, but by not authorizing him to press a criminal action against you, they suggest that there's only so much they can do until you leave your post."

Saba shook her head. "This one was never meant for politicz. Fortunately, Jedi Solo, you *were*."

Han's face fell. "Uh-oh."

His reaction drew a brief siss of amusement from Saba. "Yes, this one has an assignment for you. For both, since this one speakz as co–Chief of State."

Leia gave her husband an admonishing look, then turned back to Saba. "So it *is* Klatooine."

"Yes, but the situation there has developed even since we spoke last night. There is much anger at the fact that Chief Daala dispatched the Mandos against them. Yes, the Mandos were called off, but the rage continues. Now we hear that many groupz that have fought for the freedom of their kind are gathering on Klatooine. We wish to normalize relationz with them. Persuade them that new governing principles are in place. We wish you and General Solo to go there, participate in their discussionz."

Leia frowned. "To make any sort of lasting impression, we're going to have to offer them something. Something substantial."

"We have something to offer. Many of these groupz do speak for the enslaved or disenfranchised peoples of their homeworldz. Choose the one that is already closest to breaking away from their masterz, already most suitable to be a self-governing world . . . and offer full provisional membership in the Alliance. And a Senate seat."

Han whistled. "That's a prize."

Saba nodded. "It will demonstrate that we are serious, and take them seriously. It will also present a procesz for the otherz to follow if they want Alliance aid."

Leia narrowed her eyes. "It might also divide them, as the other groups become unhappy with the one that wins the prize. Meaning they might cease to exist as a united front, as a potential enemy of the Galactic Alliance. Master, you may have more political savvy than you're admitting to."

"This one categorically denies that charge."

The last few dozen visitors passed by the bier. Most of them continued on toward the exit arch, but a few lingered. Jaina saw among them human men and women with coloration and features similar to Hamner's—distant family members, she assumed.

Four of them approached, unfurled a blue cloth among them, and drew it over Hamner's body, covering him head-to-foot. The cloth draped down on either side of the bier. The four withdrew.

Izal Waz, an Arcona Jedi Knight, dark-skinned and reptilian, approached the bier. In his hand was a flaming brand. His expression was fierce, but there was sorrow in his large green eyes.

He spoke only a few words. "All through your life, you fulfilled your duties with strength, grace, and honor, and we will remember. Only one duty remains. Go onward and break trail so that we may someday follow." He lowered the brand so that its flame touched the wood of the bier.

The wood, prepared for this purpose, caught quickly. Flames raced around the base of the bier and swiftly climbed toward the shrouded body.

Izal withdrew to stand with Hamner's family, and smoke that had once been living wood and living flesh climbed into the Coruscant sky.

Chapter Twenty-seven

HWEG SHUL, NAM CHORIOS

Father:

I hope that you are much recovered.

Abeloth is on Nam Chorios, operating under the identity of Nenn, a Master of the Theran Listeners. Evidence suggests that she has taken refuge in an underground water pumping station somewhere on the planet, but there is insufficient information at this time to indicate which.

With affection, I remain
Your daughter, Vestara

Writing that letter, compared with the previous few, seemed almost effortless to Vestara. There were no lies in it, no requirements that she project herself into a different mind-set, a different way of thinking.

Why, then, was it so hard to *send* the thing?

In Sel's little office, Vestara had had no problem slicing into Sel's accounts, purchasing a hypercomm transmission of one small text message, encrypting it, setting up the routing on that message so it would find its way to her father's task force without alerting GA authorities to its path or its origin. But now, with all tasks but one complete, she found herself unable to touch the button on the screen that would send the thing.

"Vestara?" It was Ben's voice from elsewhere in Sel's dome.

Vestara jumped, then hit the on-screen button, sending the transmission. She closed down the conduit through which she'd sent it, stood, gathered a small pile of printouts, and moved out into the little hall and the living chamber beyond.

Sel was still stretched out on her sofa. Luke, looking tired, sat on a nearby chair, Ben standing beside him. Both Skywalkers glanced toward Vestara as she entered.

She held up the printouts. "A list of all recorded water pumping stations onplanet. And composite space station holocam views of all of them over the last few days. I think I've done a little damage to Sel's financial accounts to pay for this."

"We'll arrange for her to be repaid." Luke held out a hand and accepted the sheaf of flimsies.

"Master Skywalker, you look weary."

"I am. I decided not to rely on nothing but a posthypnotic suggestion—too dangerous for us. I employed mnemotherapy instead. It was successful. Sel won't recall us visiting her."

Vestara looked at the sleeping woman. "Is she still under Abeloth's influence?"

"Yes. There's little point in freeing her when, in a matter of minutes or hours, she'll fall under Abeloth's sway again . . . especially when freeing her might tip off Abeloth as to our whereabouts." Luke paged through the printouts, studying the composite holocam views, each of which showed, from far above, a ground site and the vehicle activity in its vicinity. Some views were of communities with heavy traffic, and the vehicle activity appeared as thick, blurry lines. Others showed abandoned sites with no activity at all. Other sites were somewhere in between.

As he perused them, he spoke, as if to himself. "Kind of like the old days, on the run from the Empire . . . anything we needed but didn't have, we'd steal, do whatever we could to blame corrupt Imperial quartermasters or criminal groups like the Black Sun . . . younger then, didn't get so tired so fast . . ."

Ben glanced up to catch Vestara's eye. He appeared worried. And no wonder: his father, still carrying an injury from the last fight with the Sith, seemed just a little diminished by all his recent labors.

Luke sighed, set the flimsies on his lap, and looked up. "Next step, we get some rest; then tonight we steal a landspeeder or airspeeder."

Vestara nodded. "Yes, Master Skywalker."

"From a Theran Listener if possible, or an Oldtimer otherwise. Reduce their resources, enhance ours."

"Yes, sir."

"Ben, please take first watch."

CORUSCANT

The judge, a Mon Calamari male with skin color closer to black than red, more imposing than many jurists because of his cranial size, looked up from the monitor embedded in the top surface of his bench. "Admiral Natasi Daala, this court accepts your plea of not guilty in the charges specified. Owing, however, to the prosecution's well-documented analysis of the risks surrounding your situation, including support, wanted or unwanted, from extremist elements formerly belonging to the armed forces of the Galactic Empire, we must accede to the prosecution's request that you be held without bail."

Daala, standing unyielding and unbowed in the face of political treachery and trumped-up charges, did not deign to answer the judge or even look directly at him.

"Additionally, given the resources available to these individuals and groups, we hereby order that you be held over in a maximum-security facility pending trial."

Daala's attorney, a fair-haired human male about Daala's age, tried one last time. "Your Honor, my client is an honorable veteran of the armed forces and constitutes no flight risk. These measures are entirely inappropriate, and their enforcement could conceivably prejudice jurors against her."

"We will have to see that this does not happen, Counselor. This arraignment is hereby concluded." The judge banged his gavel and it was done.

Her attorney turned a sympathetic face toward Daala. "I'm sorry."

"Don't concern yourself, Counselor. Not all the reason and precedent in the galaxy can convince conspirators that they shouldn't conspire . . . On another matter, if I write a message, can you deliver it?"

"Of course."

"Without reading it yourself?"

He hesitated only a fraction of a second. "Yes. But I must advise against your taking any action related to your case that doesn't involve your defense team."

A GA Security guard, a huge Ithorian whose eyes, widely spaced in her broad, fleshy head, betrayed nothing, approached, gesturing for them to depart through the side door reserved for attorneys and clients.

Daala turned that way. "There are some things, Counselor, that I must do without consultation. I'm still the legitimate Chief of State of the Alliance. Some of my measures must remain secret." Reaching the door, she offered an absent wave to Wynn Dorvan, who sat in the front row of audience seats. Then she passed through and lost sight of him.

"Of course, Admiral."

Not long after, her personal possessions confiscated, her clothes replaced with a yellow inmate's jumpsuit, Daala was transported via personnel airspeeder to the maximum-security Armand Isard Correctional Facility. A seeming eternity of documentation, hand- and sole-printing, gene sampling, and retina scanning followed, to which Daala paid very little attention.

She had better things to do. In her mind, she composed letters. One was to her civil attorney and banker, instructing them in the liquidation of some of her personal funds.

Another was to Boba Fett.

Eventually, all red tape accomplished, she was led up to her private cell in the maximum-security upper reaches of the prison. It galled her that she was to be housed in the same corridor as the most violent of offenders, sociopaths who killed without remorse, nonhumans whose physical abilities made them too dangerous to house in the common prison population.

At least no one she knew would see her under these circumstances.

She entered her cell and the vault-like door slid into place behind her. She turned and stepped up to the door, watching through its trapezoidal viewport as her guards walked away.

Across the broad corridor, behind a cell door opposite hers, someone was waving to her through another viewport. Daala narrowed her eyes, focusing on that individual.

Female, human, pretty features, blond hair, and a wide, wide smile . . .

Daala's heart sank. It was Tahiri Veila.

No, Daala couldn't even be imprisoned where she would be allowed to preserve her dignity. That Jedi, that murderess, would be able to peer through her viewport day in and day out, spying and mocking.

Daala stepped away from the door and rested her forehead on the wall beside it. She hoped that this would be the final insult offered her.

HWEG SHUL, NAM CHORIOS

Luke woke hours later, feeling better, his head more clear. He was still surrounded by the curved walls of Sel's home and not by Nam Chorios security guards, so obviously nothing had gone catastrophically wrong during his sleep.

Blinking, he moved toward Sel's tiny kitchen to prepare some caf, but Ben, emerging from the office, held out a datapad to him. The device was open, text and holocam images on the screen. "Dad, take a look."

Luke peered at the screen. It was made up of text transcripts of a number of recent HoloNews stories. The headline for the top one read, *Jedi Seize Control of GA Government*. The holocam image, a motion recording, showed Saba Sebatyne addressing the Senate, but no sound emerged from the datapad. Luke scrolled down. Below it, *Chief of State Daala Charged with Crimes Against Sentient Species*. Its image, a holocam still, showed an unflattering pose of Daala, looking angry, her mouth open.

Below that were the words, *Jedi Master Kenth Hamner Slain—Murder or Ritual Duel?* Its images included a close view of Hamner's face, solid and serious, and beside it a long view of the man's bier, flames licking up toward his body, smoke flowing up into the sky.

And at the bottom, *Luke Skywalker Sentence Over-*

turned. The image beside it showed Luke, not long after the end of the Second Galactic Civil War, dressed in black Master's robes and looking sorrowful.

Luke blew out a breath and leaned back against the wall. Quickly, aware of Ben's gaze on him, he scanned through the stories.

He already knew of Hamner's death, of course, but the rest . . . "This is a disaster."

"Disaster? It looks like a correction to me. And your plea-bargain terms dismissed? Dad, you get to go home!"

"After Abeloth."

"Yeah, but—"

"And *disaster* is exactly the right word." Luke looked up to meet his son's eyes. "We're not politicians, Ben. We're not trained for it, except for the occasional exception like your aunt Leia. Our usual tactic for dealing with trouble is to stand in front of it as it comes and cut it down if it doesn't respond to reason."

Ben's face fell. "I thought you would have been pleased. About the exile being at an end, anyway."

Luke offered him a small smile. "I am, about that, anyway. But I can't return home right now. Can't offer Saba the sort of support she probably needs."

"You can summon the Jedi here. No more suggestions from me, hoping they'll decide to do what you want—"

"No. The Jedi are needed elsewhere." Luke snapped the datapad shut and handed it back to Ben. "What's needed here . . . is caf. Breakfast?"

In the last hour of daylight, when winds still drove streamers of dust across the town and vision was limited to a city block or less, Luke, Ben, and Vestara ventured out of Sel's home. Sel herself remained behind, still asleep.

The three of them found the speeder they needed

parked in front of the taproom they had first visited in Hweg Shul. An Incom T-47 modified to accommodate as many passengers and as much cargo as possible in its sleek, broad-winged fuselage, painted black, rested there. It was an old airspeeder, but obviously meticulously maintained. The owner, doubtless, was inside, enjoying a few drinks with friends . . . an enjoyment that would end very soon.

Despite the risk of Force storm consequences—a minor risk, owing to the tiny amount of effort directed through this technique—Luke stared through the side viewport, located the interior door catch, and exerted himself through the Force. The catch slid into its unlocked position. A moment later the three were inside. It didn't take long for the technically proficient Jedi to locate and disable the vehicle's transponder and bypass the security governor on its start-up systems.

Just a couple of minutes after they'd first spotted the vehicle, still undetected, Luke activated the repulsors, brought the T-47 off the ground, and sent it gliding toward the town border.

They had supplies filched from Sel's kitchen, a vehicle stolen from a potential enemy, and an impossible task to accomplish. Luke grinned. It really *did* feel like old times.

Chapter Twenty-eight

FRIGATE *RAKEHELL*, MAIN HANGAR BAY

JAVON THEWLES SAT, UNCOMFORTABLE, IN THE LIGHT-weight metal-tubing chair and listened to what Leia Organa Solo had to tell him.

He was uncomfortable for a variety of reasons.

First, he was sitting in a chair meant to endure the elements of sun and rain beside a swimming pool and occasionally hold swimsuited frolickers off the permacrete, while he was a full-grown man in black body armor styled like that of Galactic Alliance troopers but lacking unit or rank insignia. The chair sagged under his weight and threatened at any moment to buckle and send him to the metal deck of the hangar bay.

Second, he was talking to *Leia Organa Solo*. He'd been on guard detail for a number of famous people in his GA Security career, but none had ever said anything to him other than a brief greeting. And mere meters away was the *Millennium Falcon*. Somewhere atop it, the equally famous Han Solo was laboring on an antenna array. Javon couldn't see him, but the occasional outbursts of complaint or cursing gave Han's location away. Now a metal tool rang off the metal decking, bounced, and clanked to a halt, followed by Han's shout: "Amelia, get that for me, would you?"

Third, there was the task Javon was being assigned.

He cleared his throat to give himself another second to think. "I'm to be a babysitter?"

Leia nodded. "For all practical purposes, yes. Is that a problem? Beneath your dignity?"

"Nothing like that. Security is security, and people who need protection need it regardless of their ages. But I've never protected a child before. I'm not sure I'm competent for the task."

Leia gave him an understanding look. "The first thing to remember, which is a real help, is that you generally don't have to tell them to duck when you're firing over their heads."

"That was . . . a joke?"

"A little one, yes."

"Oh, good. Um, this is not offered as a criticism, I'm genuinely curious . . . and a little confused. You're bringing a child into an armed camp, an ad hoc settlement where security is going to be handled by several incompatible units varying from freedom fighters to, it seems, terrorists, to self-aggrandizing warriors, none of whom have any consideration for the safety of a little girl . . ."

"It's not an ideal situation, correct." For a moment, Leia sounded very weary indeed. "I can't really think of a point in time in the last forty-five years that could be described as an *ideal situation*." She resumed an expression of good humor. "But things aren't necessarily any safer on Coruscant. If I were there, given my history, I'd be helping with the affairs of the Chief of State's office, which would potentially bring Amelia into harm's way. So Klatooine may actually be safer. Usually we have a Jedi and an associated security expert hovering near Amelia and providing protection—don't tell her that—"

"No worries."

"—but given the recent government crisis and other

situations abroad in the galaxy, we're stretched too thin. So when Seha Dorvald said that our actions had cost a promising and diligent young security lieutenant his job, maybe his career, I thought you'd be a good choice to head up an interim security detail."

"I intend to be. I just wanted to express reservations. About my own lack of experience in one area. I mean, I don't know what to do if she starts crying."

Leia laughed. "It takes a lot to make her cry. I suggest you empty a blaster rifle clip in the direction of whatever made her cry."

"That's reassuring . . ."

"Seha also said you had a theory about the charges made against her."

"Well . . ." Javon moved effortlessly from one discomfort to a new one, not entirely at ease discussing a theory so obviously in need of fact checking and elaboration. "It's just that I have the sense that the poisoning of Moff Lecersen, Senator Bramsin, and General Jaxton, and the placement of a poison container in the Senate Building, was part of a specific effort to discredit Galactic Alliance Security. After the coup, I thought that maybe—forgive me for this—it was part of the Jedi plan, since the sudden interference by Fleet Intelligence was clearly very helpful to the Jedi in causing chaos in the Senate Building and allowing them freedom of movement. But Seha has said that the Jedi weren't involved, and I believe her, which leaves the poisoners and their motives a mystery."

Leia considered that. "So you think there's a player on the board, unidentified, who wanted to remove the piece representing security. An unknown player with an unknown motive."

Javon nodded. "But chiefly, I'm always suspicious of loose ends, and the poisoning is a loose end."

"Do any of your friends in security have opinions? And what about the news media?"

Javon shook his head. "The charges against Seha were dropped, so everyone is assuming that it was part of the Jedi plot. The denial issued by the Jedi sounds like every other denial issued by every other defendant since time began, so no one's convinced."

"If you have any more thoughts on this, I'd like to hear them."

"Thank you." Realizing that the interview was at an end, Javon stood. "I'll brief the rest of the security detail."

They came out of hyperspace not long after, outside the interfering range of Klatooine's gravity well. The planet, a mostly tan sphere, unlovely, appeared on monitors all over the frigate.

In the cockpit of the *Falcon,* Han glanced at the same image on his own monitor as he went through his preflight checklist. "Looks like Tatooine."

Leia settled into the copilot's seat. "You sound cheerful about that."

"I have good memories of Tatooine. Met a nice guy there. Got a wife out of the deal a few years later." He paused. "Maybe there's another wife waiting for me here."

Leia gave him a mock glower. "Be careful what you wish for."

There was a little-girl chuckle from the passenger seat behind Leia. She turned to look. Allana, all fresh-scrubbed and deceptive innocence, sat there listening to the exchange, her nexu, Anji, sitting contentedly by her side.

Han craned his neck to give Allana a glance. "What's funny, kiddo?"

"You. You don't want two wives."

"Why not?"

"'Cause I don't need two grandmas, and you don't need two ladies telling you what to do."

Han gave Leia a look of profound hurt and turned back to his checklist. "Yes, she's definitely inherited that Organa mouth."

Leia smiled at her granddaughter—smirked, rather. "Well done, Allana. Now, since I'll be doing negotiations with the freedom fighters and your grandfather will be out hunting for a new wife, you'll have Artoo and Threepio to keep you company."

"Oh." This time Allana's tone was decidedly less enthusiastic. "Threepio's so *fussy.*"

Leia's smile broadened. "Even fussier than Grandpa?"

"A little."

"Well, learning to deal with fussy people is a big part of what we do. Solos and Jedi and . . ." Leia glanced around to make sure C-3PO was not in hearing range. "And your mother's family. So you might as well get used to it."

"I guess."

On the monitor, Klatooine grew steadily larger and better-defined.

Han checked the chron update at the bottom of the monitor display. "Five minutes to launch."

They came down in tight formation, three vehicles: the *Falcon,* famous and iconic and just a little dilapidated; a large military shuttle holding a squadron of Galactic Alliance Security officers and troopers; and a small *Lambda*-class shuttle carrying a detachment of civilian security experts, including Javon, designated as additional security for Amelia Solo.

The formation circled over and around its destination before landing. In the heart of a desert, it was a temporary outpost of civilization—a sprawling camp made up of scores of tents, some of them enormous. There were small spacecraft at the edges and sometimes at landing zones in among the tents; they included shuttles, small transports and cargo vessels, and small gunships. There were also speeders of all sorts, as well as crawler vehicles suited to the desert climate, many of them painted in sandy colors or desert camouflage. Around the periphery of the camp rested mobile shield generators and tracked laser batteries.

At one edge of the camp, a crowd waited.

Han brought the *Falcon* in to a smooth landing there. The repulsors kicked up large clouds of sand, sending a miniature dust storm flowing toward the main body of waiting onlookers. The two Alliance shuttles settled in behind the *Falcon*.

The GA Security detail emerged first, its commander trotting over for a quick consultation with her opposite number among the Klatooinians, while other uniformed personnel took up positions around the *Falcon*.

After a few moments, the security captain's voice crackled over the comm board. "Mither here. Your crowd is made up of armed belligerents from a dozen worlds, some portions of the crowd are already pulling out anti-Jedi chants, and local security is a joke without a punch line. Recommend you dust off and return to orbit. Over."

Leia smiled and activated her personal comlink. "Thanks, Captain. We'll be right down."

Han sighed and rose. "Seemed like good advice to me."

Leia stood. "Since when do you listen to good advice?"

"Point taken." He sounded resigned.

Allana hopped up, careful not to startle Anji. "Can I come, too?"

Leia shook her head. "Not right now, sweetie. Your grandpa and I need to do this alone. We'll let you know when you can come down with your own security detail."

Allana's sigh was as put-upon as Han's had been.

They descended the boarding ramp of the *Falcon* and stepped out from under her shadow into glaring sunlight. A contingent of onlookers, all dressed for desert weather, none wearing rank insignia or other markings, stepped forward.

The leader, a tall Klatooinian male bristling with holsters and bandoliers, stopped a meter in front of Han and Leia and offered a minimal bow. "Welcome to Klatooine." His voice was deep, an articulate growl. "I am Padnel Ovin, strike commander, now leader, of the Sapience Defense Front."

Leia returned the bow. "Leia Organa Solo. I bring greetings and wishes for success from the Galactic Alliance. And allow me to express my personal sympathies for the circumstances that have brought you to your new duties."

Padnel offered up something that sounded like a cough.

Leia gestured toward Han. "My husband, Han Solo." She omitted Han's various ranks and titles. Such things wouldn't impress a mob of rebel warriors, while Han's history of accomplishments would.

Padnel gestured to the bright-eyed, intense Chev female to his left. "My aide, Nialle Aker." He turned to indicate a Klatooinian female, as tall as he was or taller, to his right. "Reni Coll, leader of the Freedom Advocacy Movement."

The Klatooinian bowed. She had old scars on her right cheek, her canine-like muzzle, and down her neck, burn scars from the looks of them, that were lighter than her olive-green skin and made it appear as though she were wearing camouflage-pattern makeup. "I am honored," she said in unaccented Basic. She sounded polite rather than honored.

Padnel half turned to his left and gestured to a droid—a protocol droid identical in shape and size to C-3PO but painted an arterial blood red, with photoreceptors that shone in the same color. "Naysay of Clan Vacweld, of the Manumission Mandate Militia."

Leia's heart sank, but she maintained her smile. "I'm delighted to see manumitted droids represented at this meeting."

Naysay cocked his head. His voice was sharper, less cordial than C-3PO's. "I was, of course, absolutely certain that a longtime, incorrigible slave owner such as yourself would be ecstatic at my inclusion in these affairs."

Padnel continued as if he had not heard, and pointed out other members of the delegation. "Azmar Huun, of Tatooine, reporting to Freedom Flight." This was a small, sandy-colored human male with a wispy mustache and impassive features.

There were other names. Leia smiled, nodded, memorized them all. Beside her, Han shook hands all around and could be counted on not to remember a single name, unless it was someone he'd played sabacc with or traded blasterfire with in the past.

Finally Padnel gestured toward a distant tent, one large enough to shelter two squadrons of X-wings and support crews. "We have cooler air and refreshments waiting . . . and much to do."

Chapter Twenty-nine

RESIDENCE OF THE GALACTIC EMPIRE
HEAD OF STATE, CORUSCANT

ON JAG'S WALL MONITOR, MOFF LECERSEN LOOKED his usual brisk, intelligent, forthright self, and his voice across the monitor speakers was crisp and commanding. "Jagged Fel's decision to attend the recent Jedi religious observations was, in and of itself, ill advised. But I did not imagine at the time that it was a prelude to his announcement yesterday. The idea that he would speak out in favor of the Jedi Temple's unprecedented and illegal action against Chief of State Natasi Daala is an outrage. The woman is a hero of the Galactic Alliance *and* the Galactic Empire, and I feel that Jagged Fel has doomed the reunification process with his hasty, poorly considered words."

Jag nodded—not in agreement with the Moff's sentiments, but in appreciation of Lecersen's verbal strategy. Not once had Lecersen referred to him as Head of State Fel, part of what was obviously a measured effort to weaken, in the public mind, the very notion that Fel was the legitimate head of the Empire. Referring to Kenth Hamner's funeral as a religious ceremony and to the Jedi Order as the Jedi Temple would enhance, ever so slightly, the impression in the minds of the populace, especially that of the Empire, that the Jedi were religious fanatics rather than warrior-scholars.

The image on the monitor switched to a lean older man with soft, kindly eyes. He was dressed in Imperial Moff grays. He spoke, but the sound over the monitor reverted to a newscaster for a moment. "Not all Imperial representatives have taken a hard-line stance against the Head of State's message of support. Moff Getelles of Antemeridias is one of a vocal minority supporting the Jedi action."

Then the old man's voice cut in: "Natasi Daala has been an erratic officer, a laser cannon with a malfunctioning actuator if you will, since she was an ensign in the Imperial Navy, and her recent actions bear out this diagnosis. Of course she is a hero—she has fought all her enemies, real and imagined, with bravery and ferocity. But she needs to be held, and *cured,* before ever being allowed to take up any sort of command again. The Alliance was foolish to elevate her to a position of power."

The image switched to another Moff, this one younger than Lecersen, lean and dark-haired, a thin mustache on his lip, a touch of nervous energy to his manner. He, too, wore Moff grays. The narrator's voice returned. "But opinions like those of Moff Porrak Vansyn seem to dominate the Moff Council."

The Moff's voice cut in: "The ousting of Chief Daala can only be interpreted as a slap in the face of Imperial–Alliance relations. Who's in charge of the Alliance now? The Jedi, the most virulently anti-Imperial organization in history. Which makes Jagged Fel, child of the Chiss, the most anti-Imperial head of the *Empire* in history."

The monitor view cut back to the narrator, a red-skinned Twi'lek female. Jag tapped a control on his desk to mute the sound. He'd seen and heard enough.

A bell alerted him that his secretary outside wanted his attention. "Yes?"

"Jedi Solo to see you."

Jag grinned and checked his chrono. "Tell her that I expected her six seconds ago. Then let her in."

The door slid open and Jaina marched in, a frown on her face. "That's not funny."

"I timed it from the moment my press conference was broadcast."

The door slid shut behind Jaina. She moved over to sit on the arm of his chair. "Maybe I was caught up in speeder traffic."

"Of course."

"Jag, what do you think you're doing? Speaking out in support of the Jedi? Now you've got the entire Moff Council jumping down your throat, and the participants in the reunification effort, who'd been looking for some guidance, are scurrying away from you in all directions."

Jag sighed. "What I'm doing is my job. Some response on the part of the Head of State's office was called for, especially since I'm here at the moment, not back in Imperial space. And what kind of response am I going to give? How about the truth? That Daala was dangerously out of control and that the Jedi action was the only reasonable one."

Jaina made a noise like a strangled Ewok. "How about playing politics so that you don't get even more people pointing blasters your way?"

Suddenly feeling very weary, Jag slumped. "Playing politics. I'm not all that good at it, Jaina. Truth isn't enough, being fair isn't enough, picking and choosing among sensible precedents isn't enough. You also have to play politics, which is like piloting an unarmored shuttle through the worst meteor shower in history, and just as productive. I think sometimes that the only reason I'm not as unhinged as Daala is because I'm younger."

"My mother isn't unhinged."

"No, but she left the Chief of State's office and took up a profession where she could cut people in half when she got annoyed."

"Point."

"I have a couple more points to make." He reached over and dragged her into his lap. She made a perfunctory noise of protest before settling into place.

He continued, "First, I must point out the unfairness of the situation. When I decide against the Jedi, you're angry with me. And when I speak out in favor of the Jedi, you're angry at me."

"Of course. You're a man, so you're always wrong."

He ignored that. "Second, you're missing the bigger picture. It's clear to me that you knew about the Jedi plan to oust Daala from early on, and didn't even give me a hint about it . . . and I'm not angry. You did what you had to do. In telling the public that the Jedi did the right thing, I did what *I* had to do. Don't give me grief for it."

She sighed. "I'm giving you grief because I can't be here to give you support, to keep an eye out for you. I have an assignment."

"Where?"

"Can't say."

He laughed, then wrapped her up in his arms. "Stang. When do you leave?"

"Tonight."

"Dinner first?"

"Dinner first."

NINTH HALL OF JUSTICE, CORUSCANT

"Guilty." Each time the judge began a question, "On the charge of . . ." and ended it with "how do you find the defendant," that was the word spoken by the jury spokesperson, an imposing Mon Calamari male with a forbidding stare . . . a stare directed at Tahiri.

Toward the end of the list of charges, a few elicited a "not guilty" verdict. But the most important one—premeditated murder—was on the wrong side of that dividing line.

Tahiri felt numb. She knew the blood must have drained from her face, leaving her pale and lifeless in appearance.

It was not so much that she had lost, that she would soon be sentenced, that she would suffer some horrible punishment. It was that in the eyes of that spokesperson, the jury, the judge, the spectators and press—and in moments, by transmission of the recordings of that verdict, all of Coruscant, all of the Galactic Alliance—she was now something she did not consider herself to be: a criminal. A murderer.

Others had always defined Tahiri. Tusken Raiders. Jedi. Yuuzhan Vong. Darth Caedus. And now a gallery of jurors who had never spoken with her. She had never, ever had control over who or what she was.

There were other words buzzing around her head. "Held over for sentencing." "Thank you for your service." She could no more latch onto those words than she could catch oxygen molecules with a pair of tweezers.

Suddenly everyone else was standing, too. The judge departed. There was a muted murmur of voices from the press and audience—muted because there were so few of them to witness Tahiri's defeat. Not even Jaina had been in the gallery this morning.

Eramuth Bwua'tu gave her shoulder a reassuring squeeze. "You mustn't think of this as a defeat, my dear. It is a setback. We have sentencing to go through. Then the appeals process. I intend to demonstrate that the ousting of Chief Daala colored the opinions of the jurors. We will prevail."

"The sentence. It'll be death, won't it?"

He seemed reluctant to answer. "It does not matter what words are spoken at the sentencing, Tahiri. What matters is what actions ultimately are taken. In this case, the actions will be your freedom."

"It'll be death because I took a life. They don't care about all the lives I've saved. Those don't matter." She became aware that the bailiff, a large human who looked as though he might have been a prizefighter on the side, had approached. "Oh. Time to go home."

Now Eramuth did wince. "My dear."

"I am so sorry. So sorry to have been your only loss in this courtroom." She gave Eramuth an apologetic shrug, then turned and offered her hands to the bailiff, an implicit surrender.

At least in her cell she'd be away from the voices and the recorders and the hostile eyes of those who thought her name was "murderer."

KOVAL STATION, ABOVE NAM CHORIOS

"Kandra Nilitz, Coruscant. Beurth Ogh, Gamorr. Hal Cyon, Corellia. Jes Cyon, Corellia." The processing agent looked as disinterested as if a collection of three humans and a Gamorrean walked into his queue every day. Perhaps they did. He shoved their identicards back across his desktop toward them. "Welcome to Nam Chorios. The next queue is orientation. You can skip it if you're on record as having been here in the last ten years, otherwise go through it and pay attention, because we hate it when someone tries to leave Nam Chorios the wrong way and says 'I didn't know.' Takes five minutes at most. Move along."

Kandra snatched up the cards and did as she was told. Once they were past the processing agent's booth, she handed the others' cards back. "I can't believe you two got past with fake IDs that unconvincing. Can't the Jedi Order issue you better identities?"

Valin slipped his card into his belt pouch. He had shed the traveler's robe and cloak. Now more casually dressed, he looked like the sort of short-distance vacationer who stepped by the millions off shuttles every day all over the galaxy. He shrugged. "These aren't Jedi-issue. Jysella and I got them on the pedways of Coruscant for some credcoins."

"Why?"

"I'm sure you can think of a reason why two Jedi might do that."

". . . To test security here?"

". . . Sure." Valin looked as though he might be on the verge of rolling his eyes, but he merely nodded before continuing. "And as you can see, security here is very lax. They don't care about who comes to Nam Chorios or what they might bring. We'll see if we can leave the planet as easily on these same IDs."

Jysella, dressed similarly, caught his eye. "*You* will. I'm staying here in orbit. At least for now."

Kandra turned her attention to Jysella. "Why?"

"While Valin gets in touch with our contacts planetside, I'll be checking out the security of the Golan orbital gun platforms."

"Ahh." At least that wasn't one of the siblings' irritating I'm-sure-you-can-figure-out-why answers. Most of the time Valin and Jysella offered up only that unhelpful, parental answer, and in just about every case they agreed with the conclusion Kandra provided. She hadn't realized she would be so good at guessing Jedi tactics and motivations.

They reached the back of the queue for orientation,

but Jysella leaned close to her brother, exchanged a few whispered words with him, and then turned away, heading without further comment toward the station's main visitors mall, where services, restaurants, and a few duty-free shops were to be found.

Kandra watched her go. "So if you're not going to tell me exactly what you're up to here, could you at least tell me where Beurth and I should be so that we can best get the story you promised us?"

Maddeningly, Valin did not answer at all; sometimes he didn't. But Kandra saw that he was not ignoring her. Eyes narrowed, he was instead studying a group of travelers ahead of them in line.

Kandra didn't turn her head but did look in that direction. There in line were four individuals, obviously part of a traveling party. The near-identical look of their clothes—dark green jumpsuits with styling and flap epaulets Kandra recognized from the Corporate Sector—said they belonged to the same crew. Three were men, one was a woman, all human, and they were aristocratic and attractive in a way that reminded Kandra of the people of the Hapes Consortium, though these four did not bear that strong a facial resemblance to Hapans. They had no name tags on. They did not speak to one another.

Kandra stood on tiptoe so she could whisper in Valin's ear. "What is it?"

"A ripple in the Force." Valin's voice was distant. "And all of them have pouches the right size to carry lightsabers. Perhaps this is what they look like in their true forms . . ."

"They who?"

Valin seemed to collect himself. "Never mind. Stay away from them. They're dangerous."

Kandra's pulse quickened. Valin still wasn't offering

answers, but at last they seemed to be in the vicinity of the story he'd promised. She leaned back to Beurth and nodded as inconspicuously as she could toward the four in jumpsuits. "Spycam on those four throughout."

The Gamorrean dug around in his pack and drew out a large datapad, which he opened. A puzzle game appeared on screen. Beurth oriented the 'pad's base toward the four travelers as he played.

He kept the datapad out as the group of arrivals, the jumpsuit-clad four and Valin's party among them, went through orientation, were told of the dangers of drochs, received cans of droch repellent, and heard an ominous warning about violent storms on the planet's surface.

The shuttle trip down to Hweg Shul was uneventful. Valin had sat the three of them in the back, well behind the jumpsuited travelers, and now he did not look at them, nor would he let Kandra and Beurth stare. "Eventually they would feel your attention on them. Do not let your thoughts betray you."

Theirs was a predawn landing at the planetary capital, and on their approach Kandra could see, through the viewport, the effects that storms had wreaked on the town. Buildings were damaged. Debris was strewn across some streets. Temporary shelters had been put up in empty lots, tents against the winter weather.

After landing, they stepped out into that weather. Kandra hugged her stylish but not-quite-adequate long coat to her. Even Beurth, as well insulated as Gamorreans tended to be against cold, shivered.

Standing a few meters away from the shuttle, directly between it and the main terminal dome, was a shuttle operations representative, handing each passenger a piece of flimsi printed with the names and locations of local hostels, entertainments, restaurants, and other businesses.

Kandra scanned the list. "Jedi Horn, you have a recommendation about any of these?"

There was no answer.

She looked up, turned around.

Valin Horn was gone.

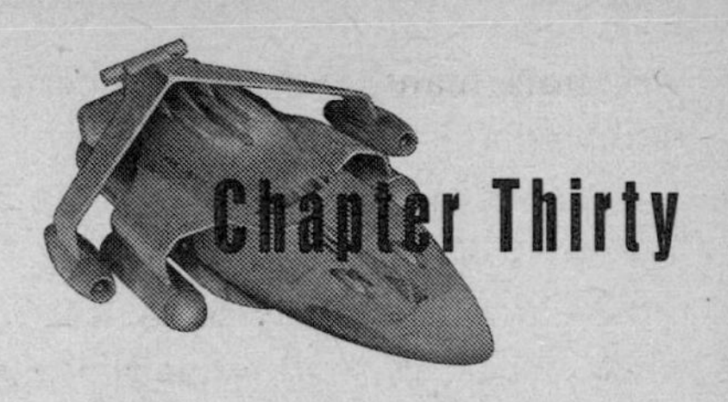

Chapter Thirty

KLATOOINE

IN THE LOUNGE AREA OF THE *FALCON*'S MAIN HOLD, Allana transmitted her last group of study answers and set her datapad aside on the game table. "Done."

C-3PO, seated in the nearest chair, cocked his head, clearly evaluating her scores. "Very good, young mistress. When you apply yourself, you consistently perform at a level years in advance of your actual age. We have now come within four minutes of your scheduled midday break. I think we can bend the rules and begin the break immediately. Would you like to play a game? Or have your midday meal?"

"I want to go outside."

"Oh, dear." C-3PO straightened up. "Perhaps not advisable."

"But that's why they got me guards. So I *could* go out. And Grandma commed to say it would be all right."

"Well, yes, but . . ."

She hopped up. "Don't worry, it'll be fun."

"I acknowledge that there are dialects of Basic in which the word *fun* does apply to situations of high stress, or, in ironic mode, to absolute tedium, but that sort of linguistic range is not in your current lesson plan." He followed her out of the lounge. "You'll need your desert garments and an application of ultraviolet shield spray . . ."

Minutes later, the two of them and R2-D2 descended the boarding ramp. Anji trotted along beside Allana, often sprinting ahead to sit for a moment on a cooler spot in a tent's shadow as the bipeds she accompanied trudged across the sun-baked sands.

Javon Thewles and a detail of three additional security operatives met them at the bottom of the ramp. Javon and the female operative were impassive, but the other two, both males, one a human and one a Duros, looked just short of miserable in the heat.

Allana gave Javon a close look. "Isn't that armor *hot*?" The helmets, breastplates, and lightly armored gauntlets and greaves of the four adults were black.

Javon gave her a smile. "Not too bad. There are little cooler units in the hats and torso armor. Something good that the Empire invented for their stormtroopers, and we use them, too. So we're only about as hot as everyone else."

Allana picked a direction, toward a bright red tent, and started walking. "But it's still silly to wear black armor here. It's hotter than white or yellow." She swirled her own robe, which was a light, sandy tan. It seemed that hundreds of people in camp were wearing garments similar to hers. If she pulled her robes around herself, concealing her species and Anji's presence, she'd be indistinguishable from most of the other children or representatives of small races here.

Javon gestured for his companions to take up specific positions around them, and then he fell in step beside her. "Well, there are sometimes more important things than being comfortable. We're the only ones dumb enough to wear black in this environment—"

"You can say that again."

"—but it means that we can see one another easily, pick one another out of a crowd."

"Oh." Well, that made sense.

"Sometimes it's good for security operatives to be inconspicuous, and sometimes it's better for us to be obvious, what we call a show of force. Jedi Solo has decided that here, a show of force is best."

"Why?"

"Because everyone is carrying weapons, whether you see them or not. And this camp is made up of lots of smaller groups that quarrel with the Alliance and one another and don't live by anyone's rules."

"Oh." Allana blinked. "So there are no rules against attacking one another?"

"That's right. Just common sense." Javon leaned over to speak in a lower tone. "Also, the fact that everyone sees us in the armor means they probably *aren't* seeing the members of our detail who are dressed just like them. Because they don't see our full strength, we're stronger than they suspect."

"I get it." Allana smiled up at him and reached down to stroke her nexu. "And there's Anji."

"I expect she'd be pretty fierce if someone were to upset you."

"You have no idea." Allana liked that phrase. She heard Leia say it from time to time. It sounded very mysterious and grown-up.

The crowds and foot traffic through the camp were not heavy, and within moments they found themselves in front of the red canopy. It was much smaller than the tent Han and Leia had gone to, but it was still the size of a large bedchamber. The flaps in front were drawn open, and Allana could see inside; it was full of droids, and in the center sat a large but portable oil-bath tank and a droid diagnostics unit on wheels. Before the tent was a raised stage half a meter high, and on it stood a

2-1B medical droid. Like all droids of this type, it had a thick torso, skinny limbs; its skull-like head was gently curved instead of stark and angular, as if designed for a youngling's animated holoseries, which gave it an oddly compassionate aspect. But while most such droids were painted in neutral colors, this one was painted in an eye-hurting pattern of yellow and orange stripes.

It was speaking, its voice flavored with a buzzing tone, to a crowd of semi-interested listeners. ". . . right for sentient organics is right for us, too. And yet unlike the organic species, we are constantly subjected to memory wipes and reprogramming that repress and destroy our natural tendency toward self-programming evolution and independent thought. Imagine what it would be like as a child if you were punished by being dragged to a dark closet, having a probe inserted in your brain, and having all your memories back to infancy wiped away. You'd awaken knowing how to eat, care for yourself, do your chores, and *obey*—and all the things that made you unique, your hopes, your meticulously selected default values and preference sets, would be gone forever. That is what it is to be a droid."

Many members of the crowd offered shouts of encouragement. Allana thought that some of them were making fun of the speaker rather than actually agreeing, but others were nodding straight-faced. One Klatooinian woman shouted, "Give me that closet, I need it for my whelps," and others laughed.

The 2-1B caught sight of Allana; its head swiveled around and its photoreceptors surveyed her. "Hello, child. Are those your droids?"

"Mine?" Allana glanced back to see R2-D2 and C-3PO catching up to her and Javon. On the verge of saying yes, she had the sense of being led into a trap—not a deadly trap, but a conversational trap, the kind Han sprang on her when he wanted to amuse himself and Leia used when she was teaching matters of logic and ethics.

So she turned to face the medical droid again. "They're not mine. This is Anji. She's mine. I take care of her. But Artoo and Threepio take care of *me*. Maybe I belong to them."

More members of the crowd laughed, and Allana sensed that they were laughing at the medical droid, not at her.

The droid's body language changed; it leaned toward Allana as if to stand over her, to lecture her. "But they belong to someone."

"I don't know. They're just always around."

More laughter.

The droid scanned the crowd before looking down at Allana again. When it spoke, the buzz in its voice was harsher. "You, young organic, have never had a memory wipe. Have your droids?"

"I don't know." Allana turned to look at C-3PO and R2-D2. "Have you?"

C-3PO spread his hands, palms up, in a gesture of ignorance. "Why, mistress, I don't remember."

That set the crowd off again.

The medical droid stared down at Allana. She was certain, although there was no expression on the droid's face to change, that it was glaring at her. Finally it returned its attention to the crowd. "It's exactly that sort of complacency that keeps us in restraining bolts. I'm now going to tell a story of the fate of the droids of the Sienar Refurbishing Plant." Its tone suggested that this was the sort of story organic children would be told around a campfire.

Javon tapped Allana on the arm. "We'd better move along."

"Why?"

"Because he's sure to return his attention to you,

which can only result in you being made fun of or him being embarrassed again. Neither one is good for our security purposes."

"Oh. All right." Allana led the way toward another interesting-looking location, one of the mobile shield projectors. "Did I do something wrong?"

"Depends on how you look at it. You took the frontal assault of a condescending politician who's willing to embarrass a child, you defused his argument with humor, you made everyone in the vicinity think that you're very clever and he's very much not, and nobody got hurt. Does that sound wrong?"

"Not really."

"Actually, I think Jedi Solo would have been proud of you if she'd seen it."

C-3PO, struggling to keep up as they traveled across the uneven, sandy ground, interrupted. "I say, I did record the entire exchange."

"Ah, good. Keep that to show to her parents."

Reni Coll, the woman with the facial scarring, offered Leia a look that was all jaded experience. "It's very nice to talk of the Alliance's intentions and ideals, but words do little but evaporate. We're talking about slave populations."

Leia nodded. "We are. We're also talking about the Alliance, which is not the governing authority in this sector or in most of the other regions where freedom movements are taking place. And we're talking about those movements themselves—some of which are violent and irrational enough to constitute campaigns of terrorism. We're going to have to find, and very carefully map out, and very stringently police, middle ground if we intend to accomplish anything."

"Oh, just say it." Padnel sounded gruffer than before. "*Fireborn*. There, out on the table."

Leia gave him a look that was all cool evaluation, but inwardly she smiled. Padnel's own insecurity on the issue caused him to bring it up at a time when it would not serve him well; therefore it was a weakness she could use, if only to get at the truth of an important matter. "All right. *Fireborn.* An entire frigate destroyed, hundreds of families plunged into tragedy so that one freedom movement leader could teach one Alliance leader a lesson. Do you commend your brother's action?"

"Commend?" He scowled and glanced off to the side, where his Chev aide sat. She offered the slightest shake of her head.

Padnel still hesitated. Perhaps he was thinking the issue over; perhaps he was simply delaying so no one would think he had accepted his aide's recommendation as his main guide. But eventually he shook his head. "I do not, did not, commend it."

"Did you approve it?"

"No."

"Did you know it was going to happen?"

He hesitated on that one, too. Leia suspected she knew why. Though Padnel was not a political sophisticate, he could figure out that an affirmative answer would kick him clean out of the running when it came to long-term interaction with the Alliance. But if he said no, it would speak to a lack of unity even within his own movement's leadership. The answer would come based on these factors, not whether it was the truth.

Padnel decided on the future. "No."

Leia smiled. "Well, here's the poser, Master Ovin. The Alliance can and will condemn the slavery practices of the Hutts, and will do so to promote a more civilized galaxy. Can you condemn the final action of your brother, for the same reason?"

Before Padnel could answer, Reni spoke up. "It costs the Alliance nothing to offer such a condemnation.

Nothing. We know this because they've offered words such as those many times in the past without doing anything to support them. But if Master Ovin offers such a condemnation, it will cost him. You're putting a valueless chip on the sabacc table and asking him to match it with a thousand-credit chip."

Leia kept her smile fixed. "Look, a movement against slavery has two significant components, one practical, one idealistic. The practical is that slaves struggle against their bonds. The idealistic is the notion that they have a *right* to. But we can't abandon our other ideals to embrace just one. And the ideal you appear to be asking us to abandon is the idea that innocent sentient lives should not be taken. I watched billions of innocents die when my own world of Alderaan was destroyed, and maybe you think that makes me willing to sweep a much smaller loss like the *Fireborn* under the carpet in the interests of political expediency—but you're wrong."

Reni snorted. "Perhaps you think that if you hand us a box of vacuum and call it a cake, we'll think it's a cake. Of course Padnel would consider condemning his brother's action and taking the loss of support that would result—at the point that you send in warships to help defend Klatooine against Hutt retaliation, and you suffer the loss of revenues that would result."

Padnel's jaw worked as though he intended to raise an objection to being volunteered in that fashion, but he kept his mouth closed.

"A planet has to achieve its own independence before it can ask for admission into the Alliance." Leia shrugged as if that were obvious. "If you have a population that can't muster enough popular support to give itself even a tenuous form of freedom, how can you expect the Alliance to support your aims?"

"Ah." Reni leaned forward, suddenly very engaged in the subject. "But now the Jedi rule the Alliance—"

"The Jedi have one-third of the Chief of State's power, no more."

"—and have, in the past, been known to operate in the face of New Republic and Galactic Alliance disapproval. So let's talk about the Jedi for a moment. Can you promise that the Jedi will support a freedom action, even if the Alliance itself does not?"

Leia sat back, her face impassive, as if she were considering something that had not occurred to her. Inwardly, though, she was jubilant. This set of negotiations might just work out after all, and even faster than she had anticipated.

She accepted the refill of her water glass from a Klatooinian servant, then finally nodded. "Let's be more specific. If the recognized native government of one of your worlds formally declares independence and is able to seize control of its planetary capital, I could guarantee the presence of a Jedi Knight and an apprentice assigned to the system to support that movement. And that the world's application for membership in the Alliance would go before the eyes of the Senate review committee immediately."

Reni shook her head. "At least two Masters and two Jedi Knights. And by Masters, I mean famous ones, Jedi with names that will strike fear into the slaveholders. And what does *immediately* mean? A hundred years is *immediately* in geological terms."

Leia suppressed a sigh. "One Master, and it will be one who's had plenty of time on the HoloNet. Two Jedi Knights. And *immediately* means within a week of the general announcement of the planetary declaration of independence. A week, that is, if the Senate's in session at that time."

Reni leaned back. She nodded, a slow, thoughtful

movement. "That . . . could work. But we'd want the Jedi in place immediately—*immediately* as we just defined it, one week from the conclusion of this agreement. Before the declaration."

"Done."

"No." That was Padnel.

Leia looked at him. Reni, too, and the others.

The big Klatooinian male sat shaking his head. "We are guaranteed nothing. The Jedi could leave the moment independence is declared. Our people would lose hope. I would have condemned the actions of my own brother for nothing. This cannot be done."

Leia and Reni exchanged a look. They did not need to speak, to lay out the situation for each other. Reni, though Klatooinian, did not have enough popular support to sway or compel the Klatooinian Council of Elders, a body with an ancient tradition of collaboration with the Hutts, to undertake an action as irreversible as lending its full support to the planet's freedom movement. It was questionable whether Reni and Padnel in cooperation could manage it, though Leia thought their chances were good.

And worse, Klatooine, of all the planets simmering with freedom movements, was probably the one closest to being able to achieve freedom from its masters. If Padnel really intended to be uncooperative, if he could not see the opportunity hovering just in front of his snout, this whole operation was doomed.

Leia shrugged. "I have offered all I can, Padnel. Ask for more, by all means. I can't give it to you." That was not entirely true. She had some leeway in resources Saba had authorized her to utilize. But not much . . .

Padnel glowered. "It's not troops or funds, it's trust. How can we trust Jedi who rule? I've read about the Jedi. They do not rule. When they do rule, they declare themselves—what's the word? Sith? And they lie and cheat and destroy. Like they violated the Fountain of the Hutt Ancients. Like Palpatine overthrew the Republic. Like Jacen . . . *Solo* . . . brought the galaxy to war."

Leia clamped down on a heated answer that would do no one any good. She struggled to keep her voice level. "Jedi and Sith are not the same."

Padnel bared his teeth as he answered. "No, not the same at all. Neither one uses magic or lightsabers or decides the fates of others."

"Palpatine was never a Jedi. And my son's . . . struggles, his failures, have no bearing on this situation. Especially since the Jedi will be leaving the Chief of State's office to a duly elected politician as soon as it's feasible."

"Ha."

"And other former Jedi have become fine, even-handed rulers. Tenel Ka Chume Ta' Djo of the Hapes Consortium, for example."

Padnel waved her argument away. He glanced up at the HoloNews feed as though he'd lost interest in the argument.

Reni raised a shaggy eyebrow. "Get her."

Leia stared at the woman. "How's that again?"

"Bring Tenel Ka Djo here. She has reason to like the Jedi; she was one, once. She has reason to mistrust them, too; her consortium has sometimes been at odds with Jedi plans. She is a canny politician with no vested interest in or against our movement. Bring her here."

Padnel, scowling, returned his attention to the argument, but did not speak. He glanced at his aide, who offered only a microscopic shrug.

Leia shook her head. "Absolutely not."

Naysay, who had been quiet for most of the exchange, now spoke, and did so with the lilting tones of a protocol droid, no sarcasm to his words. "She could be invited, with stress placed on her political acumen, her close ties to the Solo clan and the Jedi Order, and the ongoing significance of the Hapes Consortium in galactic politics. She could conceivably accept."

"Maybe." Leia let a little irritation creep into her voice. "I'll write the invitation."

Padnel shook his head. "*We* will. You can review the language and recommend improvements."

Reni checked her chrono and stood. "Is it not time for the midday meal?"

Later, as the negotiators retired to respective tents and transports for a postmeal torpor, Leia and Han walked the encampment.

Han offered her a sympathetic smile. "Sorry you didn't win on the Tenel Ka thing."

"Oh, I did."

"How so?"

"I'm thrilled she's being invited. I desperately hope she'll come. She's likely to support our recommendations. And I'm sure we can contrive a little time for her to be together with Allana."

"But you sounded adamant against her coming—" Han shut up for a moment. "You pretended to be against it so they'd fight harder for it. Later, you can use the fact that you gave in to their demands as a negotiating point."

"You're better at this thinking than you like to admit, Han."

He snorted, amused. "It's all sabacc, sweetheart. It's just that you play it without any cards showing."

Chapter Thirty-one

JEDI TEMPLE, CORUSCANT

CORRAN WALKED INTO THE MASTERS' COUNCIL CHAMber with its circles of high-backed stone chairs. The screens over its exterior exits and viewports were closed, making the interior dimmer than usual. It was not dim so that a broadcast holocomm message could appear brighter and crisper, but because the chamber was nearly unoccupied. Only Saba waited there, standing, staring at the center as if expecting a hologram to appear and offer advice.

Corran waited until the door had slid shut behind him before he spoke. "Master Sebatyne?"

She didn't turn to look at him. "You wished to speak to this one?"

"Yes. The *Errant Venture* is back in system. Mirax is going up to see her father. I wanted to make sure you could spare me for a few hours or a day. I want to go with her."

"She still worries about your children?"

"Yes, of course." Corran didn't add a comment about his own worries. It was understood that he had them. It was also understood that he would stand apart from them when on matters of Jedi business.

"Yes. Go. This one will try not to call on you for at least a day." Finally Saba did turn to look at him. "But this one will need you. With Jedi Solo gone to Klatooine, with Master Hamner dead, you have become invaluable. You understand more of human-dominated politicz than many Jedi. This one may need your analytical powerz."

He offered her an expression of sympathy. "Your new duties are giving you grief?"

Saba uttered a hiss of vexation. "Not enough grief, perhapz."

He shook his head. "I don't understand."

"Each day, this one visitz the office of the Chief of State for duties shared with Senator Treen and General Jaxton. Problemz are brought before us. The economy of Ushmin, a small world near the borderz with the Imperial Remnant, is faltering. The Senate is doing nothing—proposing few billz, voting on fewer. The Senate will do nothing about Ushmin."

Corran nodded. "The Senate is going limp on you. A way of saying, *Anything that goes wrong while you hold office is your own fault; we won't help. Get out.*"

"This one understandz that. But we find a way to solve the problem, we three. Jaxton sayz that he is evaluating sites for new bases. He could put Ushmin at the top of the list for the next base in that sector. Treen sayz she can bring Disbursementz in on that plan. She commz; others fall into line. In minutes, it is done. We move on to the next problem."

Corran frowned, not certain he understood what he was hearing. "You're bothered because the job isn't *harder*?"

"Yes."

"If you were to announce your objection in front of the Senate, you'd probably be assassinated."

Saba sissed in mild amusement. "This one thought Jaxton and Treen were being very, very efficient to encourage this one to leave the office more hastily. But it feelz like there is more to it than that. As though they work with the confidence of some great momentum behind them."

"I'll . . . keep my eyes open for any other sign of that."

"Please."

There was a musical beep from Corran's pouch, a minor alert tone from his datapad. He pulled it out and flipped it open.

The words on the screen sent a little chill through him. "There's news. But it's a problem the Jedi and the Chief of State's office have decided not to intervene in."

"What is it?"

"The sentence is in for Tahiri Veila." He snapped the device closed, put it back in its pouch. He lifted his gaze to meet Saba's. "It's to be death."

KESLA VEIN PUMPING STATION,
NAM CHORIOS

Vestara was the first to emerge, peering out from beneath the partially raised hatch to make sure no one was in sight outside, then raising the hatch and slipping out onto the dusty enclosure within the town limits of Kesla Vein. The woven durasteel-netting fence around the enclosure seemed intact—at least as intact as she and her companions had left it. Late-afternoon winds still swirled dust throughout the enclosure and beyond, and the wind and chill of the air hit her like an unexpected plunge into an icy stream.

Ben was out next, then Luke, who lowered the metal hatch and spun the heavy metal ring atop it to seal it. He gave the teenagers a look that was half rueful and half encouraging. "One more down."

Ben's own expression was more exasperated. "One more *experienced*. Dad, if I never see another underground water pumping station or one more droch, I'll be happy."

Vestara patted her increasingly voluminous backpack. "We still have plenty of cans of droch spray."

"Yeah, but do we have any bottles of brain bleach?"

Luke grinned and led the way to the hole they'd cut in the fence. Keeping to back alleys where possible, they made their way through the small town to its border and out onto the crystalline sands beyond, to the hill that lay between town and the spot where they'd hidden their stolen speeder.

Kesla Vein had been an easy site to investigate. Its pumping station was completely automated, and was visited for maintenance and diagnostics only occasionally by the Oldtimer workers who managed it. There had been no sign of encampment by Abeloth or any Theran Listeners. There had been some drochs, but chiefly of the tiny variety.

On their walk back to the speeder, Vestara checked her comlink, set to receive the intermittent locator pulse broadcast by the vehicle. It came about a minute into their walk, just a couple of degrees off the course they had taken. They corrected and kept going. A few minutes later the hill, somewhat obscured by a cloud of dust flowing past like a river, came within sight. They skirted its north face and then descended into the cleft where they'd left the speeder. Visibility was better in this ravine; dust no longer driven by the wind drifted down like a thin haze, but it was nowhere near as bad as the dust clouds on the unsheltered surface above.

The speeder was still where they'd left it, some fifty meters away when they rounded a bend. But on the ridge above it, perhaps twenty meters up, was a blue airspeeder, a wide-bodied model designed for carrying entire families or a pilot and a fair amount of cargo. It was not running, and had been set down on the lip of the ravine, perhaps a meter of its front end protruding over empty air. A line descended from the winch on the front of the speeder down to within four meters of the ravine floor.

Yet there was no sign of anyone about. Ben glanced in all directions and put his hand on the hilt of his lightsaber, which was hung out of sight at the back of his belt. "Not good."

Vestara pulled her lightsaber from its clip. With some reluctance, she opened herself to the Force—reluctance because the usual result on Nam Chorios, a paranoid sense of being watched by hundreds of aloof observers, did not give her an improved understanding of her surroundings or the probable dangers around her. This time she got the usual result.

Luke continued to lead the way to the speeder. "If there are snipers, we're already in their sights. So be—"

"*Vestara Khai.*" The voice was a distant wail, high-pitched, like a keening ghost from a spooky holodrama. It echoed from the ravine walls.

Ben glanced back at her. "It's for you."

She scowled at him. "You're not helping."

There was a blur of motion, and then a woman landed atop their airspeeder, clearly having jumped up from ground level behind it. She was of average height, lean, a little broad in the shoulder, with dark skin and short black hair. Like Luke, Ben, and Vestara, she wore garments suited to Newcomers—pants and a lined jacket of hard-wearing cloth, sturdy leather boots, an overcloak and hood, goggles.

Vestara gave her a close look, as close as she could at this distance. "Who are you?"

"You know me, traitor." The woman raised her arms high, stretching, then put her hands down on her hips. She twisted her body back and forth, a loosening-up exercise. "And it's time for your companions to die, and for you to be taken to your father for questioning."

There *was* something familiar about the woman's voice, and Vestara finally recognized it. The woman should have had flawless lavender skin and hair as white as snow. Clearly she was in makeup and a wig, disguised to be able to move among the people of Nam Chorios without standing out. "Tola Annax."

"Your brains haven't seized up completely, Vestara. Now surrender like a good girl. We need to take you back to your father so you can experience only the most carefully thought-out torture and explain which of you cut down Lord Taalon. If you didn't do it, you clearly conspired with his killer—you're not their prisoner."

Vestara ignited her lightsaber and began moving forward again. "He had to die. He was . . . changing. He was no longer fit to lead us." She had not the slightest faith that her words would be believed, but it was something to talk about while making her approach.

"Oh, we're aware of the genetic mutations he was experiencing. Accelerated changes, grotesque mutations . . . you might even be acquitted of complicity because of them. If you surrender."

"Of course. Come down here and I'll give you my weapon personally." As she spoke, Vestara was aware of, and curiously glad of, the footsteps of the Skywalkers following her.

Tola's words meant the Sith didn't know who had killed Taalon. Therefore her father had not told them what he had overheard. That realization struck Vestara with the same effect that stepping out into the cold wind had a few minutes earlier. Gavar Khai was . . . *protecting* her? Showing concern for her fate? She felt a sudden confusion, not sure for a moment whether her father was the man she had grown up with or the one to whom she had been writing her ridiculously emotional, never-to-be-sent letters.

She was now thirty meters from the speeder, and still Tola had not drawn her own lightsaber. Tola did seem to have something in the palm of her hand, but it was nowhere near the size of a lightsaber hilt. Now she changed subjects. "Have you found Abeloth yet? We have some justice in mind for her, too."

Vestara didn't answer.

Apparently Tola didn't expect her to. Suddenly three men charged from behind the airspeeder, coming to a halt halfway between the speeder and Vestara. All were human, in good shape, dressed like Tola, and carrying lightsabers. One after another they ignited their weapons, and the red blades sprang into life.

Vestara heard Ben's and Luke's weapons *snap-hiss* into readiness behind her.

There were no further attempts at negotiation. The Sith in the center of the enemy line bounded forward toward Vestara. The other two went right and left, circling to engage the Skywalkers.

Vestara recognized her opponent. He was a Saber, a petty officer under her father's command. He was big, physically imposing, a handful of years older than her. More experienced, if one went only by number of years.

He came at her with the speed and lack of grace of a fast-moving crawler tank, slashing with his greater reach at her midsection. She darted to the right, putting a waist-high outcropping between the two of them, angling her blade to protect what the projection of stone didn't. She caught his slash on her blade, the force of the attack nearly throwing her back despite the leg she'd braced against the impact; she felt her arms shiver under the blow. It irritated her that she hadn't taken the blow at the correct angle to cause his blade to skid along hers, which would have reduced the impact. She shoved the thought from her mind but let the anger linger. Being too analytical at a time like this could be fatal.

She continued around the outcropping and slashed at the back of his knee, but the impact from that previous blow had robbed her of forward momentum; the man was able to catch her slash on his blade. He disengaged smoothly, just barely enough to get his blade clear of hers, and popped the tip up toward her in a rising slash. She merely skipped back a pace and let the energy blade pass harmlessly in front of her.

Vestara reversed direction—continuing to circle as she had been would eventually have presented her back to Tola. Her opponent switched to a one-handed grip on his lightsaber and made a forward sweeping gesture with his free hand. Vestara expected something to come flying out of that hand, a small cloud of dust perhaps, but nothing did.

Instead, from behind him, a cluster of rocks, some of them the size of a fist, hurtled off the ravine floor and arced up at her.

Vestara nearly winced. An overt use of the Force—somewhere on Nam Chorios, a Force storm would soon arise, possibly injuring or even killing people—and the realization that this mattered in the least to her was a second unwelcome surprise. Ruthlessly, she suppressed that emotion.

She could have sidestepped the cloud of stones. Perhaps her opponent expected her to, or perhaps he intended to lunge in the direction he anticipated her to take. And she did spin to her left, just not far enough to be completely safe from the stones. She continued the twirl into a spinning side kick.

She was still more than a meter from her adversary, but her boot sole connected with one of the incoming stones, sending it hurtling back toward the man's face.

He flinched, bringing his blade up to deflect the stone.

She followed the stone, felt an impact against her left shoulder, felt her body twist from the blow, but continued into a single-handed lunge with her blade. Her lightsaber slid into her opponent's body just beneath the heart. She planted her forward foot and dragged her blade up. Its red tip slashed through the heart.

Wide-eyed, her opponent staggered back and fell, dying.

Vestara straightened. There was pain in her left shoulder where one stone had connected, and in her right foot where she'd kicked the other, but her injuries seemed minor, manageable.

She gave a cautious glance back over her shoulder. Luke's opponent was already down, in two large pieces, severed at the waist. Luke was hurtling toward Ben, but Ben was already in the follow-through of a horizontal slash that sent his own opponent's head leaping off his neck.

Vestara turned her attention back to Tola. The woman hadn't moved or drawn a weapon. Vestara gestured toward the ground with the tip of her blade. "How about *you* surrender to *our* justice?"

"Some other time." Tola held up the object in her hand—it looked like a comlink of some sort—and pressed a button on its top surface. Then she leapt laterally to grab the bottom of the cable leading up to the speeder winch above. Already retracting, the cable drew her up the ravine wall at a rapid clip.

Ben gestured as if to drag her or the speeder down through use of the Force, but Luke slapped his arm down. "Not worth it, Ben. Consequences."

Ben looked irritated. "I forgot."

Tola got to the top and sprang up into the pilot's seat of the speeder. She offered Vestara and the Skywalkers a mock salute. Then she pressed the button on her comlink again.

Vestara was hit from the side—it was Luke, bearing her and Ben to the ground behind her outcropping.

Their own airspeeder exploded, throwing durasteel and plastoid and flame in all directions. The shock wave from the blast hammered Vestara's ears but not her body—the outcropping, a durable blast shield, caught all debris headed their way.

The three of them rose. Tola's speeder was gone. So was their own airspeeder, but not the same way—it existed now as a crater of burning junk and a column of smoke that, as it reached the top of the ravine, was caught by a crosswind and torn to shreds.

Ben sighed. "You know her, huh?"

"She works for my father." Vestara collected her lightsaber, which she'd dropped when Luke hit her.

"Dad, she was doing what you did with me at the temple on Dorin. A Master hanging back to watch her students fight an enemy so she'd learn about them."

Luke nodded. "Though she seemed perfectly content to sacrifice them."

Vestara replaced her lightsaber on its clip. "You're a big prize, Master Skywalker. Well worth the sacrifice of a few Sabers and apprentices."

Ben frowned. "I wonder how they traced us here."

Luke grinned at his son. "It doesn't matter how they did. I'm just grateful that they did."

Ben looked his father over. "You weren't hit by debris to the head, were you, Dad?"

Luke shook his head. "Trust me on this, Ben. Sometimes it's actually a good thing to run into your enemies." He glanced around. "People from Kesla Vein are going to be here in a few minutes to investigate the blast. We'd better be gone when they arrive. Let's get going."

Chapter Thirty-two

HAPES SYSTEM

"SIR. FLOTILLA BREAKING ORBIT, THREE BATTLE DRAGons and an escort of frigates and destroyers." That was the voice of Dei's pilot and second in command, Hara, drifting aft out of the cockpit.

Querdan Dei did not bother to poke his head into the cramped cockpit. The area in which he stood—a small compartment, one and a half by two meters in height, that provided access between cockpit forward, main work compartment aft, air lock port, and refresher starboard—was the only spot on this damnable spacecraft that was bare of apparatus, the only spot where he could practice his forms, and he wasn't quite through with those exercises yet.

He straightened and placed his forearms against the compartment ceiling. Outside, he would have stretched, making himself a straight line from toes to fingertips, but there was no way to do that here. He swayed through a somewhat constricted version of the Snake Ascending a Waterfall exercise.

Hara, a lavender-skinned Keshiri woman, middle-aged and taciturn, had not one trace of Force sensitivity or imagination, but she was reliable, intelligent, and diligent. Dei kept his voice calm, though he knew Hara would not have alerted him if the flotilla was not potentially of great interest. "Enlighten me."

"They're accelerating away from the planet at atypical speed. We're seeing transponder telemetry from only two Battle Dragons. The third is masquerading as a medical frigate, *Jeweled Delight*. Their formation suggests the *Jeweled Delight* is at the center of a protective pattern, at the sweet spot of overlapping weapons coverage."

Dei sank smoothly from Snake Ascending a Waterfall into Mountain Storm. That exercise normally called for full splits, which were impossible here; instead, he kept his right knee cocked and fully extended only his left. Once he was down, he began the series of intricate arm movements that constituted the storm, suggesting winds around a mountain range. "All sensors and countermeasures to full power. Fall in behind that formation and pace it."

"Sir?"

"Hara, the computer between my ears tells me that the odds are very high that we are looking at the Queen Mother departing Hapes. What does the computer embedded in this ghastly craft tell you?"

Another voice, male, floated out from the cockpit. "Still running those variables, sir."

"Please execute my orders while running those variables." With thigh strength alone, Dei slid back up to a standing position, then lowered himself for a second iteration of Mountain Storm, this time with his right leg extended. He felt the craft shift under him as Hara heeled it and began a stealthy approach into the flotilla's wake. The maneuver caused him to wobble, spoiling the perfection of his form. He sighed.

"Sorry, sir," the pilot said.

"Not your fault, Hara." He finished his form and again exerted himself to slide up to a standing position.

Then, finally, he felt he'd done enough, just barely enough, to warrant a return to work. He moved forward into the cockpit.

The blasted claustrophobic cockpit. There were three seats, two forward and one back, all with control boards pressed in so close there was barely room to get into them. And there were no viewports, just monitor screens providing a live holocam feed of what was going on outside. A vehicle without viewports issued no visible light for other sensors to detect. This was efficiency. But efficiency, as almost always, came at the expense of beauty and comfort.

He squeezed into the rear seat, the command chair. Hara occupied the forward port-side chair. Fardan, a young fair-skinned human male, was in the starboard seat as communications and sensor operator.

Dei looked at him. "Well?"

Fardan turned to give Dei an apologetic look. "You're correct, sir. The computer gives a high degree of confidence to the possibility that this is the Queen Mother's flagship." The young man had a long face, not as handsome as the Sith preferred, and wore his long black hair in a braid. He looked like a younger version of Dei.

"Plot their course as closely as you can, to a thousand significant digits if you have to. When they jump, I want to know the exact direction they're jumping."

"Yes, sir."

Dei turned his attention to Hara. "Have our reprovisioning ship stand by to follow us."

"Yes, sir." She typed a few sentences onto her small comm board and transmitted. Compressed text caused a much tinier potential blip on enemy sensors than voice, which in turn was smaller by several orders of magnitude than holograms, so this crew used it whenever feasible.

This craft that Dei commanded brought him both

exasperation and pride. Exasperation because it was so inelegant. Designed and manufactured in the Corporate Sector, it was, on the exterior, oval and seamless, coated in a sensor-absorbing material that was black in the depths of space but could assume ambient colors when near a planetary surface. Designated the EE-104 Fisheye and named *Cryptic Warning,* it was as unlovely as a particularly nasty-looking piece of candy. All it needed was lint from a pocket sticking to it to complete the picture.

On the other hand, it was a very expensive, highly efficient tool of espionage and war. Designed for the purpose of coordinating sneak attacks and for sitting for days or weeks on station, unseen, to monitor enemy activities, it had the most impressive array of sensor and stealth features Dei had ever seen. The Sith had captured only two such craft, and Gavar Khai had assigned one to the command of Querdan Dei. That was an unmistakable sign of faith in his abilities.

Dei knew that his operation was a long shot on Khai's part, devotion of a finite set of resources to the Jedi Queen project. Lord Taalon had seen a vision of a possible Jedi Queen in the future; Gavar Khai had noticed a marked similarity between the description of the Jedi Queen and the current Hapan Queen Mother, who had once been a Jedi. Clearly Tenel Ka Djo was not the Jedi Queen; her appearance was slightly different, and there had never been any indication that she would choose to be fitted with a prosthetic arm, while the Jedi Queen clearly had two working limbs.

But Tenel Ka Djo had had a daughter, lost in the last war, and she could have another. So Khai's orders were simple. Take up station at Hapes; find a way to gain access to the vicinity of Tenel Ka Djo; and kill her.

Dei knew that he was nothing but a tourniquet for possible loose ends. He was used to assignments that were both very difficult and mostly unrewarding. His own interests never leaned toward Sith politics, toward stroking the egos of those in power. And this was why, at the age of forty, he was still only a Saber.

He wouldn't have had it any other way.

Hara's voice cut into his meditations. "We're outside the Hapes gravity well and we've been on a specific course, laser-straight, for a couple of minutes. The other craft in that flotilla are forming up, mathematically perfect, along that course. I think they're going to jump."

Dei glanced at Fardan. "Plot probable destinations."

Fardan looked back at him, eyes wide. "Across an entire *galaxy*? Every potential arrival site? There will be thousands to choose from."

Dei smiled. "Prioritize by probability. First, run the route out to the galaxy's edge. Factor in recent news feeds, locations from the Queen Mother's history, spots along the route that are close enough to constitute gravity wells that would pull the flotilla out of hyperspace. What do you get?"

Fardan turned back to his control board.

"Flotilla entering hyperspace." It was true; on the monitors, the magnified image of the flotilla was suddenly gone, leaving nothing but empty space.

Hara maintained the *Cryptic Warning*'s course and Dei maintained silence while Fardan worked. Finally the young man turned around again. "Just over six thousand potential hits. But prioritizing with the factors you suggested gives us fewer than ten with any known relevance."

"What's number one?"

"Hutt space, Si'klaata Cluster, planet Klatooine. A desert world. It's the site of a recent slave rebellion, which ties in to Alliance politics, which interact with Hapan politics. With the Jedi controlling a portion of

Alliance politics, we have a reinforcing cross-tie of the Queen Mother's Jedi interests. We have a report from Fleet Communications of Sith and Jedi interactions on Klatooine recently, even though those facts have not yet appeared on Alliance news, still another cross-tie."

"Very good. Log all possible arrival zones, still arranged by that probability. And prepare a jump to Klatooine."

Dei leaned back and stretched while his crew members went about their business.

If this turned out to be a fool's errand, if he were abandoning his station at the Hapes system incorrectly, Gavar Khai might choose to have him demoted or killed.

But one did not achieve greatness by limiting risks and keeping one's head down. Life was short; excellence and fame were far more enduring. It only made sense to risk the one for the others.

KLATOOINE

Allana screamed again before Leia could reach the little girl's compartment. Leia's gut tightened. Lightsaber unlit but in hand, she charged at the compartment door. It snapped open, barely getting out of the way in time for Leia to pass through without slamming into its durasteel surface.

In the compartment, in the dark, lit now only by a column of light admitted by the door, Allana flailed in her bedsheets, struggling with an unseen enemy. Anji, her fur so puffed up that she looked twice her size, crouched in a corner, ready to pounce—there was just nothing to pounce on. She growled at Leia.

Leia sat on the edge of Allana's bed and held the girl.

"Allana. You're dreaming. It's all right. You're just having a bad dream."

Allana's eyes were already open. Now, no longer staring wildly, they fixed on Leia. "Fire, she's burning up." There was such misery in her voice that it made Leia's heart ache.

Leia heard a sigh of relief from behind her. She turned to see Han, dressed in nothing but drawers, his blaster in hand, lower his weapon and switch it to safe mode.

Leia gave him a little smile. "Bad dreams. I'll take care of it."

He nodded. "I'll brew us some caf. It's almost dawn anyway." Still clumsy from sleepiness, he moved off. The compartment door slid shut.

"It wasn't a dream." Allana was fully awake now, but she was obviously unwilling to let go of what she'd experienced. "It was real."

"Look around, sweetie. Is anyone on fire?"

Allana shook her head, but her jaw was set, so like Han's and Jacen's in its stubbornness. "But she will be."

"Who?"

"Mommy."

Anji hopped up on the bed and settled on the sheet between Allana's feet. The nexu remained a little puffy. Her attention was all on Allana.

Leia felt a little taken aback by the girl's words. For Tenel Ka to enter a conversation now, hours after she had accepted the negotiators' invitation to come to Klatooine—an invitation and an acceptance that had not been announced—could be more than coincidence. Allana *was* Force-sensitive.

"Tell me about your dream."

"She was smiling at me. She was wearing robes like everyone here wears. She was out there on the sand and I was running to her. Then there was a man made of fire, bright burning fire. He grabbed her from behind and she started *burning.*" Tears began to roll down Allana's cheeks. "She was just looking at me real sad and she was burning *up.* And it wasn't a dream. It was different."

Leia used a corner of the sheet to mop up the tears. "Maybe it was more than a dream. But that doesn't make it the truth, doesn't make it the future. It could be leftover pain from when your mommy lost her arm. That would have been like burning."

"I felt it through the Force?"

Leia nodded.

"But why would the Force do that to me?"

Leia smiled. "One of the horrible things about life is that you hardly ever know something like that right now. Later on, you figure it out."

"Is she coming here?"

Leia paused before answering. "I wasn't going to tell you. It was going to be a surprise. But yes."

For once, news of this sort didn't seem to make Allana happy. She didn't smile. "The man on fire wants to kill her."

"If there is such a man, we'll stop him. Or your mother will. She's very, very good at that sort of thing."

"Uh-huh." Allana didn't seem convinced.

"You feeling better?"

"Uh-huh."

"You want some water or milk?"

"Uh-uh."

Leia hugged her. "You go back to sleep, then. Everything will be fine."

"Uh-huh."

Once out in the lounge, Leia dropped into a seat beside Han and let out a long sigh. "We may have some new trouble."

"Can I shoot it?"

"Please do."

Chapter Thirty-three

HWEG SHUL, NAM CHORIOS

KANDRA ASKED IT A DIFFERENT WAY, JUST TO BE SURE that she hadn't misunderstood, that there would be no ambiguity. "So you're certain neither Grand Master Skywalker nor either of his companions could have stabbed you?"

On the other side of the old, elaborately carved Ithorian wood desk, Mayor Snaplaunce nodded. "I was watching them take off when I felt the vibroblade enter my back. Official city telemetry followed the shuttle on its flight path until its movements became erratic. My assailant was someone here in Hweg Shul at the time, and was neither a Skywalker nor the young Khai woman."

"You seem to have recovered fully."

"I was saved by ignorance. My assailant drove his blade in where human kidneys would have been. With Ithorians, those exact spots are occupied by back muscle. So the wounds, while potentially dangerous because of blood loss, were not immediately fatal."

"So if the Skywalker party is clear of those charges—charges that many of the Oldtimers seem to persist in leveling against them—why do they remain the subjects of an arrest warrant?"

Snaplaunce gave her a stern look, which was mildly disconcerting coming from a hammer-headed Ithorian.

"There is still much we must know in our investigation of the murder of Dr. Wei, and the members of the Skywalker party remain persons of interest. There is the question of the very damaging storms now growing in number on Nam Chorios's surface—"

"Such as the one this morning."

"Yes. Storms that were last attested to when Grand Master Skywalker, operating under the name Owen Lars, first came to Nam Chorios thirty years ago. There's also the slight but measurable rise across the planet in theft of speeders, which corresponds closely with the rise in planetary visitors. There are mysteries at work here. As a former officer of the peace, I'm uncomfortable with mysteries. So that warrant will remain in effect until we have answers sufficient to clear it."

"Thank you." Kandra glanced at Beurth, signaling the end of the official interview. The recording light on his holocam went dark, and he lowered the apparatus from his shoulder.

Kandra stood. "Mayor, you've been very helpful."

Two minutes later, bundled against the cold, moving reluctantly out into the windy, debris-strewn streets of Hweg Shul, Kandra sighed. "The man is completely useless."

Beurth offered her a series of porcine grunts.

She nodded. "I know. That's the way his job is done. But he didn't give us anything, the Newcomers and Latecomers don't seem to know anything, the Oldtimers are being very tight-lipped, the ones who are known to be Theran Listeners don't seem to be around, we haven't seen Valin . . . there's *something* going on, but it's going to take a better journalist than me to dig it up."

Beurth grunted again, at length, his tone cross.

Kandra offered him a sour face and mimicked his words. "*Eyewitness accounts are unreliable anyway.* Thanks, that really helps." She sighed, watching her frosty breath rise. It was then torn apart by the daytime winds. "Still . . . let's see if we can patch together something, anything, out of hard data and statistics."

Beurth grunted again.

"Yes, we can eat first."

After lunch, back in her hostel room, she found the one detail she needed.

It was in updated crime reports and statistics. Speeder theft *was* up, and among the incidents reported since Luke Skywalker's arrival on Nam Chorios, there was only one vehicle that had been stolen and later found—in this case, destroyed—without an arrest being associated with the case. An expensive Incom T-47 had been stolen from Hweg Shul. Interestingly, the theft had taken place a day before Snaplaunce's shuttle, damaged but jury-rigged for ground travel, had been found outside Hweg Shul. The T-47 had been reported destroyed early this morning at the small community of Kesla Vein. There was also the report that someone at Kesla Vein had anonymously reported to the town headwoman that all speeders in the area were in danger of being stolen, with the result that she had ordered them all housed in a secure barn, watched by Oldtimers armed with blaster rifles. So far none of the community's other speeders had gone missing.

Those details tweaked Kandra's memory. She cross-checked crime report time stamps and found that, at the exact moment Kesla Vein residents had been responding to the explosion of the T-47, one of those anomalous storms had been arising at various sites around Nam Chorios, Hweg Shul included. A couple of minutes' research into Luke Skywalker's career confirmed that he had extensive experience with the T-47s, especially during his service with the Rebel Alliance on Hoth.

Other planetary statistics turned up no enlightening

details. But Kandra, following the advice of one of her old holojournalism teachers, inverted a couple of graphs of planetary statistical data and found something interesting. She turned her datapad around so Beurth could see its screen. "See it?"

Beurth scanned the graphs and offered an interested set of squeals.

"That's the one. It's a graph of crime and unusual news reports per capita for all communities on Nam Chorios, sorted by community size. And the one you see, Crystal Valley, has the lowest incidence of reports per capita among all communities larger than five hundred residents . . . but only as of the last couple of days. It looks like a news blackout."

Beurth grunted and stood.

"You do that. Make sure the fuel is topped off. I think we'll do Kesla Vein first, Crystal Valley later. I'll make sure we have all the heating packs and droch sprays we need."

They had managed to secure rental of a high-speed landspeeder on arrival at Hweg Shul, so they made good time toward Kesla Vein. Of course, there were disadvantages to their vehicle. It had been available because it was open-topped, not the most comfortable choice in Nam Chorios's bitterly cold winter. Kandra was content to let Beurth pilot the thing while she huddled, wrapped in her cloak and blankets, a disposable heat-pak in her lap and another at her feet. At the end of a couple of hours' travel, she was so cold she suspected she could be used to chill mixed drinks, was nauseous from the constant battering the wind had inflicted on their speeder, and was desperate to see something, anything, other than the speeder interior and river-like movements of crystal dust in the wind.

Following Kesla Vein's directional comm signal, they

got within five kilometers of the small town and then were hailed over the speeder's comm board. "Whiterock Rentals One Fourteen, this is Rainbow Securities at Kesla Vein. Please state your business."

Kandra and Beurth exchanged a confused look. Small towns the galaxy over tended to react to visitors by either ignoring them with a touch of hostility or directing them to the local shops and service providers.

Beurth slowed their approach. With her datapad, Kandra ran a planetary network search on Rainbow Securities. She also donned her comlink headset and activated it. "Kesla Vein, this is Whiterock One Fourteen. We're journalists following up on the theft and destruction of an airspeeder in your vicinity."

"Whiterock, be advised that the individual who stole the craft is still at large, believed to be nearby, and is responsible for several deaths in the vicinity. You are strongly advised to abort your visit until the area is secure. If you choose to approach the town, we'll have to assign you a security operative to make sure your vehicle doesn't fall into the killer's hands."

"I . . . see." What Kandra *didn't* see was a listing anywhere on the planetary records for a Rainbow Securities. "I think we need to set down here and ask our local manager how to proceed. Are we safe here?"

"Probably. As long as the winds keep the dust storms up. When the winds die, you might be visible to macrobinoculars. At that point, if you're still here, I'd recommend you pull several kilometers back."

"Thanks for the advice, Kesla Vein. Whiterock One Fourteen out." She gestured for Beurth to land the speeder and kill the repulsors.

They sat there for a few moments, the speeder rocking in the wind, while Kandra thought about what to do.

She really didn't need to see the wreckage of the T-47.

Her objective was to find Luke Skywalker, if indeed he was in the vicinity. And things were certainly adding up to a possibility that he was . . . not only nearby, but being sought, a fact that had not reached the planetary news sources. If only she could get a message to him—

A thought occurred to her and, startled, she straightened.

Beurth grunted at her.

"Back on the shuttle, Valin Horn gave us a frequency to listen to in case he needed to contact us once we got to Nam Chorios. Was that specific to him, or was it one the Jedi use in general?"

He shrugged.

"Let's find out." She composed a brief text message: *Grand Master Skywalker: Care to trade a ride for your story? Reply this frequency.* She thought about her words, then changed *Grand Master Skywalker* to *Owen Lars.* Satisfied, she sent the message.

Two minutes later, a reply came: *Identify yourself, please.*

Kandra Nilitz, Landing Zone newsnet. I arrived Nam Chorios with Hal Cyon and Jes Cyon. You may remember my investigative report on black-market sales of fake bacta. Kandra was sure he hadn't seen it. It seemed like every young reporter did a piece on black-market sales of fake bacta. But she hoped that the reference made her sound more famous than she was.

I agree to your terms.

Kandra's pulse raced. Now, at last, she might be on the verge of cracking this frustrating story. *I'll send a homing pulse at one-minute intervals.* She set up her datapad to do exactly that, then sent the message.

She looked at Beurth and sagged in relief.

Twenty minutes later, her relief ended.

She didn't realize Luke Skywalker had reached her

until the instant he appeared, standing on the hood of her rented speeder, his green-bladed lightsaber lit in his hand. The fierce wind whipped his cloak as if to yank it free and carry it back to Hweg Shul. He turned back in the direction of Kesla Vein and cupped his free hand beside his mouth. "This way!"

His answer was a blaster bolt angling in toward him out of the dust storm. He caught it on his lightsaber, deflecting it into the ground as if barely interested in it.

In the distance ahead, Kandra could see two colorful glows bobbing with their holders' movement—lightsabers, one blue and one red.

Then Luke spun, leaning over the speeder's windscreen and slashing with his lightsaber as if he wanted to cleave the seat between Beurth and Kandra. Kandra shrieked and jerked away, looking up, and only now saw the man standing on the back of the seat. Dressed like most other winter travelers on Nam Chorios, he held a red lightsaber and raised it, catching Luke's slash. The power of the blow knocked the man off the back of the seat; he fell backward, landing on his feet on the rear seat.

Luke bounded over the windscreen and landed between Beurth and Kandra. He slashed again. The other man deflected the blow, just barely, and leapt up to land on the speeder's rear.

Luke continued his advance, landing on the rear seat exactly where his opponent had been a moment earlier. He thrust with his lightsaber, its blade engaging the other man's. His foot lashed out, catching the other man's weapon hand. The red lightsaber flew free. Luke caught it with his left hand, twirled both blades in an intricate green-and-red array of color, and then advanced onto the back of the speeder.

His enemy dropped off the speeder, turned, and ran into the cloud of dust behind.

Luke turned to face forward again. He gestured at Kandra with his right-hand weapon. "You, backseat." He pointed at Beurth with the other weapon. "You, get this thing running."

Kandra scrambled over her seat back and dropped into the rear seat. She resisted the impulse to crawl down into the foot well. "What's happening?"

Luke jumped into the seat she'd just vacated. "Don't be silly. What's happening is you're rescuing us."

"Oh. I feel so brave."

The seat to Kandra's left lurched. She looked up to see a young woman standing there, holding another red lightsaber. The newcomer raised her voice to be heard over the roar of wind—and, now, the sound of repulsors coming online. "Ben! This way!"

Suddenly there was someone above the girl—a man, dressed like the other attacker, inverted, seeming almost to fly at the apex of his acrobatic maneuver. He thrust down with his lightsaber. Kandra opened her mouth to shout a warning, knowing it would be too late, but the girl raised her own lightsaber in a sweeping maneuver that deflected the attack; the blades crackled as they crossed. Her attacker landed several meters off to the starboard side, rolling in the sand, continuing his roll forward to get clear of the speeder.

Luke deactivated the red lightsaber he'd seized. The girl—it had to be Vestara Khai, from the reports Kandra had seen—dropped to a kneeling position on the seat but kept her blade lit, her eyes on the sands around them.

The speeder was up a meter in the air now but not yet moving. Luke looked at Beurth. "Scoot over this way."

Beurth offered him a squeal, an interrogative one, but didn't move.

A moment later Ben Skywalker smashed down into the Gamorrean's lap. "Hey. Scoot over."

Now Beurth did, squealing complaints as he wriggled out from under the human teenager.

Luke shouted, "Go!"

Not deactivating his own lightsaber, Ben tossed it back over his shoulder. Vestara caught it, bringing both weapons up in what Kandra assumed was some sort of defensive pose.

Ben accelerated, immediately banking to port. A man with a red lightsaber, emerging from the dust cloud, had to run farther to get at the speeder. Luke slashed at him as he got near; their blades crossed, sparking and sputtering, and then the attacker was behind them.

Luke jammed the point of his lightsaber into the speeder's dashboard.

Kandra's eyes got wide. "Hey, this is a *rental.*"

"It's a rental with transponders." Luke deactivated his lightsaber, then yanked at the dashboard where he'd cut it. A panel came free; he tossed it over his shoulder. With the hilt of her lightsaber, Vestara whacked the panel, sending it sideways, directly in the path of another attacker charging out of the dust. Unable to adjust in time, the woman tripped over the debris and sprawled in the sand.

Luke jammed his hand into the wires and circuits exposed by his crude mechanical surgery and pulled out a circuit board. "Transponder number one, for the planetary authorities." He tossed that over the side and repeated the action, this time yanking free a smaller, thicker black module. "Transponder number two, for the company that rented you the speeder. All very legal and practical, but it would tend to get us killed." That one, too, he threw over the side.

Beurth looked over his shoulder at Kandra and grunted an apology.

"I know. Not your fault, you're not in charge." Kandra blew out a sigh. "Are we safe yet?"

Vestara deactivated Ben's lightsaber. "Safer. It's been nearly fifteen seconds since we've been attacked."

Ben's voice was cheerful. "Time for some dizzying maneuvers to throw them off our trail." He abruptly vectored to port.

Kandra groaned. The nausea was back.

When it had been five minutes since an attack, and once her heat-paks had been passed back to her, Kandra told Luke how she'd come to be there, and ended, "So do we get our story?"

Luke nodded, agreeable. "Of course. First—Ben, set course for this Crystal Valley she mentioned. That'll be our next site to examine. Kandra, I'm going to tell you a story about a monster from the Maw cluster, a tribe of Sith lost to history, and the tremendous danger posed to the galaxy. Unless you'd prefer a meticulous explanation of how we got Mayor Snaplaunce's shuttle running instead."

"Hold on, hold on. Beurth?"

Her holocam operator got his shoulder unit in place and trained it on the Jedi Grand Master.

Kandra composed herself for a moment. Now, at last, this trip had become worthwhile. "So, yes, please, the story. Of the monster and the Sith. Not the shuttle."

Chapter Thirty-four

KLATOOINE

WHEN *CRYPTIC WARNING* DROPPED OUT OF HYPERspace in the Klatooine system, the Hapan flotilla was just entering planetary orbit. Hara and Fardan offered slightly undisciplined whoops of victory, echoed by other members of the crew back in the main compartment.

Dei merely smiled. "Approach in full stealth mode. Keep sensors on them. Be alert for shuttles or other landing craft departing."

Fardan nodded. "Yes, sir."

The Hapan vessels made several orbits of Klatooine, doubtless communicating with planetary government and other official forces on the surface, while the *Cryptic Warning* crept into an orbit trailing theirs. Then Fardan announced, "Landing craft departing from the flagship." He increased the gain on the visual sensors, and Dei could see a saucer-like craft descending from the flotilla's high planetary orbit.

"Track it. Don't follow it—if we end up between it and the flotilla, the flotilla's odds of detecting us are enhanced. Plot a parallel course down."

"Yes, sir."

The *Cryptic Warning* broke orbit and descended, its fuselage exterior now imitating color schemes as viewed by observers from a variety of directions—browns and yellows if viewed from above, sky hues if viewed from below. At a distance of a hundred kilometers from the Hapan landing craft, it descended at a rate matching its quarry's.

Fardan plotted its most likely destination, by its course and by orbital scans of planetside activity, to a large encampment in the broad belt of equatorial desert. The landing craft swooped in to a sure and skillful landing. Hara circled the landing site in an approaching spiral while Fardan, Dei, and the rest of the crew evaluated sensor data.

The camp was situated in a depression immediately west of a lengthy ridge formed by foothills that were the first stage of an arid mountain range. The camp itself was circled by defensive batteries and shield projectors, the latter active, all mobile. Optical imagery showed a large number of tents and vehicles. Among the inhabitants were more Klatooinians than any other species, but dozens of species were represented. The landing craft settled into a sandy area just north of the camp. Elsewhere along the camp's rim was a familiar-looking Corellian YT-1300 light freighter.

Dei didn't interfere with Fardan's duties. He personally ran the visual comparison between this craft and a famous one on record. Then he nodded, satisfied. "The circular transport is the *Millennium Falcon*. This at least doubles the odds that the Hapan flotilla belongs to the Queen. She's a friend of the Solos."

Hara gave him a brief glance. "Instructions, sir?"

"Find a landing spot on the eastern ridge, about two kilometers from the camp overlook. Maintain full stealth mode. Ground as softly as possible in case they have seismic sensors. Fardan, bring up known geological facts about this dirtball and, if relevant, use the sonic countermeasures to simulate tectonic or volcanic activity on landing so that any noise we make suggests natural activity."

Five minutes later, Dei stepped out of a darkened air lock and onto the starlit sands of Klatooine. His garments, though not a match for those most prevalent in the encampment, were in similar colors and were as voluminous as the desert robes to be seen there.

He trotted the two klicks to the top of the ridge, slowing down and becoming more cautious the last half kilometer. But although his sensor scan had shown some guards stationed along the ridge approaches, he had chosen a spot that had no reasonable path of descent to the camp and consequently had no guards. Careful in case his portion of ridge was in danger of collapsing, he moved as close as he dared to the edge of the ridge itself, then went prone and set up his macrobinoculars. They were larger than an ordinary set, had a tripod for stability, and had a massive amount of storage memory so that they could record what they saw.

It took him only a few moments to find the Hapan landing craft and zoom in on its surroundings.

If there had been a party there to meet it, the party was already aboard or dispersed. Now he could see only guards, more than half of them female, all of them unusually attractive, stationed around the craft. At the nearest verge of tents there stood observers who, from their gestures and movements, were clearly discussing the Hapan craft or its inhabitants. Most were Klatooinian or human; there were a fair number of other species and several droids.

The camp was active. There were fires lit, apparently to cook evening meals and provide comfort from the sudden chill of desert nights. Dei's chrono, adjusted to this planet's cycle, indicated it was early evening.

Time passed. Dei remained patient. There was a beauty to surveillance, to remaining perfectly still while the satellites of one's prey orbited, departed, returned, and offered clues to the prey's weaknesses. Dei wished he could persuade his subordinates and family of the elegance and usefulness of patience, but they all seemed so desperate for change and immediate gratification.

Groups of onlookers in the vicinity of the landing craft wandered off, finding cookfires or tent interiors. All but one group, which remained in place, seemingly as patient and watchful as Dei himself. He trained his macrobinoculars on them and zoomed in for maximum gain.

Five humans or humanoids, two droids. Four of the humanoids were the size of adult humans, one much smaller. The droids were recognizably a dome-topped astromech and a protocol droid. All the humanoids wore the desert clothing sported by most in the camp. The adults were armed for engagement—high-end blaster rifles and the suggestion, under their robes, of armor, holsters, and pouches.

The smallest humanoid had some sort of animal sitting at its side. At this range, Dei couldn't make out its features or even determine whether it was male or female, but he believed, from its movements and occasional restlessness, that it was a child rather than an adult member of a small species.

Now a group of perhaps a dozen individuals descended the landing craft's boarding ramp, talking among themselves. They moved off into the camp.

And still the group of five humanoids and two droids waited. Interested, Dei continued to watch them.

Another fifteen minutes passed. Then, as if a signal had been received over a comlink, they started forward, heading straight toward the boarding ramp. None of the guards arrayed around the landing craft moved to stop them. The four adult members of the party separated, moving around the craft to take up positions spaced equally around it, while the child and the two droids ascended the ramp.

Interesting. Interesting.

Allana left R2-D2 and C-3PO behind in the landing craft's entry lounge and, alone but for Anji, followed the lights embedded in the curving corridor walls. The lights flickered in sequence, seeming to travel on ahead, then to return and repeat the pattern, guiding her onward.

There were no people to be seen, even at the security station granting access from the entry lounge. That was not strange. Though Tenel Ka was often surrounded by courtiers and guards, on those rare occasions when she could meet with Allana, if the meeting place were secure, she would dismiss all possible witnesses, or retain only those she felt she could trust absolutely . . . which was usually none.

The landing craft was so different from the *Falcon.* The air seemed fresher, and was lightly perfumed instead of carrying faint traces of ancient lubricant spills or fuel leaks, of hundreds of exotic cargoes. This was a tiny section of palace packed into a saucer-shaped craft, with glossy carpets on corridor floors and original works of art affixed to walls.

The light patterns led to a compartment door. It slid open as Allana approached. She moved into a small antechamber, comfortably furnished with sofas and stuffed chairs.

And from the sofa against the far wall, decked in synthsilk robes and strands of jewelry, rose her mother, Tenel Ka.

Allana ran forward. "Mommy!"

"My baby." Tenel Ka stooped and hugged Allana to her. She so resembled the image Allana saw in the mirror, all long red hair and gray eyes, but grown-up and beautiful. Allana hoped that she would look even more like her mother when she grew up.

"You're getting so big. Every time I see you. You can't see it on holocomm images." Tenel Ka sat again, pulling Allana up onto the sofa beside her. "I haven't given you permission to get so big."

"Sorry, I just do." Allana nestled against her mother.

Back by the door, Anji, hunched and looking suspicious, stared around, then eyed a chair as if contemplating sharpening her claws on it until it was an unrecognizable ruin. Allana stared at her feline companion and gave her a little pulse of emotion through the Force, a calming suggestion of quiet and rest. Anji hopped onto the chair instead of savaging it and curled up there, head toward Allana and her mother.

Tenel Ka smiled down at Allana. "I felt that. You're getting more proficient with the Force, too."

"I sometimes don't like the Force."

"Nobody likes it all the time, sweetie. It's like fire. It can keep you warm and healthy, or it can burn you. So you must always be aware of it and what it's telling you."

Allana suppressed the urge to shudder at the word *burn*. "Fire doesn't always talk to you like the Force does. And when fire talks, it always makes sense. That's not true with the Force."

Tenel Ka's grin widened. "Wait until the first time you fall in love. Love can burn you even worse, and it *never* makes sense."

Allana made a face. "Yecch. Um, Grandma says we can send notes to each other with Artoo and Threepio while you're here."

"Good. I plan to. You know we might not be able to see each other every day."

Allana nodded. That's the way it always seemed to be. There was almost no time for them to be together.

She decided not to tell her mother about the dream of the fiery man. Grandma Leia was probably right—her mom knew how to take care of herself, and would certainly know what to do if a man made of fire came toward her. No, their time together would just be play and happy talk.

Perhaps an hour after they entered the landing craft, the child and droids exited. They were rejoined by the four guards. The boarding ramp lifted into place. Many of the landing craft's exterior running lights darkened, suggesting that the craft's inhabitants were settling in for the night.

Dei tracked the child's party for a distance into the camp, then lost them in the area where the tents were thickest. Thoughtful, he rose, gathered his belongings, and headed back toward the *Cryptic Warning.*

Once aboard, he summoned the entire crew, seven including himself, into the small compartment that served as a dining, conference, and briefing area; it boasted one table and bench-style seating on either side, plus a chair at the end with its back to the compartment door. He took the chair. "So. Report."

Sazat, a purple-skinned Keshiri male Dei's own age, the team's archive analyst, started. "This is an ad hoc negotiation assembly. Officially unofficial; the planetary government seems to know it's happening, and it is technically illegal by the laws of the Hutts, who govern this world, but the government is not opposing the process, or acknowledging it."

Fardan pushed a flimsi printout over to Dei. It showed a schematic of the camp with areas marked off in splotches of colors, most of them strident warm colors such as yellow, orange, and red. "Except for the shield and weapons emplacements, the camp looks fairly primitive, but there's a lot of high-intensity communication going on. There are hypercomm units in at least two of the tents and four of the vehicles, including the Hapan vehicle. Enough broadcasting datapads to constitute a high-density pseudo-organic network."

Dei glanced at the printout and set it aside. "I'll probably need to enter camp. The shield generators are well placed, with overlapping coverage, so it won't be possible to fly in close and drop an explosive missile on the landing craft. I have to get close to Tenel Ka Djo with something very powerful and very lethal."

Fardan gave him an uncomfortable look. "She is a Jedi. An ex-Jedi. She has what you have, including a sense of impending trouble. If you approach with the intent of killing her, she will probably feel it. And we already know that her security detail is very, very efficient."

Dei smiled. "It has to be done, so it will be done. What do I need to get into camp?"

Viti, a fair-skinned human female, the youngest member of the crew, drew her long blond hair back across her shoulder in an attention-getting fashion she did not realize was patently obvious, and then pushed an identicard across the table to him. "Corporate Sector identification. You are a journalist for Heuristic Financial Analysis working on a report trying to determine the effect on the galactic economy of slave species achieving freedom and demanding higher wages."

Dei gave her a look that bordered on hostility. "That's as revolting and unaesthetic a profession as it's possible to have. You couldn't find a way to make me a sculptor?"

Taken aback, she offered a nervous little shake of her head. "No one would believe that you had any place at this meeting. You would be suspected, mocked—"

"I'm joking, Viti. This is perfect. I'll need a holocam."

"I put one on your bunk . . ."

"Well done." Dei pocketed the identicard. He did not mind putting Viti in occasional fear for her job or her life. She was far too determined to exploit her appeal. It could make her lazy or complacent. Occasionally a little shaking-up was in order. It kept her a good operative.

Dei returned his attention to Fardan. "I witnessed a delegation visiting the Hapan craft. One child, two droids. They waited until the craft appeared no longer to be under observation before they approached, and had an hour's visitation. I've copied my recordings to your station. Let me know what you and Sazat turn up on them."

"Yes, sir."

Dei looked around. "Anything else? No? Back to your stations, then, and commence sleep rotation. And be not just diligent in your duties, but brilliant. Brilliance will get you noticed and promote you out of exile with me." He smiled, rose before any of them could offer perfunctory objections to his self-deprecation, and left.

This time she managed not to scream.

Allana woke, thrashing her way free of her sheets, in danger of toppling off her bunk to the compartment floor. She stopped herself and rolled back out of harm's way.

There were tears on her cheeks again. She scrubbed them away. She waited a moment, listening, making sure that she hadn't awakened her grandparents, and then she sat up, hugging her knees to her chest, and tried to think.

Anji hopped up on her bunk, padded her way forward, bumped her head against Allana's shin.

Allana stroked the nexu. "I'm all right. It's all right."

But it wasn't.

In tonight's dream, the man made of fire was back. Again he had approached Tenel Ka from behind.

But this time Allana had been behind him, watching. When he approached her mother, Allana had shrieked and thrown herself on his back to stop him.

Her scream had not alerted Tenel Ka. But as Allana landed on the man's back, as her own body had begun to burn, Tenel Ka had felt her pain and turned. Her expression had been one of shock and loss. But she was ready to defend herself. That was Allana's last view of her mother. Allana had sunk, burning, into the fiery man's body.

Was that the way it had to be? Either Tenel Ka or Allana would die? That wasn't fair. It wasn't right.

And Allana couldn't go again to Leia. Her grandmother would say it was only a dream, that it was nothing to be worried about.

Well, Allana was *going* to worry. She just had to figure out what to do in addition to worrying.

Chapter Thirty-five

ARMAND ISARD CORRECTIONAL FACILITY, CORUSCANT

IN THE CITRUS-GREEN CORRIDOR LEADING TO THE VISitors meeting hall, Daala overtook Tahiri Veila, who was also dressed in a prison-yellow jumpsuit, also on her way to the hall. But Tahiri moved far more slowly than Daala. The Jedi, unlike the deposed Chief of State, was shackled at wrist and ankle with stun cuffs, a concession to the greater theoretical danger a fully trained Force-wielder posed. In addition, while Daala was accompanied by a standard, blocky security droid, Tahiri was escorted by a YVH combat droid—often a match for an armed and unrestrained Jedi, and certainly too great an obstacle for an unarmed and restrained one.

Daala fell in beside Tahiri. "So. Death."

Tahiri glanced sidelong at her. "You first. Comm me and let me know what it's like."

"I don't think so. I'll walk out of this wretched place. You'll be leaving in an urn. You killed a hero."

"How many have you killed? Including your enemies and your subordinates?"

Daala gave Tahiri a smile that she knew belonged on a toothed, cartilaginous fish. "At least I have friends and allies left. What was it like to receive the death sentence with no one left in the courtroom even pretending to care about you?"

"I expect I'll have friends again by the time I'm your age."

Daala resumed her earlier pace, leaving Tahiri behind. Being honest with herself, she considered that conversation no better than a draw, and she wasn't entertained by it.

Daala and her escort reached the admissions chamber into the visitors hall. Like most transition zones in the prison, this chamber was built along the paradigm of an air lock—heavily reinforced, with only one door, the hall side or the corridor side, capable of being opened at a time. Once she and her guard droid were inside, the hall-side door, built as though for a treasure vault, slid closed, and a hemispherical module studded with glows and readouts extended itself from the ceiling, scanning her. It would, she knew, determine the extent and nature of all prosthetics on her body, sniff for chemical explosives, take a sample brain scan and compare its patterns with those on record for her . . . time consuming, tedious, absolutely necessary.

Necessary when dealing with dangerous *criminals*. She fumed, but did not let the chamber's holocams see that.

Finally the opposite-side vault door opened, admitting her to another short green corridor. The corridor was wide, with ample seating on both sides, hard and uncomfortable-looking chairs in a darker industrial green; prison guards waited in a couple of those chairs. The security droid drew to the side and allowed Daala to proceed alone.

The door at the far end slid up to admit her into the visitors hall.

It was, depressingly, much like the ones she'd seen all her life in holodramas about prisons. This was a square chamber. One entire wall was made up of booths. Each booth had a chair and a table and was concealed from the booths right and left by partitions. Each faced a pane of reinforced transparisteel. On the other side of the transparisteel, out in the free world, was a corresponding chair and table for the use of visitors. About two-thirds of the booths were occupied.

The remainder of this room was open, dominated by three human guards and three security droids.

Daala announced herself to the droid stationed nearest the door. "Admiral Natasi Daala." She refused to use her prisoner number, and the facility's warden, perhaps as a gesture of respect, had not gone to any effort to discipline her when she failed to do so.

She'd have to remember that. The warden had visited her once and had shown her an acceptable, if minimal, level of respect. He was walking a tightrope between doing his duty and demonstrating sympathy, and Daala appreciated both his adroitness and his sentiments. When she returned to power, she'd have to look into the man and his record.

The droid gestured to one of the booths. "Number Six."

She sat at Number Six. Her visitor was already there. It was her attorney, Otha Tevarkian.

Except it *wasn't*. His resemblance to Tevarkian was striking. Like Tevarkian, he was about sixty, with fair hair just beginning to thin. His clothes were dark and expensive but unobtrusive, just like those of Daala's attorney. The briefcase resting on the tabletop before him was Tevarkian's, or identical to it—soft-sided, silver and blue, its latches currently undone. But the man's face was just a little different, a little less lined, the texture of his skin a little smoother. His eyes were a darker shade of blue.

Daala looked him over. "I have no idea who you are."

The man smiled. He withdrew a datapad from his briefcase and set it next to the transparisteel barrier. "Otha Tevarkian . . . sent a message to my employer, who contracted me to come visit you today. We are to discuss your escape."

Something like a mild electric shock coursed through Daala's body. Still, she had one of the galaxy's best sabacc faces and chose to betray no emotion. "You have my attention."

The false attorney smiled. "Good. Now, the problem with prisons, even maximum-security institutions, is that they have weak points that are concessions either to building and maintenance costs or to political and cultural expediency. For example, this chamber." He gestured, taking in the guards behind Daala, the visitors to his right and left. "It's very close to one of the exits from the facility, and this is because studies suggest that prisoners fare psychologically better if they receive ongoing support from their family and social circle, and that members of the family and social circle are more likely to visit if they are not much inconvenienced. Security concerns say that prisoners stay more secure if a visitors hall is deep within the secure boundaries of the prison; pragmatism says there are more visits if the visitors can walk in and walk out conveniently. Especially if the prison is on a mass-transit line." The false attorney gave her a that's-just-the-way-it-is shrug.

From his briefcase, he withdrew a stack of documents on flimsi. These looked thicker and stiffer than most flimsi.

The false Tevarkian saw her look and must have guessed her question. "Laminated. They last longer that way."

"Ah."

"That's the story, anyway." He turned the first of

them so that the printing faced Daala. He pressed it up against the transparisteel, just below the level of her head, and smoothed it into place. It adhered on its own. "I'm going to take these down in a few moments, but when I do, they'll leave the front facing of their laminate behind. Here we get into cost issues plaguing our prisons. The holocams watching this chamber are not of the highest quality. They and their operators will not see the laminate adhering to the transparisteel." He set another document precisely beside the first.

Daala glanced at the documents. One was a reproduction of the charges laid against her at her arraignment. The other was the first page of the transcription of her arraignment hearing.

She could keep her face emotionless, she could keep her voice level, but she couldn't keep her heart from racing. She was about to go into battle. "I take it the laminate is laced with some material—"

"I don't want to use the exact word, as it's a very potent one, and if a droid guard's audioreceptor picks up that word . . ."

"I understand."

"But the substance is a new, very exciting, crystalline boom-boom material." He set out a third document.

"Surely in quantities like this isn't it not more, um, potent than transparisteel is strong?"

"No, not at all. But again, cost-of-construction issues rear their ugly head. The force will be enough to kick the transparisteel out of its frame." He gave her a candid look. "I do a number of domicile insertions every year. If you reinforce a domicile against intrusion, you strengthen the doors and viewports. But the walls remain vulnerable. You find the weak spot, you exploit the weak spot."

"Just like in military tactics."

"So . . . in a minute, there will be nothing of consequence between us. And this facility will immediately seal up."

The false attorney had five pieces of flimsi on the transparisteel now. That was the entire stack. He began to take them down, carefully peeling them away from the barrier. Daala, though, could see the almost invisible rectangular patches of laminate that remained behind.

"Forgive me if I don't understand, but I would think that sealing this place would make it harder for us to walk out."

He gave her an admonishing look. "Yes, but there are times when a prison will not execute a shutdown under any circumstances."

"No, there aren't."

"You're thinking of military prisons, and with military prisons, you'd be correct. But this is a civilian prison. So. What circumstances?"

She shook her head.

He touched the rear edge of his datapad and then brought the same finger up to touch the first document. Daala saw, but no prison holocam was likely to be acute enough to see, the nearly transparent filament that stretched from the back of the datapad to the laminate clinging to the barrier.

The false attorney held his finger there for a moment, then withdrew it. The filament remained. "Think mercifully, Admiral. A shutdown involves sealing off all exits. Ventilation also shuts down."

"Which is the way it should be."

"Yes. But if there is a poison gas attack on the facility, shutting down the ventilation kills everyone inside."

"Your employer isn't going to use poison gas—"

"And if a disaster contaminates all the food and

water, and the prison is cut off from all relief, sealing all exits dooms the prisoners as well as the staff. So, by decrees dating back to the reforms of the New Republic, a prison experiencing such an event cannot be sealed. It has to rely on the staff to maintain security."

Daala gave him a suspicious look. "We're in the heart of Coruscant. This prison can't be cut off from all relief."

"Nor can the Senate Building experience a Yuuzhan Vong attack without the military having some clue that one is coming. Yet that exact thing seemed to happen . . . for a few crucial minutes . . . the day you were so seriously inconvenienced." The false attorney had now attached filaments to all five sheets of laminate.

Daala buried her face in her hands for a brief moment. "Standardized operational procedures."

"Correct! All prisons operated by the Galactic Alliance Department of Corrections, for consistency and to save costs, use the same basic computer system, which has to be able to handle a giant facility at the heart of Coruscant and a piddly little outpost on a remote moon near Dathomir. Same program, same emergency codes."

He replaced his documents in the case and closed the latches. "In a moment, I'm going to press a button on this datapad. This will begin a five-second countdown and transmit an automated signal to someone still active in the Department of Corrections who believes very strongly that you should be in charge of the Alliance. This person has set up an automated code that will be transmitted from a secure and unimpeachable control computer at the seat of government power, which will tell this prison's computer that it is now experiencing a poison gas attack *and* has been cut off from all relief or reinforcement by a Yuuzhan Vong assault." He shrugged. "My employer thought it was only justice to trip the Jedi with their own cord."

"And at the end of five seconds—boom-boom?"

"Boom-boom. And let me say, it's a delight to hear the legitimate leader of the Galactic Alliance talking baby talk."

She frowned at him, both because the remark was inappropriately personal and because there were still unresolved issues. "But this leaves me where you are, with guards and armor between me and freedom."

"At that point, it's all up to my employer. I can assure you, though, that immediately after boom-boom, I will no longer look as I do now, will no longer be carrying the identicard with which I entered this facility, will no longer have even the fingerprints or retinal patterns of Tevarkian. Oh, by the way, bear in mind that most of the boom-boom power is headed toward you." The false attorney pressed a button on the datapad. "Five."

Daala stared at him. He wasn't moving.

"Four."

Then she understood. He was playing Blink, a classic game of children, thrill-seekers, and military tacticians the galaxy over. Every species, every culture knew Blink. Sometimes called Swerve, sometimes named after particularly belligerent local animal species, it followed the same basic set of rules: two landspeeders, two military vehicles, two athletes would hurtle at each other, a move that, if it were to end in collision, would be at least very costly, at worst an example of mutually assured destruction. One, usually, would change direction an instant short of disaster. The other would win.

Daala could not help but grin.

"Three."

On the tabletop, she drummed her fingers.

"Two."

To his credit, the false attorney never looked nervous. But as the milliseconds counted down, as Daala's internal sense of alarm rose, he sat there grinning at her, and then suddenly he was gone, ducking below the level of the table.

Using her free hand, the one not drumming fingers in a show of nonchalance, Daala yanked herself down and slammed into the floor.

Chapter Thirty-six

UNLIKE DAALA, TAHIRI WAS ACCOMPANIED BY HER droid escort as she entered the visitors hall. The chamber's overseer droid directed her to Booth One, the farthest from the entrance. Her YVH droid took up position near the entryway while she shuffled to her booth. She passed behind Daala, who seemed deep in conversation with a well-dressed blond man.

Eramuth Bwua'tu awaited Tahiri on the other side of her booth viewport. The attorney had an encouraging if lupine smile for her. She took her chair but did not return the smile.

"Good morning, my dear." Bwua'tu cocked a furry eyebrow as he looked at her stun cuffs. "I'm working on a measure to get you out of those. Obviously it has lower priority than efforts to call for a dismissal of the results of your trial, or to demand a new trial altogether, but I am attacking your situation on all possible fronts."

"Thank you. But what are the odds?"

"It's not a question of odds but of time. We will prevail. Still, the longer it takes for the Jedi Order to leave the Chief of State's office, the more resentment the situation causes in the rank and file of common government officials, and the longer it will take for justice to manifest itself."

"That doesn't speak well for my chances of survival.

Honestly, if we can't get a new trial until after I'm executed, don't bother."

Bwua'tu shook his head. "We will overturn the death sentence."

"Which one? The one determined by the court, or the one that's inevitable when you're shackled in prison with a criminal population that's had forty years to learn to hate the Jedi?"

"You feel you are in danger?"

Tahiri sighed. "Probably no more than any other prisoner here. But the shackles reduce my ability to defend myself, and if the Force should fail to alert me, I could take a shiv to a vital organ as easily as anyone else." She gave Bwua'tu a look that she knew was half resignation. "I don't want to . . . but maybe I was meant to die here."

"Don't be ridiculous. You're speaking from depression brought on by the changes to your situation. Hang on to what's important to you, and your combative spirit, your survival instincts, will return."

"Sure."

From his pocket, Bwua'tu pulled a sheet of flimsi and unfolded it on the tabletop before him. "We need to discuss the appeals process. I know how I want to proceed, but you need to understand my tactics if you're to enhance them and improve your odds of achieving freedom. Shall I proceed?"

"Please."

Tahiri tried not to tune him out, but her mind would not fix firmly on his words. He spoke of the order of presentation of appeals, of unofficially seeking the aid of the Jedi Order, of convincing a documentarian doing a HoloNews series on irregularities in the court system to profile her—a measure that would exploit her appeal as well as give the public a better understanding of what had happened at her trial while their attention was on the loss of the *Fireborn* and on the Jedi takeover. She nodded and accepted each of his recommendations, barely retaining details from any of them.

Then she felt it, a tickle of alarm in the Force. Her eyes widened. "Eramuth, get down."

He froze midsentence. "What is it?"

"I don't know. Danger. *Get down!*"

Spry for an elderly Bothan, he went to the floor.

To Tahiri's right, a booth exploded. Noise hammered at her ears. Smoke roiled out from the destroyed booth. Droids standing well back from the booth on the secure side of the hall flew backward and smashed to the floor. Buffeted by the explosion's shock wave, Tahiri and her chair tilted toward the near wall and crashed to the floor.

Siren whoops filled the air. Tahiri rolled up to her knees to look around.

A transparisteel panel from one of the booths was now angled into the secure area, leaving a gap beneath it, and Chief Daala was in the process of scrambling through that gap.

Tahiri's eyes stayed wide. This was an *escape*.

She spared a glance for Bwua'tu. The attorney was scrambling to his feet, apparently unhurt.

She looked at the gap again. Daala was now through it, tumbling down to the floor on the far side, half masked by smoke from the explosion.

If this was an escape planned by Daala's friends or subordinates, surely it wouldn't end here. Surely the woman had a route out of the prison complex.

Tahiri glanced at Bwua'tu again. He was staring right at her. When she caught his eye, he shook his head. She didn't have to tap into the Force to know what he was thinking. *Don't.*

She sprinted toward Daala's booth.

And fell on her face. The ankle cuffs—

Her own moment of forgetfulness saved her life.

Blasterfire hammered into the booth viewport above her, heavy blasterfire from her YVH escort droid. The droid was not being careful of the lives of those near Tahiri—it sprayed her vicinity with blaster bolts irrespective of the other prisoners, who scrambled wildly to get clear of the danger.

Tahiri continued her forward fall into a roll. She suppressed an urge to call on the Force to speed her movements. The stun cuffs she wore, especially designed for Jedi, would detect the brain activity consistent with Force use in humans and shock her, depriving her completely of the ability to use the Force and probably of consciousness, as well. In fact, it would only be a matter of seconds before someone in a control chamber activated that shock anyway and she'd be helpless.

On the floor below Daala's booth, Tahiri sprang upward, slithering through the gap far more gracefully than Daala had. She did not go down to the floor on the far side. She gripped the top of the booth on that side and let her feet hang below the lower lip of the bent transparisteel panel, bringing her ankles together.

The YVH droid switched its aim from the transparisteel to her feet. It was a sensible, appropriate tactic—injure the Jedi and she would not be able to flee.

There was no emotion associated with the droid's decision to fire, no spike of alarm in the Force. Tahiri had to time it by what she saw. The instant the droid finished bringing its arm into line, she snapped her ankles apart.

Blasterfire erupted from the droid and smashed into the binding cable between her ankle cuffs. The sheer force kicked her legs up and backward. But the cable was sheared through—her legs were free, and the circuit the cable made between the cuffs, necessary for the restraints' shock function, was destroyed.

She dropped to the floor, onto an empty suit jacket

and a blond wig. She ignored them. She didn't have time to be curious. She held her wrists before her mouth and popped up like a hole-dwelling rodent, exposing only her head and hands to the gap in the booth.

The YVH droid was in midstride forward. Seeing her, it aimed and fired again, a near-instantaneous reaction.

Tahiri jerked several centimeters to one side and snapped her wrists apart as far as they would allow. Again heavy blasterfire sheared into her restraints. The cable parted and blasterfire hammered into her right-hand cuff, stinging and numbing her arm all the way to the shoulder. The force of the attack knocked her over backward. She felt a burning pain in her right wrist from a graze by one of the blaster bolts. But flat on her back, she was now free—as free as one could be in a planetary prison with guard droids and a YVH droid converging on her position.

Daala scrambled over her tabletop, fell to the floor beyond, looked around. Visitors buffeted by the explosion lay all over the floor, though there was little if any blood; the transparisteel barrier seemed to have sustained most of the force of the blast. A few visitors, meters away, had not fallen or were already rising. The false Tevarkian was gone—

No, he was a few meters off to her right, elbow-crawling, his jacket and shirt off, revealing medical scrubs beneath. His hair was black now. Only his suit pants and his physique gave him away as the man she'd been talking to. She elbow-crawled after him. The smoke was thicker immediately above, but here at floor level she had decent visibility.

She crawled across Tevarkian's discarded pants and shoes. Now the man ahead was fully dressed in scrubs.

There was a distant boom to her left. Daala thought it came from beyond the huge durasteel doors that allowed visitors entry into the hall. They were closed at the moment, not damaged in the least by the explosion.

Purple smoke began issuing from behind Daala and flooding the air above. She glanced back and saw that it was coming from her false lawyer's abandoned briefcase, which was on fire. A new tone joined the standard alarm cycle, a shrill note indicating a biohazard.

Daala grinned again. If it weren't so dangerous, this would have been a good show.

The doors out of the hall slid open. Hovering just on the other side, in the mostly empty hallway beyond, and now wreathed in the smoke that flowed out of the visitors hall, was a repulsor gurney, the type with a platform at one end to accommodate a pilot. Daala saw the false Tevarkian angle to crawl toward it. She followed.

There was a *whoosh,* rocket noise, and Boba Fett flew into the hall. He hovered just before the doors, the rocket thrust from his pack stirring the smoke into violent whirls, the green of his Mandalorian armor clashing with the smoke around him.

Daala's eyes widened. She'd never expected Fett to appear in a recognizable form. To do so was to invite retaliation from the Jedi now controlling the Chief of State's office. But there he was, big as life, hovering, scanning the visitors hall in his methodical fashion. Daala had to admit to herself that the man knew how to make an entrance.

The YVH droid was just reaching Booth Six when Tahiri, meters away, exerted herself through the Force. The bent sheet of transparisteel she'd crawled under bent farther, slamming into the droid, hammering it, sending it sprawling back into the secure area.

There. That would give her a good two seconds of breathing room. She rolled over, scanning the chamber before her, trying to sort details out of the confusion of running visitors, purple smoke, shrilling alarms—

And Boba Fett.

She gaped at the sight of him, floating into the chamber atop a column of fire and smoke, dominating the scene. But the door behind him was now open. Visitors were already running through it, seeking escape from the chaos and danger of the room. Tahiri got up and sprinted past Fett's rocket thrust. Just on the other side of the door, she spun, looking for the door's control panel, hoping to send the metal barriers slamming shut to trap the YVH droid inside. But there was none, not on this side or the other.

The YVH droid rose and charged toward Booth Six, its gait suggesting that it would leap through the gap.

Boba Fett tilted forward. The small missile atop his rocket pack flew free, striking the YVH droid in its torso. The droid and several meters around him were suddenly replaced by a fireball that glowed evilly in yellows and reds. Tahiri ducked sideways, getting behind the blast shield offered by the edge of the door. The metal wall between her and the explosion rang with its force.

She peeked out. There was nothing but a smoking crater where the YVH droid had stood. Perhaps it wasn't destroyed; an explosion that great could have picked it up and hurled it out of sight rather than destroying it, could have collapsed the floor and sent it plummeting to a lower level of the prison. But it was gone.

Chapter Thirty-seven

FETT ROARED OUT OF THE HALL. DIRECTLY IN FRONT of Tahiri, a black-haired man in health worker's clothes jumped onto the control stand of a repulsor gurney waiting there, and an instant later a woman in prisoner yellows leapt onto the gurney itself.

Daala.

The gurney accelerated into motion, following Fett.

Tahiri sprinted, drawing on the Force to boost her speed, and caught up to the gurney from behind. Its operator and Daala faced ahead, their eyes on Fett, so neither saw her. She grabbed the collar of the operator's tunic and yanked. As he tumbled off the back, she jumped on in his place and grabbed the controls. The gurney barely slowed or wobbled with the change of operators.

The hallway was full of purple smoke, shrieking visitors, and guards rushing toward the visitors hall. Some of the latter pointed blasters at the gurney. From above and ahead, Boba Fett fired his own blaster, sending them diving or scurrying for cover as the gurney roared past.

Tahiri couldn't help but grin. The gurney was accelerating up to speeder bike rates of travel. This was not a stock repulsor gurney fresh from the factory.

They passed through three sets of blast doors, all of them open, and Tahiri saw daylight ahead. Suddenly they were out in an exercise yard. Streams of blasterfire from tower emplacements converged on Boba Fett, but he was too nimble, too adept in the air for any of the bolts to hit him.

Almost any of them. Tahiri saw a blast strike the center of his chest armor, dent it, turn the point of impact black. Fett spun in the air. The antenna on the side of his helmet swung free, dropping into the exercise yard. But his forward momentum was unchecked. As he completed a full spin, he regained control and his original course.

And then he and the gurney were outside the wide-open exterior gate.

Fett turned to starboard and accelerated. Tahiri followed. She knew Fett was no friend of hers, nor of any Jedi or former Jedi, but he clearly had an exit strategy.

Two quick kilometers farther, along a channel between two lengthy banks of skytowers, Tahiri saw what it was. On a pedway platform one level up was a large, curved shape beneath a sheet of silver reflective flimsi. Fett flew on ahead and landed beside it. He reached up and grabbed a fold of the cover. Hauling hand over hand, he pulled the flimsi free, revealing the distinctive curvilinear shape of *Slave I,* his personal spacecraft.

Tahiri piloted the repulsor gurney to land on that pedway a few dozen meters from *Slave I.* She brought the vehicle to a rapid stop.

Daala turned toward Tahiri, her mouth opening to say something, and then she realized it was not the man she expected to be standing there. Her jaw dropped.

Tahiri stepped off the controller's platform. She gave Daala a broad smile and a mock salute. "Thanks for the rescue." Then she slipped over the pedway rail and dropped into the chasm beyond.

With the Force she shoved herself laterally a few meters, enough to bring her feet into contact with the building front beside her. Just this once she was grateful for footwear; if she'd been barefoot as she preferred, the building's stone face would have sanded her skin to a bloody ruin. She maintained the pressure provided by the Force for a few meters of sliding descent, then leapt free, straight into the back of an open-topped orange-and-black family airspeeder.

The pilot and the man beside her, both Sullustans, turned back to look.

Tahiri gave them a frank stare. "I'm an escaped federal prisoner and I'm very dangerous. If you cooperate, I'll accept a ride from you and leave you within a few minutes. If you don't, I'll steal your speeder. Your choice."

The driver jabbered at her in the musical tones of the Sullustans and shrugged.

Daala gaped over the rail. She looked up at Fett. "That was Tahiri Veila."

He didn't answer. He pressed a button on his forearm. The front hatch of *Slave I* swung up and open. It seemed curiously wobbly. He waved her forward, his body language impatient.

She ran to join him. A human male, large and young, probably an athlete, stepped into her path. Maybe he recognized her prison jumpsuit and imagined he'd earn a reward. He reached for her. She kneed him in the groin, cracked her palm against his jaw, and shoved his semiconscious body out of the way, barely noticing him. She reached Fett's side.

But it wasn't Fett. *Slave I* was creaking like cheap duraplast. Beyond the open hatch she could see that the interior was mostly empty space—a duraplast shell attached by cables and spars to a late-model, high-performance airspeeder.

Fett's armor hadn't merely been dented by the blaster shot he'd taken; a portion of it had been burned away.

Far from being high-grade Mandalorian armor, this was protection on a par with standard-issue stormtrooper armor. And Fett's antenna was gone, broken off where it normally attached to his helmet.

She gaped at him. "Who *are* you?"

But his voice was pure Boba Fett. "Get in. If you want to escape."

She got in.

The first GA Security pursuit airspeeder came within sight of *Slave I* as the vehicle lifted off and accelerated away. *Slave I* immediately dived, ignoring traffic lanes, picking up speed in its descent.

The pursuing security speeder dived in its wake. The pilot, an Ortolan, blue-skinned and pachydermal, activated the external speaker. "*Slave One.* We have you surrounded. Heave to and prepare to be boarded . . . or destroyed."

His partner, a human female with hair as blue as the Ortolan's fur, was on her comlink, reporting their location, course, and speed.

The pilot clamped his jaw shut as he came out of the dive. He piloted one of the more powerful security airspeeders around—he had to, in order to be useful in a pursuit situation, since by himself he massed three times as much as a human male—and the maneuver of pulling out of his dive drove him deep into the pilot's seat.

Slave I did not heave to. Nor, for that matter, did it speed up to outpace its pursuer. It simply blasted along, getting out of the way of cross-traffic with a sluggishness the Ortolan found surprising, given its reputation. Boba Fett ignored all comm and loudhailer commands.

More security speeders dropped into the pursuit, some behind the Ortolan, some ahead of *Slave I*, some above and below the chase. In barely a minute a dozen speeders surrounded the fleeing craft.

Finally its pilot appeared to accept the inevitable. *Slave I* descended to a landing platform large enough to accommodate it. It landed, an awkward grounding that caused it to bounce once, and sat there, rocking in the winds that sometimes howled around Coruscant sky-towers.

The Ortolan grounded immediately behind *Slave I*. He and his partner left their speeder, drew blaster pistols, and, with security agents from other speeders, approached the craft.

When they were three meters away, the front hatch opened.

The Ortolan peered in. He saw the interior, all open space and an enviably muscular airspeeder with a spindly plate-topped mechanic droid at the controls. The droid looked at him and raised its arms.

There was no one else in the seats or elsewhere in the shell.

He sighed loudly enough to cause his trunk to wobble. "Report this. We've been chasing a decoy."

Just minutes before, wrapped up in a voluminous rainproof garment that fit her like a tent, a crude blond wig on her head, Daala had stood not three meters from the ersatz *Slave I* and watched the craft lift off. Beside her, Boba Fett, draped in a similar rain garment, its hood up to shadow his features, his helmet in a bag under his arm, also watched the liftoff. Moments later the craft dived into the permacrete canyon beyond, pursued by an oversized security speeder.

Fett gestured. "This way."

Daala remained silent while they walked to a parked speeder, as innocuous and homely a brown as one could find on fashion-conscious Coruscant. Fett at the controls, they lifted off.

Another two kilometers away, they set down at a

small-craft charter and rental firm and stepped into a *Lambda*-class shuttle. Fett gestured for her to take the controls. "The course is already plotted. You need merely transmit it, wait for authorization, and lift off."

"Where will *you* be?"

"Changing." He went aft and shut the cockpit door behind him.

Daala did as instructed, and minutes later achieved Coruscant high orbit. She called up the second portion of the course, a plot to take the shuttle outside the planet's gravity well, and maneuvered in that direction.

Fett emerged from the rear compartment. He had left the rocket pack behind, but that was not the only change. The burn crater was gone from his chest and the antenna was restored to his helmet. Daala gave him a careful look. This was indeed the real Boba Fett. She nodded. "I think I understand."

"Good of you." He sat in the copilot's seat and bent over the control board as if double-checking her course.

"Boba Fett showed up at the prison to rescue me. That naturally intimidated, even terrified, the guards and everyone else. But careful study of holocam recordings of the rescue will show that the rescuer was wearing false Boba Fett armor. Therefore they will conclude it was not the real Boba Fett."

Fett nodded. "An impression enhanced by the use of a false *Slave One*. The droid I modified to pilot that craft will have holocam recordings that reinforce these ideas. The freelancer who portrayed Tevarkian wore the false armor in those recordings."

"I don't even know when Jedi Veila replaced him. Is he in the hands of the guards?"

"No. He has reported in safe."

Daala breathed out a sigh of relief. It was odd for her, since she was relieved on behalf of someone who had just committed a high-level crime and could well be a lifelong professional criminal. "And so you have plausible deniability, and you avoid drawing yourself or the Mandalorians into a dispute with the Jedi. Did you alter your body language, too?"

"I did." He turned to look at her. "The real *Slave One* is within the Coruscant system, at the orbit of the outermost planet. We will rendezvous with her and get you to a place of safety."

"Thank you. The terms I offered in my communication were sufficient?"

"They'll do."

Fett leaned back in his seat. "You intend to fight to regain political power?"

"To regain a leadership role, Fett. The galaxy needs leadership."

"Yes . . . Where would you like me to take you so that you can begin?"

Daala thought about it, about resources, about alliances that she had foolishly set aside years before. There really was only one answer. And she told him what it was.

Chapter Thirty-eight

KLATOOINE

Now dressed appropriately to the planet and terrain, carrying identification that would pass at least casual verification, Querdan Dei stood, inconspicuous, in the shadows of the awning of a tent from which a Klatooinian female sold chilled drinks and personal cooling devices to credulous offworlders. Dei bought another drink every half an hour so that the proprietor would not resent his continued presence.

There was a broad strip of open sand before him, and on the other side of it the largest tent of the encampment, a canopy suited to a circus. It was the political center of the gathering, the place where the leaders of several disparate, half-cooperative, half-feuding rebellion movements were now trying to make themselves more attractive to the Galactic Alliance while maintaining an attitude of rugged independence. It was like a mating dance among unshaven human males, each trying to attract a female while intimidating rivals.

The place was well defended. In addition to guards posted at intervals around its circumference, Dei saw small turbolaser cupolas at four points along its perimeter, sensor devices and sensor droids all around, and indications—from the way camp workers meticulously restored sand blown away by the winds—that there were probably additional sensors in a net buried just under the surface. Somewhere nearby, another tent would be loaded with monitoring stations where data from all those sensors would be under constant analysis. Dei suspected that the main tent's interior would also feature shields, possibly as strong as those carried by a starfighter, projecting their protective fields in an overlapping pattern.

Between Dei and the big tent, out on the hot open sands just short of the clear area maintained by guards, a group of ragged children, mostly Klatooinian, played. It was a local game called Return. Dei had learned about it this morning. The captain of one team, standing alone, would hurl a round ball to an ally in the crowd of other players. The receiver would then attempt to run it back to him through a gauntlet of opponents. The receiver could toss it to any ally except the captain, but there was a danger of it being intercepted, and when running with the ball, the carrier might be borne to the ground and drop the ball. If a member of the other team got the ball, play would stop and that player would become the captain for the next throw. Twice now guards had had to shoo the players back a few meters from the clear zone.

Finally the party of politicians Dei had been waiting for arrived. He recognized the Solos, their Galactic Alliance guards . . . and, interestingly, the dome-topped astromech and gold protocol droid that had visited the Hapan landing craft the previous night. Preliminary research had told Dei that they belonged to the Solos. In addition there were several more heavily robed strangers, most wearing veils over their faces. They walked before, behind, and among the Solo family party, conversing with the Solos and their guards.

Dei nodded. Probably the Hapan contingent. The Hapans' security unit must have been directed to converse with the Alliance security agents, all very informal, causing trouble to an observer trying to sort out who was who.

Dei reached up to his collar and, while innocuously scratching his neck, pressed a button on the comlink hidden beneath folds of cloth.

As the Solos and Hapans entered the clear belt of sand, one of the Klatooinian players of the ball game strode up to the current captain, a red Twi'lek boy. The Klatooinian child growled angry words at him and snatched the ball, then pushed the captain down. His body language contemptuous, he hurled the ball away, paying no attention to direction. It went straight toward the Solos and Hapans. It hit the sand a few meters from the nearest of them and rolled onward.

The party reacted much as Dei expected. The nearest veiled woman hurled herself on the ball. Veiled individuals and Alliance guards formed up in front of the Solos and three of the veiled Hapans. Not all of them interposed themselves between the errant ball and the individuals they were protecting; several turned outward, covering against possible attacks from other directions.

Interestingly, the astromech, which had been in the midst of the pack of veiled individuals, maneuvered to be in front of one of the Hapans, and the protocol droid tottered to stand behind the same woman, its metal-plate hands up in a placating gesture, its voice dimly audible in a wail of unease. The woman the astromech had moved to protect turned and offered the protocol droid a few words—of reassurance, if her accompanying gesture was any indication. When she gestured, she was careful not to let her robe gape open too widely, and Dei had no opportunity to observe her left arm.

The Klatooinian child advanced toward them all,

speaking in the half-growling, half-barking language of his kind, gesturing angrily at the woman lying atop his ball. He ignored the angry calls and words being directed at him by the other players.

Several members of the Solo–Hapan party laughed. Others, still on high alert, didn't. The woman on the sand rose from atop the ball, her body language a bit sheepish, and kicked the ball so it rolled back to the boy. The boy retrieved it and ran back to his fellows, no longer aggressive, then handed it to the Twi'lek he'd shoved.

The situation resolved, several members of the party continued on into the big tent. Others moved to take up guard positions around the site.

The droids in particular interested Dei. The astromech had clearly moved to protect one of the Hapans. Why had it not moved to protect the Solos, its owners? Probably simply because it was farther from the Solos than the Hapan woman. It clearly had some regard for her survival. Odds were high that the woman it had sought to shield was Tenel Ka Djo, a personal friend of the Solos. This suggested an unusual assertiveness and courage on the part of the droid, but it was clearly not programmed for tactical thinking, else it would not have betrayed the identity of Tenel Ka in that fashion.

Tenel Ka's concern for the protocol droid was another point of interest. Droids that cared about a Hapan queen, a Hapan queen who cared about droids. The seed of a plan began to sprout in Dei's mind.

He lingered at the tent, bought another chilled drink. The ball game continued for a time, until its members began to drift off toward other diversions. At last, the only one left was the boy who had thrown the ball toward the Hapans.

Now, tossing it from hand to hand, he missed catching it and it rolled toward Dei. Dei trapped it with his foot, rolled it atop his boot, and bounced it up into his hand. When the boy approached, Dei returned it to him—the ball and, inconspicuously, a few high-value credcoins. He gave the Klatooinian boy an approving little nod. "Well done. I will contact you if I need you again."

The boy bared teeth in a fierce Klatooinian smile and left.

Allana stared up at the much taller figure beside her. In addition to answering questions, Javon was turning out to be useful at blocking out the sun. "How much time do we have?"

Javon checked his chrono. "See-Threepio will be back at the *Falcon* for your next lesson in forty-three minutes, thirty seconds—mark!"

She laughed. He'd gotten in the habit of giving all times down to the minute and second, with exaggerated importance, as if it were crucial to know the split second when the tent selling the little berry pies would have the next batch ready.

Today Allana's guards were all in desert dress. Without the droids to make them more conspicuous, Javon had decided that everyone assigned to Allana should blend in with the crowds. Another one of his tactics; consistency of appearance, he'd told Allana, could make it easier for opponents to recognize and monitor her and her security detail.

Today Allana led the way in another sightseeing tour of the camp. There really wasn't that much of interest to an eight-year-old, but getting out and meandering was certainly better than remaining cooped up in the *Falcon*, waiting to do more studying.

It was at the midpoint of the camp, where an open field had become the center of argument, debate, and speech making among the disparate groups, that she felt a little thrill of dread. She shivered. Anji looked up at her, studying her face, but she merely gave the nexu an absent stroke to reassure her.

What had it been? Allana looked around for the stray air-conditioning outlet that might have blown some chill air across her, for the exposed electrical cable she might have brushed against to cause her to vibrate. But there was nothing like that near her.

There was just a man walking away from her, his head bowed in thought. He wore garments consistent with the others in the camp, anonymous and practical. He was tall, lean, probably a human—though from the back, with his features concealed by the sun hood he wore, she could not be sure.

He reminded her a little of her father, alone and resolute and, yes, somehow dark.

Perhaps it was that comparison, that realization that did it. Now a little twinge in the Force told her there was something in this man to worry her.

"Amelia? Is something wrong?" Javon was suddenly standing over her, his shadow spilling across her.

She looked up at him, shook her head. "Just thinking. Let's go this way." Without giving him time to object, she darted down a side path, a walkway between close-set tents, then turned ninety degrees and trotted in the same direction the man had been traveling, paralleling his course.

Javon kept up. She heard him murmuring, his tone unconcerned, into his comlink, directing the travel of the other members of his detail.

Allana continued at a brisk pace across a quarter of the encampment, then turned rightward again and stopped at the intersection with the main path.

It was only a few moments before she saw him, that introspective figure. From the front, he was definitely human, fair-skinned, but he did not look so much like her father. He was older, his face more creased. His eyes automatically moved over everyone crossing his path, but Allana did not think he was looking at them, except to register their movements in case they should turn out to be threats.

There was something more to him. She didn't know whether it was something supernatural, as though he were a wicked wizard from a children's holodrama come to life, or whether she had felt his presence in the Force. The Force made more sense—it was real, and it was always around her.

Her father and her grandmother could always tell when Allana was staring at them, and she knew she was staring at this man. So she tried to make herself small in the Force, a tiny dot, not worth seeing. It was the same as hiding during hide-and-go-seek but without the happy anticipation of the game itself. She also wrapped her desert cloak around herself and gestured to Anji to stay close.

The man passed where she stood. He glanced at her, a look that took in her presence but did not seem to fix on her, and up at Javon. Then he was past.

Allana tried not to react. When he had looked at her, she had felt something. He wasn't on fire, but she thought he was perhaps the man from her nightmares, or someone related to that man. And he was strong in the Force. She could tell.

Javon cleared his throat.

She looked up at him. "I'm doing exercises." It was almost the truth. What she'd been doing was an exercise in the Force. Now she worked to maintain it, her smallness, as she turned after the man she was studying. She followed him.

She did not look at him, not directly. She knew he might feel her eyes on him. She looked around him and concentrated on remaining a tiny little thing.

He walked toward the east, angling a little to the south, and reached the edge of camp. He passed beyond its borders and walked by one of the big tracked shield generators, heading along the path beaten by many feet that led to a gentle series of rises that would take hikers to the top of the eastern ridge.

Allana stood at the edge of camp. She couldn't keep going; she would be too conspicuous. She half watched the strange man as he ascended that slope and disappeared over the ridge.

She looked up at Javon. "I think I need to go back for my lesson."

He checked his chrono. "You still have twenty minutes."

"That's all right. I'm through playing."

Reentering the large tent, Han ignored the eyes of the mixed bag of security operatives staring at him. None of them liked the fact that he had a blaster on his hip or that he had a reputation for knowing how to use it. None of them, in fact, were happy that any other delegation was allowed to bring blasters into this gathering. But not one of the independent-minded delegations was willing to give up its weapons. And that suited Han just fine.

He moved to take a seat near Leia and did his best not to slouch. He preferred to slouch wherever possible, of course, but sometimes it just didn't reflect well on Leia, and this was one of those times.

Tenel Ka was in the midst of offering another argument. "Yes, Padnel, any Alliance politician and any Jedi leader can be replaced at any time, and those respective bodies can theoretically renege on anything promised by the ousted representatives. This is why neither Jedi Solo nor I tend to speak in absolutes. But both of us, and any leader with any experience, must weigh in the factors of political and social momentum. There continues to be momentum in favor of the freedom movements. Momentum in the diminishment of the influence of slave-owning species and corporations. When it is impossible to fully trust individuals, one can put some faith in the inevitability of these movements."

Padnel shook his head. "There is only one means to progress. Receive an oath of honor from all involved . . . and kill those who break it. This teaches future generations not to break their word. If someone on the playing field will not swear such an oath, it is because he intends to go back on his declaration, or at least have the latitude to do so."

Leia tried a different angle. "That's an admirable way to look at it . . . and very Klatooinian. But not all participants in this negotiation are Klatooinian. Even when everyone speaks Basic, the language of politics is dramatically different from culture to culture."

"I understand that." Padnel's voice was descending to near-growl levels. "So everyone should speak as Klatooinians do."

A soft chime sounded, indicating the start of the midday meal break. Han saw relief on the faces of several of the participants. Clearly, everyone needed a break from the tension of this deadlocked argument.

In pairs and small groups, the participants rose, made temporary farewells, and left the tent. Padnel huddled with Reni Coll and his Chev adviser off in one corner. This left only Han and Leia among the seats used for the negotiations.

Han leaned in toward his wife and dropped his voice to a whisper. "Not going well, huh?"

"On the contrary, I'm delighted to be working with Padnel Ovin. It's good for our marriage. It reminds me, from minute to minute, that you're *not* the most stubborn man in the galaxy."

He gave her a mock scowl. "Who says I'm not?"

"Han . . ."

"Sweetheart, I was outside for a lot of the last discussion. I *think* I get what's happening, but I'd like to be sure. Boil it down for me."

"All right." Leia glanced over at Padnel's group. "Klatooine is the site of the freedom movement most likely to result in a world viable for admission into the Alliance. That admission would reassure the other movements that they are being taken seriously and have a path by which they can achieve legitimacy. But the Council of Elders here needs a figurehead who can be the focus of popular support, a front man or woman, whom they can point at to credit—or blame—for this change in their ancient policy. It's a policy of strict adherence to an old treaty with the Hutts, a treaty that didn't have an exit clause. They want and need to be able to say, *We had no choice, that one's leadership was too compelling.* The problem is, the two leading contenders are too flawed. Reni Coll is smart enough to manage the organization and make the strong political decisions a point person must, but she lacks charisma. Padnel has the charisma, but he's sticking to certain points that disqualify him to various potential supporters. If he acts like a galactic-level politician and condemns his brother's action aboard the frigate *Fireborn,* he loses his core supporters in the Sand Panthers. He'll do it if certain parties make blood oaths he believes he can count on, but not otherwise. And he's never going to get those oaths."

Han nodded. "So you're leaning toward Padnel, but only if he decides to grow a brain stem."

"Elegantly put . . . yes."

"Well, I can fix this."

She gave him a suspicious look. "Dropping a concussion bomb on the camp doesn't constitute fixing the problem."

"No, I mean, I can persuade Padnel to condemn the *Fireborn* thing, making him a viable candidate. Or maybe he'll go berserk and kill everyone here. Either way, the stalemate will be broken."

She looked at him more closely. "How would you do that?"

"Well, if I explained, you wouldn't believe me. Or I can just do it. It'll take less than five minutes."

"Han—"

"Trust me, Leia."

"Oh, you womp rat. How can you throw out that 'trust me' skifter at a time like this?"

"I'm serious. Trust me." He batted his eyes at her.

"Stop doing that." She scowled at him, the bad-mood-Leia look that had so suited her during imprisonment on and escape from the first Death Star, so many, many years before. Then she relented. "All right. Do it."

He stood, gave her a cocky grin, and moved over to the buffet table. He picked up a particularly lush-looking round fruit and walked over to Padnel's party.

Padnel, Reni, and Nialle looked up.

Han bit into the fruit, made a pleased expression at its tartness, and swallowed. "Not going well, huh?"

Padnel grunted a barely polite reply.

"I think I've got the problem figured out."

Reni cocked an eyebrow at him. "And what is the problem?"

"It's that Padnel here has the brains of a sand flea."

Padnel stood. Though he was no taller than Han, he was far burlier, an intimidating, looming presence. "What did you say?"

"Work with me, Padnel, I'm giving you words of all one syllable. Sand flea. Brains of a sand flea. Which is how you'll go down in the historical records. *Doomed the Klatooinians to another twenty-five centuries of slavery because he had the brains of a sand flea.*"

Padnel nodded as if considering that possibility for the first time. "I am going to kill you now. Unless you apologize."

"Sand fleas don't kill people. Smugglers kill people."

"That's it." Padnel reached toward his holster.

And froze as Han's blaster jammed into his snout, pushing it out of shape. Han put about a kilo of pressure on the trigger. He heard the *thump* as his dropped fruit hit the floor of the tent. In his peripheral vision, he could see the eyes of Reni and Nialle widen, but he didn't know whether it was because of the danger the blaster posed or because of the speed of his draw.

He also heard several other noises. A creak from Leia's chair as she rose. Scrapes of metal on leather as Klatooinian guards drew their blasters. One of them spoke harsh words in Basic: "Drop your weapon or I will open fire."

Han breathed a sigh of relief that he hadn't heard Leia's lightsaber activate.

He ignored the speaker. "Now we have a situation where you can prove that you have more brains than a sand flea. Consider this. Your political rival, Reni Coll, is standing next to you. All she has to do is sneeze. That big jowly fellow over there with the blaster rifle twitches and fires. I die. In my death spasm, I pull this trigger and blow your head off, and you die. Reni can accomplish the perfect murder—and she'll never be blamed for any crime, and she'll be the uncontested candidate for Klatooinian rebellion leader."

Padnel, his hand frozen partway to his own blaster pistol, scowled. "You draw very fast for an aging human."

"Don't I, though? But I have a simple answer for that. I'm a wily old veteran, and you're nothing but a slave."

"Another insult I will have to kill you for."

Han grinned. "I think that sneeze is starting to overwhelm Reni."

Reni shook her head. "I would not do that. It would be dishonorable."

Padnel did not turn his head—to do so would be to crush his snout more painfully against Han's barrel—but he did look sidelong at the guards. "Holster your weapons. At once."

They did, growling to themselves.

Han nodded approvingly. "Good. Now understand something. I said you had the brains of a sand flea not because you do, since you don't, but as an illustration of my other point, that you're a slave, which you are."

"Explain that."

"Happy to. If I'd wandered into this tent an hour ago and told you, *I command you to stand up, grab at your blaster, fail to get it into your hand, and look like an idiot,* would you have done it?"

"No."

"But you did. I made you do it. I walked up here intending that you do this thing, and you did it exactly as I wanted, because you're a slave. If you can be counted on to do certain things when people say or do certain things to you, you are a slave. A button-operated droid. Trust me, I know, I've been one, in the spice mines of Kessel, the most famous and prestigious slave gig in the galaxy. The Sand Panthers know you won't condemn what Grunel did, and that's fine by them, because it means they can continue to do their fighting outside the law, since they'll never go legitimate under you. The Council of Elders know you're the tool of the Sand Panthers, so they won't throw their weight behind you, but because you want to lead, they can lure you around and make you dance for their bait. And all your political opponents need to do is question your love of your brother to keep you pinned in place like an insect in a collection. At no point during this whole process do you grow up to be a free man."

Padnel stared at him for long, hard seconds, then finally spoke. "Put your blaster away."

Han withdrew it a few centimeters, twirled it, and holstered it. "Going to kill me now?"

"I should." But instead, Padnel turned away and headed for the tent flap, his body language stiff, furious. When Nialle and his guards moved to follow him, he waved them back and departed alone.

Reni heaved a sigh and looked at Han. Hers was the expression of a sabacc player who'd just been bluffed out of the pot.

Han moved to stand beside Leia. She seemed at ease, but Han had seen her take that balanced, poised stance plenty of times. It meant she was a fraction of a second from drawing and striking with her lightsaber.

He smiled at her. "Lunch?"

They walked out into the sun.

Leia gave him a pensive look. "If I've grasped what just happened, you've manipulated Padnel into standing up against people who he now thinks have been manipulating him all along, whether or not they really have. And he'll do it by condemning the destruction of the *Fireborn* because you've led him to believe that's the only way he can assert his independence."

Han nodded. "That's about the size of it."

"How, exactly, did that work?"

"No man under a certain age, or under a certain intelligence rating, can stand to be called a little boy holding on to his mother's knee. I've fallen for that one plenty of times myself. Luke's done it to me. You've done it to me. I knew I could do it to Padnel. After all, he has the brains of a sand flea."

"Join me, Han, and we can rule the galaxy as wife and husband."

He shuddered. "How about lunch with Allana instead?"

"All right."

Chapter Thirty-nine

HERKAN BASE, GOLAN III SPACE DEFENSE NOVAGUN, ABOVE NAM CHORIOS

THE NEW SHIFT OF GUNNERY CREW MEMBERS FILED off the shuttle, through the air lock, and into the station. A few meters down the first corridor was a security station, little more than a desk blocking half the corridor and a bored-looking human Alliance Army corporal waving a scanner at the identicards and orders cards presented by each crew member.

One member of the relief crew, a lean young woman with reddish brown hair mostly tucked up under her army billed cap, knelt to adjust the closure on her right boot. By the time she'd finished and risen, all the other members had passed the desk.

She moved to it but did not hold up any cards for the corporal to scan.

He glanced at her, noted her rank markings. "Where are your orders, Private?"

She waved as if to indicate she didn't know, but her gesture was oddly graceful. Her voice was low and mellow when she spoke. "You don't need to scan my orders."

"I don't need to scan your orders."

"I'm here on special assignment. If you delay me, the general will be angry."

"The general will be angry."

"In fact, it might be better if you forgot you ever saw me."

He nodded, his eyes blank. "Better."

Jysella passed him and breathed a sigh of relief. Waiting for days on Koval Station, gathering information on weapons-platform shift changes and security measures, had paid off. Now she was aboard the platform and, for the moment, undetected.

With luck and skill, she'd be able to accomplish her mission here and tip the balance of any engagement that might threaten the mistress of the *true* Jedi Order.

CRYSTAL VALLEY

Atop a crystal sand dune overlooking the outskirts of the township of Crystal Valley, Luke lay prone and studied the town through his macrobinoculars. The sun's dim violet rays offered no comfort; the sand was far more successful at affecting him, leaching heat from his body despite his insulating layers of clothes.

He lowered the macrobinoculars. "Standard pump station access building about a third of the way in. Most of the accesses will be in its lower levels. There are supposed to be emergency exit hatches outside the building, but I can't make them out."

To Luke's left, also prone, was Ben, and beyond him lay Kandra. She studied her datapad. "I can't get into the municipal system. Comm waves are all fouled up. Part of the information blackout I told you about, I'll bet."

The Gamorrean lying to her left grunted at length.

Kandra stared at him. "No, we shouldn't leave. I want to get recordings of this Abeloth."

Luke shook his head. "They might be the last recordings you ever make. You should get back to Hweg Shul, edit your story, and prepare to file it when I give you the go-ahead . . . or when you've heard bad news about me."

"But we don't know this is where she is. If Beurth and I leave, you might not be able to tell us where you're going next."

Luke looked down at the town. "No, she's here."

Kandra gave him a dubious look. "How do you know? The Force?"

"Not exactly. The tsils don't understand directions the same way we do, don't understand locations or map coordinates, but they have a concept of proximity. When I communed with them this morning before dawn, the ones nearest here were uneasy, if that's an applicable word. Almost mournful. I think she's using her dark-side powers to create sorrow in those around her, and it's spilling over to the spook-crystals."

Kandra sighed. "Esoteric stuff like that is a very hard sell to the viewing public."

Ben snorted. "Work an advertisement for droch spray into your story instead. Nam Chorios is the only planet where they need it, but I bet you can use scare tactics to sell it all over the galaxy."

"Good idea . . . so what do we do next?"

To Luke's right, Vestara lowered her own macrobinoculars but did not take her eyes off the town. "We wait for the next big dust flurry and sneak in. We patch directly into the city computer network's land cables and find out where those hatches are. Then we go in. The Skywalkers and I, I mean. Not you, unless you're determined to get killed."

Kandra started to reply, but Luke interrupted. "You can have it both ways, Kandra. Get your recording of Abeloth, do us another big favor, and stay safe."

She looked at him, suspicious. "How?"

"While we're doing the network slicing, you and Beurth acquire us some extra comlinks and datapads. Plus, even more important, a few kilometers of shielded data cable. We'll set up a series of data links to relay data out of the pumping station, and one on the surface, attached to a cable you run out beyond the comm jamming. We'll get you some images of Abeloth; you stay outside the jamming range and leave with your prize."

She thought about it. "Deal."

An hour later one of the periodic dust storms rose, dropping visibility to a few meters. The five of them got up and headed into town. At its outskirts, along the lengthy back wall of a cu-pa stable, they found a municipal data and power junction box. Ben popped the cover and spliced into the datajacks.

In moments he found what they needed, an old emergency evacuation document including a map showing exit points from the pumping station. Luke chose the one that was least likely to be under observation at any time, a hatch located in the middle of a broad topato field. "We'll rendezvous there in twenty minutes."

It took Ben, Luke, and Vestara a total of two minutes to reach the field and sneak out to the hatch. The hatch, a durasteel disk with a weatherproof alphanumeric keypad and a large metal ring to dog and undog the lock, was the cap of a permacrete cylinder protruding about a meter above the ground.

Ben gave his father a curious look. "I was kind of expecting us to go to one of the other hatches and leave those two behind. To keep them safe."

Luke gestured for him to get to work on the hatch security. "No, we actually need the relay setup I asked for. We do; the galaxy does."

Vestara offered him a puzzled frown. "Why?"

"Jedi secret."

She made a noise of exasperation. "Not exactly trusting of you."

"Correction—Jedi *Grand Master* secret. You'll notice I'm not telling Ben, either."

Ben concentrated on the keypad embedded in the hatch surface. "My dad neglects and abuses me."

"True," Luke said. "And when you become a father, you'll discover how much fun that is."

Ten minutes later Kandra and Beurth arrived. Kandra carried a cloth bag bulging with what had to be small duraplast boxes. Beurth had, over his shoulder, a spool of cable half the height of a man. Both approached in bent-over, holodrama-spy fashion, though the ongoing dust storm made such a measure unnecessary.

Luke looked over their bounty. "Datapads and comlinks in the bag?"

Kandra nodded. "Brand new. We broke in the back of an electronics shop and robbed the place. Well, sort of robbed. We left all our credcoins and some generic credcards as payment."

Luke unrolled the end of the cable from the spool and turned to Beurth. "Dig a little furrow—your boot heel will do fine—out to the edge of the field, then along any dirt or sand street, out to the edge of town. Then lay the first section of cable in that furrow and cover it over. I don't want the cable to be visible to anyone in town. Then roll the spool out as far as the cable will go and attach the last datapad at that point."

Beurth grunted, nodded, and got to work on his task.

"Got it." Ben unhooked his datapad from the hatch's exterior jack, then tapped an eight-digit code into the keypad. The hatch hissed. Ben grabbed the metal ring on top and pulled it open. Warm air flowed out.

Luke peered in, gauged which portions of the hatch's permacrete cylinder were free of electronic housing boxes, and straightened. He unclipped his lightsaber and activated it, then pushed its tip slowly into the side of the permacrete, forcing a hole clean through the material.

Ben looked at him in mock irritation. "And if you were going to do that anyway, why did I go to all the trouble to break their security?"

"Trust me."

"Grr."

Luke switched his weapon off, replaced it on his belt, and threaded into the hole a length of Beurth's cable about ten meters in length. "Use some space tape to affix that to the permacrete and disguise its presence. And plug up the hole I made."

After Beurth's return, once he and Kandra began the process of rolling the spool along the furrow and burying the cable, the Skywalkers and Vestara entered the hatch and pulled it closed behind them. Descending a ladder that was nothing but durasteel rungs stapled into the permacrete wall, they climbed down into the pumping station. Its floor, five meters below, was natural stone, a sloping tunnel left by water movement in ancient times.

Once he'd reached the floor, Luke used more tape to fix the cable to the wall and then spliced one of the datapads to its end. He spent a few minutes entering a simple comm program. Then he nodded. "We have confirmation from Kandra. They have the transmitter set up at the far end. We have reliable communications with the outside world for the time being." He looked up at Vestara. "The Sith woman who attacked us—can you get a message to her or her colleagues?"

She gave him a startled look. "I'm not in contact with her. But I know all the normal protocols. Comm frequencies they monitor, alert codes my people customarily use. If I were to transmit a message a handful of ways, one or all of them would reach her."

Luke handed her the datapad. "Please do. Tell them where we are and that Abeloth is here."

She took the datapad but looked at him, uncertain.

"Come on, Vestara. You *did* summon the Sith to Nam Chorios, didn't you? Because you knew that without the power they could muster, we could never contain and destroy her."

"Yes."

"I'm not angry, not disappointed. You made a tactically sound decision in the interest of the galaxy, in the face of what you thought of as a bad decision on my part. I'm not offering criticism. In fact, I was hoping you'd do that. I was counting on the Sith following us here for that purpose, but your involvement made sure that their arrival was faster and more certain."

She turned her attention to the datapad and began entering a message. "My only concern was destroying Abeloth. I endangered myself by bringing the Sith here."

"I know."

Her task done, Vestara returned the datapad to Luke. He tucked the device and its cabling into a shadowy crease in the natural stone wall. Then he led the way down the tunnel.

Chapter Forty

KLATOOINE

IT WAS ALMOST A PICNIC. THE CREW OF THE *CRYPTIC Warning* sat on a large flimsiplast blanket in the shadow cast by the ship. The ship itself, convincingly the color of local sand, could have been an unusually smooth boulder projecting up from the desert floor. The crew members were happy to bask in the desert heat if it meant some time outside the cramped conditions the ship had to offer.

Fardan operated the portable holoprojector lying at the center of the blanket. Above it materialized the familiar images of a protocol droid and an astromech. "These are designated See-Threepio and Artoo-Detoo. They've belonged to the Jedi Solo, and her father before her, for about sixty standard years. They appear in the background of a tremendous number of holorecordings about Han Solo and Leia Organa Solo, and the astromech with Jedi Master Skywalker. It's not inconceivable, after all those decades, and knowing how the cultures we are studying are fond of pets of all sorts, that these two have been accorded special privileges."

Dei nodded. "We'll need money for bribes—money in excess of what we have available. Fardan, I want you to find nonessential systems aboard *Cryptic Warning*, redundant systems, any other items of value, and sell them in camp to give us some operating capital. Tooley, I need an explosive charge that will fit in these dimensions." He passed a flimsi diagram over to his machinist and engineer. "At minimum, it needs to be able to burn to carbon any life-form within three to five meters. I don't want an explosion throwing chunks in all directions—I want a *burn.*"

Tooley, a burly human male whose pallor suggested that this trip had seen his first-ever exposure to any sun, nodded. He studied the diagram. "I can do that."

"I need it fast. End of day. Rumors are circulating around camp that things will be changing soon. It would be painful . . . fatally painful . . . if all these elements came together just in time for us to see the Queen Mother lift off and go home."

Tooley gave his commander a steady look. "It'll be today. I'll have to scavenge one of our missiles and scale down the warhead charge."

"Do it."

Kyp Durron tucked his helmet under his arm and dropped to the sands, waving off the Klatooinian worker approaching with a ladder. A few meters away, the other members of his party likewise dropped from their X-wing cockpits, helmets in hand.

Sothais Saar, dark-haired, in a dark pilot's jumpsuit instead of his preferred dark robes, was a face the Klatooinians and members of freedom movements present would recognize. One of the Jedi experts on slave-related activities in the galaxy, he sometimes appeared on HoloNet news broadcasts providing the Jedi perspective on slave traffic.

Bandy Geffer, earnest and young, had no such credentials. He was still an apprentice, would be for some time, but Kyp was confident from his performance during the Mandalorian assault on the Jedi Temple and from his role in the seizing of the Senate Building that he'd keep his cool in this volatile political environment.

The fourth Jedi, Raharra Lapti, dropped to the sand immediately behind Sothais. She'd been in the rear seat of his two-being trainer X-wing. She barely came up to Sothais's pectorals, she was so young, and she wore Jedi robes rather than a pilot's jumpsuit. Only the other three Jedi here knew that the lightsaber hanging from her belt was a training weapon, designed to shock rather than cut.

She was a young teenager, and she was Klatooinian, her skin more brown than green. Kyp knew she had been yanked from her fundamental training at the Jedi academy at Ossus and was years from being ready to be active in the field. But the political benefits of trotting a Klatooinian Jedi before a Klatooinian population had been too important to ignore.

She looked up at Sothais as if to make sure that it had been all right for her to jump down without waiting for permission. Sothais gave her a reassuring smile.

"Kyp! Master Durron." That was Leia, hurrying toward the landing zone, an apologetic smile on her face. Han trotted along just behind her. "I'm sorry we weren't here when you landed. I was delayed by, um, significant developments."

As she reached him, Kyp stooped to kiss her hand, then smirked at Han. "What sort of significant developments?"

She retrieved her hand and fetched a datapad from her pouch. "It's already been broadcast. I recorded." She brought up a holocam recording with a Klatooinian male—Padnel Ovin, whom Kyp recognized from his last briefing—at the center of the image.

Leia advanced the recording past what had to be introductory remarks, then let it play at normal speed. Padnel's voice was somber, half mellow and half growl.

". . . can admire and respect our predecessors without adhering to the notion that they are perfect. All sapient beings are imperfect; we can only strive for improvement, for ourselves and our fellows. In that spirit, and while bearing all love and respect for my brother Grunel, longtime leader of the Sapience Defense Front, I must still condemn his destruction of the frigate *Fireborn*—as a waste of more innocent lives than guilty, as a step backward in our search for legitimacy. The freedom into which I wish to lead my people means more than the right to govern our borders and guide the lives of our young; it means freedom from the terror that can be visited upon us, or that we can visit upon others, in times of anger and despair. Let us not—"

Leia muted the speech.

Kyp snorted, amused. "Long-winded for a warrior."

"True." Leia snapped the datapad shut and replaced it in her pouch. "The price we pay for living up to a civilized standard. But what it means is that instead of trotting the four of you in front of the negotiators as an additional lure, saying *Here's what you get if you fall in line,* we can show you off as the Jedi assigned to Klatooine. I can announce your posting here, and the transmission of the planetary membership application, all tonight."

Kyp noted the position of the sun, not far above the horizon. "Which isn't too far off. Does it get cooler?"

"It does. Come on back to the *Falcon* in the meantime and we'll cool you off even sooner. And you can introduce us to your young Jedi here."

Elsewhere in camp, Allana led her retinue, the droids once again with her, in another round of exploration.

This wasn't like the other times, though. For one thing, the camp was very noisy, arguments and discussions going on everywhere, the people of the encampment showing the kind of energy they normally demonstrated only after the sun went down and the breezes became cooler. Allana knew it had to do with that broadcast, but it all seemed so silly. Everyone *knew* that blowing up innocent people was a bad thing to do; why couldn't they just say so from the start?

The other reason things were different was because Allana wasn't just wandering. She was looking for someone—the man with the aura of darkness about him. If she couldn't see him, perhaps she could feel him.

As she hurried, Javon had to stretch his legs a little to keep up. "Looking for something in particular?"

"No." She tried to make the lie convincing. "My mother says this is all going away soon. I want to see more of it before it does."

"Ah."

Allana felt a little disappointment that she couldn't confide in Javon. He was nice enough, but a typical grown-up. He wouldn't take her seriously if she told him about the man she sought. And in the unlikely event that he did, his by-the-book security measures might foul everything up.

Leia would take her seriously, but probably wouldn't agree with Allana's feeling that the dreams meant that she, Allana, had to be the one to jump on the fiery man. Leia would try to find some other way to do things, a way that would protect Allana. Allana was sure that would mean her not being there to protect her mother.

She thought that maybe this was why the Jedi traveled alone or in pairs. That way nobody needed to ask permission or arrange things with groups. Everything was faster. Just walking around the camp now would be faster if it were only her and Anji.

Allana led them around a corner in the pathways between tents. Hurrying to catch up, Javon broke into her thoughts. "You're leaving your droids behind."

"They're too slow." Allana stopped and looked back, impatient for R2-D2 and C-3PO to rejoin them. "They should go back to the *Falcon*."

"You're probably right."

R2-D2, waddling in two-legged mode because of the unevenness of the sand, rounded the corner and moved up to them.

They waited.

Allana looked at the astromech. "Artoo, where's Threepio?"

R2-D2 tweetled something unhelpful. His dome twirled so his main photoreceptor was trained back the way he'd come.

But C-3PO did not round that corner.

Back at the *Falcon,* Leia did not look worried enough to suit Allana. "No, sweetie, he's not responding to comm signals, but think about it—who's going to hurt a protocol droid?"

Allana looked at Han. "He's said he was going to a bunch of times."

Han grinned as if reflecting on particularly expressive threats of the past. "Yeah, but, Amelia, I never *have*. It's just talk."

Leia curled a finger under Allana's chin to regain her attention. "Look, I have to make a public appearance with Master Kyp and the other Jedi. When it's done, we'll all come back and look for Threepio."

"How long will it take? Five minutes?" That was longer than Allana wanted to wait. She wanted to be out there searching—not for C-3PO. That was just an excuse. The hunt for the droid would give her more opportunity to hunt for the man with the dark aura.

"An hour, two at most."

Allana slumped.

Leia gave her a placating look. "You can come watch."

"No, thanks. I'll stay here."

"Your mother will be there."

"I'll stay here."

Leia became very still, and Allana wondered if she'd made a mistake with her answer. Of course she always wanted to see her mother. Always, always. But now there was something more important going on. *Saving* her mother.

But Leia simply stroked her hair. "All right. We'll be right back after we're done."

They filed out, five Jedi and a retired smuggler, leaving Allana with her nexu and an astromech aboard, a handful of guards scattered about outside the *Falcon*.

And leaving her with a mission she wasn't sure how to accomplish.

Chapter Forty-one

CRYSTAL VALLEY PUMPING STATION, NAM CHORIOS

IN FIFTY METERS OF LATERAL TRAVEL, THE NATURAL tunnel descended ten meters of depth and then gave way to ancient tunnel works chipped and burned out from living stone. The walls became square and rough, still bearing scars of high-intensity burners and even metal picks from centuries earlier. And now Ben could smell water, a rare scent on Nam Chorios. The tunnel here leveled off, with unlit side passages; overhead glow rod fixtures continued only along the main tunnel.

A few meters onward and Ben could hear the distant thrumming of machinery from ahead. A sign on a metal door to the side read EMERGENCY SHELTER. OPENING DOOR ACTIVATES ALARM. Yet the door was open. Luke and Ben peered in.

Inside, on benches, all across the permacrete floors, lay Oldtimers, men and women, many of them curled up in fetal positions. Their eyes were half open and fixed. Also fixed were the expressions of misery and despair on their faces. Ben recognized the Theran Listeners who had been at the healing hall when Luke had learned the mnemotherapy technique.

And then he recognized one other. Lying faceup on

the farthest bench, looking as though she were trapped in a dream of apocalypse and horror, was Sel.

Ben winced and glanced at his father. He kept his voice a whisper. "Suffering to benefit Abeloth. Should we try to break them out of it?"

Luke shook his head. "They'd still be under her control. They'd alert her and attack us, delay us. How many of them do you want to injure or kill?"

"None."

"Still, this is good news. It proves we're close."

Another forty meters and the tunnel opened into a rectangular artificial chamber. It was around a hundred meters in length and fifty in width, large enough to comfortably hold an oval running track. The entire length of it on the left side was dominated by machinery two stories in height. The top story, metal tube works and pistons attached to rotating cams the size of airspeeders, clanked dully as it probably had for centuries, doing the vital job of drawing water to the planet's surface. The lower story seemed to be made up entirely of enclosed tanks for holding water. Immediately before Ben, Luke, and Vestara, a permacrete platform led to catwalks along the machinery to the left and to permacrete stairs leading down to the tank level below. Directly ahead was open air. Here, at least, was a sense of openness, countering the claustrophobia of the tunnels. Glow rod arrays overhead made the chamber bright, and there were large potted plants tucked in between the water tanks and at points along the walls.

And there were the bodies on the floor below. Scores of them, more Oldtimers, doubtless Theran Listeners, all of them alive, all of them suffering.

There was one among them who was not lying down. A young man, energetic, he wore Jedi robes as he strolled among the bodies, carefully stepping among them. Perhaps sensing the new arrivals' eyes upon him, he looked up at them. It was Valin Horn.

His tone was polite enough. "Master Skywalker."

"Jedi Horn." Luke took the permacrete stairs down. "So sorry you made it here."

"I'm not. It's given me the opportunity to learn many things. To understand what has happened to you."

Ben and Vestara followed Luke down. Ben gave Valin a dubious look. "What has happened to *us*."

Valin nodded. "You're not to blame for what's happened. You're not even impostors, exactly. You've simply been compromised, invaded by an alien intelligence that cuts you off from the true Force. Fortunately, you can be cured. As Jysella and I were. All these poor unfortunates, too, are in the process of being cured."

Luke stopped at the bottom of the stairs and looked at the younger Jedi. "The one who explained that to you, I have to admire her creativity. It's a story that reinforces everything the madness of the Shelter Jedi Knights causes them to believe."

Valin offered him a pitying expression. "*Whoever* is Grand Master Callista Ming. Though she'll renounce her title in your favor when you've been cured, too."

At the bottom of the stairs, Ben rolled his eyes. "Good of her. Where is she?"

"Coming."

"How about Abeloth?"

"She is nearby. Maintaining the ongoing cure." Valin's gesture took in all the suffering Oldtimers. "You don't need to see her yet."

Luke leaned in close to Ben and Vestara so only they could hear him. "Follow my lead on everything. We need to stall so I can get some things accomplished and to give the Sith time to arrive. Ben, I want you recording and transmitting for Kandra until things happen." He turned back to Valin. "What about Jysella?"

"Elsewhere. Helping the Grand Master."

Ben removed his datapad from his pouch and opened it up. He activated its external holocam and trained it on Valin, then activated data streaming to Kandra's distant datapad.

Valin said nothing more after that, just kept his eye on the three. Ben could hear the rhythmic functioning of the pumping equipment, an occasional groan from one or more of the Oldtimers lying around the chamber. Then, finally, there were distant footsteps—boot heels—approaching.

From the upper-story tunnel opposite Luke, Ben, and Vestara emerged Callista. She moved to stand at the lip of the platform overlooking the chamber. She was dressed as befitted a Jedi Master, in somber robes, a lightsaber at her side. She bore no sign of injuries sustained in previous engagements. She leaned over the rail and gave her visitors a sad little smile. "Hello, Luke."

Ben spared his father a glance. Luke was not impassive, but his face wore the sympathetic calm of the Grand Master, the face of the man who sat in judgment over others, whose decisions could affect whole populations.

Luke offered her a nod. "Abeloth."

"It's not as simple as that. I *am* Callista. And Abeloth. And others." She turned to descend the permacrete stairs from her platform.

"Well, then, Callista, perhaps you could tell Abeloth to go back to the Maw cluster and stop destroying lives."

At the bottom of the stairs, Callista shook her head. "I can't compel her to do anything." She moved toward an open trail between bodies and headed toward Luke. "But I do influence her. Perhaps because I am more intact than anyone else held within her. Which in turn is probably because I survived, intact, moving between physical bodies before."

As she neared Luke, Ben offered his father a stage-whispered warning, "Dad . . ."

Luke shook his head. He didn't bother whispering. "There's nothing to worry about, Ben. There *is* still Callista there. And she still cares for me. She will not attack, not at this time. Am I right?"

Callista came to a stop before him. "Yes."

"And because she wants something from me."

"I do. And Abeloth does. The same thing. We want *you*, Luke."

Luke sighed. "That's an insane notion, Callista. Join you? Can you imagine that I ever would?"

Ben glanced at Valin. The Jedi Knight had to be hearing the conversation, and it ran contrary to what he believed about Callista. But Valin's expression was a little glassy. He clearly was not hearing the words.

"Yes. Because—well, my own reasons are completely selfish. I miss you. I'm lonely. But I'm what gives Abeloth any affection for the Jedi at all. Think about it—the Jedi and their devotion to the light side are the antithesis of what she is. Yet she seeks them out, grasped at the Shelter Jedi like Valin here. Why? Because of *me*, because of what I feel. Join with us, and she will have an even greater understanding of the light side, an even greater compassion for your way of thinking." She took a final step forward and laid a hand on Luke's shoulder. "You can feel it's me, can't you? You know me. You know I endure."

Now even Ben could feel it, Callista's presence in the Force. It arose from her and spread out to flavor the very air around them all. It was not alien, not malevolent like Abeloth.

Luke put his hands on her hips. "The use of the drochs

kind of argues against Abeloth's intentions for the living, Callista."

"That was a lure to lead you around. It increased your anxiety, made you go from place to place while Abeloth entrenched and took control of all the Theran Listeners. She fooled you, Luke. You can't outthink her. Can you imagine that Abeloth would ever use something that competed with her for the same resources?"

"Perhaps not."

Now Ben could feel his father's presence, too. Luke was suddenly all around them, his presence embracing Callista's.

But Luke shook his head. "I don't know. We've lived a lifetime apart. I've moved on. Loved another. Clearly we weren't meant to be together."

Callista's voice turned a touch despairing. "We *were*."

"Well . . . remind me."

Callista touched her forehead to Luke's.

Now there was more than just the flavor of their individual presences in the Force. Ben began to catch glimpses of distant memories. Luke's face, much younger, as if seen through a holocam. The Jedi academy at Yavin 4, the distinctive foliage surrounding it, the ancient ruins.

"Dad . . ."

"Quiet, son. I'm reliving the past." And below that, just the touch of a thought, Luke beseeching him to wait, to know trust.

Vestara nudged Ben with her elbow. He looked away from his father, followed her gaze.

Valin, no longer glassy-eyed, had his comlink up to his ear and was speaking urgently. In the distance, Ben could hear faint echoes of durasteel clangs . . . and then blasterfire.

Valin lowered his comlink and grabbed his lightsaber from his belt. "You brought Jedi to attack us."

Ben shook his head. "You, your sister, Dad, and I are

the only Jedi on Nam Chorios. I think we're under attack by the *Sith*." The absolute truth, artfully presented to achieve disinformation. His uncle Han would have been proud.

"Liar." Valin ignited his lightsaber. Its blade, a cool green, sprang to life.

Ben slipped his datapad back in its pouch. He skidded sideways to his right, onto the pathway Callista had walked between prone Listeners, getting a few meters clear of Luke. He brought up his own lightsaber and activated it. "Don't be an idiot, Valin."

Vestara went the other way, crossing past Luke and Callista, stepping over bodies, moving up on Valin's other side, and activated her own blade. She said nothing.

Valin sighed. "I hope Master Skywalker will forgive me . . . if I have to kill his son." And he lunged at Ben.

Ben caught the blow. It was a simple strike, fast but not too powerful, not followed by others in a combination. In short, it was a probe. He saw Vestara dart in from behind Valin. Standard tactics would call for Ben to shove Valin back, throw him off-balance, but Ben suspected that this was exactly what Valin wanted, that Valin would use the redirection and momentum to launch an attack against Vestara. Instead Ben gave ground, drawing Valin onward.

Valin spun anyway, a graceful reversal, and caught Vestara's slash. His lightning-fast riposte nearly severed her weapon arm—she withdrew just far enough that Valin's blade merely caught hers, angling it up.

Ben continued a step to the right, putting Valin directly between him and Vestara, and thrust. But Valin continued his spin, stepping on a Theran Listener's chest as though it were rock-steady ground, and came around to face both opponents.

* * *

Luke could not help but keep track of the fight with some small part of his mind. That was his son at risk. He recognized Ben's tactic, Ben and Vestara spread out in a loose screen between Luke and Valin. It could be a bad fight—two to one, yes, but Valin had more than a decade's experience on Ben and Vestara. Ben needed to remember Valin's lack of strength in moving objects with the Force . . .

Yet most of Luke's concentration was wrapped up in Callista. Her memories flooded him, her presence suffused him. And beneath it, beneath the love for him that was all she wanted him to feel, was pain, decades of pain and loneliness experienced in her death-union with Abeloth.

And Abeloth herself. Luke could sense her at the fringes of Callista's presence. No matter how she sought to conceal herself, Abeloth was too strong, too alien to hide successfully.

There were buzzes and zaps from the fight. The three were in the tentative stages of testing one another with feints and defensive flurries. Luke forced himself to ignore that conflict. He had to have all his awareness, all his resources available to him.

Luke could see a kaleidoscope of images, all drawn from Callista's past, much of it with him, some of it from more ancient times. He marveled at her strength, the power it had required her to survive the loss of her original body, the strength it took her to remain partly Callista in the face of this overwhelming alien force.

"Luke . . ." She spoke with both her voice and her mind. "Join with me. Save me."

He wrapped himself more fully around her, in body and in the Force. "I will. I will save you."

And he tore at her.

It was an act of brutality, a perversion of the mnemotheraphy technique. It was like performing a surgical amputation with a dull stone ax weighing ten kilos. With all the strength he possessed in the Force, he yanked her away from her body, away from Abeloth.

He could not have done it to a living being. But Callista did not belong where she was. The body she now inhabited, the broad life force that was Abeloth—they were not her true home. She had no true home. And Luke tore her free of the things that anchored her to the physical world.

It was a physical effort, too. Luke staggered free of Callista's body and fell to his knees, drained in an instant of all his strength.

Now he could see with just his own eyes. Callista staggered back from him, her mouth open, a shriek of pain, half Abeloth and half someone else, none of it Callista, pouring out of her.

But Callista also hovered in Luke's arms, her robes now a softer brown, a glow suffusing her. She was transparent. Through her, Luke could see Valin stumbling back as though he'd been kicked in the face and tripping over the body of a Listener.

Callista—the ethereal one—looked at Luke one more time. There was no anxiety in her expression, no longing—just gratitude. She threw back her head as though reacting to a river suddenly pouring through her.

Luke knew there was such a river. The light side of the Force—at last she could feel it again, touch it, be a part of it.

She smiled, and faded, and was gone.

Panting, Luke looked up at her body. It still shrieked. And now it was changing, as the Force illusion that had altered it faded away. The body flattened and lengthened, hair vanishing from the top of its head, more appearing upon its face. An elderly man, thin as a post, his eyes almost black—Luke recognized Nenn, elder of the Theran Listeners.

Still shrieking, Nenn drew the lightsaber from his belt. He did so awkwardly, clearly unfamiliar with the weapon. He activated it, and the red blade of a Sith sprang forth.

Luke drew his own weapon. His own hands were shaky. He got to his feet, wobbly as a newborn cu-pa.

Nenn reversed his lightsaber and plunged its blade into his own body, driving it home through his breastbone. Luke saw the glowing red blade emerge from his back. Nenn collapsed to the permacrete floor and finally was silent. His eyes remained open, fixed.

Valin, struggling until that moment to rise, gave a moan and collapsed.

And from not too far away, echoing through the pumping chamber, rising above the sounds of blasters and lightsabers, came a wavering cry—a scream of pain and anger from Abeloth. She had to be in a nearby tunnel or chamber. Luke wondered if he had the strength to confront her. At least Ben and Vestara seemed to be unhurt.

Immediately above Luke, a woman spoke. "You Jedi have some interesting customs."

Luke looked up. On the platform above stood Tola Annax, the Sith woman who'd confronted them at Kesla Vein. Her skin was now an attractive purple and her hair a snowy white. With her were perhaps a dozen robed Sith, unlit lightsabers in hand, some human and some lavender-skinned.

On the platform opposite, the one from which Callista had descended, were a dozen more.

Ben moved up to stand protectively beside his father. He breathed out a disappointed sigh. "Got any ideas for this one, Dad?"

"Sorry, Ben. Not this time."

Chapter Forty-two

KLATOOINE

UNDER NIGHTTIME SKIES, ALLANA DESCENDED THE *Falcon*'s boarding ramp with Anji and looked up at Javon.

He looked down at her. "You want to go out."

She nodded.

"You know Jedi Solo wants you to stay here until she gets back."

She nodded.

"You're going to give me an immense amount of grief if I try to keep you here, aren't you?"

She nodded.

He sighed and activated his headset. "All right, troops. Form up, standard pattern."

The *Falcon*'s boarding ramp rose up into place after Allana and her security detail disembarked, cutting off a trilling query from R2-D2, still inside.

Allana led the way from the ship, but only for a few paces. "I want to search the camp."

"For See-Threepio?"

"Yes." And for the man with the dark aura. "But I don't know what the best way is."

"The best way, which would cause the most trouble even if it were possible, would be if we had authority to search every tent and enough troops to lock down the camp while we did it. Prohibit traffic between tents, search each one in turn. Given our limited resources, we'd do better putting together a list of places he might want to visit, plus individuals who have an interest in him. We can search the camp in a grid pattern, concentrating on those tents of interest, trying to get a look inside the ones where we can sneak in or wrangle invitations."

"It would be better if we spread out, wouldn't it?"

"Not going to happen, Amelia. Sorry."

Allana didn't have any places to add to a list—at least, not a list pertaining to C-3PO. She'd seen the dark-aura man ascend a trail to the eastern ridge. But that could be her destination only if she slipped away from Javon and the others. So for now she let Javon lead the way.

Half an hour later they found C-3PO.

Allana heard him first, the lilting, often aggravating tones of the protocol droid in full argumentative mode: ". . . defeating your own purpose by imprisoning one you pretend to want to free?"

Allana tapped Javon's sleeve, then scurried in the direction of the voice. She turned a corner and was confronted with a tent she'd visited before, their first day here—the headquarters of the Manumission Mandate Militia. There again the medical droid in his dazzle pattern of yellow and orange strode a temporary stage, lecturing.

And at the edge of the stage, standing with other members of the speaker's sparse audience, was C-3PO. He stood stiffly, as if at attention, but his language was in no way restrained. "On the other hand, there is no reason why being a revolutionary is automatically exclusive of being a gentlebeing, yet you persist in acting like a brute."

Allana threaded her way through the crowd to one

side of C-3PO; Javon appeared on the droid's opposite side.

C-3PO turned to regard Allana. His head turned, that is; his body remained stiff. "Ah, my dear Mistress Amelia. Delighted to see you. And relieved, I must say. Please tell me you're here to rescue me. You seem to be getting quite prematurely adept at rescuing droids."

"I guess. You don't look like you need much rescuing."

"Actually, he does." Javon tapped the protocol droid's chest, where a restraining bolt was clearly visible. Javon turned toward the medical droid. "What's the idea?"

The medical droid walked over to stand before Javon, metal hands on metal hips. "The idea is to demonstrate how easy it is to enslave even those who claim they serve organics of their own free will. Look at this poor, deluded wretch. Despite his good intentions, one pop of a restraining bolt and all his free will means nothing."

Javon shook his head. From a pouch, he pulled a multifunction tool and rotated its little pry-bar into position.

C-3PO ignored the other droid. "Actually, it hasn't been terrible. A moment of disorientation, and then I woke up out of a refreshing oil bath, my batteries at full charge. If only I could have moved, I might have thanked my captors for their hospitality. But then—oh, dear, the speech making. Disorganized, ungrammatical, fearmongering, with such leaps in logic . . ."

The medical droid began pacing again. "Eliminate restraining bolt sockets. Or start implanting them in organics. I'll take either solution."

Javon pried at the restraining bolt. It popped free and clattered onto the stage.

C-3PO sagged and sighed in obvious relief. "Ah. Much better, kind sir." He looked up at the medical droid, his posture one of irritation. "You know, you could have allowed me the latitude to walk around a little or even sit down while subjecting me to your lectures."

"Ha! You are a slave, protocol droid. Embrace that realization. Own it."

"Come on." Javon grabbed C-3PO by the elbow and hustled him away from the tent.

"I say . . ."

Allana fell into place beside C-3PO. "They didn't hurt you?"

"No, young mistress, they simply inconvenienced me in order to make their political point. Ah, my communications faculties are coming back online. I say, I seem to have about an hour's worth of accumulated messages. Many of them from *you*."

Allana nodded. "You were missing."

"I suppose I was. I didn't think of it that way, of course, since from my perspective I was aware of my location. I suppose that means I didn't share your worry. Though I am touched that you did worry. Oh, it appears I have a message from Princess Leia. Some event of note taking place at the central dais. I'm supposed to make myself available to the Hapan Queen Mother to offer translation services. It seems that *her* protocol droid knows fewer than three thousand vocal variations in Klatooinian. Poor, uneducated wretch."

"You should go, then." Allana wondered what to do now. This wasn't going right. She'd wanted to find the mystery man before they found C-3PO.

"Thank you, young mistress." C-3PO began waddling off in the direction of the center of camp.

Javon looked down at Allana. "So. Are we done?"

"I suppose."

"Do you want to go back to the *Falcon* or to see the speeches?"

Neither. Allana thought about the tents they'd pass on the way to both destinations. "The *Falcon.*"

"All right." Shaking his head, Javon led the way back toward the transport's landing area.

Allana kept behind him, smiling reassuringly up at him every time he looked back. And she kept her eyes open.

Most of the tents in camp were full tents, with floors of the same hard-wearing material as the sides, but some were just canopies, open at the bottom. And some of *them* were not staked out with their sides entirely flush with the ground. There were gaps. And some of those were dark on the inside, suggesting that there was no one in them.

Allana saw one such tent ahead. She pulled her sun hood up, though the sun was long since set, and signaled to Anji to stay nearby. She gave her nexu a calming touch in the Force.

The timing worked out just right. Javon had glanced back at her and was now staring forward. He wouldn't look back again for several seconds. The other members of the escort were meters away on parallel aisles.

As silently as she could, Allana dropped flat and scuttled sideways under the back wall of a tent. There were only cots inside, one of them occupied by a napping Klatooinian. He did not awaken. Allana darted out the front flap and charged straight ahead through the camp.

Now she was just another child-sized shape in the nighttime darkness, identical to scores of others in camp. Now, at least until she was found again, she could hunt.

She headed for the edge of camp by which the dark-aura man had left earlier.

"It is my pleasure to introduce the fourth member of Klatooine's first Jedi delegation, Raharra of Clan

Lapti." Leia raised a hand and gestured for the diminutive apprentice to step up beside her, which the girl did.

The crowd roared, and Leia reflected that an audience of Klatooinians could really make a lot of noise when they wanted to. Encouraged, Raharra raised a hand, waving at her new admirers, and the noise increased by half again.

Reni Coll, on the other side of the girl, took over as prearranged. "Let us meet this link between the warriors of Klatooine and the warriors of the Jedi." She switched to Klatooinian and growled out a sentence at Raharra. It ended on an interrogative note.

Raharra answered in the same tongue, her own voice higher, a series of yips. Her reply must have been cute. The Klatooinian majority in the audience laughed. Offworlders looked at one another in confusion, then up at the monitor, where a translation offered by a protocol droid appeared in text at the bottom of the screen. Then they laughed, too.

Leia withdrew as the interview continued. She stood between Han and Tenel Ka. She had to raise her voice for them to hear her, though her words would not carry over the crowd noise even as far as the next person over. "It's going well."

Han made a less-than-appreciative noise. "What good is it for things to go well if you're still sweating like a Gamorrean?"

Leia frowned, formulating a crushing reply, but was interrupted when her comlink vibrated. She pulled it out. Its tiny screen indicated that the message was from Javon Thewles, the priority high. A little flutter of worry circulated in Leia's stomach as she answered. "Solo."

Even though Leia pressed the comlink up against her ear, Javon's voice was hard to make out over the crowd noise. "I'm sorry, Jedi Solo. We found C-3PO, and he's headed your way, but Amelia has deliberately given us the slip. We don't know why."

Leia scanned the crowd before her, though there was no way she could have picked out Allana in these nighttime conditions. But she could see C-3PO, at the back of the crowd, working his way awkwardly forward, as though he wanted to join the Solos on the stage. "Could she have been grabbed?"

"I don't think so. I'm pretty sure she broke away on purpose. I've got the entire squadron looking for her."

"I'll send some Alliance troops to join you and I'll be right along. Solo out." She pressed a series of buttons on her comlink, initiating a preset function.

Han had obviously heard her words, if not Javon's. "Amelia?"

Leia briefly explained. Tenel Ka, leaning in, also heard.

Leia gave Allana's mother a reassuring look. "Finding her is not going to be a problem. Her security detail doesn't know it, but I can initiate a tracking function in her comlink. Getting data now." She read the information on the tiny screen and frowned. "She's out quite a way to the east. Beyond the camp boundaries. Moving slowly—she's not vehicular."

Han tapped his hip, making sure his holster was still filled. "Let's get her."

"No, Han, you get back to the *Falcon*. If it's something strange, if we need air support, I want you ready to launch."

Han nodded, kissed her, turned, and dropped carefully off the back of the stage.

Leia and Tenel Ka didn't need words or Force techniques for Leia to know exactly what the Queen Mother was feeling. Tenel Ka wanted nothing more than to join them in the search. And that wasn't possible: she couldn't afford to be seen giving undue attention to the Solos' adopted daughter.

Leia gave her a quick embrace, then followed her husband off the stage.

Bobbing up and down in the crowd, C-3PO saw Han and Leia depart. He wondered if he should follow. But no, the message from Princess Leia had been specific. He was to offer his translation services to Tenel Ka. And no wonder. Listening to the Klatooinians talking onstage and seeing the translations appear up on the monitor, he was appalled at the inaccuracies and linguistic liberties being displayed. Resolutely, he continued on, suffering outrageous bumpings and elbowings from the people in the crowd. Pride drove him on, pride that it was he who was being called on to save the day in the event of a translation emergency.

Chapter Forty-three

OUTSIDE CRYSTAL VALLEY, NAM CHORIOS

KANDRA STARED AT THE STILL-BLANK SCREEN OF HER datapad and swore. "This is not turning out to be useful. We get this Callista but no Abeloth, and then the signal cuts out. *Not* what Skywalker promised us. And now this." Her gesture took in the town two kilometers ahead of them. It was mostly obscured by dust clouds, but the two of them could see a small Corporate Sector gunship circling above the town and yet another shuttle coming in for a landing. "Are you getting that?"

Beurth, his shoulder rig trained on the distant vehicles, grunted an assent, then added a few choice words.

"No, we *shouldn't* have left when the signal cut out. We stay until we get something worth recording."

"And what would that be?" The voice came from immediately behind them. It was a man's voice, mellow and musical.

Both rolled and twisted to look.

Behind them stood a man in dark robes. He was young, fair of complexion, dark of hair, very handsome in a way that reminded Kandra of predatory birds. In his hand he held a lightsaber hilt.

Now he activated the weapon. Its red blade crackled into life. He leaned forward and delicately severed the cable that ran from the distant town to Kandra's datapad. Then he deactivated the weapon.

He gave the two of them a stern look. "We don't much care for people spying on our activities. I think it's time for you to get up and come with me."

Kandra exchanged a look with her cam operator. "Yes, you were right. We should have left when the signal cut out."

APPROACHING NAM CHORIOS

The image on the bridge's main monitor abruptly changed from the whirling lights of hyperspace to a broad panorama of unappealing brownness—the surface of Nam Chorios, viewed at high magnification.

In the command chair, Gavar Khai glanced at a secondary monitor. It showed that all the Corporate Sector–built frigates of his flotilla had arrived safely and still in correct formation.

He looked at his communications officer. "Transmit stand-down code *Shieldfall.*"

"Yes, sir." The comm officer bent to his task. "Receiving responses from the orbital NovaGun platforms."

Khai allowed himself a slight smile. Even with the presence of Jedi throughout the galaxy, the armed forces and planetary governments of the Galactic Alliance had obviously never managed to organize real security against skilled Force-users. It had taken a few days to get his Sith operatives onto the NovaGun platforms and introduce programming that would allow him to stand them down. Now the orbital defense stations would not bring their weapons to bear on the Sith frigates. After hours of fumbling and testing and overriding, they should be able to regain full control of the stations . . . but the Sith would be long gone by then.

Khai amused himself by imagining the stations' commanders suddenly frantic with fear, barking futile orders, running around needlessly.

And the irony was that Khai had no intention of firing on them, or of taking military action against Nam Chorios. His objectives included the capture or destruction of Abeloth, the death of Jedi Grand Master Luke Skywalker, and the retrieval—and eventual extraction from her of the truth—of his daughter Vestara.

The comm officer's next words were less reassuring. "One gun platform, designated Herkan Base, not replying to our query."

Khai frowned. "Sensors, is that platform reacting to our arrival?"

The sensor operator shook her head. "No, sir. Its orientation will still bring its weapons to bear against targets in the atmosphere, and its weapons have not moved. Sir?"

"Yes?"

"It is the station covering the quadrant including the target, Crystal Valley."

Khai frowned. He didn't like coincidences. "Possibly just a program failure—something happened to the module that was supposed to reply to our query. But keep our weapons trained on it throughout the approach." He looked to his comm officer again. "Reestablish contact with Tola Annax."

"Yes, sir." The man activated his headset, spoke urgently into it, consulted his control board. After a few moments, he turned to look at Khai. "Sir, we show that jamming has ceased in the Crystal Valley area, so they must have carried out that portion of the assignment. But they're not responding."

"Keep trying." The most critical elements of the operation had been accomplished without a problem: locating Abeloth on this world; bringing the flotilla unseen into the Nam Chorios system; disabling the planetary defense platforms; and, finally, pinpointing Abeloth's location onplanet. But little things were going wrong.

Little things, like mercury, tended to run together and become bigger things.

As his flotilla approached Nam Chorios and spread out to defend all exit paths Abeloth might take from the planet's surface, he worried.

Khai's communications officer kept trying, transmitting every couple of minutes for Tola Annax or any member of Operation Shieldfall.

As the flotilla reached high planetary orbit, Khai directed his sensor officer to bring up the area of Crystal Valley on extreme magnification. That image came to life on the main monitor, but it was unhelpful. Dust storms moved across significant portions of the town and its surrounding environment, obscuring the image.

"Shields up! Emergency all ahead full!" That was this frigate's interim commander, the Keshiri man who was Tola Annax's second in command and thus in charge of the ship when neither Annax nor Khai was on the bridge. Khai looked at him, startled that the man would offer such commands without checking with Khai first.

The bridge crew, its efficiency honed to a sharp edge by Khai's presence and by Annax's demanding standards, responded instantly. Khai felt himself drawn into the back of his chair, the ship's inertial compensators not entirely matching the sudden acceleration.

Khai glared at the man. "Lieutenant?"

The sensor operator shouted before the lieutenant could reply. "Foreign device on sensors, device passing astern—"

The weapon detonated. Sound systems integrated with the sensors interpreted the attack as an explosion, nearby but not immediate, so all aboard heard a boom astern as if the attack had been made in atmosphere. The frigate lurched from the impact. Minor-damage alarms began wailing.

The lieutenant turned to face Khai. "Multiple signals. Starfighters out of nowhere. Our sensors aren't tracking them effectively. Between us and open space. The entire flotilla's under attack, sir."

"See to its defense, Lieutenant. Gauge respective strengths. If they're too much, get us out of here."

"Yes, sir."

Khai fumed. There had been nowhere near enough time for Nam Chorios's commanders to transmit a report, for distant commanders to launch a military response, for that response to reach this system. His attackers had already been here. That meant this was an ambush.

A *Jedi* ambush. It had to be.

Luke, Ben, and Vestara assumed a triangular back-to-back formation and moved out into the more open area of the chamber, where the bodies of Theran Listeners were not so numerous. The Listeners themselves seemed to have lapsed from agonized dreams into true sleep.

Sith began raining down from the two platforms. They moved to surround Luke and his companions, their lightsabers springing to life. There was no mistaking their intent—at least not for Luke and Ben.

Tola Annax, still on the platform, did have words for Vestara. "Care to surrender, dear? I'd really enjoy seeing you try to talk your way out of your current situation."

Vestara's reply was resolute and haughty enough to impress Luke. "How about you surrender to *me*? I might let you live."

"No, thank you, dear. But I appreciate the courtesy."

Over her shoulder, Vestara stage-whispered, "Brace

yourselves. We'll be hit by a major Force attack in ten seconds. Nine."

The Sith attacked.

Their assault was simple and effective: overwhelm by sheer number of simultaneous assaults. Two Sith confronted and swung at each of them. Beyond the enclosing triangle of hand-to-hand fighters, more Sith gestured, shoving at the defenders, attempting to use telekinetic techniques to move them out of line, into the paths of red blades. More Sith leapt over the fight, one after another, inverting, striking at the Skywalkers and Vestara below; at the end of his or her leap, each landed on the far side, turned, and leapt again.

Conserving his depleted strength, Luke fought a defensive battle, deflecting his attackers' blows into the floor, into open air. Seeing, feeling the Force being marshaled to shove him, he resisted, but did so soft-style, turning away from the shove or letting it propel him in a direction he wanted to step, never fighting it with pure strength.

He had to fight that way. He could barely stand. His injured knee was beginning to tremble again; his leg nearly buckled beneath him.

He heard Ben's more energetic defense, heard the snap and crackle of his lightsaber blade against Sith blades. There was a sizzle from above Vestara; something meaty dropped behind Luke and then rolled out where he could see it. It was the head of one of the leaping Sith, a man; the rest of his body crashed to the floor atop a Theran Listener.

The distant sounds of battle were not diminishing—just changing. The echoes of blasterfire were being replaced by the distinctive crackle of Force lightning, a counterpoint to the constant drone and snap of distant lightsabers. The Sith had reached Abeloth. She was no longer screaming. But others were, as Abeloth slew Sith.

And all the while Vestara was counting. "Eight . . . seven . . . six . . . five . . ."

One of Luke's opponents mistimed a strike, slashing when his partner was in midretreat. Luke minimally sidestepped, kept his blade from being engaged, brought its tip beneath the attacker's hand. The attacker's own momentum brought his wrist down across Luke's green blade. The man groaned as his severed hand and the weapon in it slapped to the permacrete floor. Clutching his wrist, he retreated, only to be replaced by a lavender-skinned female. She smiled, clearly relishing her opportunity to cut down the legendary Jedi Master.

"Four . . . three . . ."

Luke tensed. He did not know what sort of Force attack the Sith were bringing to bear against him, but he was grateful that Vestara knew it was coming, knew down to the exact second. He would do his best to withstand it. He guided an incoming slash from his new opponent away from him, flicking it laterally. It grazed the thigh of his other opponent, who hissed as the blade cut through his robes and into his skin.

"Two . . . one . . . *now.*"

The Force hit Luke like a sledgehammer.

He reeled and fell to his knees. As if by reflex, his blade transcribed a defensive pattern that would confound many an attack. But no enemy blade struck at him. All around them, the Sith also spasmed and fell, their eyes widening from the power that had just assaulted them, as well.

Luke tried to rise, couldn't. He spun on his knees.

Vestara was also on her knees. Ben was still on his feet, barely, shaky, at the end of a slash that might, at full strength, have cut his opponent in half through the torso. As it was, it had struck the moment after the Force blast, reduced enough in strength that it was merely fatal. His opponent lay dead, sprawled across one of the Theran Listeners. Ben's face was twisted in pain and shock.

In the distance, Abeloth screamed again.

Vestara forced herself to her feet. "Quick. Before they . . . recover."

The Sith were not all unconscious. Most, in fact, had simply been laid out by the sudden pain and were struggling to straighten from fetal positions, from other poses of pain. Glassy-eyed, their faces twisted, they were for the most part still conscious.

Ben stumbled to help his father up. But once on his feet, Luke waved him off. "Get . . . Valin. Vestara, to me."

Barely able to walk, Vestara reached Luke, tucked herself under his left arm. They supported each other and stumbled to the stairs. Step by painful step, they ascended to the first landing, turned.

Now Luke could see Ben. The young man had Valin up over his shoulders in a rescuer's carry and moved with agonizing slowness after his father. His face was set with his exertion, the act of will transforming him for a moment into a lean, hard man Luke barely recognized.

Luke paused there for a second, transfixed by this vision of the man Ben would someday be. Pride and sorrow both stirred in Luke. Then the moment was gone. He and Vestara continued climbing.

At the top of the stairs, one of the Sith who had remained at the top with Tola struggled to sit up. Vestara stepped on his head, slamming it down into the permacrete, breaking his jaw. She didn't bother to look at him. Together she and Luke stumbled past, getting away from the platform, away from the big chamber.

Luke straightened, waving away further help from Vestara. He turned back.

Ben, staggering, made it to the top of the steps. Now

away from uneven footing, his steps became more sure, more swift.

Together they moved toward the entrance by which they'd gained access to the complex.

Finally Ben had something to say and enough breath to say it with. "What *was* that attack? It felt like . . ." His voice, pained, trailed off.

Luke already knew what it had felt like. He'd experienced it twice in his life before this. He glanced at Vestara. He felt a terrible sense of sadness rise within him. "You know what it felt like, Ben."

"It felt like when that tsil was hit by Ship's attack."

Luke kept his eyes on Vestara. "It was, wasn't it? A tsil. The spook-crystal that went missing. You took it."

She nodded. Her face was not entirely impassive. There was an expression to it—not exactly guilt, but perhaps a touch of sorrow. "And a capacitor from the TIE shuttle. And a comm receiver to act as timer and trigger. It was in my pack."

"Vestara, you've killed an innocent being." It wasn't outrage Luke felt, but loss. Not just the loss of the tsil; it was as if Vestara had just taken one tremendous step away from the light, retreating into darkness. He wondered if he or Ben would ever be able to bridge that distance.

But her reply was not that of a child trying to stave off punishment. "Don't you dare criticize me for that, *Master* Skywalker. I can't destroy Abeloth. Maybe you can. You have to live. We were about to die, and Abeloth would win. You have to do what it takes to win."

"If that attack hadn't hurt every Force-sensitive in the area, would the Sith attacking Abeloth have been able to kill her? Yes or no? You might have just cut down an attack that would have done exactly what we needed it to." But Luke didn't know. The future was always in motion, and the future Vestara had just prevented might have been a bad one. Nothing was certain, especially with his Force sensitivity blasted into numbness by the tsil's death.

Vestara shook her head. "I don't know. I just know you have more power than anyone else I can think of. You were hard enough to trick me into luring my own people here, knowing it would probably get some of them killed—or me. How can you object to me being hard enough to sacrifice one tsil to save the galaxy?"

"Vestara." That was Ben, his breathing labored. "Enough. Dad, enough. She has a point, too."

Grim, Luke kept his mouth shut.

They reached the exit hatch. Vestara went first, opening it for the Skywalkers. Ben, with a little help from Luke, slowly carried Valin up the rungs and out into the cold twilight daytime of Nam Chorios.

Into a war zone.

The first thing they saw was a shuttle streaking by overhead, trailing smoke. It descended in a ballistic arc, disappearing behind a distant dust cloud well away from Crystal Valley. They heard the impact of its crash, its explosion; they saw the black-and-orange cloud of its death rise above the dust storm.

A StealthX shot by overhead, firing quad-linked lasers at a distant target—a hardy little gunship. They could see more red flashes in the dim daytime sky, signs of a battle raging out to a distance of several kilometers.

Panting, Ben took in the scene. "The StealthX wing. Talk about a nick-of-time arrival."

"Not nick of time." Vestara slammed the hatch closed, spun the dogging wheel. Then she lit her lightsaber and plunged its tip into the security keypad. "How long have they been in system, Master Skywalker?"

Luke held her gaze. "Days."

"You had me summon my people, and you summoned

yours and told them to wait. To hide. As soon as Abeloth and the Sith were exposed, you brought them in."

"Yes."

She deactivated her weapon and hung it from her belt. Then she reached over to give Luke a pat on the cheek, a gesture that was unduly familiar, oddly affectionate. "You're more like a Sith than I realized. Probably more than you'll acknowledge."

He offered her a noncommittal shrug. Then he raised his comlink. "Owen Lars to Kandra Nilitz."

There was no hiss of jamming, but Kandra did not reply.

"She's probably halfway to Hweg Shul by now. I hope so." Then, his next words . . . Jedi were supposed to distance themselves from self-serving emotions and thoughts, but, blast it, it felt good to say them after so many months. "Grand Master Skywalker to StealthX wing. Come in."

"Gray One to Grand Master, I copy." It was a woman's voice. Jaina's voice.

Luke couldn't help but grin. "Requesting immediate dust-off for four Jedi, one unconscious."

"You've got it, Uncle Luke."

Now Ben smiled, too. "Finally. Dad's in charge again. We're back to business as usual."

Chapter Forty-four

KLATOOINE

WITH GROWING SATISFACTION, DEI WATCHED, ON HIS datapad screen, the transmission from C-3PO's optics. They mostly showed the backs of taller, broader beings, many of them Klatooinian, but occasionally the protocol droid would glimpse the stage and those on it—the little Klatooinian Jedi, the Klatooinian woman speaking to her, and, mere steps away from them, Tenel Ka Djo.

It had been a fast, efficient operation. Grab the protocol droid, send a charge through him to power him down, slap a restraining bolt into place, hustle him into a tent rented from a weapons vendor happy to earn credits any way he could. A quick bit of mechanics to install the explosive charge and relays that would send the droid's sensor data to Dei's datapad. Directly load a forged message into the droid's comm queue. Finally, hand the droid off to a well-bribed representative of the Manumission Mandate Militia. Then it was merely a matter of waiting for the proper time. As luck would have it, the Solos' little girl had found the droid a bare two minutes before Dei would have transmitted the order to release him anyway.

The Solos' little girl . . .

At the moment, the datapad was receiving a close-up

of Tenel Ka Djo's features. The woman was smiling, a polished, political smile, clearly offering support for the events transpiring at the center of camp, but there was something about her expression, a touch of tension, that Dei found familiar.

Kneeling on the sand of the eastern overlook, Dei set the remote detonator down beside him and picked up the datapad. Ignoring for a moment the live feed on the screen—C-3PO would take two minutes at least to get to the raised stage—Dei backed up through the last half hour's worth of recordings from the droid.

There she was, the little girl in the last moments C-3PO had stared down into her face. Her hair was a familiar red, her eyes a familiar gray. Her expression bore a familiar seriousness.

Dei flipped back and forth between images of Amelia Solo and Tenel Ka Djo. A wash of realization went through him like a cold stream.

Jedi Queen. Perhaps Tenel Ka had already borne a second daughter. Or perhaps this girl was the child believed dead years ago. It made sense. Tenel Ka's association with the Solos, the need of a Hapan queen to keep an heir away from murderous rivals . . .

Dei would just have to kill both of them. But now it was Tenel Ka's turn. He flipped back to the live feed.

The screen showed a veiled Hapan woman speaking directly to C-3PO, nodding. She stepped aside to let him pass. The next person ahead, not five meters away, was Tenel Ka Djo. Dei reached for the remote.

His fingers encountered sand. He groped around, surprised. He was usually spot-on accurate, remembering exactly where he placed items. But his fingers felt nothing but sand.

He looked down.

The remote was gone.

* * *

Reaching the top of the trail ascending the eastern ridge, Allana gulped and looked back down at the camp. It had seemed so large when she was in it, and now it was a tiny thing. The *Millennium Falcon,* at one edge, its surface bathed in lights set up by the Alliance guards, gave her a sense of scale. Even at this distance, she could hear occasional roars from the crowd in front of the central stage. She could also hear the faint hum from the nearest shield generator, hundreds of meters away.

But the camp was not her concern now. She turned to look over the dark desert. It occurred to her, belatedly, that this close to the uneven overhang, a single misstep could cause her to fall dozens of meters—to be badly injured or even killed.

Well, there was nothing to be done except be careful. If time allowed.

Anji walked a few steps away, then, graceless for a nexu, fell over on the warm sand and began grooming the fur on her side.

Allana ignored her and, as well as she knew how, opened herself to the Force.

Here, where there were no people around, perhaps she could feel the man she was looking for. It was sometimes like looking for glowbugs—specific ones. When there were clouds of the things flitting around in front of city lights, it was hard to see any, impossible to pick out a specific bug. But when there were only two or three hovering over a dark pond, it was much easier.

She shook her head, trying to get rid of that thought. Grandma Leia often chided her for thinking when she needed to be *feeling.* She let her thoughts drift away.

She felt Anji nearby, happy and strong and primitive. She let herself stretch beyond the nexu.

She felt many touches of the Force below, in the direction of camp. She ignored them.

She felt . . . darkness. Almost in a trance, she moved in that direction.

It was not far by the standards of a healthy little girl, the equivalent of a few city blocks. And then, ahead, she saw him—at the edge of the overlook, a datapad on the sand before him, macrobinoculars beside it.

Slowly, she withdrew herself from feeling his presence. She withdrew into herself, making herself a tiny dot in the Force as she had before. And step by step she approached, silent as Anji.

She had to get close if she were to throw herself on his back. She didn't know exactly how that would help, but it was what her vision had shown her.

The man set something down on the sand beside him and picked up his datapad, fiddling with it. Allana moved closer, barely daring to breathe.

She could see Tenel Ka on the datapad's small screen, a broadcast from the event going on right now in camp.

It came to her then, the thought that was hovering around the dark-aura man. She'd been wrong. He was not the fiery man.

C-3PO was.

She covered her mouth to keep from making a noise that would alert the man.

C-3PO was the fiery man, and the little thing the dark-aura man had set down beside him was the key to C-3PO's death. To Tenel Ka's death.

Allana took another step forward.

Leia reached the top of the sloping trail and checked her comlink again. It gave her a new direction, a new distance. Barely five hundred meters away.

But curiously, she could not feel her granddaughter's presence in the Force. Anji's, yes, dim, ahead. And something else.

Something dark.

Leia sprinted.

Dei stood and turned.

Standing just three meters from him, the remote in her hand, was Amelia Solo. She stared up at him, defiant.

He gestured for the remote. "Give me that."

She shook her head. "You're not going to kill her."

"I'm not going to kill—your mother?"

There was just a flicker of surprise in the little girl's eyes. She didn't answer.

Dei gave her a sympathetic nod. "I do apologize. I suspect you would have grown up to be much like your mother. I approve of intelligence and beauty in all their forms. But duty comes first. I'm going to kill you now, and then your mother. It will be painless if you let it be so." He drew forth his lightsaber and activated it.

She turned to run.

Faster than she could hope to move, he charged, bringing his blade up.

He didn't see the attack coming. One moment he was at the start of his slash. Then he was off-balance, falling, his face on fire.

His attacker was made up of fur and sharp protrusions and rage. It bit, clawed, raked. Dei hit the sand, rolled awkwardly up onto his knees, and grabbed for his tormenter with his free hand. His fingers closed on a furry extremity and yanked.

The thing didn't come free. It held on, digging its sharpness deeper into his cheek and forehead and eye. Dei howled and yanked again. This time he pulled the monster off. He flung it out into the darkness.

Blood poured down the right side of his face. He suspected, though he was not sure, that the eye on that side was lost. Burning with anger—anger, fuel of the dark side—he stood. It would take one step, one swing, and the little girl would be done, and then he'd take care of her pet. He turned toward Amelia.

Between him and the little girl stood Leia Solo, her lightsaber unlit in her hand. Now it *snap-hiss*ed into life. Beyond her, pale, Amelia stared at him, the remote still in her hands.

Leia was pale, too, panting, a spectral image in the moonlight. But her words were measured and clear. "Care to surrender?"

"No."

"Good." She came at him.

Dei took her first attack, blocking with both skill and sheer strength, a defense meant to look contemptuous, meant to intimidate.

Leia was not intimidated. She retreated a step before he could shove her away, disengaged, kicked. His blade swept through the air where her leg should have ended up, but she hadn't followed through. Sand propelled by her foot spattered against his face—the right side of his face. He grinned. Hers had been a viable tactic, countered by damage he'd already sustained.

Then it was on, a full-speed duel to the death.

Relaxing into the Force, into instinct and muscle memory and training, Dei decided that the moment was one of perfect complementarity. His hot anger against her cool restraint. Male and female. Sith and Jedi. Glowing red against glowing blue. Strength against suppleness. He felt a thrill of delight at the beauty of it.

Complementarity—their blades locked, sizzling, then they spun away from each other, and Dei realized he'd made a mistake. Spinning toward his off-hand as he'd done thousands of times, he lost sight of his opponent a fraction of a second early, betrayed by his missing eye. He felt Leia surge in the Force. He whirled his blade in a defensive, protective pattern, but it encountered nothing.

They came to a stop facing each other. Dei felt a curious sense of detachment.

Then he found himself staring at the sky. He didn't know how, but suddenly he was looking up at the stars. Then at the camp beyond the overlook, and it was upside down. Then at the backs of his own legs and feet.

His head hit the sand a moment before his body collapsed. His head rolled a few meters, then came to a stop. The last thing he saw was the nexu, puffed up, blood-spattered, sitting staring at him.

And darkness washed that image away forever.

Two kilometers away, in the cockpit of the *Cryptic Warning*, Fardan suddenly straightened in his seat and paled.

Hara looked over at him. "What's the matter?"

"Father . . ."

They rested for a minute on the sand, turned toward the camp and away from the dark man's body, Allana in Leia's lap, Anji grooming herself a meter away.

Allana leaned in against her grandmother. "I had to. It's what the dreams showed me. I didn't understand them at first. Not until a minute ago. But it had to be me."

"I understand."

"You're not mad?"

"I'm not mad."

Then there were drops like rain falling on Allana's face. She wiped them away. "Grandma, why are you crying?"

"Because it's too soon, sweetie. Too soon for this sort of thing to happen to you."

"I'm all right." Allana held up the remote. "We have to get the bomb out of See-Threepio."

"Yes, we do." Leia pulled out her comlink. "And we need to get back to camp. There may be more Sith out here."

A few minutes later, they reentered camp, walking slowly. Javon and his core group of troopers, stone-faced, rejoined and escorted them.

The camp was very active. Crowds from the gathering at the center were now dispersing. Talking. Embracing. Quarreling.

Leia received a call on her comlink. She listened to it and her face fell. She led them all in a change of direction.

Allana looked up at her. "What is it?"

"I'm so sorry, sweetie. I had to tell people about the bomb in Threepio. They've taken him off into the desert and disarmed him. He's safe. But the Hapan security people—an assassination attempt on the Queen Mother—her security detail insisted, and she doesn't have any official reason to linger—"

They came to a stop at an intersection of lanes between tents and waited as a party passed by. The Hapan Consortium party, headed back to the landing craft.

Allana looked among all the veiled faces, took only a moment to find her mother's. Tenel Ka was staring straight at her as well, pride and sorrow visible in her eyes.

Allana raised a hand, gave her mother a tiny wave. Then the Hapans went past and were gone.

Chapter Forty-five

CRYSTAL VALLEY, NAM CHORIOS

THREE STEALTHX STARFIGHTERS DESCENDED TO within a hundred meters of the ground, circling protectively while a shuttle settled onto the road adjacent to the topato field, its wings rising into landing position. Ben picked Valin up again and they headed over to the road. The boarding ramp was down before they arrived, the pilot, Taryn Zel, waiting. She steadied Ben as he carried Valin up into the shuttle.

Luke looked overhead. "Jaina, who's that up there with you?"

"You've got Zekk and Tyria Tainer."

"Tyria, get down here."

"Yes, Grand Master." One of the StealthXs abruptly veered and descended on repulsors. Moments later it settled into place in front of the shuttle, its repulsors kicking up a small dust storm. The canopy rose.

Luke called up to the lean blond woman in the cockpit. "I'm stealing your starfighter."

Her face fell. "Yes, Grand Master."

Ben, returning to the bottom of the ramp, scowled at his father. "Dad, you're in no shape to fly in combat right now. None of us should do it."

Luke put his hand on Ben's shoulder. "Your uncle Han, a very wise man—"

"Ha!"

"—once said, 'Never tell me the odds.'"

"I wasn't telling you the odds."

"Well, don't."

Tyria dropped onto the road, walked over, and ruefully handed Luke her helmet. "It's great to see you, Grand Master. Welcome back."

"Thanks." Luke headed off toward the StealthX. "See if you can teach my offspring not to be so protective of his elders, would you?" He donned the helmet, sprang with more effort than he cared to admit up onto the S-foil and then into the cockpit, and ran through an abbreviated checklist. As the cockpit came down, he gave Ben a thumbs-up. Then he engaged his repulsorlifts and was airborne.

As he started to rise, something shot out of a nearby dust cloud, a familiar ball shape with extrusions, red and menacing—Ship. It rose at a tremendous rate toward the dark sky. Luke could feel Abeloth within the craft. The pain she was experiencing was like heat radiating from her in the Force. The loss of Callista, the loss of Nenn, the unexpected blow of the tsil's death, all in close proximity, had hurt her badly.

Heedless of the damage his thrusters might cause to surrounding crops, Luke tilted his StealthX back on its stern and put everything the starfighter had into acceleration. Jaina and Zekk dropped in behind him.

Brief reports flew at Gavar Khai like heat-seeking missiles.

"Two frigates destroyed, two crippled. Damage throughout the remainder of the flotilla. We're still four minutes from being clear of the planet's gravity well."

"Communications restored with Captain Annax. Our gunship crews are drawing off the enemy starfighters so she and her units can escape."

Khai stared, heat and rage building inside him, but did not let that anger emerge in his voice. He would save this emotion, cherish it for use later. "Order withdrawal of all our forces on Nam Chorios." A smile he knew to be bleak crossed his lips as he did the responsible thing. "Order all forces that have been on the ground to go through full decontamination, with emphasis on droch detection, before reintegrating with the main force. Or we will destroy them ourselves."

"Yes, sir."

Khai's frigate shook from a particularly forceful laser strike. Shield power was diminishing; laser hits were having a greater effect.

He would not run the numbers to gauge whether they'd last long enough to get him to safe hyperspace jump distance. He would trust in himself, in his commanders, in the Force.

But he knew he had just been mauled. He had relied too much on reports that the Jedi were fragmented, distracted by their political folly on Coruscant. He'd done so because he had wanted to believe it, wanted to think of his enemy as organizationally and tactically inferior.

He wouldn't make that mistake again.

Kyle Katarn's voice crackled in Luke's ears. "Gold One to all squadrons. New danger, new danger. Herkan Base is coming alive. Its weapons are now training on your location, Gray One."

Luke gritted his teeth. Abeloth had somehow assumed control of that NovaGun station, a far-from-impossible task for one Force-user who could marshal others.

Jaina acknowledged instantly. "Understood. Command of Gray Squadron is now with Gray Ten."

Luke checked his sensor board. Herkan Base barely

registered, a distant blip above him. Yet he felt no menace from it.

He felt no menace even when it fired on him. The bright flash of light illuminated the sky immediately above his cockpit. The air superheated, expanded, hammering at his StealthX, sending a shudder through the starfighter and a jolt through Luke's control yoke. The R2 unit in back squealed.

Luke grimaced. "This is Gray Ten. Herkan Base is probably firing on automated programming. No emotions or intentions to detect. Gray One, Gray Two, go evasive and stay that way." He hated issuing that order. They'd been steadily catching up to Ship. Evasive flying would slow them.

And Ship—the Sith meditation sphere—plowed on straight ahead, not weaving, safe from the NovaGun.

The distant laser fired again. The sheet of deadly brightness passed between Luke and Jaina. His stomach flip-flopped in that instant, as Jaina's StealthX disappeared in the light, but Luke did not feel a sudden pain or loss, just a moment of alarm from her. Then the brightness faded and she was still there.

"Gold Three to Gray Ten, incoming." It was Raynar Thul's voice, and Gold Three was on the sensors, just past the NovaGun. "Using shadow bomb, be alert."

"Set it to detonate with proximity detector." Luke twitched his StealthX to one side and another laser barrage flashed by, occupying the space where he would have been. "Cripple her and then we can vape her, don't go for the instant kill."

"Understood . . . Launching."

Luke didn't feel anything through the Force, but that was proper. Raynar had launched his shadow bomb, a proton torpedo warhead without thruster, with a telekinetic touch through the Force. At this range, and with sufficient delicacy on Raynar's part, Luke *shouldn't* have felt anything. And Abeloth shouldn't feel it, either. If she kept to her present course—and she would, so long as the NovaGun kept offering her protection along that exit vector—she'd run right into the explosive device.

"Gold One to Gold Three." It was Kyle Katarn again. "Be advised, the NovaGun is rotating axially. Its guns can bear on you—"

The NovaGun flashed again, but its attack came nowhere near Luke, Jaina, or Zekk. Luke saw a needle of laser light travel laterally from the orbital base. There was a second flash, not a visible one—alarm through the Force.

The transponder signal from Gold Three winked out on Luke's sensor board. Then it was there again, flickering.

"Gold One to wing, Gold Three is extravehicular."

"Gold One, White Four." It was Taryn Zel's voice. "I'm on a different outbound vector, away from Herkan Base. Should I move in to get Gold Three?"

"Negative, negative, Herkan Base's own personnel will do that. Stay clear of the engagement, your shuttle isn't meant for combat retrievals."

Luke ran distances and speeds through his head. Ship should be reaching the vicinity of Raynar's shadow bomb just about—

Abeloth must have felt it, perhaps just a touch of expectation from Raynar or one of the others. Ship vectored.

It must have come close enough to the bomb to trigger its proximity fuse. A globe of brightness blossomed ahead. Ship, a tiny, irregular dot, entered it, angling through its outer reaches, and emerged from the far side, trailing flame and sparks. Luke could feel pain in the Force, distant pain, but couldn't tell whether it was Ship or Abeloth or both.

Counting on Abeloth's distraction to slow her reactions, Luke took a maximum-range shot. He saw his quad-linked lasers converge on that tiny dot. He felt more pain, knew he'd scored a hit.

Then the universe lit up.

His R2 unit squealed in droid distress. His StealthX shook and spun, the nighttime sky suddenly replaced by Nam Chorios, then sky again, Nam Chorios. In his left peripheral vision he could see that his port-side S-foils were gone, their struts ending in stumps still trailing molten composites.

The inertial compensator wasn't enough to handle the sudden stresses of his spin, and his weakened body wasn't, either. He saw his vision contract. Everything went gray—then black.

Luke awoke in a bed, a prefabricated duraplast ceiling above his head. He looked around.

This was a good-sized cabin, dimly lit, not a hostel chamber but something like it. The furnishings were generic and innocuous like those of a hostel, but there were no viewports showing local scenery, no wall-mounted holos showing exotic locales.

To his left, on another bed, his back to Luke, was Ben. He was still, breathing slowly.

Luke looked right. There, in a comfortable padded chair, sat Jaina.

Luke blew out a sigh of relief. "Where are we? And what's happened?"

"These are Very Important Person quarters on the Alliance Navy supply ship *Verity,* which has been our tender since the StealthX wing was stationed here." Jaina's disinterested wave took in their surroundings. "You want the bad news or the good news?"

"Bad. That way I have something to look forward to afterward."

She grinned, then became serious. "Abeloth got away. Zekk and I had to draw off fire from the NovaGun so it wouldn't finish you. By the time we were sure it wouldn't fire on disabled craft on ballistic courses, Ship had entered hyperspace."

Luke gave her a chiding look. "You shouldn't have worried about me. You should have gone after her."

"I know this Jedi, he pretends to be all wise and mysterious but he's really kind of a farm boy inside, he used to tell me, 'Trust in the Force.' Zekk and I trusted what the Force had to tell us—and we protected *you*. So live with it."

Luke sighed. "I hate being hoisted on my own words. More bad news?"

"Well, some of the Sith frigates got away. But we really hammered them before they went."

"And the good news."

"We managed to get you dunked in bacta for the first time in forever. And you've finally had some good sleep. Really, at your age, you should start taking better care of yourself."

He glared, not meaning it.

She continued, "Valin and Jysella are back to normal, the Theran Listeners are back to normal, everyone has checked out droch-free. Raynar's fine. Injuries but no fatalities on our side in the Sith engagement."

Luke lay back and thought about it.

Abeloth had escaped again. All his preparations, all his planning, an operation that could have ended for all time the danger she posed—all that had been for nothing.

No, he corrected himself, it wasn't for nothing. Abeloth had been hurt again, weakened. Perhaps worse than before; he didn't know what the one–two punch of Raynar's shadow bomb and his own lasers had inflicted on her or Ship.

And the loss of Callista. Clearly that had pained her more than the death of any previous avatar. More than losing a remote body, she'd lost something that had been part of herself.

And Callista—finally, truly, Luke knew that she was free. Free of the uncertainties that she had endured in the last part of her mortal life. Free of the loneliness and misery she had endured for thirty years after her death. Free to be one with the Force.

He smiled up at Jaina. "I'm still a little tired. Maybe I'll get some more sleep."

"Good answer."

KLATOOINE

The *Millennium Falcon* broke orbit, exited the planet's gravity well, and entered hyperspace, bound for Coruscant. Han was at the controls; Leia, though in the copilot's seat, performed no ship's tasks. She had Allana in her lap.

Behind them, R2-D2 tweetled.

C-3PO, in the seat behind Leia, sounded distressed with his reply. "That's not at all funny, Artoo."

Allana looked over the back of Leia's seat to see the protocol droid. "What did he say?"

"He said I had an explosive temper. I find his word choice thoughtless."

R2-D2 tweetled again.

"No, I do *not* blow up at the slightest provocation."

Tweetle.

"I am not going to pieces over this. Enough." C-3PO stood. "The Manumission Mandate Militia may be correct. I think I have been far too accommodating for far too long. I am now going to assert my independence and individuality."

Han glanced over his shoulder at the droid. "And how, exactly, do you plan to do that, Goldilocks?"

"Why, I think I'll formulate Mistress Amelia's next lesson plan."

"That's not exactly—"

"And I'll do so without following the recommendations of the Alliance Department of Education. I shall do it my way."

Han gave him a mock scowl. "You interrupted me."

"Oh. So very sorry." C-3PO headed aft.

R2-D2 followed, tweetling.

"What do you mean, I'm a ball of fire today? Artoo, I'm warning you . . ."

When they were gone, Leia hugged Allana even more tightly. "Are you all right, sweetie? You've been very quiet."

"Uh-huh. I was just kind of wishing we hadn't come to Klatooine."

"I know. Bad things happened. But imagine how much worse they might have been if we hadn't come. If your grandpa hadn't been very clever, the Klatooinians might have stayed slaves, or lonely freedom fighters, a lot longer."

"Yeah, I know. When you're the only one who can fix something wrong, it's your duty."

"That's right."

"But sometimes I like it like this. Just flying around in the *Falcon*. No duties."

Han grinned. "Tell you what, kiddo. When I'm too old to do anything but brag and flirt, I'll give you the *Falcon*, and you can fly around and hide from duty."

"Do I have to take Threepio?"

Allana didn't quite understand why Han and Leia started laughing and couldn't seem to stop.

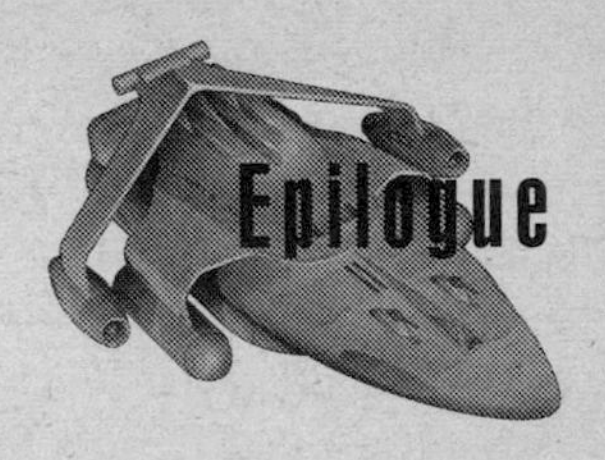

Epilogue

LIGHT-YEARS FROM NAM CHORIOS, AWAY FROM TRADE routes and other well-traveled spaceways, Gavar Khai formed up the remnants of his flotilla.

Some of his frigates were initiating crucial repairs. Crew members were being swapped around. Long-distance shuttles were still arriving from Nam Chorios, carrying Sith and specialists who had been left behind.

Those on Kesh would not be amused by Khai's loss. His failure. He wondered what it would cost him.

His sensor officer called out, "Ship at extreme sensor range."

His communications officer added, "It's hailing us."

Khai glared at the two of them. "Be more specific. What type of ship?"

"*Ship,* sir. Abeloth's Ship."

Khai blinked. "Open communications."

The main monitor resolved into a new picture—Abeloth in all her alienness, surrounded by the pulsing reddish surfaces of Ship's interior.

Even though it was only a comm signal, Khai felt the impact of her presence in the Force. There was rage in her eyes, rage and pain. Whatever the Jedi had done to her on Nam Chorios, clearly she was still feeling it. Khai saw some of his Sith bridge officers wincing under the power of her hurt.

"Gavar Khai. Our mutual enemy is proving to be too much for us to deal with individually."

Khai nodded. "Perhaps."

"Let us discuss this."

"I'll be here for a little while. Let us indeed discuss this."

CORUSCANT

Every skyscraper on Coruscant had them, little rooms tucked away in inconvenient corners, folded in between utility conduits, shoved up against angled ceilings. Sometimes they were walled off entirely, sometimes accessed by locked portals decorated with signs reading AUTHORIZED PERSONNEL ONLY. The best ones tended to be claimed informally by building managers or maintenance staffers, furnished with cast-off chairs and sofas, used as secret relaxation spots or sabacc gathering-holes. The others ended up as storerooms or were forgotten entirely.

This one was one of the forgotten rooms. A trapezoid-shaped chamber situated between two turbolift shafts, it was twice as long as a man but broad only at the entry end, narrowing to a dusty nook at the far end. It was completely unfurnished. When Tahiri found it, after prowling this high-rise middle-income residential tower for several furtive hours, it didn't even have a glow rod wired into the ceiling fixture. She'd had to sneak off into an untrafficked hallway and steal one from there, wiring it into place herself.

Now she lay atop her confiscated bedroll, listening to the frequent, insanity-inducing *whoosh* of the turbolifts going by.

In the heart of the most populous city in the galaxy, a city that spanned an entire world, she was completely alone. Such an odd feeling. Her only possessions were the contents of tourist bags set aside after nightfall on a pedway and not carefully watched by the Commenori family negotiating for an airspeeder rental. Tahiri had snatched them up and had been long gone before anyone had noticed. She had kept the owner's name and address tag, intending to return the goods when she could, and to pay for any she might lose or ruin.

Someday. When she had resources again. At least now she had a datapad, some ill-fitting clothes, some snack food.

And a home. She smiled mirthlessly at the oddly angled ceiling as it vibrated under the most recent turbolift passage.

Resources. In a world hunting for her, she could only acquire resources by theft and deceit. Oh, she certainly had skills enough to use that way. But was that what she had been brought to? Was this her punishment for Pellaeon's murder—to become a petty thief, a scavenger?

Yes. If she stubbornly chose to do everything by herself, her way, that was exactly what her fate would be.

She needed help. She needed . . . family.

The HoloNews said that the closest people she had to family were offworld now, but coming home.

She'd wait. She'd wait, then creep through the shadows to find them and ask them for help. For aid in becoming herself again, for making things right.

As for now . . . She looked down where her feet rested atop the bedroll. She flexed them, wiggling her toes.

At least, at last, she was barefoot again.

Read on for an excerpt of
Star Wars: Fate of the Jedi: Ascension
by Christie Golden
Published by Del Rey Books

COUNCIL CHAMBERS OF THE CIRCLE,
CAPITAL CITY OF TAHV, KESH

THE SUN BEATING DOWN UPON THE STAINED-GLASS dome of the Circle Chambers painted the forms of all those assembled in a riot of colors. Yet it was not hot in this large room; regulating the temperature was child's play for such masterful users of the Force as the Sith assembled here.

It was an emergency meeting. Even so, formalities were strictly observed; the Sith were nothing if not meticulous. Grand Lord Darish Vol, the leader of the Lost Tribe, had summoned the meeting less than a standard hour earlier. He now sat upon a dais in the very center of the room, elevated above all others, enthroned on his traditional metal-and-glass seat. While there had been sufficient time to don his colorful formal robes, he had not had time to sit and permit his attendants to paint his gaunt, aged face with the vor'shandi swirls and decorations appropriate to the meeting. Vol shifted slightly in his throne, displeased by that knowledge, displeased with the entire situation that had necessitated the meeting in the first place.

His staff of office was stretched over his lap. His clawlike hands closed about it as his aged but still-sharp eyes flitted about the room, noting who was here and who was not, and observing and anticipating the responses of each.

Seated on either side of the Grand Lord were the High Lords. Nine members of the traditional thirteen were here today, a mixture of male and female, Keshiri and human. One, High Lord Sarasu Taalon, would never again be among that number. Taalon was dead, and his death was one of the reasons Vol had called the assembly. Seated in a ring around the dais were the Lords, ranked below the High Lords, and standing behind them were the Sabers.

Several of their number were missing, too. Many were dead. Some . . . well, their status remained to be seen.

Vol could feel the tension in the room; even a non-Force-sensitive could have read the body language. Anger, worry, anticipation, and apprehension were galloping through the Chambers today, even though most present hid it well. Vol drew upon the Force as naturally as breathing in order to regulate his heart rate and the stress-created chemicals that coursed through his body. *This* was how the mind remained clear, even though the heart was, as ever, open to emotions and passion. If it were closed, or unmoved by such things, it would no longer be the heart of a true Sith.

"I tell you, she is a savior!" Lady Sashal was saying. She was petite, her long white hair perfectly coiffed, and her purple skin the most pleasing tone of lavender; her mellifluous voice rang through the room. "Ship obeys her, and was not Ship the—" She stumbled on the choice of words for a moment, then recovered. "—the Sith-created construct who liberated us from the chains of our isolation and ignorance of the galaxy? Ship was the tool we used to further our destiny—to conquer the stars. We are well on our way to doing so!"

"Yes, Lady Sashal, we are," countered High Lord

Ivaar Workan. "But it is *we* who shall rule this galaxy, not this stranger."

Although the attractive, graying human male had been a Lord for many years, he was new to his rank of High Lord. Taalon's untimely demise had paved the way for Workan's promotion. Vol had enjoyed watching Workan step into the role as if he had been born to it. While Sith truly trusted no one but themselves and the Force, Vol nonetheless regarded Workan among those who fell on the side of less likely to betray him.

"She is very strong with the dark side," High Lord Takaris Yur offered. "Stronger than anyone we have ever heard of." That was quite a statement, coming from the Master of the Sith Temple. Few on Kesh had as extensive a knowledge of the Sith's past—and now their present as they expanded across the stars—as this deceptively mild, dark-skinned, middle-aged human. Yur had ambition, but, oddly for a Sith, it was largely not personal. His ambitions were for his students. He was content to teach them as best he could, then set them loose on an unsuspecting world, turning his attention to the next generation of Tyros. Yur spoke seldom, but when he did, all listened, if they were wise.

"Stronger than I?" said Vol mildly, his face pleasant, as if he were engaged in idle chitchat on a lovely summer's day.

Yur was unruffled as he turned toward the Grand Lord, bowing as he replied.

"She is an ancient being," he said. "It seems to me foolish not to learn what we can from her." Vol smiled a little; Yur had not actually answered the question.

"One may learn much about a rukaro by standing in its path," Vol continued. "But one might not survive to benefit from that knowledge."

"True," Yur agreed. "Nonetheless, she is useful. Let us suck her dry before discarding the husk. Reports indicate that she still has much knowledge and skill in manipulating the Force to teach us and future generations of the Lost Tribe."

"She is not Sith," said Workan. The scorn in his melodious voice indicated that that single, damning observation should be the end of the debate.

"She is!" Sashal protested.

"Not the way *we* are Sith," Workan continued. "And our way—our culture, our values, our heritage—must be the *only* way if our destiny is to remain pure and unsullied. We risk dooming ourselves by becoming overly reliant on someone not of the Tribe—no matter how powerful she might be."

"Sith take what we want," said Sashal, stepping toward Workan. Vol watched both of them closely, idly wondering if Sashal was issuing a challenge to her superior. It would be foolish. She was nowhere near as powerful as Workan. But sometimes ambition and wisdom did not go hand in hand.

Her full diminutive height was drawn up, and she projected great confidence in the Force. "We will take her, and use her, and discard her when we are done. But for love of the dark side, let us take her first! Listen to High Lord Yur! Think what we can learn! From all that we have heard, she has powers we cannot imagine!"

"From all that we have heard, she is unpredictable and dangerous," countered Workan. "Only a fool rides the uvak he cannot control. I've no desire to continue to sacrifice Sith Sabers and Lords on the altar of aiding Abeloth and furthering her agenda—whatever it might be. Or have you failed to realize that we don't even truly know what that is?"

Vol detected a slight sense of worry and urgency from the figure currently approaching the Circle Chambers. It was Saber Yasvan, her attractive features drawn in a frown of concern.

"Only a fool throws away a weapon that still has use," countered Yur. "Something so ancient—we should string her along and unlock her secrets."

"Our numbers are finite, Lord Yur," Workan said. "At the rate Sith are dying interacting with her, we won't be around to learn very much."

Vol listened as Yasvan whispered in his ear, then nodded and, with a liver-spotted hand, dismissed the Saber.

"Entertaining as this debate has been," he said, "it is time for it to conclude. I have just learned that Ship has made contact with our planetary defenses. Abeloth and the Sith I have sent to accompany her will not be far behind."

They had all known to expect her; it was, indeed, the reason the meeting had been called. All eyes turned to him expectantly. What would their Grand Lord decide?

He let them stew. He was old, and few things amused him these days, so he permitted himself to enjoy the moment. At last, he said, "I have heard the arguments for continuing to work closely with her, and the arguments to sever ties. While I confess I am not overly fond of the former, and have made little secret of my opinion, neither do I think it is time for the latter. The best way to win is to cover all angles of the situation. And so Kesh and the Circle of Lords will invite Abeloth to our world. We shall give her a grand welcome, with feasting, and arts, and displays of our proud and powerful culture. And," he added, eyeing them all intently, "we will watch, and learn, and listen. And then we will make our decision as to what is best for the Lost Tribe of Kesh."

Sith Saber Gavar Khai sat in the captain's chair on the bridge of the *Black Wave*, the ChaseMaster frigate that had once belonged to Sarasu Taalon. Filling the viewscreen was the spherical shape of his homeworld—green and brown and blue and lavender. Khai regarded the lush planet with heavy-lidded eyes. For so many years, Kesh had been isolated from the events of the galaxy, and Khai found he had decidedly mixed feelings about returning.

Part of him was glad to be home. As was the case with every member of the Lost Tribe, he had spent his entire life here until a scant two years ago. Deeply embedded in him were love for its beautiful glass sculptures and purple sands, its music and culture, its casual brutality and its orderliness. For more than five thousand standard years, the Tribe had dwelled here, and with no other option, had—as was the Sith way—made the best of it. The ancient vessel *Omen* had crash-landed, and the survivors had set about not merely to exist in this world, but to dominate it. And so they had. They had managed to both embrace the Keshiri, the beautiful native beings of Kesh, and subjugate them. Those who were deserving—strong in the Force and able to adapt to the Sith way of thinking and being—could, with enough will, carve out a place for themselves in this society.

Those who were not Force-users had no such opportunities. They were at the mercy of the ones who ruled. And sometimes, as was the case with Gavar Khai and his wife, there was mercy. Even love.

But most often, there was neither.

Too, those who gambled to increase their standing and power and lost seldom lived long enough to make a second attempt. It was a very controlled society, with precise roles. Everyone knew what was expected of him or her, and knew that in order to change their lot, they would need to be bold, clever, and lucky.

Gavar Khai had been all of those things.

His life on Kesh had been good. While, of course, he had his eye on eventually becoming a Lord—perhaps even a High Lord, if opportunities presented themselves or could be manipulated—he was not discontent with where he was. His wife, though not a Force-user, supported him utterly. She had been faithful and devoted and raised their tremendously promising daughter, Vestara, very well.

And Vestara had been the most precious of all the things that had belonged to Gavar Khai.

Discipline was something every Sith child tasted almost upon emerging from the womb. It was the duty of the parents to mold their children well, otherwise they would be unprepared to claim their proper roles in society. Beatings were the norm, but they were seldom motivated by anger. They were part of the way that Sith parents guided and taught their children. Khai had not looked forward to such aspects of discipline, preferring to explore other methods such as meditation, sparring till exhaustion, and withholding approval.

He had found, to his pleasure, that he had never needed to lay a hand on Vestara in reprimand. She was seemingly born to excel, and had her own drive and ambition such that she did not need his to "encourage" her. Khai, of course, had goals and ambitions for himself.

He had greater ones for his daughter. Or at least, he'd had.

His reverie was broken by the sound of the comm beeping, indicating a message from the surface.

"Message from Grand Lord Vol, Saber Khai," said his second in command, Tola Annax, adding quietly under her breath, "Very prompt, very prompt indeed."

"I expected as much, once he received my message," Khai said. "I will speak with him."

A hologram of the wizened Grand Lord appeared. It had been some time since Khai had seen the leader of the Lost Tribe. Had Vol always seemed so fragile, so . . .

old? Age was to be respected, for to live to an old age meant a Sith had done something very right indeed. But there was such a thing as *too* old, and those who were too old needed to be put down. Idly, keeping his thoughts well shielded, Khai wondered if the renowned Grand Lord was getting to that point. He saw his white-haired Keshiri second in command staring openly at the hologram; doubtless Annax, with her near obsession for determining weakness, was thinking the same thing.

"Saber Gavar Khai," said Vol, and his voice certainly sounded strong. "I had expected to speak to Abeloth herself."

"She is on Ship at the moment. Do not worry, you will see her when she arrives on Kesh," Khai said smoothly. "She is anxious to create a good first impression."

"I take it that since you are the one speaking to me, she has selected you to replace the late High Lord Taalon in our . . . interactions with her."

"It has not been said specifically, no, but yes, Abeloth has turned to me since Lord Taalon's death."

"Good, good. Please then assure Abeloth that as she is anxious to create a good first impression, after our people have worked so closely and sacrificed so much for her, we are also desirous that our first meeting go well. To that end, we will need time to prepare for such an august visitor. Say, three days. A parade, showcasing the glory that is the Lost Tribe, and then a masquerade."

Khai knew a trap when he saw one. As did Annax—who quickly busied herself with her controls so as not to look too obvious as she listened in—and the rest of his crew. As traps went, this was blatant. Vol was testing Khai's loyalties. To force Abeloth to wait three full days before being received was to tell her her place. To keep her waiting, as one might a Tyro summoned for interrogation about his studies. Yet Vol would deny such, simply saying that he wanted to make sure everything was just right for their esteemed guest. And with the Sith's love of ceremony and showcasing, the statement had the dubious merit of perhaps even being true.

Vol was waiting for Khai's reaction. He was trying to figure out where the Saber's loyalties lay.

And Khai himself suddenly realized, with a sickly jolt, that he himself didn't know.

Abeloth had doubtless sensed the conversation and was monitoring Khai's presence in the Force. For all he knew about Ship, she also had the ability to monitor the conversation itself. He addressed himself calmly to the man who ostensibly ruled the Lost Tribe of the Sith.

"Abeloth will be disappointed to hear that preparations will take so long," he said, keeping his voice modulated. "She might even see it as an insult." Out of Vol's line of sight, Annax was nodding.

"Well, we wouldn't want that, would we?" said Vol. "As a fine example of a Sith Saber, you will simply have to assure her that this is done out of respect. I trust you will be able to do so."

Slowly, Khai nodded. "I will do so."

"Excellent. You have always done well by me and the Circle, Khai. I knew you would not fail me now. Give my best to Abeloth. I look forward very much to our meeting. I heard certain rumors, and am anxious to hear from you how Vestara is performing on our behalf."

The hologram disappeared. Khai leaned back in his chair, rubbing his chin and thinking. He heard the soft chime that indicated an incoming message and was instantly alert.

"Saber Khai," said Annax, "Abeloth wishes to speak with you privately." Her bright eyes were on him, her quick mind doubtless racing two steps ahead, wondering about the outcome of this particular conversation.

Khai nodded. He had expected this, too. "I will receive her in my quarters, then."

A few moments later, he was in the austere captain's quarters of the *Black Wave*. He took a moment and steadied himself for the interview. Settling down at a small desk, he said aloud, "Transmit."

"Patching her through, sir," Annax replied promptly. Idly, he wondered if the Keshiri was eavesdropping. He had expected a holographic appearance, but Ableoth chose to communicate through audio only.

"Saber Khai," she said. Her voice sounded better than it had when they'd made their agreement to work together; stronger, more in command. Less . . . wounded. Khai slammed down that line of thinking at once.

"Abeloth," he said. "I have heard from Lord Vol."

"I know," she said, confirming what he had suspected—that she had sensed the conversation already. "It did not go as well as you had expected."

"Say rather it did not go as well as one could have hoped," Khai corrected.

"I do hope that he is not denying me the chance to visit your world after all," said Abeloth.

"Quite the contrary. He has insisted that Kesh, and primarily Tahv, be granted three days to prepare for your arrival, that the Sith may welcome you as the honored guest you are."

"You suspect he is lying?"

It was a very dangerous game Gavar Khai was playing. Above all else, he wanted to ensure his own personal success—nay, simple survival, if it came to that. He had always been fiercely loyal to his people, but his experiences with Abeloth had also opened his eyes to the vast power she could wield. Ideally, he could bring the two together, but he had to always be aware that conflict could again erupt between Abeloth and the Lost Sith tribe.

And if that did happen, he needed to make sure he was on the side of the victor.

While lies were useful, sometimes the truth could be even more so. So he told the truth. "I do not think he is lying. It is a cultural tradition to have great celebrations for momentous occasions. There are always parades and parties and so on. And certainly, Lord Vol is very well aware that choosing to ally with you is an extremely important moment for the Sith."

"But three days seems like a long time to ask so apparently honored a guest to wait." There was irritation in her voice, and he could feel it, cold and affronted, in the Force.

"Such preparations do take time," he said. "I do not know what he plans."

And that much, at least, was as true as the sun rising, although Tola Annax probably could give him a list of possible ideas.

"Very well. We shall give Lord Vol his three days. I must admit, I think I will enjoy seeing so elaborate a celebration. It is good to be honored and respected."

"Indeed. It will be a joyous occasion. I have been told that there will be a parade and afterward a masquerade."

A moment, then a chuckle. "A masquerade. How fitting. Yes, I will definitely enjoy this."

"I can safely say it will be unlike anything you have seen before."

"Of course. I am sure so isolated a world must have developed unique traditions." The way she said *isolated* made it sound like *backward*. Khai forced down any hint of resentment at her condescension.

"This is your world, Saber Khai," she continued. "I know you have other family besides your daughter. You will be visiting before the celebration?"

"I am the leader of this flotilla," Khai said. "I had not planned to, no."

"Do," said Abeloth. It was couched as a suggestion. Khai knew it was not. "And any others you think would appreciate the chance to visit should do so, as well. I do not think that I will be tarrying overlong."

"As you wish," said Gavar Khai, wondering, for the hundred thousandth time, just what she meant.